QUICKSILV.

Christie Dickason was born in America but also lived as a child in Thailand, Mexico and Switzerland. Harvard-educated and a former theatre director and choreographer (with the Royal Shakespeare Company and at Ronnie Scott's among others), she has now lived longer in London than anywhere else. She has two very large sons and two small cats. Besides writing books and musical libretti, she gardens and climbs the occasional mountain. *Quicksilver* grew out of her own personal medical experience. While researching it, she spent two days shoulder-to-shoulder with a pack of North American wolves.

Quicksilver is the second book of the Lady Tree trilogy.

By the same author

THE DRAGON RIDERS
THE TEARS OF THE TIGER
THE LADY TREE

Non-Fiction

EXPERIENCE AND EXPERIMENT *(The New Theatre Workshops)*,
The Gulbenkian Foundation
PLAY GROUND (with composer Cecilia McDowall),
a musical piece for six narrators
GO FISH (an opera, with Cecilia McDowall)

QUICKSILVER

Christie Dickason

HarperCollins*Publishers*

HarperCollins *Publishers*
77–85 Fulham Palace Road,
Hammersmith, London W6 8JB

www.**fire**and**water**.com

This revised paperback edition 2000
1 3 5 7 9 8 6 4 2

First published in Great Britain by
HarperCollins*Publishers* 1999

Copyright © Christie Dickason 1999

The Author asserts the moral right to
be identified as the author of this work

ISBN 0 00 647875 1

This novel is entirely a work of fiction.
The names, characters and incidents portrayed in it are
the work of the author's imagination. Any resemblance to
actual persons, living or dead, events or localities is
entirely coincidental.

Typeset in Bembo by
Palimpsest Book Production Limited,
Polmont, Stirlingshire

Printed and bound in Great Britain by
Clays Ltd, St Ives plc

For my wise-woman sister, Cynthia

Acknowledgements

The Author is more grateful than she can say to alpha wolves, Job and Katrinka, and the rest of the pack at the Loki Wolf Refuge in New Hampshire, USA (including human alphas, Fred Keating and Debra Lennon, who slept in their den). Thanks also to Loki and Pinga at the Nereledge Inn and their humans, Val and Dave. And to Pinga's sister Tinka, who taught me a terrifying lesson about angry, anxious wolves. And to my own sister, Tess Cederholm for introducing me to these wolves and for keeping me company among them. I also thank Lynn Holm and her staghounds for letting themselves be accosted in Richmond Park and graciously continuing the acquaintance.

For help with research, thanks to the ever-helpful staff at the London Library, in particular for their copy of *The Vulgaria*, which has been quoted with all its glorious debasement of Latin. Thanks also to FEH, and to David Young for trusting me with several of his rare old herbals. To John Cederholm for American material. To Cecilia McDowall, friend, composer and music-maker *extraordinaire*, who recognised the Lydian mode in a wolf's howl, and once owned a singing dog. To my sister Cynthia Scott for her insights and for asking the right questions at the right time. I am also grateful to Paul Robertson whose work with music in healing showed me a possible way to tame the beast. And to John Faulkner for his creative listening, Dr Jeremy Powell-Tuck for medical advice, and my son Thomas (and his computer) for invaluable technical support.

And a special thanks to the London luthier, Stephen Barber, and his partner, Sandi Harris, who gave me time they didn't have, communicated their professional passion, and lent me rare historical material on the making and playing of lutes.

Always at the back of my mind while writing *Quicksilver* was Dr Ian McKenzie, former head of Neurology at Guy's Hospital, London, who taught me that it was my choice how to deal with my own beast.

Finally, as ever, thanks to Andrew Hewson, my agent, for his notes and encouragement throughout the long writing process, to Charlotte Windsor, former HarperCollins editor, for waving some invaluable red flags, and to my editor, Nick Sayers, who kept faith.

Though the reflection in the pool
Often swims before our eyes:
Know the image.

Only in the dual realm
do voices become
eternal and mild.

Rilke, *Sonnets to Orpheus*

Everything flows . . .

Heraclitus

ONE

I

I must not remember: the bloodshot amber eye so close to my own that our lashes mingled. The dry pins of bristle that came off on my tongue. The smell of its rage.

Here, now, my arms are already numb. My legs shake dangerously. I must not think about the pain.

So.

I imagine.

Another place . . .

They lay in the dim private cave of her box bed. A blue and white woollen coverlet wrinkled under their half-naked bodies, its blue stripe bleached by the sun, the often-washed wool soft on their skins. He (*that is to say, I, a self that already fades*) was completely himself then, at ease, jacket and shirt off, shoes kicked on to the floor. Marika lay with her arms above her blonde head, hands palm-up with loosely-cupped fingers, eyes shut as if asleep, but intensely still. (*And this isn't just wishful thinking.*)

He uncurled her left hand. Leaned down and kissed each of her long musician's fingers. Her eyelids quivered. He inhaled. The silver buttons of her jacket had left a faint metallic taint on her fingertips. He kissed her other hand. (*Too fast. Take your time, Ned!*)

Then he closed his own thumb and first two fingers (*right hand*) on . . . (*I think it was a green*) . . . silk ribbon that tied

13

together her chemise front (*sheer linen with embroidered scalloped edges and smelling of rosemary*) . . .

If I take it slowly enough, I may still only be stroking her breasts, which are the blueish white of Chinese porcelain bowls (but warmer), by the time my Dutch gaoler comes to spoon turnip broth into my creaking jaws as if I were a baby again.

I'm glad she can't see me here in this absurd, if painful, position: ankles hobbled together, arms spread out to each side and strapped along the top of a wooden letter T, my head turned to the right and lashed down between them. But it's so dark here in the cellar of the Amsterdam Statehouse that I can't see my own right arm and hand. My hand might or might not be as swollen as it feels.

There's a long night coming, to get through in this alphabetical pose!

Then tomorrow. And then the night again. And then . . .

It's enough to make a man ache to swing from the gallows, just to change his position.

No. Not funny.

Another place, Ned!

I resume . . .

He tugged at the ribbon. Blue, not green (*I've decided*), a little darker than the stripe in the coverlet. The corners of her mouth lifted slightly . . .

It's no good! I'm back. My thoughts flap and struggle . . . pigeons trapped alive in an oven under a crust. No imaginings will save me on the gallows. Now has me in its jaws!

In two days, I must address the magistrates in my own defence.

'Your honours, I am Edward Malise, an innocent English gentleman.' (To the Dutch can any Englishman ever be innocent?)

'Your honours . . .'

But my words dry up. Even in my imagining. In moments, I am the first to believe that I should hang at once. The world must be

14

cleansed of monstrosity, or such tiny sparks of goodness as do exist won't stand a chance.

'Your honours . . .' Deliver any verdict, so long as it makes sense of the hideous disorder that has unravelled my life!

My legs shake. If they give way, I will choke to death on my shackles. Perhaps it's a frugal Dutch trick to save the executioner's fee.

Not funny.

The worst of it is, I now care if I die. Two months ago, guilty or innocent, I would have danced up the ladder and jumped at the noose, so long as I could have killed John Nightingale first.

Not now. Marika has changed me.

Marika. When I finish making love to her, I shall sing to her. I know a month of songs.

I sing:

My thoughts are wing'd with hopes, my hopes with
   love . . .
(*When you can make love, you don't sing it.*)
His heavenly touch upon the lute ravished her senses . . .

No good! Back again! In this underground cell I can hear only the dripping of water. It's no place for music, even in the mind. Only one short hour here, and even the thought of singing stabs like a fishbone in my throat. With my head cranked forward like this, I can hardly swallow. Without a miracle, the five unfeeling lumps that were once my fingers will never pluck music from lute strings again.

Never sing. Never again know exactly where I am: safe on my note, the only safe place in the universe.

Never stroke her breasts.

Never shave away fragrant curls of pear wood to set free the lute inside.

Never eat a lemon pudding.

Never feel my cock fill and rise.

Never.

Bad word.

I suffer this painful indignity because I am considered too dangerous

15

to set among ordinary prisoners – the beggars, the common murderers, the wilfully homeless. It's feared that I might eat them . . .

Once, that fear made me laugh.

Hole in my thoughts. Wait it out.

Breathe.

The dog, the sheep . . .

Hole in my thoughts.

The child.

There's a sliver of doubt. Self-knowledge lurks just out of sight, not in its rightful lofty realm of my mind but below that hot furnace of my heart.

I burrow back into my life, sniffing after the last time I knew that I was completely innocent. My birth is as far back as I can dig, but even then, I'm not sure.

2

He lay slapped on the kitchen table between a dead hare and six onions while the wet nurse changed his soaking clouts. They were in a stone farmhouse in the Haute Savoie. It was a bright, chilly April, in 1603, between the death of Queen Elizabeth and the entry into London of James VI of Scotland as England's new king, when the English were still aiding the rebel Dutch in their long war with Spain.

He was a healthy child, though small, with the bright ancient wisdom of a newborn still in his eyes. Nevertheless, his survival was not certain, as it depended on his grandmother. And she, though still slender and with most of her teeth, but having outlived two monarchs, a husband, and five children, was dangerously close to wanting to get the whole thing over with, in order to see whether the next world would treat her better. (Or so he interpreted her words, as he grew older.) At that time few children survived neglect. Many died even with constant, loving care.

This second grandson had come a month early, with murderous speed. Catharine Malise stared at his hands, like little red spiders, and, under that unnatural crop of black hair, his crown of blue and green bruises where he had shoved against his mother's bones. A poor swap for the last member of her family who had shared her memories of England. (She had not spared him here. She spared no one, not even herself.) She looked out of the small, stone-framed window to the

17

unhelpful, rocky mountainside below the chapel where two small dark figures were scratching out his mother's grave.

The stone farmhouse was awash with bile and smelt of the boarhound that rattled furniture when it scratched fleas. The only refuge she could think of, after her son, the baby's father, had died of ague beside that lethargic stream on the northern Spanish coast. She was running out of refuges. Running out of distant cousins, like this one, here in France, who were willing to take in exiled English relatives with neither land nor money to pay for their keep.

This French cousin peered over Catharine's shoulder as the nurse wound the infant in strips of white linen swaddling cloth until he had swelled like a raw, unbaked loaf of bread. He gazed about, as if astonished by the hare, the onions, the sun-browned face of the nurse and the two paler ones of the old women.

'Who would think something so puny could kill a grown woman!' The cousin put a high price on her charity.

Catharine practised Christian restraint and pinched her lips against her reply. But she left the kitchen lest she have yet another sin of impatience to confess. In the main chamber, she knelt beside her dead daughter-in-law's chest and began to turn it out.

She shook out an embroidered jacket of cream silk, with pale blue scrolling along the edges of the front opening and the cuffs, a ghost of former lives, brought to the marriage by her daughter-in-law, but made for *her* mother in England many years before. A garden of roses and lilies in chain stitch and tiny knots bloomed over the breast. A pale yellow butterfly poised over the heart. She liked the butterfly, even though it was a symbol of frivolity. She held the jacket against herself.

'Oh, that's a good piece of stuff, with wear in it yet!' cried her cousin, leaning down for a closer look. She laid an exploring, possessive hand on one sleeve.

Silently, Catharine handed it to her.

'But it's so fine! Are you certain you want to give it to me?'

Catharine allowed the briefest pause, then closed the chest and went back into the kitchen. There, by the window, the wet nurse exclaimed in frustration as the baby's gums slid off her nipple once again. He gave a small hoarse cry that put Catharine in mind of her peacocks at Tarleton Court.

'What can you expect?' asked the cousin from the kitchen door. 'After a birth like that?' She peered at one sleeve of the jacket and picked at a worn spot on the hem, lest Catharine think that she had overpaid for her lodgings.

Catharine took the baby from the nurse – he was as light as a hank of wool – and left the house, closing the door with particular care. She wanted to slam the slates from the roof.

The farmhouse opened across a narrow, pale-grey terrace directly on to the mountainside. She climbed down a few crumbling steps and was shin-deep in pasture. Around her skirts, the grey scallops of meadow cranesbill shouldered up through the matted, winter-dried grass. Below her, the valley fell away between steep mountain walls in a staircase of near-vertical fields, not at all like the flat, damp green water meadows of her home. Cows grazed high above the house roof, udders still slack from the dawn milking. Even higher than the cows, level with one mountain rim, an eagle lay waiting on the wind.

Though cold, the air was pleasant. She had always preferred honest farmyard smells to the corrupt stink of London's streets. She set off through the stems of last year's weeds as if already headed for a new refuge. She climbed, so that when tired, she could descend. Otherwise, she would have to go down and then climb back up. Walking on the flat here, as she had once easily done at home, took her only from one rock face to another.

The child was quiet now, his blue newborn eyes pointed wide open at the sky.

'Yes, it's quite a sight when you've never seen it before.'

The bruises on his head reminded her of the crown of thorns on their Blessed Saviour, whom she had had to leave behind in England because he was too large to carry. The heavy altar candlesticks had been some of the first treasures she had sold.

A sharp stone punched through her right shoe sole. She glared at it. It had no place in a proper meadow!

She limped to a rock step in this huge staircase of a field and sat. She laid the baby safely in the long grass behind her and, after a quick look around her, hauled up her skirts. Her haunches protested as she leaned forward. Further hampered by her farthingale, which she refused to leave off like a maidservant ready to scrub floors, she was out of breath by the time she found the hole, in a shoe sole worn thinner than the skin of her eyelids.

The hole was a breach in her defences, greater than reason allowed.

Reduced to sabots like a peasant, or to a cast-off pair from her cousin.

I still have a few rings to sell and some trinkets, she thought. But there's no one here in these mountains to buy them for their true worth. I need a city. Self-made men with enough money to buy themselves someone else's past.

She sat upright on her stone, braced erect by her corset, but too weary even to weep. Thirty-two years of fighting off the truth – that what had once been would never return, including the woman she had been. All vanished. Dearest, noble William who, quite properly, put principles above his family. Tarleton Court. Her gardens. The babies. Even her memories slipped away when she wasn't looking. Clearest still were the painted garlands on the beams of her bed-chamber, which she had seen each morning when she woke up.

She raised her face to the astonishing blue sky. The eagle slid in a circle above her head. Alone because God had designed it for such celestial solitude, not because it had been deserted, however unwillingly, by everyone who mattered.

A cold hand clamped on to the back of her scalp under her thick silver hair. She would have to mention this moment in

20

confession. She had nearly given way. The devil had clothed himself in this heavy torpor to tempt her to despair.

She stood purposefully. Grit attacked her stocking through the hole in her shoe. Like the hole in her faith. She set off back down to the house in search of new resolve and a peaceful soul, with the image of her husband's beloved, self-sacrificing face in her mind.

Flags snapped in the wind. She lifted her head in the still air. Then she remembered.

She had forgotten the baby.

The eagle's talons had hooked into the tight binding strips. The beating wings flattened the grass into a shimmering halo around her grandson. Eagle and baby rose.

With a fierce, ignoble, unspeakable exhilaration, she saw release.

Take him!

Then the linen tore. The baby fell back into the grass. The eagle screamed and climbed while the baby rolled like a pebble. Catharine ran, stepped on her skirts, stumbled, fell with her arms outstretched, and the baby rolled neatly, miraculously into them. She snatched him up and pressed him to her, kissed his bruised forehead again and again in desperate remorse. It seemed to her that he did not cry until she had pressed him against her treacherous heart.

The story of my birth shifted each time she told it. The halo of grass, for instance, flattened by beating angel wings, was most likely added later. Over time, she shaped and reshaped me.

'It was an angel, of course,' she said. 'And the return to earth was a miracle, a sign of hope.' Her second grandson had been marked by God, no doubt about it. His return to earth signified a new beginning for the family . . .

'My infant Knight Templar, aren't you, Edward?'

I can still hear her voice drop as she leans near to a confidant. If I had fully understood her I would have run away.

'Not like his wicked brother. I'm too old to see it, but he will

21

do it for my sake, and his grandfather's. Re-enter Jerusalem in all our names . . .'

The eagle lifted one baby from the earth and dropped back quite another. A changeling is nothing more than an infant seen with different eyes and nourished from a different heart.

From the moment I hit the rocky ground and rolled, though less than twelve hours old, I was already a double creature.

Only my grandmother believed that my life was worth what it had cost.

'She left you in the field on purpose,' said his older brother Francis, one day without warning, as they lay on their stomachs looking down into a canal to see what useful floating rubbish they might fish out. 'You were the ugliest baby ever born.'

'You don't kill babies just for being ugly, or you wouldn't be here either!' In six years, Ned had learned to fight for his life with his older brother.

Francis conceded with suspicious alacrity. With his stick, he hooked up a submerged stocking. 'Now that I think about it, she had a much better reason.'

Francis wriggled his fingers through a hole in the stocking and looked sideways at his brother.

Get it over with, thought Ned. Better to have one's neck broken all at once like the pigeons men fed to their hawks, instead of being nibbled alive bit by bit. Francis won't let it rest until I ask. 'What reason?'

Francis threw the stocking back into the water. 'To punish you for killing our mother. If you hadn't been born, she wouldn't have died.'

For the next three days, Ned had refused to eat. His grandmother first urged, then ordered. Finally on the third evening, in anxious exasperation, she thrust a spoon of vegetable stew against his clenched teeth.

'You must eat or else sicken. And you must grow fine and strong. Our Lord has a special purpose for you.'

22

Francis raised one eyebrow in the infuriating way he had recently learned.

Ned pinched his lips tighter and closed his eyes. She had tried to abandon him on the mountainside. Now she punished him with mockery and a boiled turnip. That mysterious special purpose – whatever it might be – was not glorious at all but a part of his penance. He tried to imagine the woman whom he had killed by being born.

Catharine pressed the wooden spoon until his upper lip split against his teeth. His eyes watered. He knew that he should welcome the pain as expiation. He deserved to suffer. Instead, he felt as full and tight as a blown-up pig's bladder. The feeling pushed at the top of his skull from the inside and swelled in his stomach, leaving no room for food. A sinful feeling, for sure.

'We shall all sit here until you open your mouth and eat,' his grandmother said. 'All night, if need be.'

Francis stirred in protest on his stool but dared not speak. Friends were waiting for him on the quayside of the Damrak.

Rather than add his brother's future torment to this present one, Ned opened his mouth. Fibrous lumps of turnip swilled round in his mouth. Hard as he chewed, they refused to disappear. Finally, he forced himself to swallow. The lumps of turnip seemed to lodge half-way down his gullet, wedged solid on top of the sinful feeling.

Freed from the table at last, he thudded eagerly behind his brother down the narrow wooden stairs from their top-floor lodgings.

'Stay here!' Francis pushed him down hard on to the bottom step. 'If the Good Lord's got his eye on you, the rest of us don't want Him to see what we're up to!' The brothers reverted to street Dutch as soon as they got out of their grandmother's hearing.

'He's not watching now! I'm sure He's not!'

Francis ruffled his brother's hair. 'Don't blub and I might bring you a cake if we snatch an extra one!' He disappeared across a humpbacked canal bridge.

23

Ned sat and kicked his heels against the stair, staring gloomily into the street, ignoring the other children who played there after supper. Then he wrapped his arms around his knees. He wanted to hit Francis. He wanted to cry. He needed to do *something* or he would burst.

A woman passed, carrying a baby in her arms, with a skirted toddler on leading reins to keep it from falling into the canals.

He rose from his stair and followed them along the narrow cobbled street that ran beside the canal. He was a dog tracking them. He closed his eyes and sniffed, caught her scent of sour milk, sweat and urine. He inhaled again and imagined that he also caught a whiff of something warmer, like the dense hot smell under a pile of fallen leaves. Where you could curl up and sleep.

As he followed, she paused and bent her mouth to the top of the baby's head, seemed to breathe in its smell. Then she walked on.

Ned picked up a loose cobblestone and threw it ferociously into the water. Bent to pick up another.

'Who's going to find ones to replace those?' demanded a man's voice. 'For shame! That's as good as stealing public property!'

Ned walked away as if he had not heard, but his ears glowed hot and bright under his dark curls.

Where's Josie Jugs? he thought angrily. She worked in a brothel around the corner and often gave him sweetmeats and taught him songs. But not tonight, it seemed.

And where's my friend, the ginger dog?

Everyone had abandoned him.

He wanted to cry, but self-pity was a wicked indulgence and denied to boys returned from Heaven for a special purpose. He went back to his place on the stairs, a thundercloud pregnant with a storm.

Mynheer Warde, who owned the house, lived with his wife on the middle floor and let the two small rooms under the roof to Catharine Malise and her grandsons. At street level, kitchen and cook were lodged at the back while Warde made lutes and violins in the front room that looked out onto the canal. Francis and Ned were forbidden, absolutely, to go into this workshop.

Propelled by his inner storm, Ned now stood up, crossed the little hall and stood in the workshop doorway. From there he could see a fascinating disorder: stinking glue pots with blowsy brushes resting on their tops, tiny sharp-toothed saws, wooden mallets, bright chisels, jars of shellac, pots of wax, stacked pine planks, sweet-smelling pear-wood shavings, and blocks of sleeping wood which, like an enchanter, Mynheer Warde would awaken into instruments. Necks and rounded backs of unfinished instruments lay on his workbench like dismembered limbs on a battlefield. A finished long-necked *chittarone*, as tall as Ned himself, leaned against one wall, indolent and elegant, like a tall slender dandy wearing old-fashioned padded trunk hose.

Warde also collected other instruments and had propped or hung them amidst the disorder. Ned clearly heard their voices: the high-pitched, self-satisfied complaint of a strange, long-necked three-stringed instrument with a squashed gourd of a belly. The staccato orders of the red Chinese drum, with silk tassels and gilding that glistened like a snail's track. The noble, wavering metallic cry of the bronze gong that hung just inside the workshop door, catching glints of late sun, in a mahogany frame as high as Ned's shoulder.

The instrument-maker was at supper with his wife. The workshop was empty. By merely stretching his arm through the workshop door, Ned could tap the gong. Very delicately, with his fingernail.

The flat bronze dish shivered and released a minute clamour, almost too fine to hear. A spark of late sunlight raced around its rim and back again. The pressure in Ned's chest and belly quivered in unison with the gong.

No one came. No one shouted at him.

He tapped again, just a little harder. The gong gave another shimmer, another wonderful, louder but still muted clamour.

The gong was waiting to be struck. Why else had it been made? Each time anyone passed, it begged for a whack. Though silent now, it was rigid with the strain of containing itself.

By chance, right beside his hand, a wooden mallet hung by a cord from the frame of the gong. He watched his fingers – creatures with a will of their own – close on the handle of the mallet. The hand lifted the mallet cord from its hook. He stepped through the workshop door and struck.

The gong leaped and shivered like the sea under a gust of wind.

'THANK YOU!' it cried. The wavering clamour sliced through his belly and bones.

I'll help you, he told it. Here you are again! He swung the mallet with both hands, with a force that seemed to lift him off his feet.

'AT LAST!' cried the gong. 'WHANGanngannganng!'

He struck again. 'WHANGANNGANNGanng!' And then again. Each blow sent a grateful tidal wave of sound crashing across the wake of the blow before. The room reverberated like the inside of a giant drum. The *chittarone* hummed with sympathetic pleasure. Two ebony string pegs leaped from the workbench to the floor. The sleeping pear blocks stirred in their dreams. The marrow shivered in Ned's bones.

'WHANGANNGANNGANNG! WAR! THE SPANISH! THE SECOND COMING!'

He shouted in unison with the awesome magnificence that he had freed, the splendour flung out by that grateful bronze dish. His child's voice grew huge and deep. He was the gong. He was God raising a storm, Jove flinging thunderbolts. He struck again and again. He struck aside all petty interference, struggled in the instrument-maker's arms, stretched and twisted, still trying to strike the gong yet again, and wept in fury as he was lugged upstairs to his grandmother, who was already on her way down to complain about the furore.

26

'My grandson?' Catharine's indignation gave way to disbelief and apology, under which Ned could hear a growing rage, and disbelief that he had been so ostentatiously wicked. Erred, not by careless inattention but by wilful design! Committed trespass and wanton disobedience, and then called such public attention to his sin!

His grandmother should have terrified him but she seemed distant, as she and everyone else had been distant when Francis once gave him strong wine at an inn. The gong still shivered wonderfully inside him.

Catharine led him into the single bedchamber which they all shared, pushed him on to his knees at her bedside. 'You will stay here and beg God for forgiveness – and contemplate your coming punishment – until bedtime prayers.' She locked the door as she left.

But he still quivered with a metallic clamour. Felt huge and powerful. Not in the least sorry.

However, if he didn't repent, he would go to Hell, which was like burning your hand on the poker but all over and forever.

If he did repent, he stood a chance.

He tried to drop back down into his everyday self. He tried to pray.

His grandmother was very, very disappointed in him. Nearly as bad as being damned, and much more immediate.

And yet. He still quivered.

He became a dog. A ginger one with a curled tail. Like his friend.

The dog – not Ned – was still too exhilarated to pray. The dog felt no guilt. The dog saw quite clearly that the East Indian gong had wanted to be struck. He had done it a favour. Broken the evil spell of silence that the instrument-maker had cast on it.

Oh, the relief, the shivering in his bones! How time had held its breath while his magnificent clamour shook the air!

The dog had done it! Not Ned Malise, aged six and sure

27

to be damned. The dog had sinned, not he. And while dogs could be whipped or penned up or hanged, they could not be damned, because they had no souls.

Nevertheless, the dog swallowed against a chilly, fretful queasiness. He growled gently in his throat.

Pah! A noise fit only for that unfriendly little spaniel who trotted by most Tuesdays and Fridays. He opened his throat and growled *basso*. Better. He growled again.

A staghound. Long-legged, with a noble arching muzzle (quite like his own Malise nose). With a rough grey coat. Fast and fearless, able to bring down a running stag with the help of only one other dog . . . a brother would do.

Madam, his grandmother, reared away in alarm on her slender doe's legs. He chased her in long easy bounds, darted at the pale fur of her throat, dodged the cutting edge of her hoofs, snapped at her flank to turn her, and made for her throat again. His fangs snapped shut. He felt the exquisite warmth of her throat between his jaws, smelt her delicious scent . . .

He stopped abruptly. Shifted his weight to his other knee, uneasy.

He began again. His grandmother (herself again) cried out for help as she cowered before a footpad with a sword. Without fear, the dog nobly flung himself between her and her attacker, ears laid flat to his head, fangs bared. The thief fled.

'Brave, good dog,' crooned his grandmother, stroking his rough grey head. Tears of relief and gratitude ran down the fine taut skin of her cheeks. 'Good boy. You saved my life!' She tore off the breast of the partridge on her silver plate and fed him with her own hand.

With satisfied dignity, the dog rose from his aching knees and stalked across the room, waving his great scimitar tail, to lean on the sill of the open window and sniff at the dusk. He read the air from top to bottom, left to right, as his ginger-furred friend did.

Peat and coal smoke. Canal slime, night soil, a whiff of rotten meat from the knacker in the next street, and a faint unexpected exclamation of rosemary. Waves of horse manure, decaying straw, human piss and stale beer rose from the courtyard below him where the instrument-maker's hens whirred and settled their feathers for the night under their basket cages, and the house mastiff turned in his straw in one corner of the yard.

A carpet of orange light suddenly unrolled across the cobbles from the open kitchen door beneath his window. The last pans and crocks clattered in the kitchen of the instrument-maker, over a lazy murmur of Dutch. Only half-dog now, he leaned from his window and tried, without success, to hear if the women in the instrument-maker's kitchen were gossiping about his crime. He rested his chin on his hands.

The heavy pulse of the day had stilled. No churns or hammers thumped. No rasping saws, ringing harnesses, hoofclaps on cobbles. Instead, the faint forced cheer of fiddles in a *musico*. Two distant drunks in the street bawled a musical inventory of female anatomy. A bat slipped past his head.

I should try again to pray, he thought. But all his senses were too alert and turned outwards into the night.

Then: on the neighbour's roof, a howl, a screech, a second jaw-trembling caterwaul, and the scrabble of cats' claws on tiles. The mastiff in the yard below him sprang to its feet. 'Howhoomp!' It gave a bark as deep as wind blowing down a well. A smaller watchdog from the neighbouring house barked inquisitively. Then there was silence again, an accidental conjunction of pauses, as profound as the silence after the gong had died.

The silence waited, a field of fresh snow in need of a footprint. A glassy pond poised for a stone.

He growled.

The mastiff's claws clicked on the cobbles. It split the silence wide open with its deep hoarse voice. 'Howhoomp? Who the devil are you?'

The dog in the high window opened his throat, like an organ pipe. 'I'm the biggest dog in Amsterdam,' he barked. 'Quake before me, you villain!'

29

'It's my courtyard! My court! My court!' The infuriated bellow reverberated around the brick walls of the yard.

'Pah! Lapdog!' he tossed back down with delight.

The hens woke under their baskets. 'What's wrong?' they squawked. 'Who's there? Is he hungry?'

'Now look what you've done!' cried the mastiff.

'Howhoomp!' bayed Ned the dog. 'Howhoomp! Howhoomp! What will you do about it, lapdog?'

'Kill you,' the mastiff bayed back. 'Kill you!'

'Lapdog! Lapdog!'

The frantic hens flung themselves against their woven basket cages. 'Death! Disorder!' they shrieked.

The neighbouring watchdog now joined in, raging at the wall that stood between it and all the fun. Another more distant dog added a tenor yelp.

'Help!' Ned yelped back across the rooftops, beside himself with pleasure. He braced his paws on the sill and leaned farther out. 'Help! Come help! Join the fun! Howhoomp!'

As he stared back down into the mastiff's eyes, the hair on his neck bristled straight up with pleasure and a real, growing rage. His white teeth gleamed. 'Kill you back!' he bayed down at the mastiff. 'Kill you back!'

Two more dogs joined in from across the alley which ran behind the house. The message spread across the neighbourhood, in soprano, alto, tenor, bass. War! Fun! War!

'Quiet, sir! Be quiet!' a man shouted to his dog. Women stood alarmed and curious in kitchen doors.

Ned drew a breath and listened to what he had made: a thick, rich delicious soup of sound that filled the low night sky, a hunting pack in full cry. *Basso* mastiff, as steady as a ground bass. Howhoomp. Howhoomp. Yips, yaps, howls and barks. A riot of canine convulsion spreading from street to street. Even, from the chamber just below him, the high yelps of the fat, flatulent, rheumy little beast that slept on Mevrouw Warde's pillow.

The key turned in the door.

He flung himself from window to bedside, but too late. His grandmother's purpose was set firm by this second public humiliation. She had her strap in her hand.

'Please say it,' she begged as she beat him. 'I never expected such a thing of you – a Malise and no better than a beast! Say it! Ask God to forgive you!'

He gritted his teeth and pressed his face into the bed.

'If I can't hear you, neither can God. Say it, please!' She wept with each blow.

He bruised his clamped lips against the mattress, flinched under the slow rhythm of her arm and waited for her to be done.

'Please ask the Lord to forgive you! Dogs are for guarding and hunting. Man is their master, set above them and all the other beasts by the decree of the Lord. Only Man looks up to Heaven. Beasts look down to Satan. I must tame the beast in you, Edward, for your own sake. For the family's sake!'

Fortunately, she soon grew too tired to lift her arm. There was a long silence while Catharine stood despairing and her grandson knelt with his face pressed into the coverlet.

'When you are older, you will thank me.'

When the key had turned in the lock behind her, he curled up on the floor, teeth clenched so hard that for some time he forgot how to part them again.

Why will I thank her? I never will!

Wicked or not, he tried and tried to become a dog again. But he was back, merely himself. Still curled on the floor, he slid towards a heavy, imperative sleep.

Who would want to be a boy? Boys can be both whipped and damned.

31

3

There are other ways a child can disappear. That she has vanished doesn't mean that I ate her!

But then, I welcomed the dog into my soul, did I not? And, if a dog, what else?

'Come, boy! Here, boy!' whispered Francis at midday dinner the next day when their grandmother's back was turned, clearing away their vegetable stew.

'French or English, Francis!' Catharine had not looked at Ned all morning but moved about her tasks with distant eyes and a preoccupied frown.

'This morning the whole *burt* knows that I have a looby for a brother,' whispered Francis. 'What possessed you?'

Catharine heard and turned on him in fury. 'He is not possessed! Don't dare say such things!' She raised her hand to slap him.

Francis stood up, faced her, daring her to strike.

Catharine drew a breath, looked up at her older grandson, now nearly a head taller than she. Then she shrugged and dropped her hand. 'Get out, Francis. Go do whatever it is that you do with your ragamuffin friends all day, but don't dirty your younger brother with it! Let him be!'

Francis turned and sauntered to the stairs.

Ned curled tight on his stool, trying to be a snail and hide inside his shell, away from the list of his miseries. He was

32

damned. His grandmother would not even look at him. And now Francis would never speak to him again. Or take him to inns or to gamble on board ships anchored at the docks.

Perhaps he really had managed to make himself invisible, for his grandmother prodded the fire and then began to slice an onion as if he weren't there.

Leaving the onion half-sliced, she went into their sleeping chamber and returned with a large book, which she set on a stool. Then she lowered her stiff hips on to the single wooden chair.

Though she still had the figure and bearing of a much younger woman, disappointment and poor food had set her joints rigid. The damp sea air made her right hip grate in its socket with every step, so loudly that Ned could hear it.

'Stand here by me.' She picked up one of the stumpwork panels which she stitched, whenever she was not needed at the leather shop, for a tailor to apply to the fronts of coats. 'Closer. There. Learn to stand respectfully, as you will have to do for many hours at a time at court.

'One hand behind your back, the other resting lightly on your breast bone, just touching the string of your collar.' She eyed him critically, then held her work close to her eyes. 'How the pattern wriggles! But at least I can see the black threads against the canvas.' She winced as she pushed her needle through the canvas. The ball of her right thumb had swollen painfully. 'How old are you now?'

'Six, madam. And three months.'

Catharine nodded. 'Your brother is out in the streets all day, every night, and not yet twelve years old.' She held her stumpwork close to her eyes again. 'Too handsome by half. And quick on his feet in every sense. I hope you don't study his manner, Edward. There's a touch of flippancy there that alarms me. And a hardness to his ambitions that doesn't suit a gentleman.'

'No, madam.' Ned felt a guilty stab of confused, unworthy pleasure at hearing her criticise his beloved older brother. He

33

shifted his weight to his other foot. The backs of his legs still smarted from last night's beating.

'You, at least, must be groomed into a Malise and not allowed to dwindle into a foreign street rat like your brother.'

Ned dropped his eyes. Given the choice, he preferred to be a street rat.

'You both need more tutoring than just the English and French that I can give you! And while Father St Hugh can no doubt manage the catechism perfectly well, I have no faith in his Hebrew and Greek. Nor much in his Latin except for prayers. Take that book.'

Ned hefted it with dismay. He knew at once that this volume was to be another penance. A weighty one. *Vulgaria*, said the title on its spine.

'Sit down.' Catharine pointed to the stool. 'That's a text for learning Latin, with Latin and English written side by side. I'm too old, and only a frail woman at that, the lesser vessel, but I'll do what I can. Start with the first page and read to me.'

She held the stumpwork up into the light of the window. Then dropped it on to her lap. 'Three hundred years behind us, all gone. With William, alive, in England, still at Tarleton Court, it would be simple. I would know what to do with you. William should never have died as he did. *Homo lupus homini*. That's one Latin precept I learned all too well! Man is a wolf to man.'

She stabbed at her needlework for several moments in silence, while Ned waited on his stool with the *Vulgaria* open on his knees, the black letters as dense and heavy as a ship's ballast of stones.

'I sometimes feel that William did not love me enough to choose otherwise.' She gave Ned a sly, frightened sideways look, as if she had just uttered an obscenity. Then she adjusted her face to its usual smooth calm. 'How can I think ill of him, after the way he died? I'm a wicked, wicked woman. Aren't I, Edward?'

34

He wished she wouldn't talk to him as if he knew what she was talking about. As if they were in collusion.

'God, forgive me . . .' she began. But she was off. Now the others came into her head, as they often did. '. . . My beautiful twins, with that pale duckling hair and little hands that clutched at my knees. Richard, my second son, dead of ague in Spain. And his poor, poor wife who split like an overripe peach when you were born.'

He began to close the book very, very slowly.

She laid her hands on her knees like a pair of plates and studied them. 'So red, no matter how many unguents . . . those dyed leathers every day . . . no matter how I wash.' She turned them over and gazed at her knobby palms. 'Who could have foretold . . . ? When I was a girl, they were white and soft. What a journey . . . getting here.'

Ned looked over his shoulder at the door.

She stood up abruptly. 'When I fled from England, I had to walk like this . . .' She leaned her small frame forward against the remembered drag of gold plate, necklaces, the altar candlesticks, the coins sewn into her petticoats. 'You must listen and remember!' She turned on him. 'A leather pouch of gold coins dug into me here, under my stomacher.' She pressed a hand to her ribs. 'All sharp knobs and edges. Can you feel it? Try to imagine!' Her eyes probed, as if she wished to transfer her memories along their beam into his head.

He ducked his head and looked at the floor.

She sat back down and picked up her needlework. 'I can see that you don't understand. Read to me now. We shall do this every day.

'Good morrow,' Ned began obediently. '*Bonum tibi huius diei sit primordium.*' It seemed a long way to go about a simple greeting. 'Good night. *Bona nox.*' That's better. *Bona nox,* he repeated to himself silently. 'How fare you? *Qua valitudine . . .*' He saw that his grandmother was not listening and lifted several pages to see what lay ahead.

'I am weary of study,' he read silently. '*Tedet me studij.*'

35

He looked at the next page. 'I am almost beshitten. *Sum in articulo purgandi viscera.*' He inhaled with startled delight. Then he found, 'You stink. *Male oles.*' Then, farther on, 'He hath married a wife. *Duxit uxorum.* He is a cuckold . . .' Then, an unimaginable list, the parts of the body. 'Lungs, stomach, heart. *Hic pulmo, hic stomachus, hoc cor.*' And just below those, '*hec nates, hic podex, hic penis.* Buttocks, arsehole . . .'

'And what has delighted you so?' demanded his grand-mother. 'I told you to read it to me aloud.'

He jumped with guilt and flipped back to his starting page, but even there his eyes first landed on 'A turd in thy teeth! *Merda dentibus inheret.*' He could not let her take away this wonderful book! He searched the page.

'Beggars be ragged and bawdy,' he read at last. '*Mendici scuti and squalidi sunt.*'

'That's true enough,' she said.

He sagged with relief. Searched the page, chose carefully. 'Take heed to thyself. *Cave tibi.*'

'Take that one to heart,' she said. 'I fear so for both of you in this city. When I first came here to Amsterdam, I believed that I was saving us all from death by the slow dripping of bile in that French farmhouse. But I saw the error of my choice of haven even before I found lodgings. What comes next?'

His eyes skated wildly over the page looking for something proper enough. 'I go into the city. *Confero me in urbem.*'

'I must speak to you of that.' Catharine set her needlework on her lap again. 'This city is not ours . . .'

Amsterdam was at the centre of the East Indies trade, peopled with sailors, foreigners and all other manner of shady dealers, Catharine told him. Also, The United Provinces of the Netherlands, of which Amsterdam was the chief city, were caught up in the long, long war with Spain and her Hapsburg rulers. Dutch soldiers, mercenaries of all breeds, and their attendant evils crowded into the taverns, *bordeels* and *musicos*.

She drew a deep breath. 'They roar, piss and even fornicate in the streets.'

36

Ned was nearly as amazed by this uncharacteristic frankness as he had been at the anatomical list in her book. Her information, however, came as no surprise to him.

But she had not finished. A scarlet tide rose up her neck and cheeks. 'These men also . . . sometimes they solicit unwary children . . .' She glared at Ned. 'I wish William were here, but he's not, so I must speak for him. These men may urge you to . . . carry doubtful messages. Or worse.'

Ned scratched his small blunt chin. Grandmother didn't know the half of it. Francis earned much of his money on just such errands.

'And then there are the sinful women,' she said. 'Does your book warn you against them as well as against beggars?'

'I shall look, madam.'

'Do that tomorrow. You may go now.'

With relief Ned escaped down the narrow stairs into the street.

That afternoon there was still no sign of Josie Jugs and her red feathers and rich animal smell. Or her friend, Catryn the Corset. He walked a little along the canalside, kicking a fallen potato with alternate feet. Then he heard Josie laugh, and spotted her in the murky shadows of an alley. A man had pressed her back against a wall with her skirts heaped up over her hips. Ned's breath tightened. He wanted both to watch and to run. With a jolt he realised that Josie must be one of his grandmother's sinful women. He took one last quick, oblique look at the thrusting hips of Josie's customer and walked on.

He whistled for the ginger dog with the curly tail. When his friend trotted around the corner, they set off on a hunt together.

'Prey!' whispered Ned suddenly. Silently, he and the dog stalked closer and closer to a little girl, about Ned's age, dressed in pink silk, who sat blowing bubbles from a mussel shell on the *stoep* of a big house a few streets away. They were lithe and hungry hunters, stalking an unwary prey. Two bubbles in succession burst without lifting free of the shell. The little girl

37

cursed like a sailor and went back into the house. At the last second she flashed a blue-eyed look at Ned.

She had seen them after all. Had chosen to ignore her danger, as if they were of no account, made them look like fools. Ned blushed hotly.

The hunters then let themselves be drawn away by the delicious butter and cinnamon smell of the *wafflewife* in the next street, which reached them even before her call.

Ned ran to meet her.

'Hello, good-looking.' She smiled and gave him his usual gift of broken and overdone waffles.

On the canal edge near his lodgings, the ginger dog now waited to have its ears scratched. Ned gave it the last piece of waffle, then offered his hand, and then his face, to be licked. They sniffed at each other, then settled together under a tree where he could see both the canal and the street that rose up over it on a hump-back bridge. For a time, Ned was perfectly happy. Temporarily safe from any special fate, he and the dog watched the noisy, busy streets of the city which his grandmother said he must not call his own.

He leaned over and made a face at his reflection. Dared the water to reach up and grab him again.

'Three days after you stood up for the first time, you tried to touch your reflection in the Singel,' his grandmother had told him. 'Your skirt hem slipped from my fingers. Eight feet you fell . . . down into that dark water until all I could see was a little white ghost beneath a floating shoe. Thank the Lord, a passing cabbage-seller fished you out.'

He forced himself to hang there, above the thing that still waited down in the darkness to get him. All the hungrier because he had cheated it before.

That same afternoon, when he had been about fourteen months old, she had had a leather harness made, with a long rope attached between his shoulder blades. Then she had tied him to the table leg. He remembered the bite of the harness.

38

'You may blub,' she had told him. 'But how else am I to keep you alive and out of trouble?'

At first, whenever he raged, leaning out on his taut rope like a sailor in rigging, she beat him. Not hard, as he was still very young.

'You'll understand,' she told him in frustration, 'when you're older, why you, even more than most children, must be tamed away from your natural wild and sinful bent.'

He made another face at his reflection now. He hadn't asked to be singled out.

He wished Francis were there. His brother knew everything that he himself was still too young to know. But Francis was off on his search for whatever it was that he could never find to make him content. Ned closed his eyes and saw his brother's handsome face skewed by a permanent secret bitter joke.

After a while, Ned knelt with his forearms on the cobbles and became a dog too. He sniffed the air and listened, reading the day as the dog did. Flowers, pigs and chickens trailed their smells past them, below on the canal. Ale and tobacco smoke from the inns and *bordeels*. He looked at the sky and waited for the bells.

Almost at once, church bells from eighteen churches lurched into a spasm of metallic clamour. Three o'clock. Some days, like today, the bells took him over. Rang in his bones and twanged at his sinews. He became a bell, as he had become the gong. Sometimes more, sometimes less. Sometimes he could stand back and merely listen. And still other times the bells joined with the rest of the city to batter painfully at his senses. On those days he fled back home, into bed and pulled a blanket over his head to muffle the pounding of the world.

When the bells fell silent, he looked at passing faces for recognition of what had just happened. He thought everyone heard, smelled, saw and tasted the world as keenly as he.

At the docks, he and the dog sat on a coil of tarry rope, looking out at the great merchantmen moored beyond the double palisade of dolphins which protected the harbour. Ned listened to the shouts, bells, whistles, the sharp crack of snapping canvas, the duller thump of ropes, the rumble of barrels being unloaded down wooden ramps. He delivered a letter for a ship's officer and earned five *stuivers* which he spent on a meat pie. Then he and the dog settled again on the canalside near St Anthony's Gate and listened to the morose slap of water against the canal walls, the suck and splash of oars, the agitated, staccato drip of water running off the oars, the slurp and belch of drains. The dog licked between his fingers for the last traces of salt and meat pie.

A little after the four o'clock bells, a fiddler in a nearby *bordeel* began to practise a new bawdy tune to please the customers later that evening. Not knowing the lyrics, Ned sang along in pure sound. The bones of his face vibrated pleasurably. Music made in him a calm, secret centre, a sense of balance. He wished that Francis would deign to sing.

The dog skewed its ears as the fiddler's bow slipped and shrieked across a string. Sometimes Ned could induce it to howl as he sang, but not today. He then slept with his head on the dog's warm, pleasantly smelly flank.

'Edward!' his grandmother called down from their window. 'Come up to supper and bed!'

But he was a dog, and dogs ate and slept in the streets, just like his friend here. Dogs had no secret purpose that they didn't understand.

'EDWARD! I can see you down there! What are you doing with that filthy, flea-bitten beast?'

As he did not want to risk another beating like that of the night before, he stretched his head and foreparts upwards just as the dog did, yawned doggily, then rose reluctantly on to two feet.

40

4

For the next year, he read to his grandmother in the mornings, and spent his afternoons in the streets. His grandmother often studied him in a way that made him uncomfortable. Then she would suddenly seize his hand, or touch his hair.

One evening when he was seven and a half years old, she called him in earlier than usual for supper and bed.

'Stand as I have taught you to do in my presence.'

While Ned watched, one hand resting on his breast where the string of his collar would be if he were wearing one, she chose an iron key from the ring on her belt, unlocked the cupboard built into the wall, and took out a heavy, cloth-shrouded bundle. She removed the cloth. In the wavering firelight, the figures engraved on the gleaming surface moved as if alive.

'Solid silver. It's very fine, is it not?'

He reached out, then looked at her.

'You may touch it. It's your right.'

'What is it?' he whispered.

'The Malise Salt, from our table at Tarleton Court.'

He touched one of the dolphins that leapt around the silver pillow of the base. Then he stroked the bishop's robe worn by St Mark, who balanced unsteadily on his lion's back as if it were a stepping stone in a bog. On the other three sides of the shining square tower that rose from the base, he saw Matthew, Luke and John (whom he knew by their lamb, ox and dictating angel) struggling through overgrown silver

41

gardens. Silver flowers snared their ankles and twined around their feet. Silver gadrooning, and festoons of acanthus and ivy closed in from all sides.

He was sure that they must also feel the weight of the vast silver dome above their heads, where a battle raged between horned demons and angels in Spanish uniforms. And of the column above that, on the very top of which perched a single lonely figure in Ancient costume, a foot and a half above the table.

'You poor things.' He grasped the column and lifted the weight of the battle from the saints' heads.

'Yes,' said his grandmother. 'That is the bowl for the salt itself.'

Under the dome, in a silver hollow, nested a small, blue glass bowl, the tiny, vivid heart of the amazing edifice.

She sighed with remembered pleasure. 'I always polished the Salt myself and set it on our table at Tarleton Court on Saints' Days and whenever visitors came.' She peered into his eyes for a reflection of her memories. 'I don't know how I carried such a thing from England! I hardly knew what I did as I prepared to flee. Yet my hands chose well enough by themselves . . . rings, gold, silver . . . and when I opened my bags in the Savoie, there it was!'

She found an oiled rag among the cloth wrappings and began to rub at the lion, fiercely, as if to wipe the slightly simpering smile off its face. The metallic tang of yielding tarnish crowded out the stink of hot animal glue from Warde's workshop down-stairs. Her single candle bloomed into forty tiny reflected ones.

'Imagine it, Edward. A table twenty-six feet long, of polished oak the colour of honey.'

As she spoke, their own small, rough table grew, stretched out into the shadows and gleamed with her own beeswax polish, made from wax from the estate hives. Her candlelight fell on velvets, silks, pewter and silver plates, silver-rimmed drinking vessels of horn. It broke into stars on the surface of the Salt in the centre of the table.

'Imagine, my darling.'

Ned was there with her at Tarleton Court, their family's old home, which was Paradise on earth.

'Above the Salt, your grandfather William, me, guests, our bailiff, and Father St Fiacre . . . the late sun through the tall window always reflected from his bald pate. Below it sat my waiting women, our clerk, the boys' tutor. And the musicians, of course. The dogs under the table and benches, except for little Aphrodite curled on my lap. I saw to it that the chamber always smelt of fresh-cut rushes and new bread.'

Her voice changed. 'Men will destroy anything to get what they want, even kings. Even William in his own way.' She reached out and took the dome from him, rubbed fiercely at one of the oddly helmeted angels with the dome lid braced against her stomacher.

Ned was jolted back to Amsterdam, found himself watching her polish the Malise Salt while she stayed at Tarleton Court without him.

He knew that his family had once been wealthy enough to eat meat every day, for she often said so. They had once owned estates in England and held powerful positions at the court. Something terrible had happened, so that she and he and Francis lived in Amsterdam now. But none of that explained why she wanted him to watch her polish the Salt.

Other things puzzled him almost as intensely. Why, for example, were the angels disguised as Spaniards, who were enemies of the Dutch?

With a rattle of silver on wood, his grandmother set the dome lid down and leaned on the table.

She looked so odd that Ned cried out, 'What's the matter, madam?'

'A bee is buzzing in my chest.' She looked frightened. She stared at the edge of the table with such wide eyes that Ned looked too.

Death poked his head above the table. With prickling scalp, Ned saw the white, naked teeth and hairless crown.

43

'GOT YOU!' Death said. 'I'm really here. Any time now. As quick and unexpected as this. BOO!'

But after a moment, Death pulled his head down and stayed out of sight. His grandmother resumed her polishing. Ned could see that she was somewhere else again. He watched for Death to pop back up, not knowing what he would do if it did.

Without looking at him, she said, 'Go to bed now, Edward. I can see that you're still too young.'

He kissed her smooth, dry offered cheek.

'What am I to do with you? I haven't much time.' She smoothed back his hair. 'My little falcon chick. You're all that's left.'

He fled to their single sleeping chamber, pulled the bed he shared with Francis out from under her bed and yanked the coverlet over his head. Wonderful as it was, the Malise Salt filled him with alarm.

The next evening, when Francis and Ned climbed the stairs for their supper, the Malise Salt stood on the table. Huge and shining, a gleaming cathedral rising from a squalid slum. She had never set it out before.

They looked at each other. Ned's stomach tightened.

'Sit down,' said their grandmother.

They sat but continued to stare covertly.

'I can't remember how I carried it from England.' Their grandmother placed an earthenware bowl of vegetable stew on the table and sat down on her stool. 'Your father had all of my gold and diamond eardrops sewn into the sleeves of his little jacket. And Mary . . .' Her small mouth closed on the inventory of dead children whose weight her arms still seemed to feel. Abruptly, she folded her hands and bowed her head.

'Lord, who nourishes the least of your sparrows,' she sang.

'Give us our daily bread.' The boys' voices joined hers.

'And fish on the occasional Friday, if that's not asking too much,' whispered Francis so that only Ned could hear.

44

She served the vegetable stew into their clay Delftware bowls.

'Now. This spoon is made of silver.' She lifted her wooden spoon. 'And this . . .' she tapped her flat earthenware bowl '. . . is pewter.'

Ned and Francis gawped at her. They glanced at each other, then at their plates. It was well known that old women often went mad.

'Look at me! This . . .' she touched her spoon to a turnip '. . . is a quail. Which is *une caille* in French.'

Ned began to flush with misery on her behalf. Surely she must know that she had gone mad!

'How would you set about eating it?' she demanded.

'As fast as possible, given the chance,' said Francis.

'Edward?'

In spite of his bravado, Francis flushed at this dismissal.

'I'm afraid that I've never eaten one,' said Ned with careful civility.

'Time that you learned. God will send you back to England one day and you must be ready. First, take some salt.'

While Francis crossed his arms and sat back on his stool, Ned gazed helplessly at the Salt. The figure perched at the very top of the slim round column above the dome looked giddy, as if he wished he could climb down to somewhere safer.

'Edward!' Her voice was throaty and commanding for someone of such small stature.

He straightened.

'I said, please take some salt. Have you forgotten all your English?' She smiled to soften the rebuke. 'Remove the dome with your left hand . . . Yes. Now, take up a little salt on the tip of your knife and put it in a single mound on the side of your bowl. Never directly on to your food.'

He did as she said, carefully.

'Now you, Francis. You might as well learn, too. And try not to snigger or you will spill it.'

45

Ned stared at the silver jungle nearest to him. The silver vines grappled on to his ankles as they did St Luke's.

'. . . never give such small bones to the dogs; they will stick in their throats . . . Edward!'

He had missed something. Francis slouched on his stool again with his arms crossed.

'Hold your knife, so. As I just showed you. Insert the tip into the leg joint . . .'

With burning ears, Ned dissected his turnip, skewered from one side by the intense eyes of his grandmother and from the other by the ironic ones of his older brother. She nodded approval. He laid down his knife with relief and began to wipe his hands on his thighs.

'No!' Her brow contracted. Her voice cut. 'A sailor or ploughman might have no other choice. But you will have a serving man, who will offer you linen and rosewater, from your left. Turn a little, like this . . . shoulders only. Dip your hands gently – don't scrub as if just back from the stables – and dry like this.'

She seemed to see the serving man, basin and linen towel. She gave Edward one of her rare, astonishing smiles that showed her still good, white front teeth. 'Go ahead, my pet. You may feel foolish now, but you will be grateful to know these things when the time comes.'

While the boy repeated her dumb show she watched critically, with the odd cud-shifting movements of tongue and jaw that Francis swore were proof that she padded gaps at the back of her gums with wadding.

'You may now wipe your knife on your bread.'

He did, with relief. The ordeal seemed to be over.

'Now drink me a toast.'

He flushed as red as Francis had done earlier, and shrugged helplessly.

She sighed with restrained impatience. 'If you had been born and raised at Tarleton Court as you should have been, you would know how.'

46

'Sorry,' he mumbled, then thought how stupid he was to apologise for having been born in the wrong place. His red ears throbbed so that they seemed to beat against his skull.

'. . . In the Tower Chamber, where there is light enough for the midwife to see. My favourite room, with garlands painted on the beams. You will love it too. Your father was born there, and Mary. I kept my wedding chest there, which is why I had to leave it, too heavy for me to carry down those stairs alone.' Her eyes turned to the Malise Salt. 'The Lord knows how . . .' Then she looked down at her hands on either side of her plate of turnips and potatoes.

Francis made the mistake of drinking from his mug.

'Oh, yes . . . the toast,' she said. 'Close your eyes, Edward. Try to see it. You hold a silver tankard. The points of your sleeves are tipped in silver. Fine shoes on your feet, not those dispiriting clogs. Your grandfather is here beside me, where you will sit in time, in his carved chair-of-grace, on a blue silk cushion that I embroidered myself and stuffed with the finest wool from our own sheep.'

Ned opened his eyes, now certain that he, too, would see his grandfather, the way he had seen the table grow and gleam in the candlelight the night before. But all he saw was the usual scrubbed wood and the remains of his turnip.

Francis smirked.

'Yes, William here.' She laid a hand tenderly on the rough empty table beside her. 'And Father St Fiacre there. Then Cousin Ambrose and his second wife – the first died, of course, when their second child was born.' Her large eyes now looked into the air. 'Cousin Cecilia who played the lute . . . After dining, we sang and danced. I'm sure that the Lord was pleased to see His children in innocent diversion. He asked to be praised with music, did He not?'

She rose to her feet and sang, '*Au premier jour du joly moys de may* . . .' Her voice was light and husky but still true. 'Sing with me!'

They joined in obediently. Francis croaked but Ned sang

47

high and clear, and with delight. He felt the secret pleasure of music begin to flood his body. His grandmother smiled into his eyes and he smiled back. He was pleasing her. Everything was all right again.

Suddenly she leaned on the table, arms braced.

'Are you ill, madam?' Both boys spoke at once.

Ned thought he saw a flash of white bone whip back beneath the table edge.

'My heart was as light as my petticoats then.' She placed one hand against her stomacher as if in pain, still leaning on her other arm. 'How my skirts drag! And the pouch digs into my ribs. Mary in my arms and little Richard holding tight to my sleeve.'

'Yes, madam.' Her grandsons helped her to sit again.

'Drink a little.' Francis held her mug up to her lips. Insolent or not, he had no other family.

A small, cold hand clamped on to Edward's wrist. '*You* drink. Do as an old woman asks.' Her eyes pressed a message into his.

He looked to his brother for help.

'Is it so distasteful to toast this poor shadow of what I should have been?'

'No, no,' he mumbled.

'Don't lie. *I* find it distasteful. Age is quite demeaning enough. It's unbearable also to have become so much less than I expected. You should mind! You should hunger, both of you, for more than another piece of bread or – if God is kind – a roasted capon!' Her rage grew with each word. 'You should hunger!'

Bang! Her wooden spoon hit the table. 'To be.' Bang! 'Your rightful selves!' Bang!

Edward flinched. The table was his head and she meant to pound her words into it like nails. Everything was no longer all right.

He was an unspeakable item that she had just spied in a ditch. He looked away, tried again to meet her large eyes, which could

48

once have found her another husband easily enough if she could have stomached a foreigner. Then he looked at the Salt, and then he studied his chipped bowl which in no way resembled pewter. His ears burned once more. On balance, he preferred to be whipped.

Even Francis was still, his brow unarched.

That night he could not sleep. To get away from his grandmother's snores and Francis's grunts in their shared sleeping chamber, he flew out of the window to sit on the stable roof, where he sang the *Chant des oyseaux*. He was a lark, a nightingale, an owl.

'Forgive me.' She suddenly held out her hand from her chair where she was listening to him read.

He looked up from the *Vulgaria* at the reddened, knobby hand. Her face was so different, pale and taut as parchment. With her silver hair and her body like a girl's, something both seductive and imperative in her manner made him uneasy.

'I was harsh with you at supper.' She waved the hand impatiently for him to draw near.

He put down the book and crossed to her slowly, with an instinct to resist and the craving for her touch at war in him.

She caught his hands and held him prisoner while she studied him.

'Seven and a half years and already growing tall. Fine dark hair, like a crow's wing. Like my dearest William. Light eyes with dark lashes. And your face will grow to meet the nobility of that Malise nose. It will sit very well one day. You will be a handsome man. As handsome as your grandfather.'

While he flushed with helpless pleasure, she dropped his hands and gave him a small key. 'Open the cupboard and take out the Salt.'

He lifted it out, very carefully. It was even heavier than it looked.

'It is yours.'

49

He dropped it on to the table, then grabbed the giddy stylite on top of the column to steady the wobbling dome.

'Not Francis?' As the older, it should be his by right. Ned knew and didn't really mind.

'I'm sure that you know your brother even better than I do. Would you give him the most valuable thing you own?'

Her unexpected candour shocked him as much as the gift, as if she had blasphemed, or cursed like Josie Jugs. She had not only flouted the usual order of things, she wanted to engage him in a conspiracy, with Francis on the outside. And, in spite of Francis's rough teasing, Ned adored his brother.

But she was right. Francis had dealings in the Amsterdam streets and brothels about which he had been sworn to silence in blood.

'You, not Francis, will return the Malise Salt to its rightful place on our table at Tarleton Court,' she said. 'I know. I have known since you were born. Ever since the eagle.'

There was nothing safe for him to say, so he kept silent. He felt more and more agitated.

'Do you remember why I had to flee from England, Edward?'

'Grandfather died.' He looked at her warily.

'Died!' She half-rose from her chair and subsided again. 'To say "died", as if he were no more than a pup being drowned!' She put her hand on her heart. 'It's buzzing again, under my ribs . . . I was there with him, in my last act of married devotion, begging him to breathe deep of the smoke!' She stared at her grandson, who could never, not ever, no matter how often she told him, imagine how it had been.

'Madam?' Her eyes had gone oddly opaque.

'The Queen murdered your grandfather. For books. My husband chose to die for *books*!'

The boy nodded and stared at his toes.

'I can see that you don't understand. In your place, I wouldn't either. It's no use! I can't do it. Go away!'

'But, madam . . .' Did she want him to put back the Salt?

50

After a moment, he did. She ignored him and sat staring at the window with blind eyes, but then called him back before he reached the stairs.

'Sit there.' She disappeared into their sleeping chamber.

Ned hovered near the stairs. He had had enough now. Wanted to escape into the bright morning in the street, to Josie Jugs and his ginger-furred, curly-tailed friend. He might even decide to run away.

His grandmother returned and handed him a worn, folded piece of parchment. 'Read it.'

It was in English. At first, his reluctant eyes saw only an account. Then he read it again, carefully, wanting not to trust his reading.

Item:

For 10 loads of peat to burn him		40 shillings
For a half boll of coal		12 shillings
For a stake and the dressing of it		17 shillings
For 2 fathoms of tow		2 shillings
For a barrell of tar		7 shillings
For the executioner, for his pains	4 pounds	12 shillings
For the carrying peat and coal to the marketplace		3 shillings
For showing the instruments of torture		16 shillings
For the first degree of torture		3 shillings
For the horse and cart for taking what remains		8 shillings

Count given out by Henry Nightingale in London in the year of God 1580 for William Francis Malise of Tarleton Court Hertfordshire, his execution.

'Do you remember your grandfather's crime?'

Ned shook his head helplessly. 'You said, books.'

'He died for remaining true to the Holy Church of Rome. He dared to distribute books written in the Catholic faith. And this act of Christian duty was called treason!'

51

She leaned over his shoulder and pointed with a trembling finger. 'And while the executioner was paid a mere four pounds and twelve shillings for disembowelling my husband and then burning him while still alive, the man who signed this account . . . Henry Nightingale . . . burn that vile name on to your heart . . . was given Tarleton Court – your family's house for one hundred and seventeen years – by his grateful monarch!'

She was weeping now. 'Is that account a fit gift to give a widow just five minutes made, while her husband's ashes were still smoking? For immediate settlement! And my eyes could scarce read it. They still saw his hair flaring up and imagined his skin blistering inside the tarred hempen coat. And my nostrils still wide with smoke and the scent of his roasting flesh!'

'I'm sorry, grandmother. I'm so sorry!' Edward burst into tears. 'What can I do? What do you want me to do?'

'Put it right.'

TWO

5

Ned still did not understand exactly how his grandmother thought he would put things right, but for the next four years, he schooled himself as well as he could to be ready for whatever he would have to do.

He practised civility at all the times when he remembered. He crammed down Latin and as much Greek as their priest, Father St Hugh, could manage. He learned to bow gracefully to his grandmother and then, without smirking, led her out in a pavane or galliard in their smoky low-ceilinged chamber. He mastered, earnestly, in both French and English and with a straight face, the carving of imaginary woodcock, duck, goose and swan. He lifted the bones cleanly from his grandmother's real fried fish.

This paragon also practised sword play with Francis (who had learned it who knows where and not in its purest form), prayed in three languages, and, under his grandmother's critical eye, mastered the handling of a borrowed hat. He read the lives of the saints when he wanted to be out in the streets. He kept his feelings about everything firmly to himself, including some that even he himself didn't know he had.

The other Ned – street-rat Ned, or Dab Ned, as Francis called him when feeling amiable – was still friends with whores, still caught fleas from dogs, still frequented inns with his brother and, as he grew older, began to deceive his grandmother.

When she believed that he was memorising moral precepts

55

from the *Vulgaria*, he was in fact enlarging his vocabulary in both Latin and English with every wickedness he could extract from the warnings and prohibitions in the book: *matula*, pisspot; *fedo*, a fart; *mulier portentosae libinis*, an exceeding strong whore.

He tried to learn such improving observations as 'Striped kerchiefs and shirts be instruments of pride and lechery'. But willy-nilly found himself staring at words like *hic penis*: a man's cock, his tool, his instrument, his yard. He searched furtively for the Latin for breasts, babs, paps, jugs, Cupid's drums.

Inexorably he always arrived at *hic vulva*. Still the great mystery, in spite of his half-accidental spying on whores. *Locus ubi puer concipitur*. The place where children are conceived. The silk purse, the flap, the slit, the Paradise (even more unimaginable than Tarleton Court) which he must also one day enter and take.

In the streets, he began to find himself peering at women's skirts as if his will could turn them transparent. He began to blush whenever he met Josie Jugs or Catryn the Corset, and could think only of the dark secret they carried so matter-of-factly between their legs.

With trembling hands, he leafed through the pages searching for every variant of that basest word of all, to add to the words he had learned in the street. Fuck, fiddle, swive, play at pickle-me-tickle-me. To occupy, vault, spike, mow and mount. Poke, tumble and trounce. Prod, stretch the leather, dance the buttock jig.

His small boy's instrument (tool, sword, club) sprang to rigid attention. He was still too young to know what to do about it and, even more than the fear of damnation, the shared bed and bed chamber prevented experiment.

He soon found himself trapped in a tedious cycle of confession, penance for sinful thoughts, and helpless reoffending, while his grandmother imposed his harshest penance by praising him for his virtue and hard work. His deepest agony was to stand civilly in the street while her friends wished, with sighs, that their own children or grandchildren were more like him. However, with all its sweaty discomforts, he was later to remember this time as one of perfect joy and a purer, distracting passion.

The instrument-maker, though a preoccupied, unsmiling man, had soon forgiven him for the episode of the gong, and one day at last invited Ned into the workshop to hear how the other instruments could speak. Warde had let him beat the red Chinese drum with its polished, red lacquer beater, and had watched unsmiling as he made his eardrums bulge trying to blow sound from a long wavy wooden horn.

The next day the man pretended not to notice when Ned hung silently in the workshop door watching him work. Ned reappeared the next day, then the next. As Warde never objected, nor even seemed to notice, Ned rushed down to the workshop door every day for the next several months after his morning studies.

He loved the smells – stinks and all – which plaited themselves in the air like notes of a song. He loved the different coloured woods which hid secret peg blocks, or long necks, or sounding boards or round curved lute backs locked inside their rough-featured blocks and planks. He loved the shining bottles of oil, the jars of brushes, the milky beeswax chunks. He loved the way Warde lost himself in his work, the care with which he chose just the right tool for each task, the way he caressed the emerging shapes of lute, angelica and mandolin as if they were beloved children. Or women.

He loved the scraping irons which were often shaped like leaves or flattened bells. Loved the knives with brass and steel blades, some arrow-straight, some half-moon scimitars, and the rest in as many curves as there are in the leaves of a tree. Almost more than anything else, Ned loved the wonderful ranks of chisels and fine-toothed saws with polished wooden handles, some of them tiny and delicate enough to be used by a miniature angel, each of them as beautifully made as the instruments which they helped to release. His hands ached just to touch them, one at a time. The thought of using one of

57

those chisels to pare a curled shaving from a block of pine as smoothly as butter or to lift off a black wafer of ebony inlay made tears of excitement stand in his eyes. He hated Warde's intense, busy apprentice, who still did no more than sweep the floors and tend the hot glue pot but would one day learn such skills.

One day, about a year after the gong incident, Warde laid out his parchment patterns on his workbench to begin a new instrument. He rummaged among his piled woods, and pulled out a long flat board, which he dangled by his ear between two fingers. He tapped it, first with a short metal rod, then with a wooden one. Even from the door, Ned could hear the faint answering voice from inside the board, a dull, thick, sullen response. Warde set aside the board and picked up another.

'What are you doing?' Ned burst out. He had seen Warde do this several times before but feared to speak lest he be shooed away.

'Come listen.'

Not believing his good fortune, Ned stepped once more into the workshop with its master's blessing.

Warde held the pale, fragrant sand-coloured wood near Ned's ear and snapped it with his forefinger.

This block, unlike the first, gave a high, clear ringing 'tock'.

'It wants you to use it!' cried Ned. 'Listen. Hit it again!'

Warde gave him an odd look. Again, the clear 'tock'.

'What did you hear?' asked Warde. Unsmiling in any case, he now seemed poised as if he might suddenly pounce.

Ned blushed, afraid that he had been uncivil, even impudent.

'What did you hear?' Warde asked impatiently. 'Why did you say that it wanted to be used?'

'It's happy,' mumbled Ned. 'Not like the first one.'

Warde chose another board and gave it to Ned. 'Translate this one for me.'

Ned tapped it. Another sullen fellow. 'No,' he said. 'No. It sounds like the first.'

Warde took the second board and fastened it into a vice.

'Do you only use the boards that sing?' asked Ned.

'Only those without knots.' Warde did not look at him again as he meditated over his choice of saw. Nor did he ask Ned to leave.

'What mischief have you been making with our landlord?' Catharine demanded as she served their evening potato and cabbage broth. Her spoon shook with contained rage.

In warm weather they ate their evening meal with the table shoved over into the light of the single unglazed window, which looked out over the street and the canal. At the last minute, Francis pounded up the stairs and slid on to his stool.

'Mischief, madam?' Ned's ebullience withered into the premonition of despair. He had misread Warde's kindness. Been a nuisance after all. The man had complained to his grandmother. He would be forbidden to watch from the doorway ever again. At the best.

'He went so far as to come up here to speak to me himself.'

Ned kept his eyes on his bowl.

'He had the effrontery to misunderstand our straitened circumstances.' Catharine banged the iron pot back down on to the hearth with a dull clang and rattling of spit chain. When she returned to her own seat, she began to eat her broth silently, with angry brow and distant eyes. She shook her head to herself with a single, dismissive jerk of her chin.

'How so, madam?' He had to know his fate.

'He offered to take you as his apprentice.' She spat out the words as if Warde had wanted Ned for a groom to empty piss-pots.

Ned let out a breath of delight. Apprentice, yes! Yes, yes! Earthly Paradise had invited him to stroll right in. His hands already searched, like Warde's, along the row of tools, feeling for the one that asked to be used.

'I told him civilly – for he controls the roof over our

59

heads – that, contrary to what he seems to imagine, you are a gentleman, and gentlemen, in England at least, where such things are understood, do *not*, in any circumstances, ever consider learning a trade!' She sipped her broth and shifted her cheek padding with her tongue. 'One must be civil from charity too. There are no gentlemen in Holland, only this dreary, intolerable equality!'

'But, madam, Warde would pay for Ned. Might even take less rent,' said Francis recklessly.

'Edward is not to be bought by anyone, tradesman or otherwise,' snapped Catharine. She turned her eyes on Francis. 'I've long since given up on you, my boy. With your raggle-taggle friends, quick eye and greedy fingers. You imagine that there's an easier way than honour and duty. Don't think I don't guess what you get up to.'

Francis's face went white. Then he smiled. 'I bow to your word as always, madam, and remain a hopeless case. But I want what you want, even if you don't believe me, and even if I am younger and see a different way than you how to achieve it. We need money. If you don't like the way I earn my share of what we spend, then let your darling Ned earn it any way he can!' He fled down the stairs leaving his bread and soup uneaten.

For a long time, Catharine sat straight-backed and silent, her hands out of sight in her lap. Ned froze on his stool, unable to eat or even move.

He was to be banned from Paradise and his brother hated him. He was in danger of hating his grandmother.

'Well,' said Catharine at last. She wiped her mouth delicately with her napkin. 'What was I saying? The presumptuous Mynheer Warde . . .'

Ned blinked back tears.

'. . . then said to me that, as you were a gentleman, you would need to know how to play a musical instrument for your own delight and that of others. And offered, as an act of charity, to teach you. It seems that he plays the things as well as makes

60

them. I agreed to his condescension in this case. A gentleman must have music. Music brings man closer to God.'

'It's like this,' said Warde the next day, 'I already have one officially registered apprentice, but I need a boy to deliver strings and run other errands . . . exercise my mastiff. Can't pay you of course, but I could teach you to play the lute when work is finished for the day. I'm not a fine musician, but I know enough for a beginner like you. Of course, you'll need an instrument for practice . . .'

'One of those!' Giddy and reckless with his wildly swinging fortunes, Ned pointed at the long-necked *chittarone*.

Warde glared. 'In your place, I'd start with something closer to my own size. A *mandola*, perhaps. And you'll have to make it yourself.'

A delicious warmth seeped from his scalp down through his chest and into his gut as Ned stared back at the man, unable to believe what they seemed to have just agreed.

When he wasn't delivering strings, fetching pegs from the wood-turner or walking the mastiff along the canals, he watched. Warde first allowed him to scrape leaves of wood into the right thickness, then to polish them with rushes to a perfect smoothness. Ned learned to sort gut for the strings from gut for tying frets. Then to heat glue to just the right liquidity. He learned to use the saws and chisels. At last he was allowed to draw the shapes of the tapered ribs that made up the back of the lute on to thin air-wood boards, to shave them out, and to bend them around the hot curved bending iron until they sat precisely together on the wooden mould shaped like half a pear.

At the age of eleven and a half he owned a lute, made mostly by himself, although Warde had carried out the most delicate operations, and perhaps even made secret corrections. Just as intensely as he was still disturbed by visions of female private parts, but far more innocently, Ned fell in love.

61

He sat for hours on the narrow staircase of their lodgings with the half-pear of his lute cradled across his body and his back against a stair, practising the correct posture Warde had taught him, learning to hold her with his right hand alone so that his left was free to work on the frets, feeling silently for her frets, tuning her, stroking the strings, running his hands again and again across the satiny smoothness of the great curved back.

She was plain, without decorative inlays or ivory edgings, and had some slight flaws in both construction and finish, although each of her five coats of varnish had been lovingly applied and polished. Her tone was perhaps not perfect. The modelling on the rose, or knot, cut into the wood of her belly just under the neck, was not as delicate as it might have been. But she was his, had grown under his hands, been released from the maple and pear wood by his will. When he made music, she already knew his hands.

His grandmother seemed to accept the show he made of protracted lessons with Mynheer Warde. She did not question his long absences from their lodgings. She taught him all the French and English songs she knew, and took pleasure in his growing confidence as a musician. The sight of Warde, however, always made her purse her lips.

Francis refused absolutely to let Ned keep his lute in their shared bed by day, even though Warde said that this was the best way to keep a lute safe from the damp sea air which would loose its glue and soften its strings. So Ned learned next how to make her a case.

Catharine began to drown in her own phlegm, in the spring that Ned turned thirteen and Francis, twenty. Day by day the liquid rose in her lungs. After five days Francis picked three pockets so they could call in a physician. The man peered at her urine, sniffed her breath, bled her, cupped her, then shrugged and took his fee.

Her voice dwindled until it scraped out of her throat like a breeze through dry twigs. When she sucked at the air, Ned

62

could hear a thick boiling deep in her frail chest. In the second week, she refused food, believed that she was in her bed at Tarleton Court and talked only of William and the babies.

'I can't bear it!' muttered Francis. 'I'm off for the night . . . to find somewhere I can sleep without listening all the while for her last breath.'

He began to stay out every night.

Left alone with his grandmother, Ned dozed, heard silence in his sleep, jolted awake in terror, hung over her, unable to breathe himself until she heaved and twitched and sucked again at the reluctant air. Each night he imagined that the silences grew longer. By day he wiped her damp face, read aloud to her, sang to her, held titbits to her closed mouth and cajoled.

'At least drink!' he begged. 'Please, madam!'

Although he could not bear the idea of her death, a vicious, unworthy thought began to tap at the back of his mind. If she did die (and the Lord forbid it), he might not have to put things right after all. Or at least, he could decide for himself what to do when the time came. If it should ever come.

But her soul will still know if you fail her.

He flushed with guilt and set the cup of water on the floor. Then looked back at the set of her jaw. Even in Heaven his grandmother would find a spyglass and never let him out of her sight.

Three weeks after falling ill, she pushed away the cup of ale in Ned's hand. 'Breathe the smoke!' she ordered. She paused, drew a breath as if heaving at a boulder and stared into his eyes, her face stiff with terror. 'Please, God! Breathe deep and end it!' She stopped so abruptly that he thought she had died. Then one of her eyelids quivered.

'*Gran'mère!* I'm Edward!'

She frowned and was briefly again the woman whom he had feared as well as loved. 'Of course, you fool!' she whispered. 'I know who you are. Well, I can't do it, so you will have to.' She

63

sucked at the air. 'Tarleton Court, Edward. Its soil and rock are your flesh and bones. Don't forget.'

'I won't.' That much he could safely promise.

'Where's my crucifix?' The dry twigs scraped in her throat.

'By your hand, madam.' He picked up the diamond-studded cross on its gold chain and put it into her reaching fingers. She fumbled it back into his hand, closed his fingers on it and fixed him with her eyes. She drew another painful, bubbling breath. 'Edward, you must . . .'

Please, no, he thought. Don't ask me to swear to the impossible.

'How is she?' Francis interrupted, entering brightly from his night away. 'Look, *gran'mère*, what I've brought you – sweet rolls from the baker. Do you good, if only you'd choose to eat.'

She turned her face away. The dove claw of her hand gripped Ned's arm as if she feared to fall. 'Edward! Swear to reclaim Tarleton Court!'

The words were a rustle of dry leaves.

'Well, you eat it then.' Francis stuffed a roll into Ned's free hand, chewed his own and regarded them both. 'What a dismal sight, the pair of you! How about a song for our grandmother? You know you like to hear Neddie play and sing, and I'll croak along as best I can.'

She glared at him but let go of Ned's arm.

Gratefully, Ned went into the main chamber to fetch his lute.

His grandmother's eyes followed him.

'And none of your gloomy church maunders this morning. Look!' Francis whipped a posy of yellow primroses from behind his back. 'Don't fear. You needn't eat these . . . just sniff.' He laid them on the coverlet over her shrunken lap. 'First of May today. There's only one fit song and I've heard you sing it yourself, so don't scowl and purse your lips. Off you go, Neddie!'

She lifted the crucifix again and thrust it towards Ned.

He ducked his head and began to sing as best he could around

64

the knot in his throat. His brother joined in with great vigour and no sense of pitch.

'*Au premier jour du joly moys de may . . .*' The knot loosened enough to allow the song to escape. And, in spite of everything, he suppressed a smile. Francis did croak. Music was the sole art in which Ned excelled him.

He risked a glance at his grandmother. To his relief, she had let the crucifix fall back on to the bed and was nodding as the delicate notes sprang away from Ned's fingers. He was giving her pleasure. And she had forgotten her oath.

'. . . pleased to see His children in innocent diversion . . .' she whispered when the song was done. Then she sucked at the air again. Each word drained her strength. 'After supper, we must push the tables back to the wall. The twins will dance together like a pair of angels. Oh, William . . .' She now turned on Ned one of her rare smiles. 'We must swear to each other never to forget this moment.' She reached out and grasped his wrist in a trembling but fervent grip. 'This is Paradise on earth, and we are the luckiest of mortals. We must never forget. Promise me, my love . . .'

Then she stared, dropped his wrist abruptly and covered her face. 'Where's William, when I need him most?' she demanded angrily. 'Where IS he? Where are we? I don't like it! You silly boy, I want to go to Tarleton Court!'

'Madam . . .'

'Take me there at once! And don't tell me that the coach journey is too long! Send for Culver. Tell him . . .' She fell asleep suddenly, exhausted by so much speech.

'I've had enough of this,' muttered Francis. He vanished down the narrow staircase to the street.

In mid-afternoon her eyes opened and fixed on Ned as if all her dwindling force beamed through them. 'Swear to me that you will reclaim Tarleton Court! Restore the Malise Salt to its rightful place on our table!'

If he did not respond, she would use herself up entirely with trying to speak.

65

'Yes, madam,' he mumbled.

She shook her head and lifted the crucifix a quarter inch. The effort visibly moved her a little closer towards death.

Quickly, before she could slide any farther, he took the crucifix.

'I swear by our Blessed Saviour on the Cross that I will reclaim Tarleton Court in the Malise name.'

'The Salt . . .' she wheezed.

'And put the Malise Salt back in its rightful place on the table in the great chamber.'

A huge weight pressed down on the top of his head.

She closed her eyes again, satisfied at last. Soon after, while lighting a candle against the dusk, he stiffened and lifted his head to listen. The silence in the room stretched out longer and longer. He ran back to her bed. She stared through him from under half-closed lids. The silence still went on.

Breathe! he urged her.

Silence. Huge and hollow. Voices in the street outside wove themselves into a shell around the silent void where he stood, at the centre of enormity. He pushed at her arm.

Not asleep.

He stared back at her for a moment, then turned and hurled himself down the stairs into the street.

'Francis!'

6

My time on earth shrinks towards nothing. My hands are numb. My legs shake. My shoulders burn with a restless pain that makes me want to tear them from my body. I need an argument to save my life. But it grows harder and harder to think — my body shouts so for attention. After only a day. I believe . . .

How can one tell the days in this subterranean darkness? I can't hear the bells. Just rats scuffling and the sighs of the earth. I smell only mould, my own body, the rough damp wood under my left cheek. I've already begun to lose fresh waffles and the perfume behind Marika's ears and on the insides of her thighs . . .

I must not lose my mind, or not that part of it which is still Man. Must not let pain squeeze it dry of thought and shrink it to a small hard useless stone. Must not lose my reasons for staying alive.

Don't wander. Think!

Could I have killed the child?

Hole in my thoughts.

Wait it out.

Breathe.

What horror am I capable of?

Silence in my mind! Silence in my mind. Silence. Void.

Sweet Lord, here it comes! A memory I don't want.

Hold it off. Hold it off!

67

7

Ned's vow weighed him down each night as he sank into sleep and greeted him sourly when he woke. His grandfather William visited in his dreams, as bright as a torch in his burning pitch-lined hemp robe, holding his opened belly together with fingers of flame.

Ned lay awake in the dark, conjuring up the twisted faces of the enemy – the Nightingales. He rehearsed their vileness and crimes against his family. He played and replayed his first meeting with Henry Nightingale, who had signed his grandfather's bill for execution, never thinking that the man might already be dead of old age.

He approached the great barbican gate of Tarleton Court, between two shining towers (in one of which was grandmother's painted room), his feet hollow on the moat bridge that he imagined. Nightingale himself answered his thunderous knock and saw at once that Ned was his fate. Ned thrust his Spanish steel blade cleanly through the evil heart. Then he (perhaps) cut off the hand which had held the fatal pen.

And found himself miraculously seated at the great, gleaming, honey-scented table with the evening sun falling on the Malise Salt and the priest's bald pate. Everyone singing.

He always broke into a sickly sweat, trying to imagine even the first step in such a momentous crusade. Instead, Warde took him on for a low wage as a workshop assistant in addition to the properly registered apprentice.

68

Warde taught Ned how to lay out the Platonic diagrams of harmonic proportion on the leaves of belly wood. He introduced Ned to the sawing and cutting of fine inlays and began to let him work with precious woods – sappan, the tight burr of Amboyna wood, heavy, spicy ebony, and rosewood which smelt of roses and vanilla when it was shaved. From the first, the instrument-maker always asked Ned to listen to the blocks of wood singing before finally choosing the ones to make a lute.

Maple gave an instrument a soft voice, Ned learned. Ebony, a loud, cold clarity. The voice of rosewood was also loud but warm.

'But ash is the queen of woods,' said Warde, forgetting himself and speaking with passion. 'It bends easily, glues well and has an incomparable bright, crisp tone.'

Ned also found that ash gave out a faint harmonious ringing sound if he held it near his mouth when he sang.

'It's your wood,' said Warde. 'You must make yourself another lute, of ash.'

Then, at age fourteen, Ned found, to his delight, that with music he could earn enough to help pay for their daily needs. He began to sing at night in the Blomsloot *musicos*, where the whores made the assignations that were carried out in nearby brothels or in their homes. He already knew many songs from his childish days and evenings on the canalside, not just bawdies and love songs, but also stirring, patriotic celebrations of the beauty, virtues and prosperity of Amsterdam.

Josie Jugs praised him to her friends, Catryn the Corset and the Dainty Dane, who passed him on to others. The whores smiled at his dark curls, pale amber-flecked eyes and still coltish legs. Men stuffed *stuivers* into his fist, clapped him on the shoulder and called him Ganymede or a young Apollo. He barely believed that he was paid for the pleasure of making his lute speak, first of martial pride, then of lewd abandon, and then of melting tenderness. Together he and his lute sweetened every sort of encounter, from sentimental tryst to animal rut, with no experience of either except observation.

True, by fifteen, he burned and lusted in secret. He felt ready now to take the earthly Paradise. He returned to the *Vulgaria* to seek out all those vile words again, then tried to numb his senses with an excess: penis, vulva, tool, yard, slit, leather-stretcher, pizzle, fuck, fiddle, swive, occupy, mount.

He then tried to walk off the choking restlessness that followed these scholarly ventures. But in the streets he saw only trembling breasts, inviting curves of wrist, parted lips. Even the glimpse of a shoe inflamed him, connected as it was to the leg that climbed up to the mossy bank. With little chance for solitude and sharing a sleeping chamber with his brother, he lacked opportunity for relief, even if moral teachings had not damned the sin of Onan.

All the same, he said 'no' when Josie offered, in gratitude and friendship, to take his maidenhead. His grandmother's teachings, a natural fastidiousness, and terror of the pox held him back. He had seen the pustules, the oozings, the stranguries, scalded heads, and dosings with mercury that some of the whores' clients suffered. So instead he burned.

His older brother had taken employment as close assistant to a mountebank who peddled skin lotions from Constantinople, love potions brewed from Cleopatra's secret recipes, abortifacients made of who-knows-what, and so-called cures for the plague. Unlike his master, he was clear-sighted about what he did.

'People believe what they wish,' he would say. 'And do as they wish. Surely, it's better for them to buy my concoctions, which are sometimes even efficacious, than to turn their faces to the wall and die of despair.'

It did not take him long to decide that he should go into the business for himself.

He sold walnuts for the headache because they resembled the afflicted part, the brain. Hound's Tongue leaves against dog bites. The tooth-shaped seed pod of henbane against toothaches. Mandrake and unicorn's horn to urge on reluctant husbands and lovers. Juniper berries or a concoction of white poplar bark and mules' kidneys to procure abortion. He asked

70

eagerly after any new plagues, pursued women with coughs, wens, or pallid cheeks, and charted the progress of disease in the city as keenly as if following commodities on the Bourse.

'I shall sell to the women!' he said. 'It's the women who buy.' So he invested in nutmegs, which were said to aid abortion, in frankincense against wrinkles, and in a 'sacred nectar' from India compounded of spices and hemp for easing childbirth. Like the mountebank, his former master, he also sold mercury for dosing the pox. He was not a guild member with either the apothecaries or physicians, but found his customers among those who were too poor or too desperate to care, and those who valued his absolute discretion. At first, therefore, he was happy to make good use of Ned's presence in the *bordeels* and *musicos*.

A little shorter than Ned, with lighter colouring, Francis was now a handsome fellow who knew how to use his eyes and tongue to woo new customers and soothe any failed cases who had survived their ills. Ned never saw him with a woman, however, except his female clients. Nor did he show any interest in the mousers among Ned's acquaintance. He pined only for wealth. And to gain it, he studied the wares of the apothecaries and had himself introduced among men of commerce who might lend him money or invest. He experimented with recipes for 'magic' potions and salves. From time to time he sent Ned to deliver a hair rinse or love philtre.

'Don't give it to a maid. Insist on putting it into the hands of the mistress herself,' he sometimes said. 'As we rise, I mean to make a better use of you than as a delivery boy! I've found our quickest way back to England. You shall marry money.'

With alarm Ned heard in his brother's voice an echo of their grandmother's steely purpose.

71

8

'A rabbit for each of us to chase,' said Francis. 'The sister for you, her brother for me.'

It was the same house, Ned was absolutely certain. Though the tree where he and the ginger-haired dog had lurked was both taller and wider.

Now Ned thanked the Lord that he had spent four hours dressing, had changed his collar for another, changed it back again, examined his cuffs, found a spot of soil, changed them, polished his shoes three times. Rubbed his teeth with a sprig of rosemary until his gums bled, and then chewed a scrap of cinnamon bark to sweeten his breath.

He had sniffed his armpits and splashed on yet more orange water.

'She's nearly fifteen,' Francis had told him. 'Wild and spoilt from too much money and no mother. A brigand for a brother and dangerous good looks. Experienced beyond her years from her dealings with her brother's cronies. A true challenge, my baby brother!'

Ned braced himself for a knowing demi-harlot.

'My sister Marika.' Justus Coymans stepped aside to let the young woman move forward.

Ned inhaled deeply, as if someone had just opened a door on to the scent of a spring morning and let in the sense of wellbeing and delight.

Since she had last sat on her *stoep* blowing bubbles from

72

her mussel shell, Marika Coymans had grown tall and broad-shouldered for a woman. Her eyes were not so far below Ned's own and looked straight into them. Her waist was small, however, and her bones light. The moon-pale child's hair had turned gold like her brother's, and curled with an even greater vigour. Scandalously uncapped, it sprang away from her temples, like his, giving them both the air of being always in motion even when standing still.

Ned bowed, English-fashion, then straightened to see that she held out an egalitarian hand to shake. It was small in proportion to the rest of her, and very warm. Her bones felt as frail as flower stalks. He looked back into her eyes, which still looked into his with curiosity.

She was his fate. He knew it at once, without a doubt. All the forbidden words buzzed dangerously in his head, but it was more than that.

I should have known it all those years ago, when I thought that I merely wanted to observe another child who seemed to have no parents.

He broke away from her gaze to look at the rest of her, to see more clearly what the woman was, who had been cast in this sudden new role.

A high, smooth forehead much the same pinky cream as the pearls around her neck. A few sweet shadows – under her brow bones, and a delicious one cast by her full lower lip on to the upper curve of her firm, rounded chin. Blue eyes set farther apart than her brother's, and far more candid.

A face of open spaces and clear skies, he thought. No sign of taint. Francis maligned her.

He couldn't determine whether or not she was pretty. But it didn't matter, he had no choice. His life had gaped open and she had stepped in. He observed himself, too, from a slight distance, astonished. He was a boat swinging out into a strong current without a rudder. He wanted to touch her again. He tried to ignore the beastly stirring of his prick in his breeches. He was again in love.

73

'Another one gone,' said Francis under his breath to Coymans. 'Do I lock up my brother, or do you lock her?'

'My sister chooses her own sweetmeats. I merely see that they're not poisoned ones.' Polite but chilly, Coymans turned to his sister. 'As Master Ned is here, why don't you take him into the parlour while his brother and I discuss some necessary business matters?'

They sat in two chairs near the front window which looked out over the street. They smiled at each other. Ned drew a deep breath. He almost wished she weren't there, so he could cool down and examine in detail his amazing new state of existence. She offered him a glass of hock.

He took it and drank in silence. I used to watch you almost every day, he wanted to say. You looked so sad.

Impossible. But he couldn't think of anything else to say.

'Do you dance?'

'Badly, mevrouw.'

She gave him a false, radiant smile.

False, for sure, as he knew that he had done nothing so far to deserve it. But, oh, the delicious little curve in each corner of her mouth. Her smile lifted her cheeks a little towards her eyes.

'A man with your shoulders and reach must be a fine swordsman, then.'

'Francis is your better man for that.'

I must look away from her mouth, he thought.

'You don't much like conversation, do you?' Her dry, cool tone was disconcertingly accompanied by a warm glance. Perhaps she felt sympathy rather than disdain, but Ned was not entirely certain. 'So, what shall I do with you until we dine? Do you sing?'

'I try.' He wanted to beat his head against the wall in frustration at his dumbness. But he dared not open his mouth too much or those evil words buzzing round his mind like horseflies would escape out into the room.

'We progress.'

74

As he followed her from their chairs by the front window to the virginal at the far side of the white-plastered room, he thought that her strong wide shoulders should make her less desirable, but in fact they merely accentuated the smallness of her waist.

If this were a *musico*, if she were the Dainty Dane, and he a ship's captain, he would ask if she cared for a fumble and that would be that. How the devil was he to set about explaining to her how things now stood between them? *Musico*s were no place to learn the skills of gentle wooing. And for all their tutoring of one sort or another, neither his grandmother nor Francis had thought to teach him how to woo a well-placed but badly-reared young woman.

'Shall I play for you? It would spare us the need for tiresome conversation.'

Was she being uncivil? He didn't care. She would learn in time that she was as caught up with him as he was with her.

'. . . as a special gift.' She was waiting for his reply.

'Forgive me, mevrouw . . .' Not pretty but beautiful, he decided. And much more than handsome, though some men might call her that. The linen over her breasts, above the top of her bodice, was so sheer that the flesh glowed through.

He clenched his fists to keep from reaching out to touch the soft quarter-globes.

Her breasts, bubs . . . Stop it, Ned!

'Am I so tedious even before I begin to play?'

I love you, he wanted to say. What shall we do about it?

'You know that you could never be tedious,' he finally managed to say.

'I don't know it. We are all taught to be so civil to each other that we can never learn the truth about ourselves.' She lifted the lid, inside of which was painted a scene of the bathing Artemis and peeping Actaeon. Horns already blossomed on the young man's head, and, in the far distance, behind trees no taller than the first joint of Ned's thumb, the hunter's own dogs already

75

cast about for his scent. A naked, white-haunched Artemis groped for the concealing veils, dropped in her alarm.

I'd gladly turn beast for such a glimpse. Ned blushed and hated himself. Quim, slit . . . Oh, God!

'My brother told me that you were reared in the streets,' she said. 'Does that mean you're ill-bred enough to be willing to tell the truth?'

'I love you.'

She laughed with delight. 'You don't need to exaggerate. But I think I may safely conclude that I'm not tedious.'

His nerve failed him. He smiled instead, as if he had just made a successful sally. At least she did not seem to mind that he had been reared in the streets.

'I was saying to you before, when you were gawping at Artemis and not listening, that this virginal was made in Antwerp as a special gift for my mother. Look!' She lowered the flap in front of the keyboard. Inside, it was doubled. Two keyboards, end to end, where usually there was one.

'This upper one, on the right, lifts out, to take with you when you wish to visit friends who have no instrument.' She played lightly up and down each keyboard. 'I play the lower one. Friends of Justus's sometimes play with me on the other.' She sat on the chair in front of the virginal. 'Dowland. English music, just for you.'

Her body grew still, then her hands pounced like attacking cats. Her face was intent. Her hands thundered, raced. From time to time, she suddenly swayed forward as if about to throw herself from a cliff top. Then, finally, her hands lifted away from the music like the last of a departing mist off water under the sun. The stillness held them.

His love turned to helpless adoration. The vile stirrings of his cock and mind gave way to a purer ecstasy.

'So,' she said after a moment.

'That's no mere graceful, gentlewoman's pastime.' He felt that he had already drunk too much.

'No.'

76

'You play exceeding well.' (Tedious, Ned! Tedious!)

'I try.' Dry as her voice was, her eyes flicked to his in pleasure. 'There are few things in this world that I take to heart, but this inscription is one.' Carved into the lowered front flap: *Ars usu iuvanda*. Art comes through effort. 'I practise.'

'But I know that it doesn't feel like labour!' Could she intend the double meaning?

She nodded.

'If only I had brought my lute, I could return the compliment with a Dutch song for you. I don't play half so well . . .' No wooing was going to be needed. No explanations, after all. She would see as clearly as he already did that they had been yoked together by fate. Music would serve them instead of treacherous words.

'We'll send for it at once.'

She stood and called into the hall for a servant.

'Fetch that chair from the window,' she ordered him. 'If you like, while we wait, I shall teach you to play the virginal.'

He sat beside her on her right, his left shoulder ablaze where it brushed hers. He grew stiff as a tent pole under his breeches, but she seemed not to notice.

'Put your first finger there. That is "ut". Now the next finger, on "re", then "mi, fa" . . . finger over . . . "sol, la". Keep playing up, three, four, three, four . . . splendid, keep going.' She leaned forward, watching his fingers intently. He smelled the rosemary water with which she had rinsed her hair, and a warm, fleshy gust which seemed to rise from under the sheer linen over her breasts.

'Now, play back down. Start with the fifth finger.' She leaned back in her chair. 'No! No! Fourth finger over coming down! Like this.' She leaned forward again. Ned swivelled his eyes up to the ceiling and breathed deeply. He closed his eyes and played down, his whole being crowded into his left arm, which pressed against the side of her bodice as she reached across to guide his fingers.

'Mynheer, your lute.'

77

He embraced his instrument gratefully and sheltered its curved, half-pear body against his own. With it, he felt complete. He bent his head to listen as he tuned the strings.

Oh, my soul, he begged the sounding post. Help me now.

For a moment, he could not think of a Dutch song that would be suitable, and grew uncertain again. Then he remembered a Psalm of David, by Sweelinck, which he had learned to please the musical family across the canal from their lodgings. His voice arrived full and round, miraculously clear of phlegm or nerves. His left hand found the sweet spots on the frets with easy authority. The fingers of his right hand danced as he felt his body could not. He was a window through which the music shone.

She sat very still while he sang.

'Another, please,' she ordered, when he had finished. 'English this time.'

'All ye whom love or fortune hath betrayed . . .'

'You do sing well. And you are quite transformed when you sing.'

How? How? He wanted to beg, to hear her tell him. 'For the better, I hope.'

'Of course.' She reached for her pet monkey who had been hiding under her skirts, betrayed only by the dark tip of its skinny tail. 'Did I hear that you sometimes sing in the *musicos*?'

'Francis hoped that secret was buried.'

'My brother learns everything about people he does business with . . . Did you?'

Ned nodded.

'Sing me some of those songs . . . to annoy your brother, if you dare.'

'I don't think . . .' He rummaged frantically through his repertoire. Found a drinking song. Rowdy but not bawdy. 'We be soldiers three . . .'

When he had finished, she said, 'That's not the worst that you know.'

78

'You didn't ask for the worst.'

'I do now.'

He lowered his head, touched the strings. 'As the scabbard for the blade, so woman for man is made . . .' That one had always earned him a generous *pourboire*. He looked at her in dread as he played and sang.

She smiled, and, to his delight, a slow-rising tide of delicate pink spread up from beneath her linen collar.

A reckless flush washed him head to toe. His fingers flew. He finished the song and began the tune of a tavern catch. 'To thee, to thee, and to the maid/That kindly will upon her back be laid.'

'I think I've caught it!' she said, and picked up the last verse, without words. Their voices plaited together two strands of the meltingly sweet tune, while he played the third strand on his lute.

They had now flushed as pink as each other.

'You are the most unlikely . . .' she said. She looked down at the keyboard and then sideways up at him with devastating, if perhaps calculated, effect. 'What is the most bawdy song you know?'

He shook his head.

'A challenge,' she said.

Of their own will, the fingers of his right hand leaped over the strings, choosing the song. 'I have a gentle cock . . .'

'Listen, my sweet,' she murmured to her monkey. 'An animal song.' She smiled down at the keyboard and waited.

Ned raced on, a man running downhill out of control. The verses seemed endless, wallowing in the barnyard. His voice sounded too loud in his ears. '. . . and every night he percheth him, in my lady's chamber.'

She had looked down at her lap. Her left hand stroked the monkey's hard, bony little back then fell still on the grey fur.

Ned heard a small, sharp puff of exhaled breath.

'Have you experience of the business?' she asked.

Ned distrusted her meaning, looked into her eyes, saw that

79

he had been right in the first place. He hesitated, then shook his head. '. . . If I understand you. Is that good or bad?'

'Will you take my maidenhead?'

He blinked. Then gaped like a clubbed trout.

'You are free to refuse. You will still be given dinner.'

'More than anything,' he said. 'I mean, that I would like, more than anything . . .' Trembling, he set his lute on the floor and bent to kiss her at last.

But she rose to her feet in alarm on the far side of her chair. The red cut-velvet chair back stood between them like Thisbe's Wall. Then she smiled again and shook her head charmingly. 'Later. We'll get to all that later. Come eat now.'

He would have liked to remember his first entrance into Earthly Paradise as an erotic triumph. But when it came to it, the moment was an odd salad of panic, lust, and taking pains. And she made him pull out of her just before he climaxed. In the end, he lay panting, flat on his back, dazed as a leaf sucked through a millrace. Marika seemed pleased enough, however, and inclined to talk.

They lay in her box bed, a comfortable cavern that smelled of pine, wool, and beeswax candles. Justus had gone for two days to Antwerp, though Marika assured Ned that her brother wouldn't be angry if she told him not to be. Nor did she think that any of the servants would dare report them to the police, for positions were scarce and her brother paid well.

Her pet monkey sat with its tail draped across one of Ned's ankles, inserting a black finger again and again into its fur in search of fleas. Marika lay naked on her stomach, chin on her hands. Ned stroked her back and fingered the bright, wild hair in curious wonder, while she chattered. From time to time, she interrupted herself to lean forward and kiss Ned's shoulder or the top of his arm.

'. . . I reign here already and Justus dotes on me,' she was saying. 'We keep merry company.'

He examined her left ear. It was as perfect as her navel.

80

He wondered what she would say if he wished to enter her again.

'Who wants to be some man's prisoner and pop out babies until you split like a dry seed pod? I like my life as it is, with Justus, my sweet pet here, my virginal and my garden. There are plenty of would-be husbands who come to my brother's table. Old men who try to flirt and pay me compliments. I hear the jests – they imagine that I don't overhear, and if I do, that I won't understand.'

'Does Justus want you to marry?' He wondered how to get her to stop chattering and turn on to her back again.

'Justus would like to keep me with him always, but he feels he must do his duty by me, find me a good husband. And of course it would help him if I were to marry someone like Johann Pietersen who owns six lighters and a large ship as well. But for a wife, these men want only perfect goods. *Intacta.* Justus has said that he will never marry and would be lost without me. So, for his own good, and my pleasure . . . With your help, I am out of the marketplace. I mean never to marry.'

She rolled on to her back at last and arched her spine, which brought a pink nipple within irresistible reach of his mouth. 'Just so we don't mistake each other, please don't imagine that I shall fall in love with you and marry you either.'

His second erection, which had come hard upon the death of the first, now died by itself. He lay back on the pillow and threw his forearm across his eyes. He felt her shift on the coverlet beside him.

'Don't mistake me, darling Ned.' She paused for a second as if listening to herself speak the endearment. 'Dearest Ned!' Her hand lifted his arm firmly away from his eyes. 'I enjoyed it much, much more than I had feared.'

'Feared.' He turned his face away from her.

'Dammit!'

Shocked, he looked back. Her face was frowning, very close to his.

81

'I'm trying to be honourable with you. Don't sulk. I believe that a maidenhead is not a trifling gift, whether or not love comes with it! I've waited and chosen carefully.'

'That must be the queerest compliment a lover has ever been paid!'

'Did I displease you?' Her voice and eyes were anxious.

'Oh no! No, no!'

'Then why are you so angry?'

'When I should be grateful, you mean, to have been given a thing that you didn't want?'

She sat straight up, away from him. One of her nipples had been creased by a fold in the coverlet. His thumb ached to smooth it out.

'I thought that you would be more worldly, with your experience of the *bordeels*,' she said. 'I didn't imagine . . . I'm sorry, I seem to have made a mistake . . . Come.' She held out her arms to the monkey and the little beast dropped into them from the curtain of the bed.

'Please don't apologise. I'm grateful for what I have been granted.' He sat up too. 'I should go.'

She played with her monkey's tail. 'If you think it best.'

He passed a sleepless night. He had been a beast. Though their love was meant to be a union of souls, he had polluted not only himself but her. At the same time, in spite of her deflating words, he wanted to do it again and again and again, like the crudest, most potent billy goat.

At breakfast Francis eyed him and asked if he were still young enough to need an introduction to Milady Five Fingers.

'Go to hell!' said Ned. He went to his chamber and spent three hours writing and rewriting a note.

He went to deliver it himself. Not to see Marika! He would not go in. Merely hand it over to the maid. But he would at least know that it had arrived.

Should he wait for a reply? The question vexed him all the way to the Coymans's house on the Old Side.

82

As he mounted the stone steps to the Coymans's *stoep*, he met their maid coming down.

'Mynheer Malise! You have saved me a walk.' She handed him a sealed note. 'I'll go tell Mevrouw Coymans that you're here.' The woman winked.

'We read at the same time.'

He nodded. The parlour was silent except for the sound of tearing paper. Both letters trembled slightly as they read.

'So?'

'So.'

They stood and smiled at each other. 'Forgive . . .' they both said at the same time, and then laughed.

A foolish laugh, thought Ned. But I don't care.

Nothing had changed. But the terrible ending to the previous night had been miraculously reversed. Nothing else mattered. He was filled again with wellbeing and delight. They played a duet to cement their reunion.

But she never let him enter her again.

'Babies,' she said shortly. She then kissed the corners of his eyes and swore that she loved him even if she would not marry him.

At last, driven nearly mad with frustration, he could not help himself and introduced her to Mevrouw Fist, to whom she took with apparent pleasure, even sitting at her virginal, while he nearly expired in blissful terror of a passing maid or groom. And once, when Justus was away again, she was happy enough to let him spend himself against her flat, smooth, naked belly. She was never more tender than when he lay afterwards with his arm again across his eyes, relieved but appalled, trying to will into her the force of his intense love.

He took heart from their playing music together. That, at least, was unarguable. And pure. A product of the higher self, not the polluted charnel of his fifteen-year-old flesh. Music would lead her to the truth and him to virtuous love.

83

Then, without warning, came another note, in which her true youth appeared.

Dearest Ned,

I am grateful to you for your Help in Certain Matters. But as my Brother frowns on our Liaison, I think it best if we end it Now. And be done, not to suffer protracted Anguisshe. Forgive me for the Coldness in onley writing to you but I fear that If I see you agayne, I will Weaken and Suffer all the more. I beg you to forgive me if this should give you cause for Greef. Yours in Friendship and Gratitude,

Marika Coymans

He did not tell Francis. He would have killed his older brother for so much as opening his mouth.

He wrote back, but had no answer.

Perhaps I haven't behaved enough like a Dutchman, he thought. Too much like a foreigner. So he tied a bouquet to her door knocker.

The next morning he found it tossed into the street. He pounded on the door but spoke only to servants. (One maid dared to giggle.) He raged, he begged, both in letters and aloud in his sleeping chamber.

She did not write back.

He scorned to suffer, then changed his mind and borrowed from a literary gentleman who frequented Josie Jugs, copies of *The Aching Heart Express'd* and *The Post Office of Cupid and Mercury*. Alone at home again, he searched their pages for examples of a perfect model letter to express, better than his own inadequate words, the scalding pain of his wound. When he found one, he copied it out four times by candle light until satisfied with the balance of his hand and the spacing of the lines. Then he delivered it at once, in the middle of the night.

Still no reply.

84

He sent two more – The Aching Heart Despairing and The Mournful Shepherd. Still without reply.

There can be only one cause for her silence, he decided. I revolted her with my beastly lusts. Disgusted her with my vile fluids and overheated appetites.

He would remind her of their pure connection through music. The soul of the lute would become his soul, and transform the deepest tremors of his being into an exquisite disturbance of the air.

He found a tenacity in himself that he had not known he had, and spent three agonised days teaching himself to write her a song, both words and tune. A lover's praise this time, not complaint:

> In her are seen pure white and red
> Not by feign'd Art but Nature wed,
> To celestial Smiles, an Angel's Face,
> Affecting Gesture, unforc'd Grace.
> A fair smooth front, free from least Wrinkle,
> Her eyes (on me) like stars did twinkle.
> All beauty out from her doth shine,
> In her, all perfections do combine.

Though the last two lines did not satisfy him, and he was a little uncertain about 'twinkle' and 'wrinkle', he was impatient to try the power of his song. That night he sang it, a little shakily, outside her house, accompanying himself on his lute. After a short time in which no one came to either door or window, he began to sing it again.

Someone stirred at the first-floor window. He flung himself to his knees on the damp cobbles. Her brother glanced out, then closed the shutters. Then the owner of the neighbouring house leaned out of an upper window and threatened to throw water on Ned if he didn't stop his tom-cat yowling.

Ned limped home on bruised knees, feeling a fool. If only

85

he could have perfected those last two lines! And replaced that doubtful couplet!

The next morning, he woke up enraged, skipped breakfast and surged without direction for most of the day around the Amsterdam streets. He wrote her name in the dirt and scrubbed it out violently with his foot. She was a flirt, a jock teaser, a witch. A spoilt brat.

No!

She is Aphrodite whom, in my myriad shortcomings, I have failed to please. The Queen of Love who has exiled me from her court!

He sprang into the air beneath a canal-side tree and caught hold of a low branch, which broke under his weight. Without caring who saw, he wrenched it from the tree, snapped it in half and threw it into the canal.

No matter which way he looked at it, one truth remained: a chit of just fifteen had turned him inside out, then thrown him away. She had hardly given him satisfaction, when it came to it. He wished the pox on her, every painful pustule and lump.

By the next day he had found an excuse to pass her house, then fled with burning ears and thudding heart, to hide in their lodgings with his faithful lute. All that afternoon he sang and re-sang to himself ayres of cruel passions, of unquiet thoughts, of Cupid's wounds and bursting tears. He could have wept with the force of a sudden revelation: even in heartbreak there is enlightenment. For, now, with mature age and bitter experience, he had come to grasp the true, deep profundity beneath what had before seemed to be shallow modish words.

That evening, he punished her by singing the song he had written her in a *bordeel*, to Josie Jugs and some of the other whores.

'That's lovely! *Bene, bene!*' cried Josie. 'You'll melt some hearts with that one.'

He told them.

'I'll walk with you past her window,' offered the Dainty

86

Dane. 'In my best petticoats and apron, with my nose in the air and my pearl-edged cap.'

'She wouldn't care,' said Ned. 'But thank you.'

He looked again at the Dainty Dane. A fair-haired, unspoilt young woman, not long ago arrived in Amsterdam, with her pale blue eyes firmly fixed on a permanent role as doxie to a rich man. She didn't yet look much like a whore. He accepted her offer after all, and they agreed to meet on the Damrak the next afternoon. Ned rushed home to borrow his brother's one silk suit, cast off by one of his customers. Francis was so preoccupied with his own affairs that he even agreed to the loan of his hat.

Though it threatened to rain, the Dainty Dane wore a grey silk dress and her pearl-edged cap, both gifts from a client and speaking well for the eventual success of her ambitions. She had left off her red apron and feathered hat. Marika would never guess what she was.

'What if she doesn't see us?' Ned asked, as he avoided an egg-seller and a pyramid of cabbages set out on a cloth.

'We must promenade until someone in the house does see us. A maid is as good as the mistress in this case,' the Dainty Dane pronounced firmly.

Ned offered her his arm as they entered Marika's street. Together they made a sweet rustling of linen and silk, a flowing rush of folds and swags, punctuated by the tiny harsh scrapings of the Dane's iron clogs on the paving stones.

Ned affected a trace of swagger. Dressed like this, the Dane was almost as beautiful as his disdainful mistress. Marika's heart would twist in pain when she saw that the man she had thrown away was already entranced by another woman.

To his amazement, Marika suddenly came out on to the high *stoep* of her house as they drew near.

'Steady!' whispered the Dainty Dane. She clutched his arm as he staggered on the uneven paving.

'Has she seen us, d'you think?' He could hardly speak for the jolting of his heart up into his throat.

87

'There's a carriage waiting for her,' said the Dainty Dane. 'Do you want to go on?'

A carriage inside the city! You needed money and position to be allowed that luxury.

Marika walked elegantly down her steps and was handed up into the carriage. Which drove on straight at them. The Dainty Dane pulled Ned out of its way.

As it jolted past, Ned stared through the nearside window at the profile of a middle-aged man. A creechy-breathed old fart in black silk. Marika was sitting beyond him with only the top of her head visible.

Four horses! thought Ned miserably. A rich old man who dared to think of touching Marika's peachy flesh. For what else could he be thinking? A young girl didn't ride out alone with a man in his carriage innocently, not even when as careless of gossip as Marika and her brother were. She had agreed, after all, to marry the owner of the lighters and ships. And wasn't honest enough to tell him, after all her warbling about truth.

It made Ned want to vomit.

When the carriage had turned out of sight and then rumbled out of earshot, the Dainty Dane looked closely at Ned. 'Come with me!' She pulled him into the main street, down an alley and into a dark, comfortable tiled room filled with men and tobacco smoke, where she bought two large glasses of *ginèvre*.

Francis, though distracted by his own problems, finally noticed his brother's anguish. One evening as he unwrapped a roasted chicken he had bought, he said, 'Your wits have sunk into your rig. She was for practice only. That's not the marriage you should make.'

'She wouldn't have me in any case!' Ned slammed the door as he left the room. All the way down the stairs, he cursed her. His rage refreshed him. At the bottom of the stairs, he stopped.

What a fool I've been! he thought with a warm rush of hope.

88

I've gone about it all wrong! I never asked Justus for her hand! He doesn't know that I mean to marry her!

The following day he borrowed Francis's suit again, this time without asking, took his lute and went to call on Marika's brother.

'News, bratling . . . !' Francis stopped at the top of the stairs.

Ned was sitting in the dark in their lodgings, the fire nearly out, with the Malise Salt, slightly tarnished, gleaming hazily on the table in front of him. His lute too lay on the table. Several sheets of crumpled paper and sheet music had been scattered on table and floor.

Francis lit a candle from a coal in the fireplace, then took the candle to the table. He bent and picked up one of the crumpled papers, looked at it, then tossed it into the dying fire. 'Does your face represent the Aching Heart Express'd or a toothache rampant?'

The paper flared and the fire leaped back to half-hearted life. In its light, the crevices and crannies of the Salt sprang out in high relief. The Spanish helmets glinted.

Francis sat opposite his brother and pulled a sheet of music to him. '"Come, Sweet Death"? Surely not! No skirt is worth so much. In any case, why waste your time on a Dutch cunny? I hear that English women are as hot as goats.'

'I shall simply stop . . .' said Ned, '. . . die from the lack of will to live. My life has no purpose. I've failed every way!'

His brother lifted off the silver dome and peered into the empty blue glass bowl. 'Don't you want to know my news?'

Ned sank his head into his hands. 'I've made such an ass of myself! Justus Coymans saw me off!'

Francis replaced the dome.

'His precious sister must marry a man of substance,' cried Ned. 'A man with a right to own a thing like that salt. Not a "jumped-up guttersnipe who plays the lute in brothels".'

Francis cursed under his breath and walked to the top of the

89

stairs, where he stood looking down. 'Do you seriously want that little demi-whore?'

'She's not! And yes, I do. As my wife.'

'I wager I can make you forget her.'

'She's my fate! I have no choice but to love her.'

'Then clutch together the gaping wound in your self-esteem and listen to my news! I have great plans. Even without that bastard Coymans, I mean to prosper. Man will always be ill and always need cures. I mean to raise us both so high by that trade that men like him can't wrinkle their noses in distaste. And then you can decide whether or not you still want his sister. I will need an assistant whose loyalty I can trust absolutely. Who better than my own blood?'

He came back to the table and put his hands on Ned's shoulders. 'I'm a thruster and I work hard. But Coymans is right about singing in brothels. A brother who whittles pegs for strings and serenades rutting tarts and sailors in *bordeel*s is a drag anchor at my stern. Forget saws, chisels and catgut, bratling. Join with me in the nostrums trade.'

Ned groaned into his hands and shook his head. While his heart was dissolving with anguish, his brother talked of business.

'I've never seen anyone work so hard at being miserable,' said Francis. 'If only a man of substance can bed Marika Coymans, then join with me and make yourself into one. Justus might change his mind if his sister were to be mistress of Tarleton Court.'

Ned raised his head.

'Yes, my little Knight Templar. You can't die of love, you see, for you must get ready at last to go on crusade.'

9

Here it comes. Can't delay it any longer. The story is a hook lodged in my guts. It may kill me to spit it out.

Though I swallowed his excuse of a profitable venture in England, I knew. I told myself that we were merely gathering intelligence about our enemies, but dread sat in my stomach like a cold stone.

I wish the eagle had taken me.

They landed on the Norfolk coast in a heavy fog and slept in an inn at the port. The next two days, while the sky dropped sheets of rain, they walked fifteen miles.

With or without rain, England seemed at first very like the Low Countries. The same flat land, flooded by sheets of water. Similar windmills, low hedges, familiar grey skies. Then Ned began to notice that the edges of the landscape were a little rougher, the villages farther apart. And then they moved away from the coast and reached the trees. Thick and untidy, undergrown with scrub and bramble, they crowded in on the track, ebullient and undisciplined as they were never allowed to be at home.

Francis left Ned in a second inn and went off to accomplish a profitable ambassade. He had kept a closed mouth, but put on a mysterious mien about the identity of his customer.

'Well-placed, that's all I will say. With a badly-timed case of the pox that could prevent a marriage. She's afraid it would become known if she sought help at home. If my dosing

91

works, she'll help me to get where I want to go.' He left with his rattling mahogany case of vials and swore to be back by midnight. Ned was not to leave the inn.

Restless and shivering, Ned paced their tiny, cold room and peered out under dripping eaves at the grey soggy country that was his birthright. He tried to imagine the delights of Tarleton Court: the tower chamber with the flowers painted on its beams, the long table gleaming in the late sunlight. The singing and dancing.

And they sought only intelligence, not battle. Still, he could not shake off his sense of dread.

He went down to the main public room of the inn, sat in a corner by the smoky fire and breathed the words of Dutch songs. When the innkeeper banked the fire for the night, Ned went back up to their room, wrapped himself in a damp, odorous wool blanket and lay down on the mouldy straw to try to sleep.

Francis kicked his brother awake at dawn. He looked pleased with himself. 'That's a business begun well. Now for Tarleton Court.'

'Francis, let's not go.'

'Have you lost your reason?' Francis's scorn could sound very like his grandmother's. 'When we've come this far already!'

Francis had hired two horses and tossed the groom a coin with easy disdain.

For a time Ned set aside his dread and gave himself over to learning a gentleman's skill that he had not yet mastered. In wonder, he stroked the tender velvet nose of his sweet-natured grey mare and let her lap at his hand with flapping lips. But when he prepared to mount for the first time, he hesitated.

This riding business was implausible. Surely his mare would protest at the tight leather girth and wicked, pinching metal in her mouth. Why should she, or indeed, the powerful bay gelding Francis was riding, agree to God's fiat that they were created to serve Man?

'We'll buy you tutoring in Holland,' said Francis in exasperation as Ned paused on the mounting block. Francis sat on his own hired horse as easily as on a chair. 'A gentleman must ride.'

Why did such magnificent, powerful creatures not rebel? After all, Man, their master and moral superior, rebelled often enough against the word of his master, God! Ned had often wondered idly on this subject as he watched horsemen in the Amsterdam streets. Now that he was meant to be the master, the question turned urgent.

I'm sorry, he silently apologised, and swung into the saddle.

The mare did not object.

To his amazement, he and she were soon in an accord which he felt he had done nothing to earn. She turned when he wished and stopped and walked at his will. And, as his first panic died, he noticed that he could feel every movement of her mouth trembling along the reins to his hands. Then he learned to send messages back to her the same way. His waist muscles began to loosen and move with her stride. By the end of the morning he risked kicking her into the shared exhilaration of a canter.

How had he lived his whole life this far and not known that such joy existed?

The nearer they travelled to Tarleton Court, the more antic Francis grew in disposition. On their second day on horseback, he suddenly pointed ahead at the rutted mud of the track that led through the tunnel of trees. 'Look, there! Our footprints, waiting for us to step into them!'

Ned let the cooing of a wood pigeon crowd out Francis's voice. Today, the sun shone. He turned his head towards a sudden shuffling of pale green leaves and felt the first shiver of a familiar ecstasy. He had never seen so many trees at once.

How the air changed once you moved among them!

It lay so still against the earth that each of the hundred plaited

93

sounds was set off like a jewel, distinct and bright. And he was moved by the mists of bluebells seen unexpectedly between dark trunks. Then, as his mare plodded gently onward, his eyes were held by the acid green heads of wood spurge.

'We're close now,' said Francis over his shoulder, 'if the directions in that last village were right.'

Like any mortal poised for revelation, Ned was filled with panic.

'God's blood! There it is!' Francis kicked his horse forward out of the green tunnel, then reined it in. Ned followed and blinked in the late afternoon sun. To the west, with the sun behind it, stood Tarleton Court.

Ned aimed his eyes and opened his spirit like an empty sack. Beside him, Francis was also still.

Ahead, the forest had been carved back to make fields. In the centre of these, an irregular house of rusty brick sat like a cake on a flat green table. House, forecourt and gardens were enclosed by low brick walls with the gleam of primroses at their base. Outbuildings wandered like children from an unworried parent, linked by grassy lanes and dried rivers of mud punched deep by the hoofs of cattle. Here, a grain store leaned companionably shoulder-to-shoulder with a cow barn. There, a pig house squatted alone with only a few outdoor pens for company. Beyond the house rose the chapel tower. The undersides of the few remaining trees had been barbered flat by browsing cattle and deer.

So much green, thought Ned. So much solid earth in its rightful place, not a usurper, as in Holland, straining to hold back the displaced, yearning weight of the sea. 'Paradise smells of cows and damp hay,' he said at last. Not as I expected, he meant.

Francis shook his head angrily, as if one of the bees in the hedgerow had flown too near his head.

It was a small, pleasant manor house, not frightening at all but friendly and workaday, built as a hall house in the days of the old barons, and added to, piece by piece, as need

94

arose. It spoke of goodwill and honest labour not of betrayals, executions, and exile.

Where was his grandmother's palace? His barbican gate? The bridge on which his footsteps would echo? Where was his field of war?

His grandmother's tower was merely a corner piece that balanced the chapel on the far side of the house.

A man's voice called faintly to a horse team in a field to their left. A distant dog barked.

'I should be master here,' said Francis. 'Look! There above the gate.' He pointed. 'The Malise eagle and keys have been cut away and the Nightingale device carved instead.'

Ned stirred uneasily. His mare bobbed her head to loosen the rein and stretched down to eat the new grass. Then he saw that the source of his dread lay not in that pleasant, modest house but in his brother's voice.

'Let's leave!' he begged.

'Too late now, ungrateful bratling.' Francis kicked his gelding forward.

The dog came out of the open courtyard gate, a large deerhound, all leg and sweeping curves. As they advanced, it stepped forward with its ears pricked and its tail stiffly raised. Keep away!

'It means for us to wait here,' said Ned.

Francis kicked his horse again.

A boy came out of the gate to stand at the dog's shoulder, which was nearly as high as his own. He laid his hand on its neck. Clean, confident, well-clothed with a lace-trimmed collar. The enemy at last! thought Ned. Whom I must displace and destroy. A perfectly ordinary, well-bred boy.

'A fledgling Nightingale?' muttered Francis. He called, 'Any chance of a bed for the night for discharged soldiers on our way home up north?'

'I'll fetch my father. Hold them, sir.' The boy disappeared.

'Snot-nosed lob,' said Francis. 'The young master himself, no doubt.'

95

Ned half-turned his mare. 'This is a dishonourable, sneaking way to come here,' he said to Francis. 'I won't enter Jerusalem under a false name!'

Francis dismounted. 'Look there on the gateposts, again, where our family's device was chipped away!'

'I don't want to do it like this!' Ned said passionately. 'Let's go now!'

'Off you go then, if you haven't the stomach for the game! But I mean to sleep here! One night at least in my rightful place. I shall couch at last at Tarleton Court!'

Ned grasped his reins irresolutely.

'Here they come,' hissed Francis. 'How many beds do I beg? Where was the honour in our grandfather's death? Or the Nightingales' theft of our house? I stay. Are you with me or not?'

It is that easy for the need to please someone we love to turn the course of our lives. As the man and boy approached, Ned swung down from his horse.

Just one night, he promised himself. Then, no matter how Francis sneers, I will make him leave at first light tomorrow.

'Nightingale himself, I warrant,' said Francis under his breath. 'Grandson of grandmother's Henry, I would say.'

For, of course, Henry, who had signed the bill of execution, would almost certainly be dead by now. With shame at his own ignorant imaginings of drawbridges and clean sword strokes, Ned watched the Nightingales approach – a pleasant, well-favoured man with level eyes, and his equally level-eyed son. The man was older than Francis, the boy a child of his middle age.

'Vultures.' Francis smiled at the man. 'He'd best not expect me to tug my forelock. We're soldiers who have been fighting for the English cause, are we not? Worthy of respect along with our mattress and crust. Lie-safe-abeds like those two should bow and scrape to us in gratitude!'

Francis sounded as if he believed his own fiction nearly as much as he clearly enjoyed it.

Ned's ears blazed a warning beacon for any who knew how to read the signs. The dog stalked over on its long legs and sniffed Ned's ankles, then considered the hand that he offered.

'My son tells me you're discharged soldiers who need lodging.' The man studied their faces, their clothing, their swords. He looked at Ned's ears.

Yes, headed home to York said Francis. The King lacked funds to pay them any longer. Hard times. Would probably have to sell their horses for lack of money to buy feed. Not used to begging charity, but needs must. Willing to work for bed and food. A proud man fallen on hard times – he did it well. His covert rage gave his words a believable edge.

Ned stroked the dog's rough noble head. He imagined saying, 'I'm not a discharged soldier, I'm Ned Malise.'

'His name is Mars,' the boy said to Ned.

'I'm Humphrey Fox,' said Francis to the man. 'And my cousin Ned. Ned Gool.' He tapped Ned on the shoulder, as if to show off a sound piece of goods. 'I expect a good kiss and a down coverlet from my aunt for delivering him back in one piece.'

Don't talk so much! begged Ned silently. Don't tell lies for the fun of it!

The dog now turned to Francis. It stood very still, its questioning nose pressed to his knee and ears folded close to its head. He pushed it away.

The man tilted his head slightly, as if listening for a sound he had not quite caught.

He has doubts, Ned thought. I can see it in his eyes. But he's going to say yes. He's too kind to turn us away. But the dog knows.

The boy was watching the dog with sharp hazel eyes.

'You're welcome,' said Nightingale. 'If you don't mind the stables. They're warm enough this time of year, and there's plenty of food in the kitchen.' He led them around the house into a stable yard.

97

'Cutt,' he called.

A stocky man with hair like a shorn sheep raised his head up from behind a broken cart.

'Show these two soldiers where to lodge their horses and see them right for the night themselves, in the loft. Then send them to the kitchen for dinner.'

'A cosy den for a pair of foxes, eh?' Francis leaned both of his hands on a crossbeam and looked down from the hayloft. The threshing floor below breathed a permanent haze of dust. The loft was nearly empty, as the winter hay had not yet been cut. Their two straw-stuffed mattresses and woollen coverlets lay alone on the wooden floor, with only a stack of leather-hinged flails and four hay forks for company.

'I notice that he didn't invite us to eat with the house family. Here we are, among the dumb beasts, as suits our station! I should have dubbed you Ned Bullock. Or, better, Ned Pusscat.' He slapped the beam with both hands and straightened. 'Let's go sniff around before we head for our trough to feed.'

He made a detour through the walled garden whose gates stood trustingly open. 'This would have grown to be my peach.' He plucked a pale pink blossom from a fan-trained tree against a red-brick garden wall. 'Or my apple . . . who knows which?' He tossed it away. 'May the fruit stay green and give them the gripes!'

Ned looked around for the dog. 'Let's go to the kitchen,' he said. Francis was ripe with an unspoken intent which terrified him. 'Eat and get it over with.' Unlike Francis, he was desperately grateful that they had not been asked to sit with the house family at a long polished table smelling of beeswax.

'The Spanish always kneel to cross themselves before they take aim,' said Francis. 'So that's when you must attack . . . while they are trusting to God and not their own right arms. And did you know that their Infanta vowed never to change her shift until the English are defeated? Her courtiers keep their

98

distance from more than respect.' He cranked the spit from his stool beside the fire while the laughter died.

The large shadowed kitchen was warm and friendly. Loaves of fresh-baked bread stood cooling on a long scrubbed table. The thick slice in Ned's hand was still warm. His brother's lies rang discordantly among the sounds of the fire and roasting meat, and the cheerful, unsuspecting voices.

A wide-eyed kitchen groom turned to Ned on the bench which had been pulled in front of the fireplace. 'Where were you fighting the Spanish? How many did you kill?'

Ned made hard work of his mouthful of bread, to buy time. His cheeks were already flushed by the fire.

'The South Netherlands,' called Francis, swift but vague in the rescue. 'Border forays. Move in like shadows, that's what we do. Strike and run!' He cranked the spit again, perfectly at ease, already melting into the house family.

The cook, a woman, bent across him to baste the huge joint being roasted for the next day's dinner. She leaned her hand on his shoulder to balance herself. 'Is it true that the Netherlanders sometimes have webs on their fingers and toes?'

'I swear that I once met one with gills.' Francis cranked hard enough to rattle the chains. 'For decency's sake, I won't say here how I saw them. But believe me, I was close enough to her to be sure!' He flashed the woman an oblique look which Ned recognised as his false professional flirtation.

Ned swallowed the last of his beer, stood up and backed over the bench.

'But then, the Hollanders think that we English eat nothing but joints of meat.' Francis cranked again. 'I tried to tell them that some of us must make do with bread and turnips. Not all of us can be the masters.'

Ned thanked the cook and fled. He preferred dangerous ignorance to being witness a moment longer to his brother's invention.

He found himself in a small irregular courtyard enclosed by the kitchen wall and three outbuildings. To his right a cobbled path led back along the wall of the house towards the front. Beyond that lay open fields and the forest from which they had emerged.

To his left another cobbled path ran between an open-windowed still room hung with grey and lavender bunches of herbs, and a tile-roofed woodstore with open walls.

My grandfather must have stood here once. Just where I stand. And perhaps my father, as a tiny boy. The thought made him feel odd.

As he tried to conjure up the rest of them – the angelic twins, the dead uncles, the priest – a farm worker carrying two heavy, slopping milk buckets came into the courtyard past the woodstore and still room.

Ned's heart raced. But the man, with a curious glance, merely greeted him and staggered on into the kitchen. As blind as the servants in the kitchen with their curiosity, and their host in his goodwill.

Only the dog has wit enough to suspect us.

He took the path to the left, past the stillroom, trying to imagine that he had walked it all his life and knew where it led. Beyond the still room he passed a sour-smelling dairy, then turned sharply to the right into an open courtyard rimmed with roofed pens.

The dog yard. In use – a thick dogginess crept to the back of his nose, balanced precisely between pleasant and unpleasant – but one pen stood open. Inside he saw saddles, cracked wheels, stacked timber cut into varied lengths, frayed rush mats. All the broken things and projects that need a temporary home while waiting to be repaired or finished. The days on the estate were not long enough to mend and knit all that kept inexorably unravelling.

He sniffed the smell of oak shavings and felt a jolt of connection with the place and with the people who lived there, an unwelcome pang of kinship for the man who had not yet sewn back the torn stirrup strap nor yet jointed the sides of an unfinished cradle.

A busy but still pleasant life here, for certain. *Can I imagine living here?*

He was beginning to understand his grandmother's nostalgic grief.

A mastiff thrust its huge dew-lapped jaw and old man's eyes over the gate in one of the occupied pens. It sniffed at Ned's offered hand, yawned and dropped back to the ground with a loud thump.

Beyond the dog yard stood the coach house and its yard. Ned lingered in the shadowed passageway and looked out.

Three men were climbing over a wooden coach which had been pulled out into the open air. A boy polished the wooden spokes of one great iron-rimmed wheel. Another, on the black, pitch-sealed roof, brushed vigorously at the hammer cloths. One of the men flung the scent of honey into the air as he waxed the brass-studded red leather panels of the sides.

'We don't want those soldier visitors to think we only go about in carts,' said the waxer loudly, with a sidelong look at Ned in the shadows. 'No, we don't!'

Ned nodded shortly. He would have liked to linger and talk in the late, low sunlight but was too ashamed. As he fled across the yard into the nearest alley, he heard a muffled comment and resulting gust of laughter.

A rooster tracked him from the top of a wattle fence with a cold amber eye, past a moveable wicker chicken coop and a midden that buzzed with flies. Outside the milking yard the orchards began. On his right, lines of apple trees played tricks with his eyes. One minute, the quincunx pattern was a confused maze, the next, it suddenly resolved itself into straight parallel corridors, carpeted with bluebells.

At the top of one such sudden corridor, he climbed the low stone wall to be among the trees. After a few strides, the lines of trunks became a pattern of oblique lozenges moving away to his right. Another step, and all was disorder again. He paced forward until the geometry reappeared. Risked disorder with a few more strides. Regained order. Walked on into chaos again. Then he stopped, shin-deep in bluebells.

The boy lay on his back in the long orchard grass, flattening the bluebells. The dog stood over him, forelegs on one side of his body, hindlegs on the other, while the boy scratched its breastbone. The dog swayed gently with the rhythm of the hand. Both seemed half-asleep, eyes closed, dreamily content, lost in a perfect present, with no past and no future weighing on either.

Ned dodged into the shadow against the nearest pinkish-grey, knobbled trunk. Then he decided, I shall tell him who I really am. Apologise . . . He stepped from behind the tree.

The boy looked up and saw him. Their eyes met. The boy was crying. He half-smiled at Ned, then turned his head quickly and wiped a forearm across his face.

Ned took a step forward, started to speak, backed away again, stumbled in the long grass, then turned and bolted. He leaped the low orchard wall, found their barn, flung himself up the loft ladder, and burrowed into his hay-filled mattress, where he tried to regain command of himself.

There, in the orchard, he had had a dreadful, blasphemous thought. He hardly dared remember it now. For the time of their brief exchange of glances, he had thought that, though they were of different ages, he and that boy could become friends.

Tears started into Ned's own eyes. A sickening metallic weight dragged at his heart. He finally understood his grandmother's Paradise. Not the grandeur that he had imagined. Not the abandoned gold plates, nor altarpieces too heavy to carry. Not the privilege and wealth, for these seemed modest enough here. He wept instead for the peace and permanence and for the sense of safety. He wept for the ordinariness of it all, for the smell of honey and for the dog stall full of unfinished work. For the possibility of the smell of roses and vanilla and the spice of ebony shavings.

The Malises had been thrust rootless out of this Paradise. His grandmother had left her true self here, stuck to the place and people she left behind, and never found a new place. Through her teaching, a part of him was stuck here also.

I know now what I want for myself, he thought. This peace and safety. A place where my unfinished work can afford to wait for me. A place for perfect stillness.

But to keep its peace, I must earn it fairly. Buy it back honourably. It was simple now that he had seen it. It didn't matter any longer that the Nightingales had gained Tarleton Court unfairly. He would still set the Malise Salt on the table. Grandmother would still be satisfied. But no more wars now. No more blood. Suddenly, he felt equal to the task even if he did not yet see exactly how he would achieve it.

Buy back the estate. Somehow. He would bring Marika here, as his wife. They would stroll after supper in the orchard. Perhaps with the boy, grown to a man, who would visit from his new estate, with the dog, or its progeny, trotting alongside. I will confess the ill will we brought here in our hearts and how I went away again a little changed by seeing him and the dog in the orchard.

As he drifted towards sleep, he saw the two of them leaning over the pen in the dog yard to examine a new litter of staghound pups.

Footsteps crossed the threshing floor below and the ladder creaked.

'You didn't need to run to earth,' said Francis. 'Those toothless hounds in the kitchen were more likely to fall over with tail-wagging than to bite.'

Ned breathed slowly, as if asleep.

A foot prodded his kidney. 'You didn't drink enough for that, my darling brat. Sit up and pay attention. I have conceived a wondrous plan!'

103

10

'No!' Not now, after what he had just decided.

'For sport! A jest,' insisted Francis. Ned smelled ale on him.

'Men hang for sport like that!'

'Only when caught. And even if we were – which we won't be – I wager that even Nightingale would see the just humour of it.' Francis lay back on his mattress. 'Listen! Can you hear? Those should have been my sheep. And that rustling over in that corner . . . my very own rats.'

Ned closed his eyes. If he could sleep, his brother would temporarily disappear. Or, at least, change his humour by morning. He clung to his vision of the dog pen. Burrowed deeper under his coverlet.

'A purse. Nothing more,' said Francis. 'And every coin in it plucked from this estate. It follows, by reason, that the money is mine, in God's sight if not in the Nightingales'. I will merely take it back. A very little of it.' He stared at his brother's shadowy back for a few moments. 'Better that than burn down a barn or two from bottled spite.'

'They set a mastiff loose at night,' said Ned's muffled voice. He didn't really think that Francis would torch a barn, but one could never be sure. 'Anyway, they would know that it was us.'

'Here, yes. But on the road, they won't!' Francis sounded as

104

pleased as if Ned had just offered a final argument in favour of his plan.

Ned listened to the rustling of hay, braced for more argument. Even when he heard Francis's quick breathing turn steady and slow, he could not sleep. For a moment, before Francis had come, he had felt eased, as if something had been resolved. Now he again felt the cold, heavy dread.

The loft was still dark when Francis prodded him awake with his foot. He was already dressed and held two mugs of beer in one hand and a chunk of torn bread in the other.

'York is a long way, my dearest Cousin Gool. I told the cook that we had to be away early. The Nightingales plan to lodge at Hackney tonight, and, if we are to beat them to the ford that I have in mind, we set out now.'

Francis had not changed his humour.

I'll obey now, just to get him safely away from here, thought Ned. Then I'll refuse to take any part in this dangerous, lunatic sport of his.

I I

Afterwards, I chose differently, again and again. I defied Francis and rode straight back to the Norfolk coast. I refused to help shift stones into the ford. I betrayed our blood tie and shouted a warning. I seized his arm in time. But in fact:

'Where do you think you're going?' called Francis, knee-deep in the river above the ford. On the bank below the ford, Ned dragged a wool stocking back on to his wet foot.

They had ridden fast after leaving at dawn. Once they had arrived at the ford, Francis had driven them both hard, rolling boulders from the stream bed into the shallow crossing, to block the way of the Nightingales' coach. Now, as the sun fell, the shadows under the trees were growing cold. The shadowed river already ran black between the stones of their blockade. Their exhausted horses were hidden at a distance in a thick stand of oaks.

Head down, Ned wrestled on a second stocking over wet skin. 'Leaving.' He yanked on his boot. He flinched even before the blast of his brother's incredulity hit him.

'We've not finished yet!'

'This can't be what *Gran'mère* intended us to do,' Ned muttered. 'It's certainly not what I promised.' He pulled on his other boot and stood up. His wet breeches dripped into the dry boots.

'You can't leave now!'

106

'I've done too much already! I should have refused at the start.'

'I can't do this without you.'

'I know.'

For a moment, they stared at each other across the dark, fast water. Ned felt an icy dampness begin to soak his stockings. His brother's face was colder still.

Then Francis reined in his rage. 'Don't tease, Neddie. This is a venture I'd die for.' He grinned up at his brother on the bank. 'Which would make it the most capital jest of my life. But it won't come to that.'

Ned snatched up his cloak from the bank, and buckled on his sword. Francis was not going to give it up.

I must go at once, before he wheedles me round into staying as well, Ned thought wildly. Can I get back to Amsterdam without him? I must get to my horse. Then what? I've no money for my passage. Francis controls our purse strings.

'Come on, Neddie. I know our men well, after last night among 'em. Nightingale's their only swordsman. This jape is a token of our greater intent. Of course, grandmother wouldn't approve, but she'd be secretly pleased all the same. Help me win this one small satisfaction.'

He's talking too much, thought Ned. I know him. Be careful . . . and I shall just have to try to earn my passage back to Amsterdam. Scrub the decks. Gut herring.

He shook his head and tried to remember exactly where the horses were hidden.

'I shall do it alone then.' Francis bent and began to heave another rock end over end through the water. 'With or without you.' He looked up. 'Go then! Alone, I may well be killed. With two of us, there's no danger. I need you at my side, little brother.'

There is no word more seductive than 'need'.

But even then, Ned still resisted. He even turned to go.

But as he turned, Francis called urgently after him. 'Leave me to risk death alone, then! I only came to this cursed place

107

to assist your cause!' The rock splashed into place.

'There!' said Francis. 'That will do.'

Ned watched him wade to the bank, his own clear purpose now blurred by layers of the many different brothers who waded towards him: ruffling his hair, bringing sweetmeats, tormenting him, taking him out with older friends to inns, thumping bullies and then teaching him tricks to win fights, stealing money to give their grandmother for food. That approaching shape was the warm body against which he had curled at night on their narrow bed. His tutor at both swordplay and picking pockets. His world-explainer. His only family.

'We can take our positions now.' Francis touched his brother lightly on the elbow. 'They should be here soon.'

With his mind clamped shut against the truth of what they were doing, Ned bowed yet again, but for the last time, to love and to his brother's stronger will, and followed him into the cover of some oak scrub near the ford.

The river gurgled and thumped between its stones. A cloud of gnats hovered at the water's edge.

All will be well. All will be well.

Ned crouched behind a holly bush in the cluster of oaks, clutching his sword, kerchief knotted at his throat and his hat pulled down over his ears.

Only a jest. Just as Francis says. Only a jest. An exchange of a few words, a few moments. A purse.

Nevertheless.

Please let all go well! Please let it be over and done with!

The air chilled as the dusk thickened. He shivered and pulled the wet fabric of his breeches away from his skin. The leather of his boots was cold and slippery with damp. The river drummed in his head. Every rock and pebble seemed to vibrate with a low deep booming note.

Frogs began to tune up. A fox yelped far away in the forest.

He heard the horses before Francis. A faint metallic clinking

108

of harness. Then the sound of hoofs on hard ground and the creaking and screech of wood and leather.

From where they lay hidden, they could see only scraps of dark leather passing across gaps in the leaves, fragments of darker horse, the interrupted orange glow of two lanterns and swinging flickers of yellow light. Then a coachman's cap and the glinting arc of a wheel as the coachman reined-in at the ford.

'Why have we stopped?' called Nightingale's voice above the sound of the water.

'Rocks in the ford, sir. We'll have to shift them.' The voice of the man who had been polishing the studded leather panels.

Francis clenched his fist on his sword and lifted the kerchief tied around his neck to cover his nose and lower face.

'Can I get out and look?' asked the boy's voice.

His mother's reply was too soft to hear from outside the coach.

Two men's voices spoke together at the water's edge.

'Now!' breathed Francis. 'Stay close.' He pulled his hat down to meet his kerchief. They broke out of their cover.

Ned saw all that followed as if by lightning flash, between the bangs of his heart which blurred his eyes and plugged his ears.

Pale in the dusk, two startled faces looked up at the bank. Nightingale stood at the water's edge. The coachman was already knee-deep, bent over a boulder.

Francis's voice, pulled up from his belly in disguise. A small loss, a great favour. Merely a purse. Please oblige. Then free to go.

Then Ned screamed, 'FRANCIS!'

Francis turned. Close behind him, a white-faced groom wrestled with a heavy pistol, his hands turned rebel with shaking. Faster than thought, Francis lunged and tilted their fates with his sword.

Ned felt a yell of protest rise into his throat but could not unleash it. He saw his brother's face, clearly identifiable, without its kerchief which had been dislodged in the brief fight.

'Ned! Stop him!' Francis pointed at Nightingale. 'He's going for his sword.' He pulled his own sword from the groom.

Nightingale knocked Ned aside and climbed up into the coach. Francis hurtled past after him, followed by the dripping coachman.

Ned stood dazed. The dying groom was more than a jest. Then, with a sickening lurch of his gut, he understood what that glimpse of his brother's naked face now meant.

A sheep bleated behind him. Ned turned.

The coachman had launched himself back towards Ned, teeth bared, eyes terrified, falling forward as if dragged by the heavy sword he held upright in both hands. He gave his bleating battle cry again.

'Don't!' begged Ned. 'You don't need to.'

A woman screamed inside the coach.

The coachman swung viciously at Ned's head.

Practice with Francis had put Ned well above the coachman's standard. He knocked aside the man's sword, almost too easily. He paused. They stared at each other. The evening before, one had joked while the other had fled with hot ears and a desire to linger for company. His nostrils flared to the smell of burning pitch.

'Kill him, you blockhead! He knows us!' Francis leaned akilter, braced on rigid legs against the single coach door, face contorted with his effort, his teeth bared.

'No,' said Ned. But he had waited too long to finish his rebellion.

The coachman's seat cloth was on fire. Flames shimmered across the pitch-covered wooden roof of the coach.

Nightingale thudded against the inside of the coach door, trying to dislodge Francis from the outside.

Francis dropped the lantern with which he had set fire to the coach's trimmings.

'Francis! NO! The woman and boy are inside!' Ned turned from the coachman in horror, to pull his brother from the door.

But the coachman mistook Ned's intent. Rage overcame his fear and he set on Ned with the ugly uncontrolled energy of a dogfight.

'Let me by!' Ned shouted. It was no longer Francis who blocked escape from the burning coach. His brother had been replaced by a snarling beast. Ned struggled to escape the coachman. He must destroy the beast.

But the coachman was deaf with panic. His sword sliced past Ned's ear. Ned turned and gave himself to one of the short deadly bursts of coherence that make up a battle. For a few moments, in the need to save his life, he lost his fear and horror. Fighting against a less-skilled opponent made him feel powerful and raw. He parried and stepped past the coachman, turning to parry again. Each sweep and grab of his sinews cut a clear, absolute shape in the air. All his senses fused into a single burning beam turned on the coachman. He was a lion. The man could not touch him. Their swords rang together. He bared his teeth, panted, and parried. The clash of their swords juddered through the bones of his arm. He was invulnerable, propelled by a wild elation.

Smoke surged between them, then blew back. They circled through the dark drifting veils. Then the smoke laid a towel across his face. He coughed, blinded, his eyes streaming.

The woman in the coach screamed. A blade sliced past him in the smoke. He swung blindly. His sword smacked into flesh. The sharpened edge near its tip sliced. Then the smoke blew clear and he fell in a sickening swoop from the height of his elation back into himself.

The coachman had stopped as if Ned were no longer there. Looked at his arm, then sat down on the ground and pressed the severed muscle back into place with his hand. Ned stared, appalled, first at the coachman, and then at the blood on his sword.

Ropes of smoke twisted between them again.

'I'm sorry!' cried Ned. He jumped back, away from a sparking firework launched by the pitch roof. He coughed and wept with stinging eyes as smoke from the coach rose, curled, and fell back down in dark bolsters that unrolled across the ground.

The wooden coach was now fully ablaze. The clearing around it glowed with a wavering orange and yellow light. Tree branches above it had begun to smoulder and drip fragments of glowing leaf.

The woman still screamed and screamed as her shadow danced in the heart of the fire. The horses screamed and reared, then broke free from the burning traces and crashed away into the forest. Ned heard their own horses whinny with fear from the thicket where they had been hidden.

'They know us!' yelled Francis. 'They've seen my face!'

The beast's face at the coach door.

Ned stared in disbelief as a comet curved through the air from the coach window.

The boy. Thrust through the window, his hair on fire. He landed heavily. Black smoke covered him.

'Kill the whelp!' shrieked Francis. 'Kill them all now, or hang!' The abscess of his rage had finally burst.

'MOTHER!' screamed the boy. The blazing dandelion clock of his head rose like a swimmer above the black smoke, then sank again.

Ned tore off his cloak and threw it over the boy. He squinted against the smoke and hot orange light at the dark shadows inside the burning coach.

'Go on, kill him, God damn you! Kill the boy!' cried the beast.

Ned put up his sword. The coachman lurched past him into the smoke and with his good arm began to drag the boy away from the coach towards the bushes at the edge of the track. The screams inside the coach had finally stopped.

'KILL HIM!'

Ned stepped into the beast's way. They collided, grappled. Francis threw Ned aside and thrust his sword at the coachman's back.

The blade slipped, caught in clothing, then found the space between two ribs, where it jammed. The man screamed. Francis cursed, yanked, finally abandoned the sword to beat the bushes beyond the track, but the boy was gone.

Francis returned to the writhing, keening coachman. Put a foot on the man's back to yank out his sword. Finished the job. He stood over the body, suddenly slack. He seemed almost to sleep upright.

Ned looked away. It was his brother Francis after all.

The clearing felt very silent. The inside of the coach was still except for the crackling of flames. The river grumbled. An iron wheel-rim glowed red. A blackened circle in the overhanging branches smouldered, dropping flakes of ash like black snow.

The orange-lit bodies on the ground looked both real and implausible, like actors at the end of a tragedy.

Ned felt cold and numbed. Sick with remembering his flash of exaltation. They were both beasts. Grandmother had surely never intended this carnage. And he had forsworn more wars. His shaking body yearned for the heat of the fire, but a gust of roasting meat, pushed at him by the evening breeze, made him gag. Grandfather's fiery execution at the stake had been revenged with a hideous precision that he had never imagined.

At last Francis said, 'What possessed you to let the brat go? He can hang us both.'

Homo lupus homini, his grandmother had said. Man is a wolf to man. And he and Francis were no better than the worst of their enemies.

'Who are you staring at?' demanded Francis. 'Ned?' He moved towards his younger brother.

Ned sat down suddenly on the river bank. He felt distant from the scene, nothing like a triumphant knight. And very far from the painted tower room where children were born. He gazed in disbelief from far away at the two small figures still upright on the battlefield.

Francis stopped uncertainly.

An owl gave its first evening cry.

Ned closed his eyes. Became an owl. Flew up through the dusk away from the fire. He circled on silent wings, staring down, trying to understand what he saw. Trying to think where to fly next. He caressed the air with his wingtips, flew higher. But couldn't fly high enough to escape the smell of charred meat.

THREE

12

Reason says that I should have killed the boy. If I had obeyed Francis, he would still be alive and I would most likely not be here now. But I have never obeyed Reason as I should.

I think this is my second day here. How many meals?

My hands are unfeeling blocks. I must tear my burning, aching shoulders from my body.

Another place . . .

No! I must give all my attention to staying upright. I try to stiffen legs that I can no longer feel. They will give way soon.

What can I say to the magistrates?

I snatch at dream fragments. Sitting down. Swimming. Fragrant wood shavings. A few words someone once said that might hold my salvation . . .

Hole in my thoughts.

The door scrapes open. I see the orange reflection of a light on the wall beyond my right hand. Someone's here with me.

I don't imagine!

All my hair prickles. Perhaps he'll unshackle me!

A man's voice speaks, but not to me. He's angry. Another voice, surly, disclaiming. They leave again.

I think that it was Maurits. But why didn't he speak to me?

Maurits. Must wrestle what remains of my mind around to him. Timon Maurits van . . . something. Hole in my thoughts . . .

Knees!

Maurits van Egmond. My would-be saviour. As well-born as a man can be in these damp egalitarian provinces. Stinking rich. Spoilt. Fearsomely clever. I feel a hope as tangible as heat begin to suffuse my bones.

Maurits came here. Into this underground cell. Something will happen now.

Can I stay alive and in my right mind until then?

I will go to meet him.

13

To Ned it seemed that, with those deaths at the ford, Francis had put Tarleton Court out of his reach forever. And, therefore, Marika and the fulfilling of his vow. Even worse, Ned had had a glimpse of his own nature that appalled him.

Once memories are made, they stick. Again and again, on the journey back and ever since, Francis's orange-lit face shrieked, 'Kill the brat!' Again and again, Ned felt a hideous elation as he swung his sword and sliced into another man's flesh. Again and again, the coachman clapped the severed muscle back against the white glint of bone.

Twice on the boat from London he had caught his brother studying him along the ship's rail with an uncharacteristic unease in his eyes. He himself often looked at his brother in astonishment that by daylight his features were their former, unchanged selves.

Now, here in the White Cat in the Old Side, liquor loosened Francis's tongue. He had been dipping his beak all evening and was as soaked as an owl.

'For the love of God, take off your funeral face, bratling! All the day, every day. What do you want me to do? Nothing's gained by regret.' He glanced quickly again at his younger brother, then drank deeply from his beer glass. 'That cursed groom should never have brought weapons into it. Then I took fright when things went wrong, that's all.'

Ned bent his head to his lute which he had been fingering.

Since their return, it had seemed to resist him. And his voice, which had so far defied nature, croaked and rasped as if about to break after all.

Ned's fingers moved laboriously in an act of will that brought forth only dead, mechanical sound. Dried flies falling from an old basket. He looked at the wall above his brother's head. 'Any moment now, you'll tell me that the whole massacre was the coachman's fault.'

In the silence, on the wall above their heads, a chained yellow-green finch hopped from one end of its perch to the other. 'Pink, pink,' it said. A chipped, mournful note.

'Indeed, if he hadn't attacked you . . .' Francis looked at his brother's face and stopped.

Ned set aside his lute. He picked up a white clay pipe from the planked table-top and pinched some tobacco from an open box. His hands trembled as he tried to light it with a coal from the clay pot on the table.

Francis went red. 'Hell's teeth, bratling . . . !' He glanced around and lowered his voice. 'We can still do it! Go back. No one knows our true names. No one survived but a brat of six years.' Francis refilled his green glass *roemer* from the jug on the table. 'There's no cause for us not to go back.'

Ned's hands jumped so that he could not light his pipe. His heart suddenly felt as hot as the coal he was trying to set to the tobacco. If he looked at Francis, his gaze would sear his brother's flesh.

Francis leaned close across the table. 'No one who would be believed could know us again for that pair of ragged soldiers turned highwaymen.'

'Francis, shut your mouth!'

Francis snapped his mouth closed. Pulled his head into his shoulders and stared back in disbelief. They were both equally astonished.

Ned felt that his merest touch would burn.

Then Francis flung out an arm and seized a passing skirt. 'Josie Jugs! Come help us drink a toast! Where's your friend, the Dainty Dane?' Francis refilled his brother's glass. 'You too, Neddie!'

Josie rumpled Ned's hair fondly and sat beside him on the bench. 'We miss your singing in the *musico*,' she said.

The Dainty Dane, who followed behind her, sat beside Francis.

'Get your glasses, ladies,' cried Francis. 'I want to drink to a house . . .'

'Francis!' Ned pushed his own glass aside and stood. 'We must go now!'

Francis seemed to spread a little wider on his bench like a toad. 'Our house . . . ours . . . you and me, Ned, the last of the Malises.'

Ned glanced around the inn. While it was unlikely that an English spy was drinking there at just that moment, the sea between was not so wide that you could afford to blab.

'I have the means!' crowed Francis. 'Neddie there is cross with me, because he doesn't yet know what I know!' He tapped his nose ponderously, a little unsure of its location but pleased to have found it all the same. 'We shall be drinking toasts with the King and Queen of England, I swear it!'

Ned closed his eyes and became the finch that dragged its tether ring from side to side along the perch rod.

Pink. Pink. Pink. How vile those large wingless creatures are, the finch thought. Think what they've done! Yet they imagine that they have souls while I do not. But with my sharp eye I can see their teeth and muzzles through the smoke. Pink. Pink.

'Secret,' said Francis. 'My secret. If Ned's a good little boy, I might tell him too.'

But, at sixteen, Ned thought, I'm no longer your good little boy. If I have become clear about anything, it's that.

As Ned rolled him into bed later, Francis said, 'Soon, bratling. Show you my secret. Key to England.'

14

I don't like this tale. But it will continue with or without me.

Francis accepted his brother's revolt in the White Cat with surprising docility. He returned to his traffic in miracle cures, and found new lodgings among the artists and artisans of the New Side, overlooking the muddy cut of a new canal – the Prince's Canal – which was being added to the concentric half-rings that cupped the city. This morning, eleven months later, he was his old bumptious self.

'I won't take nay from you! You shall come!' he said.

'I'll make no more sorties with you, dear brother.'

'Do you remember a secret investment I made, shortly before we went to England?'

'Our "Key to England"?'

'My healing genius has just now completed his first experiments. We have been called to witness.'

Ned crossed to the window and looked down. Early as it was, buckets of muddy water already travelled from hand to hand along four chains of excavators. Two teams of men were lowering great oak piling posts into holes that refilled with water as fast as the buckets emptied them.

'Francis,' he said, 'didn't you hear me? I am no longer with you in your ventures! None of them!'

'Why on earth not?' cried Francis. But for a few seconds there was a large hole of silence in the air of the room.

'When you see what I hope to show you,' said Francis, 'you'll get back your appetite for our ventures. If this cure is efficacious, we are made men! You'll be singing to countesses and queens, not pickpockets and whores.' Francis joined his brother at the window. 'What disease do fair women fear even more than they fear the plague? Ah, you must wait to learn! At least come see! If you still refuse, then I will have to accept it.'

They sailed by public canal boat through grey, damp air to a house outside The Hague. Not a country mansion, but a small ornate wooden hut, built in one of the country pleasure gardens which many Amsterdammers bought because space in the city was too cramped for gardens and entire country estates cost too much.

Francis rattled the wooden gate, yanked at the bell rope, peered through the cracks, and demanded what could be taking so long.

At length the owner himself appeared to unlock the gate. In his fifties, thin, with skimpy, faded beard and moustache, he had that pinched, mended, slightly soiled look of disappointment and acquired poverty.

Ned glanced at his brother in dismay. Was this his healing genius?

As soon as they were through the gate and he had locked it behind them, the man grasped Francis by the sleeve and said with excited pride, 'Mynheer Malise, the secret is in a virgin's blood!'

Again Ned looked at his brother.

But Francis flushed with pleasure. 'In truth? How did you conclude this?'

'Patience. Patience. You shall soon see.'

Inside, the hut was equipped as a physician's study, with books and bottles. Ned also saw an apothecary's still and a rack of surgeon's knives and saws. A tiered muslin sieve. Scales and weights and many implements of steel and iron which he

123

could not name. No black coat in evidence, however, nor silver-headed cane.

Perhaps a physician once, thought Ned sourly, but most likely no longer. Perhaps he overdosed a poxed provost with mercury or failed to save a stateholder's child.

The man had laid out ready a large book with pages covered from margin to margin with words and numbers. He turned over the pages at the front. 'These were my first assays. You can see how many I made on your behalf before I discovered the miracle. At great expense.'

'I know all this!' said Francis impatiently.

The man shot Francis a glance. 'You may now read here . . .' he pointed to the page '. . . how I at last thought to mingle the pure blood of untainted virgins with the blood of those who had suffered the contagion. Look how many.' His finger ran down a list of the names of both men and women. 'An entire dozen. And all have so far remained well while members of their families have contracted the disease and many have died. And the reason for this miracle is clear: the principle of maidenly purity has routed the dragon of contagion!'

'What is this disease?' asked Ned, interrupting. That fair women fear more than they fear the plague.

'The small pox, of course.' The man looked startled at his ignorance.

Ned was surprised at his brother's gullibility. Such talk of virgins' blood rang of country superstition, not an apothecary's careful science.

Francis, however, seemed well satisfied and clapped the man on the shoulder. 'It's well that you labour here in the country. You'd have trouble finding many virgins for our purpose in Amsterdam!'

'I don't need so many. One moment please.' He called from the back door of the hut. 'Hanne!'

A young girl of no more than twelve or thirteen came into the hut. She was solid, rough-handed and stank of soured milk. But instead of a dairy maid's expected rosy complexion, even

124

under cheeks burned by the sun, the skin of her neck and wrists was a translucent and unhealthy grey. She curtsied, then stood tranquil and smiling while the three men looked at her.

'Our miraculous fountain, our source,' said the man. 'I've made myself her guardian. Paid her parents as handsomely for her wardship as if she were an heiress. They were overjoyed.'

'Do they know that you drain their daughter's blood?' asked Ned sharply. Under her sour milk, the girl smelt cold, like a damp stone.

'No!' The man looked suddenly anxious. 'We've sworn ourselves to secrecy, haven't we?' He smiled at the girl. 'I promised that if she stays with me for two years, and holds her tongue, I'll buy her two cows of her own, one for each year.' He nodded at the girl. 'You may go now.'

She curtsied again, as if they were all fine gentlemen and left.

'Twelve trials is not enough for absolute certainty,' said Francis.

'I believe that it is.'

'It's not, and I won't buy.'

After a short and eventually amicable negotiation, Ned and Francis took their leave. 'I shall visit some of your "miracles" to see for myself that they're still alive and unblemished,' Francis warned.

'He's killing that girl,' Ned said, as soon as they were out of earshot of the gate.

'Don't be an ass. He's doing no more than a good physician who lets blood to cure a fever or headache. He may need to be reminded from time to time who's the master, but if he does as I say, I trust the cure.'

'I've witnessed your miracle and I still want no part in it!'

'You will, dear bratling, when you know fully what I intend. I can't tell him why I need more trials because I don't want him to know how high my stakes will be. I must be patient because I must be absolutely certain! A hundred trials would hardly be enough to satisfy the lady I have in mind.'

'As you're bursting to tell me, spit it out!'

'The woman in my sights must fear the loss of her fair looks more than any other madam in Christendom – a Catholic unhappily married to an Englishman who ignores her. She needs to win his heart and to breed heirs. She must escape the scars of small pox, she needs love philtres, she needs potions to make her fertile with males. She'll welcome true, loyal help where she can find it – Her Majesty Henrietta Maria, the English queen.'

Francis was in earnest. Mad, perhaps, but in deadly earnest.

By the time they reached their lodgings again, Ned had decided.

There had been too much blood already. Tarleton Court must not be bought back with still more, even that of a complaisant virgin. He was not clever like Francis. He had no head or taste for business. He was still not quite seventeen and his education had been severely flawed. He would use the only weapon he had, untrustworthy as it now seemed to be.

Ned went back to Warde.

While he waited for the doctor to make the new trials, Francis made expeditions to Spain and the Spanish Netherlands where he bought pieces of dead saints in jewelled cases to sell to wealthy, exiled German Catholics. Ned sometimes wondered whether his brother carried gold or guns across the borders as well as pharmacopoeia and relics. His brother's hunger might not be satisfied merely with Virgin's Blood and lavender water, particularly with the English queen in his sights.

Whatever he might be buying and selling, Francis worked hard, if furtively, and prospered. With a little money now in his purse, he sought introductions everywhere, won invitations and invested openly, with some success, at the Amsterdam Bourse.

Ned again led a double life. Francis had forbidden him to sing in the *musico*s or to engage in any work that did not suit the attendant moon of a planet rising. Although his voice still slid off notes and cracked in unexpected places, he learned to choose his songs to favour his faults. In place of the *musico*s, he began to sing in private houses and lodgings, though still to enhance the act of fornication. As the men who could afford to keep mistresses or bawdy lodgings paid even better than sailors, students and labourers, he too prospered, and saved every *stuiver* and guilder. He had to tell Francis that he was working for Warde again, but did not tell him that he had begun to save money to buy passage back to England.

'I won't have my brother sweeping floors for a mere craftsman!' insisted Francis. 'How do you imagine that you can ever turn gentleman?' But otherwise he left Ned alone.

Ned did not tell him that Warde had now made him a properly registered apprentice, but not merely to sweep floors. The joints of the lute-maker's hands had begun to swell and throb with age and he needed Ned to become his hands instead. Now Ned did the most intricate and careful work. Warde began to trust him to work unsupervised and finally gave him, to make alone, a commission from a nobleman in Utrecht for a thirteen-course lute in bird's-eye maple and plum wood, with an ebony-veneered neck and peg box and ivory half-edgings.

As Warde paid him barely enough to cover his dinners, Ned often went without midday food in order to add to his tiny but growing hoard of guilders. But Warde gave Ned knowledge, a reward even greater than money. Also, under the instrument-maker's renewed teaching, as he finished his fourteenth lute, Ned began to regain his sense of internal harmony. With Warde, he laid out the perfection of Platonic diagrams on the wooden leaves that would become the sounding board, so that the finished instrument would resonate in accord with the same harmonic patterns that governed the heavens themselves. When his whole being guided a chisel, Ned was again briefly in concord – his hand, the chisel, the wood on which he worked – with the universe itself. The growing sureness of his hands and eye was born from the same perfect stillness as his music had been.

'I won't have it!' Francis once tried to insist. 'Only today I dined with a man who told me that you had put new strings on his wife's mandolin! I could barely keep my composure!'

'I can't imagine you being outfaced by anything or anyone, Francis.' Ned had begun to feel as steady as a young tree which had wrapped its roots around a rock. The end of his purpose now felt certain, but was still so distant that it had lost its terror.

'You must join with me, Neddie! I've the brains, Neddie. But you've the looks and bearing to win the women, now that you're nearly a full-grown man, with your dark curls and height. You must learn to use those light, piercing eyes of yours. They're made to shoot Cupid's darts!'

'Which missed the only target I ever wanted to hit.'

'I thought you'd forgotten that Dutch cheese! You can aim higher than the spoilt sister of a notorious rogue.'

'We were in perfect harmony.' Or so he now sometimes seemed to recall.

'Pah! A good marriage is more than twiddling at a lute, my dear brat.'

Because he had begun to feel safe from Francis's pull, Ned agreed from time to time to carry a parcel for him as a gesture of peace. For, in spite of everything, Francis was the only person on earth who loved him. Even in his rough, hugger-mugger fashion. They were tied by blood and years of sharing a cot, like two puppies.

Though Warde snorted with amusement at the idea, Ned began to attempt a perfect lute or, at least, the best that had ever sung under human fingers. For himself, to join his adored but flawed first darling. A new-style, larger, ten-course lute, with nineteen strings, which his long fingers could play without difficulty. If his own voice was flawed, his lute's soul would sing for him.

Of ash, he decided. His wood. Hard but flexible, with a bright crisp sound. And of a simple design, with a little decoration but not over ornate.

128

First he rapped and tapped at scores of ash planks until he found the perfect ringing tone. He carefully sawed the plank into two wide, thin leaves for either side of the belly, and nine narrower leaves for the ribs of the back. He found just the right piece of ebony to make thin black stripes between the pale ash ribs, and for the pegs.

'Beware of attempting perfection,' said Warde. 'It smacks of arrogance.' But he gave Ned ivory for edgings.

Ned designed a new pattern of his own for the decorative rose cut into the belly to free the sound inside, and carved a printing block of this design. He and Warde spent a pleasant hour in debate about the exact size for his lute, and which of the many limewood moulds he should use to shape the body.

One day, as Ned was smoothing the assembled back of his lute with a piece of sharkskin glued to a block, he felt Warde watching him.

'This will be your master piece,' said Warde. 'I shall tell the Guild and make them reckon in the years that you worked for me before. I've known one or two others as young as you.'

A master luthier! Ned beamed at Warde, flushed and speech-less with joy. That end was enough in itself, even without the use he intended to make of it. He began at once to design his own maker's mark to set on the belly just above the rose.

Sometimes, instead of singing in the evenings and when it was too dark for the workshop, he went back to the Blomsloot just to stroll by the canals or sit with his back against a tree and watch the street. It was the only home he had known, but he was not allowed to claim it. His ginger-furred friend had vanished, but another dog, a short-legged, brindled chimney-brush creature, was often happy to join him in exchange for a scratch.

He shared an occasional friendly gin with Josie Jugs or the Dainty Dane. Catryn the Corset had bought her own *musico* on the other side of the seaport, they told him. Not, alas, thriving, or so gossip said. He went at once to visit her, then returned to play and sing for her customers for free.

'He's a saint! A musical angel!' she would cry. 'Aren't you all a fortunate crew?'

Word of this free entertainment spread, and Catryn's clientele grew.

Francis be hanged! thought Ned. I don't care if he learns. This singing gives me pleasure.

His chief fear at that time was that he might meet Marika. The sight of her might dislodge his precarious new sense of balance. At the same time, he listened avidly for any scrap of gossip about her.

'Not married so far as I can learn,' said Josie.

He sometimes imagined that he might visit her again. But the memory of past humiliations changed his mind yet again.

Just once, he allowed himself to walk past their house, veiled by the dusk, when the Coymans had guests to supper. Through the window he watched her laugh and touch the hand of the man beside her. He fled. He had been right to avoid her. His pain flowed through him again like a fiery river.

At night he still dreamed that the Nightingale boy and his dog came to their lodgings, burning as brightly as torches but able to converse from the heart of the flames. Sometimes his grandfather waved a charred arm from the ruins of the coach. His ashes blew into Ned's eye.

In the morning after such dreams, he fled to Warde's workshop as a safe haven.

One night in the late spring a year after their return from England, Francis opened his mahogany case and showed Ned eight glass vials filled with a dark ruby liquid.

'Eight vials of pure gold,' said Francis. 'From my doctor. The blood of his bucolic virgin. I'm nearly satisfied. Need to make one last trial of my own. Then we'll sail for London!'

'But I haven't finished . . .' Ned cut himself off.

In the following weeks, Francis sold all eight vials. Then he waited.

'It will be proved,' said Francis. 'I feel it! This is my good

130

fortune at last.' He stared into the mahogany case, whistling between his teeth. 'The man's a gifted physician, but a child at business. He needs me to take his cure out into the world.'

Ned told Warde of his brother's plans, and worked on his lute from dawn until he squinted with even three candles and an oil lamp.

He counted his money. Enough to buy passage to England. The first step.

Then they waited for three months. Ned finished his lute in good time after all, and Warde submitted it to the Guild. By the end of the summer, when all diseases flourished in the crowded cities, not one of Francis's clients had contracted the small pox.

Francis went back to his man and returned with five more ruby vials.

'Now for Her Majesty and Fortune!'

'I'm more sorry than I can say that I'm leaving you,' Ned told Warde.

'I, too.' Warde glared. 'But you're eighteen. Time to be your own hands, which seem to know all they need to know. I have received your lute back.'

Ned did not breathe.

'And your certificate from the Guild. No surprise to me, but I daresay that you're pleased. Too bad you won't be here long enough for the . . .'

'Yes!' shouted Ned, beyond civility with joy. 'Oh, yes!' Then he recalled himself. 'I thank you . . . !'

'And also,' Warde bent and heaved a small wooden chest up on to the workbench, 'my master's gift to you. For England. Until you can make or find your own.'

Ned lifted the lid. Inside was a set of eleven chisels, four planes, three saws, a small piece of sharkskin for smoothing wood, five knives of different sizes, a bundle of minikins from Munich for tying frets, several thin leaves of ash and maple, a strip of ebony, a small block of brazil wood for pegs and his own rose pattern block.

131

'There is just room for one mould,' said Warde. 'You may choose which you want to take.'

While Ned was still incoherent with surprise and emotion, Warde also gave him a purse. 'You've worked for love and in some kind of penance which I don't wish to understand. But here is the balance of your proper wages. Use them to buy time. Don't sing in English whorehouses just in order to live. Buy time to choose. Don't betray your true part in music!'

'Never!' said Ned. 'I just pray that she doesn't desert me!'

'What the devil's in there?' demanded Francis when Ned came home with the chest.

'Some tools that old Warde gave me, which he has no use for.'

'Well you won't have any use for them either, as the brother of a gentleman!'

'Things don't always turn out as you intend,' said Ned. Their eyes met. Francis looked away first.

So Ned set off for England in the company of his brother, but not in concord with him, to seek out the enemy and recapture Jerusalem honorably with only his hands, his lutes, his chest of tools, and his flawed voice.

FOUR

15

In London, Francis at once took extravagant lodgings at Covent Garden, where the Earl of Bedford had already begun to build houses for gentlemen and 'men of ability' to the north of his own Bedford House garden.

'What are we but men of ability?' asked Francis when Ned protested at the cost. 'Malises can't live in Shoreditch.'

They bought rich, fashionable clothes to suit their new status, and hired servants whom Francis dressed nearly as well as himself. He presented letters of introduction, including one from his satisfied client in Norfolk, and began at once to entertain lavishly in order to recreate and improve on the growing network of acquaintance he had left behind in Amsterdam. From his Dutch savings he invested modestly in other men's ventures, to make himself felt rather than in hope of great returns, as all his hopes lay with the Dutch doctor and his dairymaid. Ned protested that they lived beyond their means, but Francis swore that they must.

One evening he set the Malise Salt on their dinner table.

Ned eyed the great silver bulk with unease. 'It belongs at Tarleton Court!'

'I want it seen here in London. To help us to Tarleton Court. What men see is what they believe. And what they believe is transformed to the gold of reality.'

Francis also began to spread rumours of his small pox cure.

'Three ladies of the highest breeding whispered to me today

that they wish to learn more!' he crowed at the end of a picnic he had laid on in St James's Field.

Within six weeks of arriving in England he had disposed of all five vials and sent to Holland for more.

Ned set himself to writing songs.

Francis also used his new acquaintances to gather intelligence. 'John Nightingale still lives at Tarleton Court,' he reported after one dinner. 'He's the master there now.' He bared his teeth briefly. 'Seems never to come to London. And certainly doesn't move in the circles we already nudge at. A country bumpkin. A rustic with no taste for leaving home.'

Small wonder, thought Ned. After his first taste of travel!

The story of the deaths at the ford seemed to have died.

The boy was an impossible obstacle between Ned and Tarleton Court. In John Nightingale's place, Ned would never agree to sell the estate! Least of all to an old family enemy. But whenever he tried to harden himself to think of all Nightingales as the enemy, to be outdone in some other way, remembered the boy lying on his back in the grass of the orchard scratching his dog and wiping tears from his eyes. Then he saw the arc of his fall from the coach window, and again heard him scream, 'MOTHER!'

If he won't sell, how am I ever to take the place from him? Without dishonour?

I'm the tortoise to Francis's hare, he decided. One step at a time.

He practised his lute and wrote more songs. He fell in love with London. Many afternoons, he walked the streets as he had in Amsterdam. Sometimes among the booksellers of St Paul's. Sometimes to Thames Street and the wine and roasted meats he could buy there. Sometimes among the docks and quays belonging to all nations, which reminded him of Amsterdam. Spices and frankincense from the Indies. French wine. Russian amber and furs.

He often visited the cattle market at Smithfield, where horses could also be bought. Young unbroken horses, mares and beasts for pulling carts and ploughs. Amblers and pacers for gentlemen. He stroked soft noses and promised himself that at Tarleton Court, as well as a staghound, he would have a splendid horse.

Sometimes, after listening to the ballad-sellers bawling out their wares on street corners, and learning both tune and words, he would hang on the sea wall above the Thames and watch the wherries stitch together the two banks of the glittering river. While he did not share Francis's hunger for the society of St James's Fields, he often strolled across London Bridge to Southwark, which reminded him of the Blomsloot. He felt comfortable there among the rogues, the whores and *bona robas*, and often sat in the friendly company in the Rose and the Bear, listening to the talk and laughter, joining in, as one does, with strangers sharing a drink. Before long he was greeted by name and could, himself, shout out greetings to faces he knew.

He still did not bed any of the whores, though in his new male adulthood he sometimes felt he would explode with lust. His old inhibitions held. By now he had seen even more of pustules and swellings, stranguries and scalded heads. And more than any other sign of the *morbus gallicus* or great pox, he now feared the damage to his voice, which was settling again. He tried to imagine himself as a secular monk sworn to his music for both joy and purpose.

One evening a troupe of players were drinking in the Bear after their performance. Three of them began to sing songs from their play.

With one of the whores, Sukie, leaning on his shoulder, Ned joined the song.

'Sing it louder,' said Sukie. 'You've a lovely voice, mister. Shut your cake-holes everyone!' she shouted. 'We've got a real singer here!'

Ned stood up. Someone handed him a lute. It was battered and out of tune, but he tightened the pegs and eased the frets along the neck until it sang true for him, unperturbed by the shouts of derision and impatience from his audience.

'Ahhhhhhhhhh!' He tested his voice against the low ceiling of the inn. After his years of experience in the Blomsloot, he knew exactly what he was doing in this smoky room full of drinkers. The roughness of his voice did not matter. His height gave him command. He was comfortable here.

'Sing! Sing! Sing!' The drinkers pounded their mugs on the tables.

'Ohhhhhhhhhh!' he teased them, still testing his voice. It arrived, open and full. His cheekbones vibrated. Just as well. He needed full volume. The lute made too delicate a sound for this room and these rowdy enthusiasts.

'Sing! Sing!'

Still teasing, he sang a rousing Dutch drinking song with a simple accompaniment. The last note brought applause but also shouts of protest.

'Give us English music! A good English song! No more of those foreign herring-eaters' dirges!'

'A good song?' demanded Ned. 'Like this, d'you mean?' He began a hymn and let the catcalls wash over him. 'Why don't you English ever say what you mean? Here's good-and-wicked, then.' His fingers danced and he sang, 'Man is for Woman Made'.

This time he got cheers. Even better, his voice was once again his friend.

He sang, 'I Have A Gentle Cock'. Then every filthy English song he knew, mixed with a few of the street-corner ballads. At last, when his voice cracked, he called for mercy and a mug of ale, and threw the lute back to its owner.

In the furore of back-pounding, compliments, four offered ale mugs, a kiss from Sukie and demands for more songs, he heard a voice he knew. Well-spoken, young.

'I know you!'

'Me?' asked Ned, all innocence.

'Malise! Ned! Francis Malise's younger brother! What the devil are you doing here?'

138

'Same as you, I should think.'

'No, I can't sing for my supper, let alone for a fuck. Wish I could.'

'Not something Francis approves of.'

'Well, I won't tell your brother I met you here, if you don't tell my father.'

They clasped hands on it and Ned taught William Shaw the words to 'I Have A Gentle Cock'. In spite of his disclaimer, Shaw proved to have a light, true voice, a good ear and considerable gusto for both music and ale. By the time they stumbled home across London Bridge, they were sworn friends until death and Ned had promised to teach Shaw how to play the lute.

Young Shaw at once set himself to lifting the basket from what he saw as Ned's hidden light. And Francis pushed him forward in society just as eagerly, for his own reasons. Ned began to be known as an obliging, nimble-fingered musician who knew every fashionable song as well as a number of other improper but most amusing ones. He was soon in wide demand among their growing circle of acquaintance. Furthermore, though he did not see it, the daughters of at least two wealthy merchants fell wildly in love with him.

Who, they whispered to friends, could resist that charming accent, that fine figure, with those long legs, those strange pale eyes that made one shiver deliciously, those dark curls, those hands? Who could watch a young man like that caress the smooth rounded wooden body of his instrument and settle it against his own body without having improper thoughts? And how tenderly his hand curled around the neck!

One or two of the older women were even more taken by the way he tested and tuned his strings with a remote, rapt expression in those eyes of his. The fierce blade of his nose and dark heavy brows only served, in their minds, to hint at something a little dangerous behind what was, to be frank, an over-civil and mild demeanour. Except when he played and sang.

★   ★   ★

Six months after they arrived in London Francis had a letter from his doctor.

'Hell's teeth! I cannot credit it! I'll rip the man's guts out with my bare hands!' Francis kicked a joint stool across the floor of their great parlour.

'I take it that something's amiss,' said Ned. He observed his brother's bear-like temper as if from a distance.

'He let the girl, Hanne, die! Did he think she was a polder to be drained quite dry?' Francis stood at the window, leaning on the scarlet, silk-velvet drapery, clenched fists pressed together on the sill. 'I already have four more ladies panting for the cure, including one on the fringes of the court, all desperate to save their fair complexions. Now he says that he can't send the blood. Must find another virgin, he says. Whom he can buy like the last one. I've already begun my campaign to achieve Her Majesty. The delay will ruin me.'

'Ply your old trade until he's ready,' said Ned. He knew better than to suggest that he might set up a workshop himself and make lutes.

Francis turned and sent a wave of his rage surging towards his brother. 'Turn mountebank cure-pusher again, d'you mean? I've risen higher, bratling! And even if I wanted to, how easy do you think it would be, eh? London's more closed even than Amsterdam!'

The English apothecaries, surgeons and physicians, while hating each other, nevertheless joined fiercely to prevent any selling of remedies by non-members of their guilds. Ancient wise women and midwives were regularly fined and pilloried for stepping over the line. Some alchemical quacks were even imprisoned. So, any trafficking in cures that Francis might wish to do would have to be as clandestine 'favours' granted to special friends or to friends of friends, for which he might, perhaps, accept small tokens of gratitude.

'I can whet appetites, but I won't risk my new social position. Not when I'm so close to success.' Francis looked at the letter again, as if the force of his will might change what it said.

140

'I must wait for this fool in his garden to find a new virgin to drain.'

Meanwhile their living costs continued to eat up their small accumulation of wealth.

Just before their second Christmas in England, Ned wrote a short masque on the Judgement of Paris for Francis's acquaintances to perform. He was feeling his way forward. He knew only that, however he advanced towards his goal, he must always stay in harmony, must never again allow that terrible discord in the universe which he had felt after the evening at the ford. If he could keep the harmony, Tarleton Court would one day be his. The belief was part honourable conviction, part superstition.

At the first rehearsal he spoke lightly and laughed like a man without care while, with dry mouth and thudding heart, he exposed his private thoughts to public view and criticism. The performance in a private house was much applauded by its performers and their friends. But Ned saw then that it was a hollow shell, a patchwork of borrowings, concocted in order to flatter two heiresses with the roles of Athene and Aphrodite, and a wealthy widow with the more matronly one of Hera. Still, it was a first venture, which he seemed to have survived.

No pleading from goddesses or brother, however, had persuaded him to play the part of Paris.

'It will soon be time for you to set about planting little Malises in English soil,' Francis told Ned in exasperation soon after the performance. 'Our Athene would have you if you played her right. If we can't make money, we can at least marry it!'

Ned laughed and shrugged. Francis mistook the overlapping of their ambitions for collaboration.

Without intending it, Ned sharpened his laugh and gained a new sardonic manner which made a better match for his misleading look of danger and grace than his previous gentleness had done. Ambition, however masked and gentle, was giving

141

him an edge. As the brothers lived among new acquaintances, no one but Francis remarked the change.

In those first years in London, Ned grew still more to a man's full imposing stature, and also broadened. Francis saw his brother's tall piratical elegance as a valuable social asset, if only he would stir himself to real wooing and flirtation instead of being content with the false passions of the latest songs. When that damned Dutch doctor finally sent the virgin's blood, Francis meant to put his brother to work at once in the outer Catholic orbits around the unhappy young French queen. Then Ned shoved them upwards in a way he had not planned and did not even recognise as an advance until much later.

'Play that last again!' commanded the young Mistress Ann Woodvine, as Francis's guests sat amusing themselves after supper in the great parlour.

Ned obliged with the same sweet watery flow of melody.

Mistress Woodvine closed her eyes. Her lightly freckled face was even paler than usual. 'Again,' she murmured. 'I vow that your music is easing my headache when every apothecary in London has failed!' She managed a wan smile. 'Can you also sing away my freckles?'

A week later, she sent for him urgently to come to her father's house near Clerkenwell.

'Well done, bratling!' exclaimed Francis, reading the note over Ned's shoulder. 'You're on your way with that one! I thought as much the other night. No beauty, but her father made a fortune in wool.'

Her maid showed Ned into a private parlour where the young woman sat on a cushion-covered bench, in the darkest corner of the shuttered room.

'I feel the megrims beginning to attack.' She cupped her small hand to her brow in agitation.

Indeed, she did look pale and strained.

'I hate most noise at these times, but I keep remembering

142

how you eased my headache the other evening. Can you drive this one away with your music too?'

Ned began a fashionable tune.

Mistress Ann screwed her eyes tightly shut and winced.

He thought hard, then began again. This time, a tranquil liquid song he had written, from a lullaby he had once heard through an open window as he sat on the canalside with the ginger-furred dog. He teased the notes softly from the strings, as if reluctant to disturb the air with their vibrations.

Her brow unclenched.

He finished the song and began it again. Even more softly. He imagined a perfect stillness within himself which the music expressed. As her face grew smoother, he played more and more softly until he barely nudged the air, trying to create for her that perfect stillness of the soul.

'However can I thank you enough?' she murmured. 'I hardly dare believe . . .' She lay back against the cushions, her eyes still closed.

When he heard from her breathing that she had fallen asleep, Ned rose and tiptoed from the room.

Mistress Woodvine not only escaped the megrims that day, she talked – even more than young Master Shaw. Both of the besotted merchants' daughters sent at once for Ned's help, one suffering with headache and the other with melancholy, both of which he was able to ease at the time. The melancholy, however, returned just as soon as he had left the house. Then one of the fathers, having heard his daughter's claims, asked for relief from a toothache which did not let him sleep. Successfully lulled, the merchant also joined in the chorus of praise for young Malise's near-magical musical power.

'Don't make enemies, bratling,' warned Francis jovially. 'Or you'll be arraigned as a wizard for putting enchantments on their women. And don't enchant too many of those, or we'll never keep you safe for just the right wife!'

Even Francis's ribald amusement was tempered when the wife of a very wealthy ship owner called urgently for his

143

brother to ease her pangs of childbirth, from behind a screen. Though Ned succeeded at some times better than at others, he had only one outright failure, a woman who was dying of a canker. But even she graciously allowed that although the pain gnawed just as viciously, her agitated spirit had been a little stilled by his singing.

'I was able for a few moments to think again of God.'

Ned's secret intent and Francis's ambition to rise from Dutch street rat to English court gentleman were more obviously aided by the open warfare being waged at that time in the Palace at Whitehall. Six monarchs after Old King Harry's split with Rome, England had found itself possessed with the marvel of a French Catholic queen.

Henrietta Maria, daughter of Henry IV of France and Marie de Medici, had arrived at Dover in a fleet of twenty ships. These carried, among the others in her train, a Grand Chamberlain, ushers, a Grand Almoner and twenty-four priests, scores of French ladies-in-waiting and as many gentlemen, her nurse, cooks, grooms, a surgeon, apothecary, perfumer, tailor, embroiderer, clockmaker, eleven musicians and a fool.

Ever since the royal marriage, there had been angry rumours, inflamed by gifts made to Henrietta by the Pope, that she had married King Charles solely in order to convert him to the Church of Rome. The huge rabble of French, with their bright new fashions, painted faces, frivolous continental pastimes, Catholic worship and passion for meddling in English politics, had convinced many of the King's faction, including the Bishop of London, that the Great Whore of Babylon herself had moved to Whitehall.

When Francis and Ned arrived in London, the Queen, after a shaky start to the marriage, had just lost the King's favour altogether, either through her tantrums and wilfulness (according to his people) or through his native coldness and shortcomings as a husband (according to hers). The Duke of Buckingham, who had been a favourite of the King's father

144

and was now the King's, also played his part in it, as he did not care to share the young King's affections, even with a royal wife.

The Queen's faction were therefore ready to welcome two handsome, Catholic brothers with a French name, who spoke passable French and carried a tang of the Continent. After his opening attack on the wealthy merchants of London, Francis burrowed like a ravenous deathwatch beetle towards the goal of an invitation to Somerset House, the Queen's chief residence. He dared to hope that he might even, in time, achieve the Queen's private presence itself.

He flirted with the court ladies. For a small consideration, he had both Ned and himself presented to the Sieur de Montelet, the Queen's chief usher, by whom they were cordially received. Ned's masque, given another showing in a noble private house, went down very well in these circles. He was even congratulated by Nicholas Lanier, a royal musician and singer.

Word of his more private musical powers, too, must have reached Whitehall, for one evening he had a late-night summons, in which he was asked to allow himself to be blindfolded in order that he might not see where he was taken.

Ned hesitated. No man cares to trust himself, sightless, into the hands of others.

But these others, though only grooms and well-muffled from recognition, were muffled with the finest wool and wore excellent boots.

'Go, brother!' Francis's eyes were wide with speculation. 'We don't refuse invitations like this one!'

Ned and his lute were taken by coach only a short distance from their Covent Garden lodgings and let in through what was clearly a back gate of a very large house. Inside, an uneasy serving woman led him up three flights of stairs and around several turns in the corridor. Then up another, narrow flight of stairs with walls that he could feel on either side. Then, telling him to remove his blindfold, she opened a door.

As he stepped into the room, a child began to scream.

Ned froze. It was a boy, of about five years, dressed in silks but also wearing a leather harness. The harness was chained to a bed.

The boy rushed at him, mouth wide, uttering wild animal screams of rage. The chain jerked taut and held him. He struggled against the chain, threw himself forward again and again, screaming all the time with a hot, blind fury.

'Can you soothe him?' the serving woman asked. She gave the boy a sidelong glance and furtively crossed her fingers against the evil eye.

'Mistress, I fear that . . .' He remembered how he himself had raged against his tether. But this was more than rage. The child was lost in an internal pandemonium.

'If you succeed, you will be well-rewarded. Nothing else will help him. He doesn't know even his own poor mother.'

'I mean only that I have no magic powers, nor even medical ones, only those of a musician.'

'His mother has heard that you can do wonders.'

'Only the wonders which naturally arise in the realm of music.'

Though wild, the child looked well-tended and well-fed.

'How do you feed and dress him?' asked Ned.

'I must wait until he wearies too much to fight me.'

It was an impossible task. The boy would not even hear. But a sudden fierce compassion outshouted common sense. Ned shed hat and cloak, sat on a stool and set his lute across his lap. He played Dowland. He played Sweelinck.

Without effect.

The boy sat on the floor and thrashed his legs, kicked his heels against the floor. He threw himself face down, drummed with clenched fists. And kept screaming.

Ned played 'Soldiers Three', and then the latest, most fashionable jig. Nothing silenced that terrible, agonised animal noise.

146

Ned stood up in despair. 'Mistress, I might as well not be here. I'm sorry . . .'

He refused the payment she tried to press on him and let himself be taken home again, where he went straight to his own chamber, avoiding his brother.

But Francis knocked on his door almost at once. 'Could you detect whose household it was?' he demanded eagerly. 'How did you fare?'

'Ill.' Seated in his high-backed chair, Ned stared into his fire. 'That child needs to be touched by a special grace. I don't dare even to presume to as much. Nor can you dare ask it!'

All the same, their luck at first seemed almost over-generous. Not only did they suit the court of the lonely Queen, they had also arrived at a time when everything from the Low Countries was in fashion. Dutch pattern books were the rage for all new buildings. Noblemen and wealthy merchants hired Dutch painters, Dutch craftsmen and Flemish weavers to adorn their newly-built Dutch-style houses. In London salons, *cognoscenti* admired the paintings of Mytens, van Belcamp and van Stalbemt and gained credit for speaking knowledgeably of studios in Amsterdam. One evening, Francis exchanged mutually-assessing civilities with Mynheer Van Dyck, a Fleming turned English court painter.

Their steady social rise frustrated Francis all the more.

The Dutch doctor still had not sent his cure.

Though their savings began to reach an end, Francis had found that there was little he could do to make more money. Everywhere, he met severe limits on his freedom to trade and to invest. He was not a member of any guild, and the process of becoming a member was both seven years long and very expensive. And even as a guild member, in order to trade in anything, from gold to mousetraps, he would need a licence from the King. These were not merely expensive, they were unobtainable, even if you could pay – all such licences already

147

being held. To raise desperately-needed money for the Crown (having disbanded Parliament, the King lacked its help in raising taxes), the King also sold monopolies. In short, England was oversupplied with money and undersupplied in ways to invest it.

'How does anyone build wealth in this accursed country?' became Francis's nightly lament. 'Unless you can buy land – which no one will sell – you might as well have a chest filled with stones!'

Only Ned knew that Francis again got out his mahogany chest, his scales, his measures, his mortar and pestle and worked in secret at his recipes. He did not advertise these wares among any of his new society acquaintances. Even Ned did not know where he went, alone and on foot, from time to time in the night. Then, he begged Ned to go in his place on one of these furtive errands.

'I am invited to dinner with a new acquaintance who cannot be slighted. Please, bratling!'

Reluctantly, Ned agreed.

'Go in through the courtyard. They'll expect you there, and urgently,' he told Ned. 'Don't dawdle. And if you meet a friend nearby, say that you've been visiting a whore.'

On his way, a little irritated by his brother's high-handed instructions, Ned stopped in the light of a tavern window and took from his purse the small stoneware jar that he was delivering.

It was sealed shut with wax.

Francis still expected him to obey without question. Even now, he never found it worth the trouble to explain or to let Ned make his own judgement.

He took out his knife, carefully sliced round the seal and removed the top of the jar.

A green unguent, of pounded herbs and grease.

He sniffed.

A sickly, slithery smell. A little green, like the leaves which had been pounded into the grease, but with an undertone of

148

thick, purple sweetness that suddenly leaped out and caught at the back of his throat.

He replaced the top, smoothed the wax seal with his thumb and found the entrance to the rear courtyard of a large house in Clerkenwell. He knocked on the kitchen door, then listened to the unbolting and rasping of two locks.

Not like the Dutch, who prided themselves on having nothing to hide.

An old serving woman opened the door half-way.

'Is he here yet?' called a young voice from behind her.

Ned peered over the old woman's shoulder. A beautiful woman in her mid-twenties sat hunched on a stool in the kitchen, in her petticoats. She wore diamond eardrops and rings, and bracelets of gold. The shutters were closed and the room was dark except for the low cooking fire.

'Have you brought it?' the old woman asked.

'Did he bring it?' the younger woman repeated.

'Don't speak!' the serving woman told her sharply.

As he dug the jar from his purse, Ned looked again at the young woman on the stool, half-naked but in her finest jewels. Her face wore an odd and dreamy expression. The kitchen smelt sour like a prison or poorhouse, though it clearly belonged to a rich man. The smoke that lingered in the upper air had a strange bitter smell. The two women were alone. No cook, no maids.

He felt suddenly oppressed and in haste to leave. At the same time, curiosity made him want to stare at the young woman.

'Keep your eyes to yourself!' said the serving woman as she paid him. She gave him a deep steady look with her own dark-blue, wrinkled eyes, as if memorising his features. 'You might wear them out.' Then she bared what remained of her teeth in a mirthless smile.

Though he managed a dignified stroll, he wanted to run as he left the courtyard.

'What did I take? Who were those women?' he demanded later.

149

Francis tapped his nose but looked uneasy. 'Hush, Neddie. Best if you don't know. Forget that you ever went. But I assure you, she's not the only one. Women sometimes want strange things, even the most gently bred. And not just the women either.'

To Ned's astonishment, after his clear failure the first time, he was called again to sing to the tethered boy, who, just like the time before, began to scream as soon as they entered the room.

This time, Ned asked the serving woman to leave them alone.

The child drew breath as the door closed behind her. There was an instant of silence, then he began again to scream and rage. Filled with the sound of his cries, his small body vibrated like an instrument itself.

Ned tried soft music. He tried loud. Sacred hymns. *Bordeel* bawdies.

The child seemed to grow even angrier and angrier, until Ned began to fear that the small red face would burst open with the force of inner rage.

'Stop!' he begged. 'Please stop before you do damage to yourself!'

The boy howled. He shook so hard with the force of his cry that he could hardly stand.

I can't bear it, thought Ned. He stood up. Looked about desperately as if he could find what to do.

'*Stop!*' The voice of the gong rose in his throat and clamoured through the air. For a moment he and the boy vibrated in unison.

As they both drew breath, there was total silence.

And then for the length of another breath. The boy did not look at him, but stood with his head cocked, as if listening.

Then he gave another cry. Then the screams began again. But to Ned's ears, with less than a whole heart. A little uncertain.

His own breath grew short with excitement.

150

As the door closed behind him, however, the force of the screams was redoubled.

'I want to come again,' he told the serving woman.

But in two more visits, in both of which he again created silence with the voice of the gong, he gained nothing further than one quick glance from the boy which almost met his own eye.

It was enough, however. For the moment, Ned set aside his vow to his grandmother for a greater purpose. If, with his music, he could make the child smile, if he could lead him to the perfect stillness, he felt that he would in some way have put right a little of the evil done at the ford.

At last, another letter came from Francis's doctor. After a long search, he had found a new girl – the daughter of a clean-living fisherman – but there had been an unexpected problem: two women who had received the blood of his new girl had contracted the small pox. Nevertheless, he assured Francis, it was a temporary setback. He had already procured another fisherman's daughter of unblemished virtue. He persevered in full confidence of eventual success. And would be grateful if Francis would please arrange a further payment . . .

'Fortune has turned trickster!' Francis crushed the letter in his hand. 'What has happened to our luck?'

Ned visited the boy again a week later, and thought of little else between visits. This time, he no longer wore a blindfold but walked freely to the house which, he learned from the arms moulded on the firebacks and carved on to pillars, belonged to a wealthy baronet, a ship owner with a title bought from the King's father. He still entered by the small back gate, but the boy's mother, the baronet's wife, met him outside the child's door and thanked him in person for his saintly Christian devotion to her unfortunate son.

'He sleeps better when you have been. And I imagine that his cries are milder.' She offered payment again.

Ned blushed and refused. 'I do it for myself, madam.'

'Then may God reward you as you deserve.'

On his sixth visit, when he and the boy again combined their voices in a terrifying warlike bellow, he had an inspiration. Though terrible to hear, they nevertheless were in accidental concord. When the boy shrieked again, Ned imitated him. In pitch and volume, but without the rage. As with the voice of the gong, the child stopped in astonishment. Seemed to listen. Then continued more weakly. The pandemonium had begun to ebb.

Ned imitated him again. The boy hesitated.

A dog barked somewhere in the house. Ned imitated the bark. So did the boy.

The serving woman must have been listening at the door, for when Ned left, she looked at him in astonishment and surmise.

On his next visit, Ned sang the door creaking, and the boy creaked back.

Then Ned sang the first melody any human learns, the plaintive fall of 'Ma, ma!'

With his head averted, the child imitated Ned. 'Ma, ma.'

Suddenly, for the first time, the room was absolutely still, only for a flash. But they both heard it and each knew that the other had heard it. Beyond all doubt, the boy was listening.

Outside the door, the mother embraced him, in tears. 'He said "Mama"! You induced him to say, "Mama"!'

Ned protested that the boy did not know what he had said, that the change, if any, was slight, and had only just begun. But the grateful mother just nodded and said that miracles had begun to happen.

He did not tell Francis of his progress with the baronet's son, but it may or may not have been by chance that Francis announced a fresh turn in their luck only a few days later.

When Ned argued that they had no money left to invest in two-year sea voyages to the Dutch Indies, Francis shouted him down. 'I'll not let the chance escape me to join a company such as this! I've already borrowed what we need. And you're coming with me. It's the least I can ask in exchange for the blind eye I've turned to your Southwark slumming!'

Francis woke Ned at five on the morning of their triumph. He had already been shaved and put on his finest linen shirt. His eyes glittered and his hands were cold.

'Let me smell your breath.' He sniffed. 'Pah! Go scrub your teeth with a rosemary twig!' Then he watched to see that his brother sprinkled rosewater on his groin and rubbed a handful of herbs under each armpit. He himself trimmed the hairs in Ned's nose, then tugged and patted at his dark curling hair as if his younger brother were still two years old and didn't now stand an inch and a half taller than he did.

Having once agreed to go, Ned accepted the fuss with good grace.

When Ned had been dressed by his manservant in a new suit of rose silk, Francis himself checked to see that all his points were tied, the bows on his heeled shoes set precisely square across the insteps, his stockings unwrinkled, beard close-shaved, nails clean.

'You'll do,' he said. 'But no singing today! Just keep your mouth shut and leave the talk to me.' Then he clapped him on the shoulder to take the sting out of the words.

Francis had hired a carriage, although it was an easy half-hour's walk from their lodgings in Covent Garden to Sir George's house on the Thames west of Whitehall. Ned would rather have swung his long legs across the stones of the city streets, but he allowed Francis his show of triumph without protest. He couldn't help catching a little of Francis's excitement.

'The morning gleams like our prospects,' said Francis, looking out through the open hole of the carriage window.

Ned leaned forward, listened, and thought of the boy tied up in the attic room. He would sing him the sound of water slapping, of shouting boatmen, dogs, cats, and horses' hoofs. Birds.

153

The sun flickered on the distant Thames as they trundled along the Strand. Inside the coach they were sunk in murky light, swamped in the creak and rustle of silks and buckram and squeaking leather. They had to sit opposite each other to leave room for their clothes. Francis's cloak had now rucked up behind his collar and stood stiffly out around his shoulders so that his head seemed set on a blue silk platter with a frill of cream lace instead of parsley.

His forehead was damp, Ned noticed. And his lips were outlined in white.

They eyed each other in the silent speech of lifelong intimacy. They had come a long way from exile in the Blomsloot slum.

Francis had worked hard to make it happen. Ned had to admit it. The evening at the ford would always separate them, and Francis chose ways of working that Ned would not. But it seemed churlish not to give him credit at a moment like this.

'Grandmother would be pleased,' he said, as an offering.

Francis nodded and flushed with pleasure. 'Yes.'

They stared out through opposite window holes, thinking, not altogether happily, of the slim, silver-haired terror who had raised them for such a moment but seemed to have put her money on the wrong grandson.

Sir George Tupper's massive Thames-side house was still being built. Buckets of mortar and heaps of rubble lay strewn about the courtyard. Their new shoes stirred up a fine lime dust as they climbed the wide stone steps to the heavy door. The entrance hall smelt earthy and clean, not yet tainted by human sweat, smoking lard candles, dogs.

'I shall build one larger,' said Francis under his breath, but loudly enough for the manservant who led them to hear.

Outside the mahogany double doors, carved with panels in high relief of English merchantmen in full sail, they paused and glanced at each other again.

'It's not your execution, brat.' Francis tapped Ned's sleeve in encouragement. 'Smile. Think of all those richly-endowed

154

daughters.' He grinned, then wiped his forehead with a lace-trimmed kerchief, stared at the dampened linen as if reading it for signs, stuffed it back into the interior of his clothing.

The manservant opened the double doors.

'Remember, Neddie, who your grandfather was . . . and that Sir George's father was only a fletcher.' Francis walked through the doors into Sir George's great parlour, with Ned close behind.

Faces turned to stare. Poised in that short unguarded moment before men begin to shape their behaviour, Ned saw an eyebrow lift and felt his stomach clench.

No more need for that now, he told himself. Life has been changing for months and today marks the public acknowledgement of the change. One way or another we are new men. He put on his pleasantest face and tried to stare comfortably back.

Fires burned in the two fireplaces against the damp, even though it was daylight. There were no women in the room. The men, mostly older than Francis and all of them older than Ned, stood or leaned, with glasses in their hands. A few already sat with papers at the long trestle table set up in the centre of the room where business would later be carried out.

That first moment passed. The men moved again in a shifting sheen of black silk, lightened by flashes of dark green, blue and burgundy, the glint of glass. Most of them still wore old-fashioned doublets and heavy sleeveless coats. A few even wore white stiffened ruffs. The worthy members of the South Java Company. Men of substance and influence, who were about to welcome the Malises into their number. Who would help Francis to make his wealth grow at last. The men among whom Ned must learn to live.

'Malise!' shouted a stocky man with a long-nosed face so like that of an ageing ram that Ned could have sworn the man had bleated 'Maaa-aaaa-lise!' He wove towards the brothers between the well-upholstered bodies of his colleagues, his bulk jouncing above small feet.

155

'Sir George.' Francis clasped his hand.

Ned smiled in spite of himself. Above his long Roman nose, Sir George also had sheep-like tightly-curled grey hair.

'Master Francis. And your brother. Master Edward, I'm happy to make your acquaintance at last.' He seized and held Ned's hand in a fierce grip while his slightly protruding eyes sized him up.

'Sir James . . . and William . . .' Sir George grabbed a nearby sleeve '. . . let me present Francis Malise, our new investor. I've been intent . . .'

As Sir George dragged them around the room, he showered them with names until Ned felt dizzy trying to keep track of the men behind them – so many different faces, voices and smells. This man, with round face and white eyebrows, had recently smoked tobacco. This man had already drunk too much. This one had a sour sick smell. This one had recently made love. The room reeked of woodsmoke, civet, citrus oils, male sweat and the cedar and lavender used to keep moths from their clothes.

Francis glowed. His smile was mercurial, deferential one moment, collusive the next. He met assessment with assessment and dispensed pleasantries as densely as a wet dog shakes off water drops.

Ned followed more soberly, trying to unravel the open, friendly voices from the tight, withholding ones. To link in his memory the rasp of catarrh with a long, lined face and the clear, resonant voice of another singer with a balding tub of lard.

The voices became a blur of sound. Mouths flapped without meaning, his brother's among them. Then, in the midst of all the others, he met the baronet, the father of the boy. From tact, he gave no sign. But the baronet surprised him.

'I already know Master Edward Malise by reputation,' the man said warmly. 'His music brings lightness to our house. I'm much obliged to you sir, and wish you and your brother well in your association with us.'

Ned bowed, flushed with pleasure. In the corner of his

156

eye, he saw Francis look from him to the baronet in startled surmise.

On an order from Sir George, two menservants began to fill all empty glasses with ale and wine from silver jugs.

Ned found himself standing beside a ship's captain. He mistook him at first for a general, until the man told Francis that he sailed in six weeks for Timur, and they began to trade knowledgeable words on tonnage and seasonal winds. When Francis moved away, to fill the pause, Ned asked the captain whether he ever carried passengers on his voyages.

'We need all the space for chickens and pigs.' The captain gave Ned an inquiring sideways glance. 'Planning a sea voyage?'

'Not just now.'

They held out their glasses to a manservant.

Then why did I ask? Ned wondered. Having raised it, he now considered the thought. To go somewhere new!

His old eager spirit twitched and stirred. He felt a jolt of hunger to sail off the map, a sudden lust to fling himself blindly into a new world.

To leave Francis to his investments and the past and remake myself through adventure . . .

His nightmares of the ford might not follow him that far.

He saw himself as a sea captain returning from the East Indies with a cargo of nutmegs and cinnamon. He moored his great-bellied, high-tailed galleon outside the dolphins of the Amsterdam harbour and sailed in the lighter through the canals right to the door of the Coymans's house. For a moment, Marika did not recognise him, full-grown and in such splendid uniform . . .

He wondered if she had married the man in the carriage after all.

'. . . a welcoming toast to our new investors!' proclaimed Sir George.

Startled back to the present, Ned began to raise his own glass as the captain was doing, then realised that he and Francis were the subjects of the toast.

When the toast was drunk, and Francis had replied, the captain turned to Ned again. 'Well, if you ever do decide to endure two years on board a ship with poor food, slimy water and the stink of the men, speak to me. I sometimes miss civilised company.'

The captain would not have spoken so agreeably to the Amsterdam guttersnipe, thought Ned a little sourly. Two or three years ago, he would have offered to sign me on as cabin boy to scrub pots in the galley. Even so, he felt the shape of another possible future begin to grow. Make a fortune abroad, then return to buy Tarleton Court. He might be dead before his music could take him as far.

'My friends,' said Sir George to the gathering, 'Master Francis Malise here, and his brother, Master Edward, have not only bought into our next voyage, they come hot from Amsterdam, the entrepôt of Holland – the very heart of our enemy's commerce. Our governments may have signed treaties, but we all know that it's still war on the seas. And I swear that not even the East Indies Company can boast members who could also serve as spies against the Dutch!'

There was laughter. But Ned saw an exchange of looks here and there.

Sir George concluded less roughly, with a formal welcome. The company drank the brothers' health again. Francis and Ned locked eyes briefly across the room.

He has worked hard, and sometimes dangerously, to bring us here, thought Ned. I should tell him I'm grateful. He raised his own glass to his brother, just a little, but Francis had already turned away.

The double doors opened to admit two late arrivals, an old man and a youth of about fourteen or fifteen. Ned tried to see them better but was distracted by a man dressed in black Puritan silks with a face made as rough as oak bark by small pox and who smelt of soured linen.

158

'How long have you lived in Amsterdam?'

The new arrivals were now masked by two broad backs. Even with his height, Ned craned to see.

'How uneasy it must have been for you there, as an Englishman. Though I expect you speak Dutch. I'm afraid that I can't manage any foreign lingo – only plain unvarnished English for me.' The man's tone was civil but he meant to start the slow dripping of blood. Ned did not hear.

I must get another look at those two! 'Pray excuse me,' he said. Then, through a chink in the crowd, he saw the youth's face.

Francis, beware!

Ned pushed forward urgently. There were too many men in the way! He would not reach his brother in time to warn him.

Francis turned. Stared past the shoulder of the man to whom he had been speaking. His face drained of blood until it was as white as a haddock's belly. Ned heard the melodious crash of his glass on the stone floor.

'NED . . . TAKE CARE!' Francis's shout froze the company into startled silence.

Not Francis in danger, but Ned. Ned had been waiting for the last six years. It was almost a relief.

The youth careened off shoulders, sent a wine glass flying. Teeth bared under tight white lips, eyes wide with fury, he collided with Ned like a runaway cart. They staggered backwards together. For a moment, Ned could not resist. As his left temple smashed against the stone fireplace, he heard the dull deafening thud inside his head, saw a flash of red, then black.

When his senses began to return, he was pressed against the fireplace, held up by the youth's weight, his body insisting on its own will to live. Unable to breathe, he clawed at the youth's hands which gripped his throat.

As his blurred mind cleared a little more, he tried to seize hold of a little finger, to bend it back, break it, as Francis had taught him. But the youth gripped so hard that Ned's fingers

159

could not find purchase. Though smaller and slighter than Ned, the youth was powered by savage rage, while Ned suffered the disadvantage of not wanting to kill him in return. In the corner of one eye, Ned saw Sir George. Francis. Heard shouts almost in his ear. Then the grip on his throat loosened so suddenly that he nearly cracked his skull on the fireplace again.

He blinked a red fog from his eyes, saw the youth shove violently at Francis's chest. Francis tried to catch himself. He staggered, then danced backwards, his feet rushing to catch up with his head.

Someone shouted a futile warning. Francis toppled backwards as slowly but inexorably as a felled oak.

With all the desperate force of his will Ned tried to freeze the Universe, to set its fluid dance in iron, to suspend his brother there, angled above the stone-flag floor forever, still alive.

Francis's head hit the floor with the succulent thud of an overripe melon.

In total silence the members of the South Java Company watched a dark wet stain spread across the front of his blue silk trousers.

'Francis?' Ned spoke steadily. To act as if all was well might still make it so. 'FRANCIS!' He knelt beside his brother. His head hurt. His eyes were still blurred. But he could see enough.

One grey eye looked straight into his, the other a little over his shoulder. Francis's jaw hung open and askew. A chilly current washed through Ned's chest into his limbs and belly. His hair lifted on his scalp.

'FRANCIS!' His voice was angry this time, as if Francis were refusing to listen. Ned pushed his shoulder, as Francis had pushed his to wake him that morning.

'Master Malise . . .' Hands pulled at Ned's shoulders.

A man knelt on the other side of Francis and felt the back of his skull.

'Is he dead? Have I killed him?'

Ned raised his head and met the youth's eyes.

160

No, I killed my brother. When I disobeyed him and refused to kill you.

The murderer stood limp, like an old coat on a hook, arms and legs still gangling under his fine clothes, all the rage gone from him. He looked very young, almost as he had in the orchard. His left hand, clutching the front of his coat, was bleeding from Ned's nails.

Does he remember the orchard too? Ned wondered.

They stared at each other with ferocious curiosity, each the shaper of the other's future, marking in each other the beginning of a terrible new course.

Go ahead, thought Ned. Finish it!

'These men killed my parents.'

FIVE

16

I don't know, I say, yet again.

The officer sucks his upper lip. Then he slaps shut his tablet and calls the gaoler to let him out of my cell. The door slams with a terminal thud that reminds me of swords hitting blocks.

The magistrates want a confession so that they can hang me with light hearts. There's no doubt that I killed the dog. But I will not confess to the child! Whatever evil corrupts me, I swear that it does not infect my soul that far!

The officer was angry. I would like to help him feel the satisfaction of a job well done but how can I swear to tell any truth in my present confusion? I think that the magistrates are as perplexed as I – though less urgent in their perplexity. Thank God for the humane moderation of the Dutch, who eschew torture. The English or Spanish would not be so patient.

At first Ned did not recognise retribution for what it was.

John Nightingale was arrested for the murder of Francis Malise but never stood trial. Even before he could be examined, he vanished from his prison cell as if he had walked through the walls. Searchers could not find him at Tarleton Court, which now belonged to him, nor at the remote country estate of his uncle, the older man who had brought him to the meeting of the South Java Company.

Ned heard gossip of witchcraft and magic. He also heard more plausible rumblings that the case was an embarrassment:

165

accusation and counter-accusation between a returned Catholic exile and the Protestant nephew of a powerful merchant and landowner. And how many of the witnessess and how many of the English magistrates had estates acquired in the same way as the Nightingales? No magic was needed to keep that one quiet!

Wherever Ned protested the injustice of young Nightingale's escape, he met blankness, as if the natural sense of justice had been wiped from men's minds by a Lethean spell. He himself was questioned by a magistrate about the old unsolved murders at the ford.

For a moment, after John's accusation, surrounded by the members of the South Java Company, he had wanted to cry, 'Yes!' To spill it all – his grandfather's execution, his vow to his grandmother, the awful mischances at the river, his sudden, terrifying, wicked rage at his dead brother and at himself for not resisting hard enough when he knew that he should. He felt in advance the lightness of throwing off those weights.

But something choked him. The ghost of the noose or block. Reason.

Francis was dead and could not be killed again, even to satisfy the law. No one, least of all John Nightingale's parents, the groom and the coachman, would gain from the public savaging of Francis's body, even if the courts ruled it. He himself had tried to stop the murders. His chief crime was to have failed.

So, to the examining magistrate, he denied everything passionately. He argued that the accusation was absurd, that John Nightingale would have been too young and too terrified to remember the truth. That he and Francis had been living in Amsterdam at the time.

His examination was informal, as among equals if not friends. His music had brought him patrons with wealth and power both in Whitehall and in the City. Among others, the baronet gave witness to Ned's good Christian character and his opinion carried weight. Nightingale might have his protectors, but Ned had his own. His arguments were accepted.

166

But even as he saw the success of his denials, Ned felt chilled. With these half-truths, he had missed his last chance to speak and live truthfully, wholly as himself, however briefly.

When John Nightingale never reappeared to stand trial after his escape from prison, Tarleton Court and his other estate in Norfolk were both forfeit to the Crown. Rumour then began to place him in France, in Somerset, in the Americas. He was dead, turned ranter, disguised as a titled lady in Scotland.

Within a year, society forgot the murder of Francis Malise, but Ned still offered a reward for word of any sighting – no matter how much later – in the City and its Liberties, in the stews and gymnasia of Southwark, the street markets of the City, the wool-tenting fields of Hackney.

In spite of the lingering suspicion which tainted him in some circles, Ned found that his life continued mostly as before, if more frugally. The South Java Company voyage in which Francis had invested would not return for two years. Until then, he must live on what he already had, and what he made from selling most of their Convent Garden furniture and all of Francis's silk suits. One evening, he unwrapped the Malise Salt. If he sold that great heavy silver weight, he could live in luxury for five years at least. But then he put it away again. He often opened the chest and looked at his tools. He was launched now as a gentleman. The tools would bring a good sum. But he could not bear to part with them either.

He moved from Covent Garden to cheaper lodgings in St Martin's Lane among other artists and musicians who wished to be near to the court. Although John Nightingale's accusations had made some acquaintances fall away, he soon saw that if he held firm he need not change his purpose in seeking royal favour. In some ways, his task was simpler. The Crown now owned Tarleton Court. Royal will had once taken the estate from the Malises and given it to the Nightingales. Now, if only he could win royal favour, royal favour might give it back. The bulk of Nightingale's supporters were King's men. Therefore,

Ned set his sights, as Francis had done, on the lonely young French Queen.

Meanwhile, he dined and gamed with William Shaw and his friends, sharing wine, hemp cakes and hilarity. He improved his riding skills on horses owned by acquaintances, though he remained as amazed as ever at equine complaisance. He sang with the many quartets and consorts formed in wealthy and noble houses by their inmates for the delight of the singers themselves. From time to time, he also went back to Southwark to sing at the Bear to shake out the kinks in his spirit made by too much civility. (Here, when no one he knew from the court or City was there, he was not too grand to let an occasional *pourboire* be forced into his hand.)

He still visited the boy, who could now sing his own name, James, and was learning simple tunes which he sang even when Ned was not there. His father offered Ned any honourable service he cared to ask. Ned thanked him warmly, but refused all reward. It was enough just then to have such an ardent patron, not least, one prospering as the baronet was from building ships for the English navy.

Without fee, Ned taught music to the daughters of rich men. He even tried to fall in love with one of them. However, he felt something growing in himself which was too dark for the light frivolities of such a courtship.

Within a week of Francis's death, he had begun to have violent headaches once or twice a week, which left him weak and in need of sleep. He believed that they were caused by the blow when his head had struck the fireplace, and would improve with time. After several months, without relief, he began to grow angry, then despondent. At last, in spite of scepticism learned from Francis's dealings, he consulted a physician. The physician peered at a flask of his urine, bled him with Thames leeches, agreed that the blow to the head was the likely cause, and charged him the price of five music lessons.

The headaches continued.

Then Mistress Ann Woodvine, with whom he had formed

a slightly flirtatious but harmless friendship, recommended an apothecary who had sometimes helped to relieve her megrims. The man sold Ned a decoction of willow bark which did seem to help at first. But each time, the pain finally swamped the remedy.

Ned tried another apothecary and, back in his lodgings, swallowed the prescribed paste of walnuts (to heal the brain, which the nuts resembled) and antimony. Within an hour, he began to sweat profusely, then he vomited. For the next two days, he sat on his chamberpot. He also coughed violently, as he had been warned. This remedy did nothing to purge the painful humours from his head. On the contrary, the paroxysms of coughing set off one of his fiercest headaches ever.

In desperation, he at last consulted a cunning woman in Southwark who had a good reputation among the whores.

'Take off your shoe and let me see it,' she ordered him.

Whilst Ned stood on one foot, with the white, knitted silk stocking of his other foot held clear of the filth on the old woman's floor, she peered into his shoe, held it to the light, sniffed, turned it over in her hands, then closed her eyes and mumbled words over it. Thereupon, she gave a satisfied nod, wrote out a secret charm on a scrap of paper, and made Ned eat the paper. But the headaches still continued.

In the painfree ease of the times between them, he pursued the Queen's favour, with some success. He wrote a civil but pleading letter to the Sieur de Montelet, who had received him and Francis so cordially. The Sieur wrote back words of hope and encouragement. Also, Mistress Ann Woodvine married a title and insisted that Ned sing and play at the wedding supper, which brought him to the notice of several of the Queen's courtiers.

Twice, he was asked, in a low voice, both times by men he knew only slightly, whether he could procure any of his brother's Sacred Salve of Egypt. Though this was the first Ned had heard of the Sacred Salve, the requests put him in mind of his errand to the grand house, where the young woman had sat in the kitchen dressed only in her petticoats, begging to know if 'it' were arrived yet. When he protested that he could provide no miracles except the accidental ones of music, he saw a sudden wariness in the eyes of the askers and found that both of them then cooled towards him and kept their distance. Most often, however, he and his lute were enough to ease the mind and lift tedium.

In spite of his small advances, Ned felt his character begin to grow unpleasant, as if corrupted by pain. He sat for hours in his chamber, fingering his lute but afraid to sing lest it set off the black pain in his temple again. The world outside his lodgings often seemed misted and unreal. All his own desires seemed trivial. His thoughts churned without end around his slowness in fulfilling his vow to his grandmother and what revenge he might still owe his murdered brother.

Francis had been guilty, but not by cold intent, Ned told himself as he often lay sleepless at night. He was another Malise destroyed by a Nightingale. Twice was unendurable.

He would rise, pad naked and on bare feet to the window of his bed chamber and try to see the Thames, down the hill to his right. Sometimes the London air at night felt thick as syrup in his lungs.

Long after Francis's death, a letter arrived for him from the doctor in Holland, brought by a servant from the new residents of their former lodgings in Covent Garden.

Ned turned the letter over in his hands for a few moments. The sight of his brother's name, written by someone who did not know of his death, gave him sudden ghostly life, which stirred both grief and rage. Ned set it aside.

If he opened it, he knew that Francis would once again direct his life.

But his death directs it already, he thought. If I leave it unopened, I deny him again.

At last he opened it.

The doctor prayed that his patron was well and was, if he

170

himself dared deduce from Mynheer Malise's long silence, pre-occupied with far greater affairs than their own. Nevertheless, after many trials, he was now certain that the small pox cure was proved efficacious beyond question. He commended himself to Francis and asked for another small payment to defray his costs.

After long thought, Ned sent the asked-for money, using his brother's name. He could at least settle his brother's debts, even if he had no intention of ever using the Virgin's Blood.

King Charles finally stripped the Queen of her trouble-making 'messieurs', including de Montelet. Lady Ann (formerly plain Mistress) told Ned over sweet wine and nuts one evening after dinner that Her Majesty was now reduced to her dresser, Mme de Ventelet, her old nurse, twelve musicians and a single Scottish priest.

'She'll be bound to welcome a young man who can speak French, sing French songs, or is otherwise less than wholly English.' She eyed Ned with her head on one side, then said to one of the other ladies there, 'I'm sure that you'll support me in this: if he also has a noble bearing and the unshakeable ability to hold the tune (as I myself will swear), Her Majesty will no doubt go so far as to command him to play in one of the masques which she writes herself and produces at Somerset House.'

Ned responded with a joyful cascade of notes from his lute, then a song praising the beauty and virtue of an inaccessible lady, in which the ladies and gentlemen joined.

A short time later, Lady Ann sent her own maid to Ned's lodgings with the news: the Queen wished to see him with her own eyes to decide whether or not to permit an introduction. Ned was to present himself at evensong that same day in the Queen's Chapel, which was attached to Somerset House, the Queen's principal residence.

By miracle, it was a pain-free day. Dressing, sweetening his armpits and breath, made him think of Francis.

I'm sorry you're not here for this fulfilment of your deepest

171

ambition, he told the ghost of his brother. In spite of his brother's sharp dealings, Ned felt in some ways the less innocent. Because he had no inner music, Francis had depended entirely on the outer world for his joys.

How much more Francis would gleam and dispense words and courtesies to court ladies than to sober merchants and their daughters! Ned could see his brother's face, alight and wide-eyed at their closeness to the healing power of Majesty.

And I may be close at last to laying down the weight of my vow!

Washed and dressed in his best red silk suit, with ribbons on his shoes and Brussels lace cuffs on his stocking tops, Ned entered the large plain brick building attached to Somerset House where the tennis court had once been. But as he passed through the high, arched door lined with pale Purbeck marble, he stopped and stood, mouth a little open, staring up like a child. He forgot the Queen. Forgot everything. His soul soared as high as the dove that hovered at the very top of the painted sky above the altar.

Below the dove floated seven layers of cloud. On each layer stood painted archangels, cherubim, seraphim, in their hundreds, more than he could count, all lit by constellations of hidden candles so that they seemed to be among the stars. Some of this multitude knelt or leaned forward in eager adoration. Most of them sang, or played viols or pipes. With uplifted eyes, some released the pure sound of their angelic souls. Others, with eyes cast down to see the strings, embraced their instruments with a heavenly tenderness. In the quivering glow of the hidden lights, and the warm radiance of several hundred wax tapers, they breathed and moved.

Lightness filled him. He imagined, just then, that he would not only propitiate his brother's soul and be forgiven the tardiness of revenge, he might also one day be given a chance himself to begin again.

Slowly, he entered the chapel, found a place in a pew, without dropping his eyes from the angelic choirs.

172

The anthem swelled. The angels' voices were doubled and redoubled under the high ceiling. The music surrounded him, filled him. He opened his throat as if his own voice might pour from his mouth, whole and pure again at last. Tears blurred the candle flames so that the altar, too, looked like a star-filled sky, lit by the flaming sun of its red, oval lamp. Then a faint sneeze from the organ side of the altar betrayed the hidden, earthly choir.

He blinked, closed his mouth for a moment. His tainted voice had no place among those others, mortal or immortal. But surely, he thought, a moment like this is one of redemption. Heavenly or human, those voices welcomed him into their concord. His ecstasy did not ebb. His soul still floated among the singing angels.

There was a flurry at the door behind him. He recovered his wits enough to bow deeply with all the others already there, whom he had hardly noticed in his elation. Queen Henrietta Maria, Queen of England, daughter of Marie de Medici of France, entered the chapel.

Under his dark brows, he watched the pretty young woman who had arrived in a foreign country, to a foreign husband, at the age of fifteen. Dressed entirely in white, she still looked like a girl, with pale skin livened by rouge, large, dark eyes and tendrils of dark hair framing her oval face. In her pale silk dress, with lace frilled at each wrist like a carnation she would have looked like one of her angels, except for the red lacing on her bodice, a red ribbon in her hair, and a lively gleam in her eyes.

Lady Ann, in the royal party, winked at Ned as she passed. Then, as the women arranged themselves at the front of the chapel, she whispered in the Queen's ear.

Between the Queen and the singing angels, Ned hardly heard the words of the service. He breathed in the sweetly resinous incense, quivered with each sounding bell, waited for the angels to sing again each time they stopped, while the resonance of the music in his bones made his long fingers twitch on the polished wood of the pew back, on an invisible lute.

173

As she left at the end of the service, Henrietta turned her head to look where the countess pointed and smiled on him with her small pink mouth. As he bowed so deeply that his nose almost touched the lace cuffs on his stocking tops, he was already asking her in his mind for the arrest and trial of John Nightingale and for the return of Tarleton Court.

There, Francis, it's almost achieved!

Lady Ann ran quickly back from the chapel door. 'The Queen wishes you to sing in her own Shrovetide masque!' she whispered triumphantly. 'This is a mark of the highest favour! And I am to play Iris!' She rushed away again.

He knelt again, overcome with too many pleasures, of both the mind and senses. Then, as had happened before, the sounds around him blurred into a single clamour. But when the music ended abruptly, the clamour died. The chapel suddenly became a dark empty void. He stared at a dancing candle flame. Without the music to hold him aloft, he felt himself start to fall, plummeting down from the sky among the angels, down into a cold, dark current like the icy water at the bottom of a deep lake.

A belch of terror rose from his stomach and jammed against the underside of his vocal cords.

He gripped the back of the pew in front of him. What is happening to me? He was filled with a rush of terror and foreboding. Kept falling. The pew, the floor, the space around him dissolved and swirled like oil on water. His orderly pulse was scrambled into noise. He was filled with noise. His being dissolved into dissonance.

I am dying.

This is death.

His nostrils flared at the scent of burning. His ears sharpened so that all sounds had keen edges, like broken glass.

He clamped his attention on to the suddenly-precious details of the world. The sticky wood of the pew back. The hovering mist of incense. The candles. The dove.

A giant fist squeezed his chest, closed his throat so that only a thread of air could get through. He tore at his collar and shirt. A nail of pain drove through his skull.

The thread of air grew thinner. He struggled as the dark current sucked at him.

I'm not sure how long I can last.

Then he was no longer alone in the swirling, dissonant darkness. Something was coming. He felt a shadowy beast there with him. Behind him. On his shoulder.

No!

But he was not himself. Had no will left to fight it. No strength. The beast pressed into his head, insinuated itself into his sinews. He felt the muscles of his scalp and face shift as it grew through his bones like coral, reshaping him in its own image.

The bubble of horror spread up into his throat.

I'm . . .

I . . .

But he no longer had words. He was the beast.

'Malise, do you hear me?'

He crouched whimpering, shaking, curled on the dark cold floor against the pew back. A round face floated above him. A halo. No, fair hair like a halo, luminous with candlelight behind it.

'Master Malise! Can you understand what I say?'

Other faces. Mouths moving.

He had torn off his shirt. And trousers. Bare skin against chilly wood. He shivered in the cold air of the dark chapel. Still couldn't speak. He could think the words now, but something had cut the string between thought and tongue.

Who are those faces? Why are they so frightened?

'Like an animal,' said a voice. 'He can't speak a word. Doesn't know any of his friends!'

The beast was going.

'Malise, can you understand me?'

Another voice: 'Ned, do you know me?'

175

Lady Ann. But he could not answer her.

His teeth began to clatter together. He was coming back. Coming back. He wrapped his arms around his knees to hold himself together. He was a fragile shell around an ebbing pandemonium. Just hold on.

His eyelids drooped. Too heavy. The beast had taken all his strength. Sleep flooded into the hollow space left behind.

He jerked awake on his pillows, his heart jolted into a gallop. His eyes widened and he struggled to sit up. A strange man was in his bedchamber, standing at the end of his bed, watching him.

'Who the devil are you?' Ned demanded. He could be a thief, a murderer. Anyone at all! And how did I get here to my bed?

I'm still confused. Know the face. Round face with a halo of wiry blond hair. Pink cheeks.

'Maurits van Egmond.' The man was older than his plump, flat child's face made him look at first glance, in his thirties at least. He wore black, like a physician, scholar or Puritan. 'I helped to bring you back from the Queen's Chapel last night. I'm happy to say that you seem more yourself again now after a long sleep.'

Ned remembered the familiar ecstasy, then the unexpected, hideous plunge into a sense of death, of horror and transformation.

'What ailed you?' asked his visitor.

'I don't know.' Ned closed his eyes. He dared not say that he had known himself to be dying, that something had invaded him, slowed his thoughts like cold molasses, made him no longer himself. 'I was noise.'

'Noise? How do you mean, you were noise? Do you mean that you heard noises? Were they voices?'

Ned shook his head. It could not be explained. 'Was there a fire? I also smelt a fire.'

'No fire. Unless you mean the burning candles.' Van Egmond

came to the side of the bed. 'Had you drunk too much? Eaten any hemp cakes?'

'No!' Ned said indignantly.

'May I examine you?'

'Are you a physician?'

'The Lord forbid! But I am a student of Man in all his particulars.' Without waiting for permission, he leaned his face close to Ned's.

Ned had the disquieting experience of gazing into a pair of pale blue eyes that looked no farther than the surface of his own. Annoyance cleared his head. He had enough to unsettle him without this stranger's familiarity. Dutch too, by his name and accent.

'Forgive me, van Egmond, I'm most grateful for any assistance you gave me last night, but I'd like to rise and dress now.'

Van Egmond stepped back but gave no sign of leaving.

Why's the man staring at me like that? thought Ned with irritation. And why is he still here, for that matter? 'I was unwell. Lack of sleep maybe. Now regained. And, now that I think, I may have drunk too much as well. I'll keep close to my lodgings for a day or two.'

I'm most likely mad, he thought with a sickening lurch of his stomach.

When the man still did not offer to leave, but stood with his head a little on one side, Ned threw back the covers. 'If you tell my man where to find you, I'll call on you and repeat my thanks when I'm fully recovered.' He called his manservant and asked him to offer his guest a glass of ale on the way out, then to bring breakfast here to his chamber.

At last, van Egmond bowed and left.

Ned lay back against his pillows again, then suddenly got up to dress. Who else had been there? Whom he knew and could trust? He had to find out what had happened and decide what excuse to make. Though he might have gone mad, he knew better than to say so.

★   ★   ★

177

On her housekeeper's advice, he had found Lady Ann strolling with two other gentlewomen and their maids in St James's Field, near the menagerie.

When she saw his face, she excused herself from her friends and took his arm. 'You were half-naked by the time I came back,' she said, colouring slightly. 'Didn't know me, nor anyone else.'

'How many saw?' The caged beasts were making him uneasy. He steered her away, back along the path towards Whitehall.

'Perhaps four others. I was too alarmed to heed them. Most had left directly after Her Majesty. I came back to say that you must come next Friday fortnight to a meeting of our cast, and there you were on the floor, with that Dutchman calling your name! You were making the most fearful sounds, I could hardly believe that it was your own sweet voice. And crouched like a cornered beast! As if a witch had cast an evil spell on you!'

Ned avoided the dangers of too much truth. 'I admit that I felt wretched. Too much wine perhaps. Not enough sleep.'

'You poor thing.' She gazed at him thoughtfully.

'Who is that Dutchman? I woke up and found him perched like a plump raven at the foot of my bed, staring at me. I seem to be in his debt for seeing me safely home.'

'You should be honoured,' said Ann drily. 'He's terribly famous in the Low Countries, or so he'd have you think. Wealthy and well-connected for certain. He boasts that he means to be the youngest Praelector of Anatomy at the University of Leiden, which sounds terribly dull, as he himself is, if you try to discuss anything but his science. I've tried every topic I can think of and throw my hands in the air in despair. God keep me from his side at dinner!'

'His breeding's no better than his conversation,' said Ned sourly. 'I almost had to ask my man to throw him out before he took the hint and left.'

'Well,' said Lady Ann, still studying Ned. 'He may carry a good name, but I've heard that it's not rightfully his, that his family adopted it as they rose in society. Still, he's a friend of

178

the Royal Hen's physician, and several of our noble amateur scientific enthusiasts clamour to sit at his feet and listen to him rave against his professional rivals . . . I must say that you seem a little weary but otherwise quite yourself again.'

While Lady Ann seemed to have accepted his story of excess wine, and would doubtless tell it to others out of goodwill if not conviction, Ned still felt in himself a churning pandemonium that reminded him of the baronet's son in the early days. He wanted to scream in rage and terror. Could not make sense of what he had felt. Knew only that he had become something else. Had torn off his clothing, crouched, whimpering, unable to speak. All so unlikely that he began to think that it might not really have happened. That he really had suffered a passing ague or drunk bad wine. Unless, of course, he was mad.

His grandmother's Latin tag came into his head – *homo lupus homini*, man is a wolf to man. He could not shake the words from his head again, nor the insidious thought that he was paying for past beastliness by truly turning beast. He was more frightened than he had ever been in his life.

As he expected, he soon heard the gossip from friends of friends who, of course, could hardly bear to repeat such a thing: Ned Malise, the handsome Orpheus who could raise the heaviest spirit back to life, that paragon of civility, that almost-too-good-to-be-true *nouveau arrivé*, had been blind, staggering drunk in the Queen's Chapel! In Her Majesty's presence! It proved her infinite goodwill that she did not have him sent back to Holland at once!

Ned groaned inwardly when he heard, but bad as the gossip was, it was better than the truth.

Two camps soon formed. One, chiefly the Queen's women and their friends, held that he was a gentle miracle-worker, suffering the bad luck of passing ill health. Harder views, held by many husbands among others, were that he, like his brother, was a drunken, murdering, blackguard foreigner. There were other darker murmurings which Ned did not yet hear.

Ten days passed. He began to hope that the horror in the chapel was a single happenstance.

Then, one night in an inn where he was gaming at a table near the fire with William Shaw and four other acquaintances, the beast found him again.

'No!' he cried, just in time, while tongue and words were still connected. But he could not fight it off.

Again, the clamouring, jagged glassy edges of sound, the piercing smells. Again the fist that crushed the air from his chest, and again the belch of terror that lodged at the base of his throat. The invasion of his body. The shifting of his muscles on his skull. The beast. But without the fall from ecstasy this time. A direct hit. Straight into darkness.

He stood up blindly, knocking over his stool, towered for a moment over his astonished companions, helpless with rage and terror, trying to speak, tearing at his clothes. Then he fled into the darkness of the street. He heard them calling, calling, more and more faintly, but kept going purposefully along a long straight Roman road towards the final cutoff of the horizon.

'Damn you, Ned for frightening me like that,' said Shaw the next day. 'I searched all London for you, thinking you might come to harm, the state you were in. And found you sound asleep safe on your own doorstep at four o'clock in the morning! What the devil ails you?'

'Could you not see?' asked Ned warily.

Shaw shook his head. 'You were gone before I could even blink.'

This time, Ned imagined that he could bring back memories of his time when he was not himself. Dreams of roaming. Narrow dark spaces. The smell of sewage, salt water and rats. The creature's memories. It stood his hair on end.

'William, if you're my friend, learn what the gossip is now!'

Friday. He was to attend the first rehearsal of the Queen's masque.

180

I can't go! he thought in panic. What if the beast comes again? Before all those courtiers . . . before the Queen!

It would finish his hopes.

But you must go, said another voice. Listen to reason. This chance of advancement won't be offered twice. Somehow, you must keep the beast as your own terrible secret.

He closed his eyes and tried to think why it had come.

Twice. Both times at night.

Then he realised that his headaches had stopped. The beast had eaten them and taken their place.

Devil or madness?

His thought stuck there, like a wheel in mud.

In this unhappy state, he presented himself for the first rehearsal of the Queen's masque. One of the royal music masters arrived to teach the cast the music they would sing. Ned was the only newcomer.

'You come highly commended,' the music master said. 'And are trusted with the most demanding role of the shepherd, Lycidas. I hope you will be worthy.'

Lady Ann fluttered her sand-coloured eyelashes ironically but smiled warmly at Ned.

Two other ladies looked at him askance and whispered behind their hands. He knew what they must be saying. Shaw had come back with the grim news that one of the gamesters from the inn had flapped his mouth all over London about the terror he had felt when Ned Malise began to transform before his very eyes and then fled into darkness before the extent of his corruption could be revealed.

If it had not been for his vow to a dying old woman, Ned would have fled again now from this elegant white room with its Roman pillars and plague of sharp, interested eyes.

As they prepared to sing and he saw the music master's eyes on him, he felt a fear that had not struck him since he sang for the very first time, at the age of eight, in an Amsterdam *bordeel*.

What's wrong with you? You sing as easily as you breathe!

181

But you've turned beast. May still be part beast. And beasts cannot sing. For Art, you must have a soul, and beasts have no souls.

He felt a choking grip on his throat that cut off the sound. He tried to swallow, to loosen his throat, but had forgotten how. Suddenly, he was battling with a thick lump of rebellious muscle that threatened to block his throat altogether. When at last, he managed to swallow, his relief nearly brought tears to his eyes.

'Master Malise, are you ready now?' The music master lifted his hands to begin again.

Ned opened his mouth. And could not sing.

He survived the rehearsal somehow. Managed to cobble together a tale of agues and phlegm. Mouthed the words and nodded constantly in a show of eager understanding.

'I swear that you're only teasing us!' cried one of the minor goddesses. 'To make us swoon all the more when we hear your true voice at last!'

But Lady Ann frowned at him in puzzled concern.

As soon as he was alone, he tried again to sing. But Art does not always bend to human will. Every time he opened his mouth, the choking grip tightened on his throat. He tried again to sing before he slept. But still the grip on his throat prevented the music from rising up. Ned Malise, as he had once been, had gone.

He began a new, terrible double life, always alert for signs that the beast approached. He grew sly at making excuses to get away from human company when he imagined that he felt the threat. Though the beast did not visit a third time, he always felt that it might. He stopped going out at night, left gatherings before dark, for he at length worked out that he felt safer in darkness than in fire and candlelight, in the open night air than in close, smoke-filled rooms. He yearned to go to mass and repeated prayers from his childhood, but he now feared the chapel, and all other churches, more than anywhere in the world.

He began to hear the gossip for himself. At Ned's insistence, Shaw had violated his own good nature and repeated all that was being said.

'Drunk' had been forgotten. 'Mad' was the kindest word. 'Under a spell' was heard. And whispers of 'Devil' and 'possessed' had grown more frequent. Even his friends tacitly acknowledged that something was wrong, for they made excuses and explained how he had been distracted by his brother's death. Ned knew that a fearful danger lay in all those whispered words, but did not know what to do.

He had been unravelled, as if a firm thumb and forefinger had taken hold of an unnoticed loose end and pulled. The stitches came undone, row after row. Suddenly, where there had been an identifiable garment, full of little quirks of pattern, turnings, false starts, joins, and one or two stretches he could take pride in, was nothing at all. A tangled heap, knotted, confused, the strands kinked. Try as he might, nothing joined up right.

Madness or the devil. A bad pair of choices.

He recognised retribution now. Ned Malise might have escaped prison or the gallows for the deaths at the ford, but these same fates still hungered for the madman, the possessed lunatic, or the devil's own thing.

He had immediate urgent need to conceal his loss of voice, to avoid exile from the protection of the inner circle of the Queen's court. It was too late even to plead the ignoble excuse of syphilis. He feared not only the end of his hopes for Tarleton Court but also the possibility of arrest. No one had yet said 'wizard,' aloud in public, but it was only a matter of time. One more visitation would see him in irons.

He thought of throwing himself into the Thames. The Queen's favour depended on his singing. Tarleton Court depended on it. Justice for his brother depended on it. His entire life depended on it! It was the way he knew himself. His chief joy. The source of his peace. And with the music had also gone the perfect stillness that followed it and out of which it grew.

183

When, at the second rehearsal of the Queen's masque, he could produce only a coarse sound filled with phlegm, the music master moved him to a smaller, more suitable part as a demon. And Ned heard the whispers growing louder and bolder. He might have found himself in serious danger if the court had not been distracted by a case of small pox among the Queen's waiting women. For fear of spreading the contagion, rehearsals were temporarily suspended.

After an evening of pacing his floor, Ned sailed for Holland. Francis had had a hand in bringing him to this dangerous state. In desperation, he would turn to Francis for help. In Holland, he went straight to the house of the Dutch doctor, who swore that he was completely satisfied with his testing of the Virgin's Blood. Ned bought ten vials. The whole journey took him only nine days. Back in London, he called at once on Lady Ann.

'One of my brother's miracle cures,' he told her urgently. 'I feared that it had been lost, but recently got word that it could still be had. From a medical scholar whom Francis befriended, who is too unworldly to take it out into the world himself.'

He opened the wooden box and showed her the gleaming dark red vials that lay cushioned on green velvet. '"Virgin's Blood against the Dragon of Contagion." I don't myself understand its power, but both my brother and his doctor swear that no man or woman who mixed this pure blood with their own had ever suffered the small pox. He always intended it to be a token of his love and respect for Her Majesty.'

'The Royal Hen will be delirious with joy,' said Lady Ann. 'Things go better for her now with the King. To be scarred and lose her looks now would be cruel beyond all words!' She lifted out a vial reverently and held it against the sunlight. It flared and gleamed darkly, like a fine ruby. 'Perhaps I might test it myself.' She looked at him in question. 'Is this cure as costly as I fear?'

'Not to you!' said Ned. 'I owe you more than I can possibly ever repay. Take that vial, it's yours already.' He rearranged the remaining vials in the chest.

184

'Neddie!' She leaned and gave him a quick kiss. 'I've not done much except try to protect a dear and worthy friend. But if this miracle of your brother's truly does prevent the small pox, you'll never need worry for your position or safety. The Hen will see to that.' She grinned suddenly. 'Even if you are the devil himself!'

Shortly after Lady Ann delivered the vials to the Queen on his behalf, Her Majesty, to Ned's astonishment, sent one of her own physicians to visit him.

'Her Majesty has asked me to restore an invalid Orpheus to his proper self, so that his voice might give her joy.'

He was a tall man in a physician's black coat and white collar, with intelligent, cool eyes.

While Ned made the required protestations of unworthiness, gratitude, etc, his heart raced with a sudden, irrepressible flare of hope, which he quickly snuffed out.

Take care! he warned himself. This man is most likely an intelligencer, come to learn whether the Queen risks showing favour to a madman, or to a man possessed by the devil.

He pissed into a bulbous glass flask, which the physician sniffed, then held up to the light.

Then Ned repeated his tale of phlegm in the throat. And agreed that he had also, much earlier, had a severe blow to his head.

'The phlegm hardly explains the rest,' said the physician. 'Your odd behaviour . . . Why do you tear at your clothing and run from the light?'

Confirmation, if Ned needed it, that the gossip had reached Somerset House.

'A fever . . .'

'How do you feel now?'

'Very well.'

'Are you a man or a beast at this moment?'

'I would hope there's no doubt! I'm a man!' But before he could stop himself, Ned glanced down at his hands and

185

legs. They were indeed human parts. 'Is it not clear?' After a moment he asked, 'Why the question?'

When the physician did not reply, Ned swallowed uneasily. His tongue threatened to thicken again, as it had at the music rehearsal. He tried to think of not swallowing, for the physician was watching his efforts with interest.

'Are you often thirsty, Master Malise?'

This seemed a safe enough question. Ned nodded.

'And is your sleep troubled?'

For certain! He nodded again.

'And you have a pale complexion and sunken eyes. By your own testimony, your mouth lacks saliva. All the signs . . .'

'Of what?'

'Patience. Now please turn around and lift up your shirt.'

Ned nearly balked but, to keep the man's goodwill, such as it was, he obeyed.

There was a long silence, while the physician examined his back. Ned felt his fingers at the base of his spine.

'You have the aphrodisiac tuft,' said the physician at last. 'Here, just above the cleft of the buttocks.' He raised his voice. 'Do you remember turning beast?'

'I don't know what I remember.' Ned swallowed before he thought to worry that he couldn't. 'But I don't say that I turn beast!'

'But you feel changed in some way?'

Reluctantly, Ned nodded again.

'I find your case to be quite clear,' said the physician.

'Am I mad?'

'You have a sootiness in the black bile. An overflowing of melancholy.'

'But what are you saying?' demanded Ned.

'That tuft of hair on the base of your spine, the aphrodisiac tuft, indicates a lupine disposition which has been precipitated by the blow to your head into a form of distraction.'

'Distraction? You are, in fact, saying that I'm mad.'

'With a special form of madness, which we call lycanthropia, from *lycos*, the wolf, although the animal may take any form.' The physician spoke with authority. 'Men and women in such a state of distraction often believe themselves to be dogs, cats, hares or, most commonly, wolves. I believe, without doubt, that the last is your case.'

Ned shook his head, testing the feel of the word, madness, now that it had been pronounced with such certainty.

'Like a waking dream,' said the physician. 'With all the sense and habits of the beast in question. Such distractions are common, and very often after blows to the head.'

'What is the cure?'

'Restraint. So that you may do no harm either to yourself or others.'

Ned had seen them, the poor lunatics, caged and chained. 'Surely madness is constant!' he said desperately. 'I have suffered only twice, for a few hours, then returned to myself. I swear that I do not feel like a madman! You can see that I live as a perfectly ordinary gentleman. Here we stand now in reasonable conversation!'

'Such disbelief and disclaimers are further infallible signs,' said the physician. 'You must believe me! I have heard swearing of such oaths, and innocent weeping and gnashing of teeth from people who a short time before were crouched barking or mewling Adam-naked on all fours!'

Ned drew a deep breath and bit back the oath he had been about to utter. 'Is there not another cure for such afflictions, a cure more rare, perhaps beyond the pocket of many men?'

The physician studied him thoughtfully.

'There is another way. It's possible that your case is not yet too far advanced to be reversed. I myself have perfected a way of opening the skull with a small hole to relieve the pressure of excess melancholy on the brain.'

'No!' cried Ned. Then steadied himself. 'Perhaps,' he said evasively. 'Should such measures become necessary. I am deeply grateful to Her Majesty for her concern, but I had begun already to feel myself mending.'

187

'There is very little pain.'

'I've no doubt! And I would put myself into your hands with the fullest confidence.' Ned mustered every ounce of self-possession in order to make this man see that he was not – could not possibly be – mad. 'May I offer you refreshment? A small token of my gratitude? Please . . .' He indicated a chair. 'I forget my manners in my delight at meeting a man of such wide and excellent reputation.'

When the physician had left, Ned found that he had to sit down on a stool.

There it was! Madness. Lycanthropia, in which distraction, he – turned madman – believed himself changed to a wolf, with all a wolf's senses and habits. Indeed, his senses had sharpened. He had seemed to hear and smell as a wolf might hear and smell. He remembered the musty reek of mice in the Queen's Chapel.

The diagnosis fitted in many ways: with the feeling of being reshaped into a different creature, the almost painful clarity of sound and smell, the need to flee, as the devil's own dog would need to flee, out of light and into darkness.

Faced with the physician's calm authority, he now remembered what he had so far kept pushed out of his mind. When he . . . after the belch of horror and certain knowledge that he was about to die . . . after his sensation that the beast had invaded him . . .

I remember that I seemed to see with eyes that were not my own, hear with ears that were sharper than mine. Smell . . . The man had smelled the incense, the phantasmic wolf had smelled the mice under the pews.

And yet, a small part of him still resisted. Even beyond the fervent desire to escape chains among other madmen or a hole drilled into his skull.

I do not feel as I always imagined madmen to feel, he thought. But then, according to the physician, that's certain proof of my madness.

But what's my other choice? he asked himself. Would I

188

rather believe that an invading demon casts out everything that makes this fleshy shell into Ned Malise, then occupies it and animates my sinews and bones with its own fiendish will and purpose?

If I'm not already mad, I may go mad now.

He stood for a long time at his window looking down into St Martin's Lane. He wondered what the physician had made of him and what he would report.

Four days later, his manservant left. Ned went to bed in the evening and when he called for his man the next morning, no one came. The man's mattress was folded away in its chest, his few belongings were gone.

'What the devil's going on?' he asked Shaw, whom he visited that afternoon. 'Why wait until now to leave?'

Shaw flushed and stared at his hands.

'Is the news that bad?' demanded Ned. 'Out with it! Is it time for me to run?'

'I don't know, Neddie. It's just servant talk. My man told me. A maid, who had been in the chapel, overheard the physician speaking of you. I don't know what he said, but the servants are all aflutter, saying that you're not mad at all, or possessed, but a shape-shifter.'

After a long silence, Ned managed to say, 'I hadn't thought of that. Do you mean that they think I really turn into a wolf?'

Shaw nodded miserably.

'But that's wizardry. Witchcraft!' Among reasonable men, surely it could never come to that!

Wizardry was punished by death.

'It's only servants' gossip. And among just a few of them.'

'So far.'

'Don't be an ass!' said Shaw. 'No one of any consequence will believe such superstitious nonsense!'

But what of my enemies? thought Ned. The King's men who favour the Nightingales' cause? Would they cavil at a fine point like belief?

189

'In any case,' said Shaw, 'you're safely lodged among the favourites of the Queen herself!'

But precariously, thought Ned. Clearly, this friendly intelligencer of his had missed the juicy news that this favourite had lost his voice. Apart from Lady Ann, no one but the Queen seemed to know how else he had tried to keep a grip on his position.

Well, Francis, he told his brother's ghost. I owe you thanks after all. And an apology for my dragging feet. Not just my success but my future safety seems to depend on those vials of blood.

Fortunately, the arrival of summer bought Ned time and made his affliction easier to hide. London was emptied of society. The annual plague brought more urgent concerns than any over a mad musician whom the ignorant were calling a shape-shifter. Anyone who could afford a second house in the country moved self, family and servants, with their certificates of health, away from the narrow streets, crowded kennels, bad airs and stinking ditches of London, which were thought to spread contagion. The inmates of the slums in the Liberties which encircled the city, and any of the indigent fortunate enough to have places in Alleyn's, Emanuel, Sion College and the other alms houses, had to stay and take their chances. Some years were worse than others, but each summer at least a few houses carried locks and the red cross. A number of bodies always waited on plague carts to be buried in pits dug near the parish churches.

Early every summer, the vendors went into action, selling snouted masks with scented herbs sewn into the muzzles, astringent pomanders, plague waters, cupping glasses, and amulets of all sorts. Saffron, walnuts, bayberries and goat's rue grew scarce in the marketplace. Cow dung was treasured and saved to strain with vinegar. Every June and July saw the mustering of searchers, who would enter houses to detect whether the plague had already visited. Chosen women carried food and water to afflicted houses. The streets were sluiced with buckets of water every night.

Ned stayed in the emptied city and contented himself with two spoonfuls a day of a medicine recommended to him by Sukie from the Bear, brewed from sage, rue, red bramble leaves, white wine and ginger. And every night, he rinsed his mouth with an infusion of rosemary and vinegar.

He decided to manage without a manservant during the summer when there was no one there to wonder. After all, he thought wryly, I lived a good many years without any servants at all. In truth, he was relieved not to have another pair of eyes always watching him, with that wary expression which he had noticed more and more. He was also relieved not to have to pretend that all was well, when it was not.

He often told himself that he should run. But where? The beast might find him anywhere. In London, he at least had a few friends and the chance of the Queen's protection if the cure for the small pox worked.

Avoiding Westminster and Holborn, which were often among the most badly hit parishes, Ned dined well for a shilling in the taverns, strolled in the quiet streets without fear of meeting acquaintances, gazed at the closed warehouses and ships still unloaded in the docks. He was waiting for the beast to visit again. He could feel it, in the shadows just beyond reach of thought, biding its time. To quiet his mind and get through the hours, he set himself to making a lute.

With an unfamiliar sense of pleasure, he unpacked his tools and precious pieces of wood, the leaves of ash and ebony, the block of Brazil wood. He had a smith make him a bending iron for curving the ribs of the lute and bought a charcoal brazier to heat it. Then bought a rough table for his workbench. He found an apothecary to sell him glue, varnish and coloured stains. From a merchant in West Chepe who sold fine and rare woods, he bought a block of Hungarian pear wood for the neck. He laid out his drawings and templates, printed his design for the rose on to a square of paper, and set up the

191

lime-wood mould for the body of the lute. Then began a pleasingly Spartan life.

At first his hands were clumsy from lack of practice. The scraping irons and planes bit too deeply, his knife wavered while scoring lines on the wood. But the ease and pleasure soon returned. He ate and drank no more than he needed. Worked all the long daylight hours. At dusk, when failing light made mistakes more likely, he put away his tools and walked for an hour or more along the Thames, to admire other people's lights safely distant and small, the stars in the water of the wherrymen's lanterns, the reflections from the windows of the houses on London Bridge, which stretched and shimmied on the surface of the dark river. Then he slept long and well, undisturbed by the usual racket from the now-quiet streets. His beast seemed to withdraw to a greater distance, into deeper shadow. Some days, he almost managed to forget that it still waited. He told himself that he was not lonely, but fortunate to be left in such peace.

One day, at the end of August, when he had begun to string his new lute with the German gut Warde had given him, an unfamiliar manservant brought a letter:

Malise,

I believe that you still owe me a Courtesie Visit. As you no more than I have not left with the Sheepe for Safer Pastures, please dine with me in two Nights Time. I promise to amuse as well as feed you.

The Witness of your Misfortune in the Queen's Chapel,
And Good Samaritan,
. . . Maurits van Egmond of Leiden

The man even writes an irritating letter, thought Ned. But I suppose that, from civility, I must go.

He would much rather have stayed quiet inside his safe private bubble of solitude and work.

Ned was shown up the great staircase to the Dutchman's rooms,

192

in the noble house on the Strand where he was lodged while in England.

When Ned came through the door, Maurits raised his head from a book. 'Look here, Malise!' he said, as if they were old friends and merely continued a conversation.

Politely, Ned looked. The right-hand page was filled with a wood engraving of what looked like a flower, with five thick fleshy petals. From its centre grew a thick tube that divided and then divided again into a ferny net.

'The liver, as described by that great god of anatomists, Andreas Vesalius!' Maurits glared at the book on the table in front of him. '*Sanguificationis officina*, the workshop of sanguification, with its mesenteric tributaries.'

No table had been laid. No bottles and glasses stood waiting for a guest.

He has forgotten that he invited me here to dine, thought Ned with a mixture of irritation and amusement. I should have expected such a trick after our last meeting.

'"The chyle," says Vesalius, "is converted in the liver into blood, the so-called first of the four humours" . . . Ha! We shall see!' Maurits seized his pen, took some ink and made a forceful scribble on the offending site. 'Vesalius goes on to say that the liver then extracts yellow bile, or choler, and passes it to the gall bladder, here . . .' His halo of fair hair quivered with indignation. His face was red with passion.

'But, alas, now we have one tiny difficulty: if the impure blood then moves on to the spleen here . . .'

Ned's eyes moved to what looked like a slab of bacon trapped in the ferny net of the mesenteric tributaries.

'. . . as the unassailable Vesalius claims, how,' Maurits demanded of Ned, 'is the resulting black bile discharged into the stomach? Eh? You show me! Go on! Find me the conveying duct!' His blue eyes glared in challenge.

Ned flinched under the ferocity of the question. 'I'm not even at your beginning, let alone your destination,' he said mildly.

193

'Then can you at least tell me how many lobes you see to this liver?' Maurits pointed to the fleshy petals of the main picture.

'Five.' That much, seemed clear. And Ned now understood Lady Ann's dining-table despair.

On the other hand, a dining table did not seem to play a large part in Maurits's thoughts at the moment.

'Ah, yes! But how many lobes here?' Maurits pointed to a smaller engraved image on the top right corner of the same plate, labelled 'The male organs of generation'.

Minus the man. Kidneys, bladder, testicles and penis hung like fruit from a tree of liver and portal vein.

'How many lobes d'you see here, heh?'

There was a trick here, a trap. 'Only two.' Ned waited for the metaphorical crack across his knuckles which, he was sure, van Egmond would not hesitate to give.

'You are absolutely right!' cried Maurits loudly and triumphantly. 'You see, my friend, even Andreas Vesalius wavered in his blind loyalty to Galen and the Greek authorities! There . . .' he pointed to the small drawing in the top corner of the page '. . . where he clearly says "generational organs of man . . ." *viri* . . . of *man* . . . couldn't be clearer! Here, he shows a true image of only two lobes – but very small, as if hiding some vice of the mind. Whilst here . . .' he pointed at the main engraving again '. . . in this chief work from which all teaching is done, he still shows five lobes to the human liver – a false figure set centuries ago through examining dogs!'

'Hmm,' said Ned noncommitally.

'In all my morbid anatomies, I have never seen more than one or two in man! But, alas, the ancient authorities say otherwise. And who am I to dispute it?' Maurits thumped his clenched fist against his breastbone like a bad actor. 'I share Cassandra's rage. Like her I am given the gift of seeing truth but am cursed to be forever disbelieved!' He turned expectant eyes on Ned.

All this rage for the number of lobes in man's liver!

'It's a small detail surely?' Ned murmured. Was this lecture what the man had meant by 'amuse'?

'On the contrary! It's the heart of the matter! What's true of that "small detail" is true of all knowledge now possessed or ever to be possessed by Man!' said Maurits triumphantly. 'Don't you understand yet? Vesalius saw the truth, but denied it! Denied the evidence of his own eyes, because the ancient authorities said otherwise. And the great professors still follow his example, lecturing with one hand in a book and eyes tightly shut. "Five lobes in man," squawk these sage old parrots, echoing their masters. "Must be so . . . written here . . . ancient authority says so . . . squawk, squawk! Bow, at any cost, to the classical authorities and play Judas to yourself."'

Maurits wiped the tip of his pen on a scrap of cloth and corked his ink. 'Shame on you,' he said unexpectedly. 'To make me summon you for a visit that you promised so long ago.' He looked more closely at the suppressed irritation on Ned's face. 'I apologise for my preoccupation. Janni, my assistant, says that I have no breeding at all.'

'Janni's right,' said Ned pleasantly.

'But who could value breeding above the truth? Neither you nor I, my friend, I'm sure! And truth is why I called you here.' He closed his book and stood up from the table. 'I should think, from what I hear, that you are confused.'

'I'm entirely lost,' said Ned, startled into frankness by the brutal change of direction and the direct gaze that now pinned him to the spot.

'You're not mad.'

'What then?' asked Ned, now a little frightened as well as startled.

'I can help you.'

Ned laughed. 'My troubles are far greater than the number of lobes in a liver. Two physicians, and two apothecaries have been equally certain they could help me, one way or another. Why should I trust your hypothesis any more than theirs?'

195

'Hypothesis?' Maurits was outraged. 'Hypotheses are merely ways to plug the gaps in our understanding. I abhor hypotheses!'

'I mean only that my troubles lie outside your realm of reason. I believe I suffer a corruption of the soul.'

'The soul lies in the body, at a site not yet proved, though some speculate and say the pineal gland, others the heart. I won't waste time now making myself clear. Come to my demonstration of morbid anatomy next week. A condemned criminal will be hanged on Tuesday morning, and I can have him by the afternoon. Come, let me show you fact, not hypothesis. See for yourself what I offer in the way of answers. You will be satisfied.'

Maurits looked at his watch, an intricate golden marvel produced from the folds of his black scholar's robe. 'Now, I'm afraid I must go!'

He had indeed forgotten that he had invited Ned to dine.

'How do you know that I will be satisfied? You know nothing of who I really am.'

'Oh, yes,' said Maurits, looking up from his watch. 'I know very well who you are.' For a second, the child-blue eyes sharpened and skewered Ned like a pair of pins. 'I also know that your beast can be governed by Reason.'

As he walked back to his lodgings, Ned paused to look at the shadowy figure that gazed back from a darkened window. An indistinct bulk trapped in another realm, real but not real. Most likely entirely human, but he could not be sure.

He leaned closer, saw the gleam of his eyes and the black lines of his brows. Bared his teeth, saw the pale flash in the window.

I have never seen myself clearly, he thought. Although I've stared into looking glasses, still water and dark windows as much as any one else.

The physical man was easy enough: handsome (he was told), with pale grey eyes and black lashes and brows. A strong nose, sensuous mouth (female opinion). Taller than average, with

196

slim legs, well-muscled arms and fine hands. A man so favoured should have been a prince. Conversation should have stopped when he entered the room. But Ned saw himself differently: one minute he wasn't there; the next, he was there, inserted diffidently into a crack in other people's lives. Smiling in a friendly way, a little awkward, hoping he could stay.

The shape in the window did not look diffident now, more like the alarming, piratical creature who had sometimes looked back from other reflections and seemed very little related to the rather shy, music-loving kernel of himself that blushed easily and enjoyed solitude. He was always surprised to learn that he had alarmed an acquaintance or that a maidservant had been frightened to approach him.

I'm like one of those blurred canvases, he thought, on which the artist has painted a second, or even third, version of a portrait without entirely wiping out the first.

He was his grandmother's infant knight and family redeemer, Francis's annoying street rat of a younger brother, the clumsy, brutish seducer of Marika, the berserker who had briefly gloried in battle at the ford, the contented, solitary lute-maker, the healing Orpheus of Whitehall. All at the same time and now joined by something dark and terrible, very like a wolf, perhaps mad, perhaps worse.

Maybe grandmother was right, he thought with a twist of fear. Perhaps I corrupted my human soul as a child, when I revelled in pretending to be a dog.

Even without his affliction, he would have been a little seduced by Maurits van Egmond's offer of objective clarity. The possibility of a true likeness, drawn with pure reason. Call it vanity if you like, but few people could have resisted the hunger to learn more about themselves.

I will go to his demonstration, he decided. But as much from curiosity as from hope.

SIX

17

Francis, what are you doing here? If I could lift my hands from the wooden crossbar, I would strike you . . . Leave me!

Hear how I rebel? Better late than never . . .

Maurits! Not Francis at all. Maurits moves into my line of sight. In the flesh, again, here in my cell. A gaoler too. Therefore, I don't visit Maurits in Leiden. Orange arcs fall on the damp stone walls and wooden pilings.

My ears quiver under the pressure of a corporeal voice.

'Have courage, Malise.'

'He won't live to hang if you keep him like that,' Maurits says to the gaoler. 'He won't survive the trial!'

Under his direction, the lantern is set down and two gaolers unstrap me, prise me free of the wooden T, and lay me out all of a piece on the floor, like a man I once saw lifted frozen solid from a snowdrift.

A ball of orange light now floats somewhere near where my head used to be.

Maurits rubs a salve on some part of myself that I can't feel. Then I scream with the pain of life returning to my legs. Then to my arms. I lie on the floor, whimpering in an invisible fire, but free of that alphabetical torment.

'Can you hear me?' Maurits whispers softly, beside my face, as he looks into my ear. 'Can you hear? Do you know me?'

It hurts even to try to swivel my eyeballs in answer.

He says something, and the light grows larger. I recognise a lantern. A quiet light trapped in a glass cage, not dangerous.

'Cut off my arms!' I beg him. 'I don't want them! They will kill me!'

He lifts my head and gives me a bitter drink. 'I have a plan to get you out of here,' he breathes in my ear as he holds the vial to my mouth.

'Alive?' My cracked lips shape the word.

Hope returns with as much anguish as the sensation in my fingers and toes.

I don't regret either the sensation or the hope, however painful.

When my gaoler arrives at midday, he stretches out his hand with the spoon from such a distance that half the grey broth slops on to the floor. He watches me, ready to leap back. I see his fear of me clearly as my flopping neck tries to reach the spoon. His fear proves my new degree of freedom.

I no longer stand. I can move my limbs, within limits. I have been freed from the wooden T. I don't mind the chains on the iron bracelets around my wrists and ankles, all joined at the centre like a piece of my grandmother's lacework and bolted to the floor. I am already giddy and careless with Maurits's brew. The icy cold stone under my buttock, thigh and shoulder fills me with ecstasy.

Maurits is a magician, after all, if he can accomplish this miracle of freedom.

With the ebbing of pain, I begin to think again. Not well, but more than before. I keep feeling Maurits's warm breath against my cheek.

'Trust me.'

How soon the body forgets! Hardly more than an hour can have passed and I already dare to think that the stone floor hurts my hips. I shake with cold. And I can't remember how it was different before, when I was tied upright. I have already begun to petrify. My flesh seeks union with the stone of the floor.

'Trust me.'

September brought an easing of plague danger and London regained its society. The crowd of spectators arriving for the

202

demonstration shouldered and jostled up the increasingly narrow staircases. This private theatre of anatomy, the *theatrum anatomicum*, was on the top floor of the London house of the lord with whom Maurits was staying.

A crowd as if at a real theatre for a performance of *Lear*, thought Ned, or for a parade of new exotic beasts from a recent Indian voyage. For the week of waiting, he had been in two minds whether to come or not.

I've come to the wrong place, he thought. This is society not science. Society come to gawp as some well-connected Dutch anatomist cuts up an executed villain.

The stern black suits and the sheer linen collars of witnessing physicians pressed upwards among plumed hats and careless cloaks. A frightened monkey clung to its owner's hat above the crowd like a shipwrecked sailor on a rock. Several men and the one or two women carried small dogs.

He would have turned to go down again, but was forced upwards by the crowd, step by step, with his nose pressed against a pair of shoulder blades that smelt of musk and rosewater.

This is not how grandmother saw me rising in society.

At the top of the final staircase, a pair of doors opened into the back of the theatre itself, at the top of a small wooden amphitheatre, three tiers high. Once through these doors, Maurits's guests expanded gratefully, shook out their cloaks and skirts, and disposed themselves downwards on to the tiers, calling to each other, laughing, clasping hands, kissing cheeks.

'Judith!' exclaimed a fellow just below Ned, in yellow silk and flowing French-style curls. 'Congratulations on your latest commission! Are you come all this way to give truth to your Marsyas?'

A tall, dark-haired woman in a red cloak and starched cap accepted his homage, then fought her way politely to a prime place on the bottom tier.

Ned sidled along the top tier, stepping over a dog, to a place on the waist-high railing which ran around its front edge. He peered down between the bobbing hat plumes and arms upraised in greeting.

Daylight poured in through two glazed windows set into the roof so that the interior of the wood-panelled room was almost as bright as the street. In the far wall, opposite the entrance door, a pair of tall, open windows admitted light and cool air into the room, which was already growing warm. On either side of these windows hung a human skeleton clutching a banner in white bony fingers – the City of London on the right and the family's arms on the left.

A short set of steps led down to a flat circular wooden floor embraced by the horseshoe of tiers. In the centre of the floor squatted a heavy, rectangular wooden table, as scrubbed and workmanlike as a kitchen bench. Five black-coated physicians stood talking beside it. A large box of sawdust was tucked away beneath it.

Through the ale, civet, rosewater, musty wool, leather and sweat, Ned smelled stale blood.

The woman called Judith now set up a drawing board on the railing in front of her, and pinned a sheet of paper to it. Two men on the lowest tier also readied themselves to draw. Ned waved at William Shaw, who stood opposite him in the middle tier. Shaw waved back and began to make his way in Ned's direction.

A young man in a soft, blue velvet Turkish cap and cloak slung from one shoulder, leaned on the rail to Ned's right. 'Is this your first demonstration? I haven't seen you before.'

Ned nodded curtly, too much a-jangle to make easy chat.

Undeterred, the young man asked, 'Are you here to rage or to learn?'

'Idle curiosity,' said Ned, a touch sharply.

'Well, I come for the pleasure of hearing Master van Egmond rage at the authorities, including his own teacher, Fabricius. And to rejoice in being an Englishman. In Italy, he would have been burned or sent on a penitential pilgrimage to Jerusalem.'

'Do they share your pleasure in his raging?' Ned nodded at the chatting physicians clustered around the table.

'He's also a good teacher, as it happens. Even the grandest physicians attend his demonstrations.'

Some grounds for the man's arrogance, then.

'And unlike many others, he always manages somehow to lay his hands on subjects,' went on the young man. 'It's not easy to get human subjects, even with a church as forgiving as ours.'

Ned looked around uneasily. 'Who is she?' He indicated the woman in red.

'Aha,' said his new companion. 'Judith de Keyster. A Dutch painter. Our host wants her to paint The Flaying of Marsyas on his main staircase. She's come today to learn what lies under our skin.' He blinked at the sudden intensity of Ned's gaze. 'Artists prefer van Egmond's demonstrations to any others – he doesn't just mumble to cronies at his elbow, like many university professors.'

Under the skin . . . Ned's heart seemed to beat now in his throat.

Through a small door in the bottom tier, an overturned beetle came on to the circular floor.

Ned blinked. The beetle became a man with a table balanced on his back.

The crowd fell silent and watched. The man set the table down near the tall open windows, then left by the same small door, disappearing down some steps like a demon descending into Hades in a play. He climbed back up into the arena with a white linen cloth, which he spread on the small table. And left. After a moment filled only by murmurs, he reappeared yet again with a polished wooden chest. Everyone jumped at the sudden metallic clatter as he dropped it with undue relish on to the small table and left again.

The crowd in the amphitheatre grew very silent. Shaw slid to the rail on Ned's left.

Then the small wooden door was bumped open by the

livery-clad rump of a manservant backing up the steps. After a second, Ned saw that he carried the head of a plain wooden coffin. A second servant followed at the foot. The scuffing of their shoes on the wooden floor filled the silence in the amphitheatre. With a heavy thud, they dropped the coffin beside the table and exited.

The spectators now stared at the table, the heavy metal-filled chest and the coffin, silent except for their breathing and the sighing of their clothes. A boot sole squeaked on wood. Someone murmured something and the tall woman artist in the red cloak laughed.

The young man leaned his head close to Ned. 'He plays an audience better than any fairground flim-flammer.'

Exactly what I would have expected of the man, thought Ned.

Then the crowd on the lower tier stirred. At last Maurits, robed in black, climbed up the steps from Hades on to the stage. He was closely followed by a young woman, also in black, who stood as tall as he. One or two people applauded. Two of the physicians stepped forward to greet him.

Ned watched the Dutch anatomist shake their hands, then, smiling, make a regal progress around the front of the tiers. Set against the solid dignity of the physicians, he looked to Ned like a precocious child aping its elders. An academic clown.

'The woman's his assistant,' said Shaw.

'They say . . . and who knows what else?' the young man murmured. 'She seems deft enough at morbid anatomy.'

Ned listened absently, glancing towards the young woman.

'His assistant. They say,' the young man repeated, when Ned did not respond to his first insinuation.

Ned saw her now, as she opened the wooden chest and, with strong pale hands, laid out the instruments and tools inside: saw, chisel, mallet, long steel needles, tongs, scissors, several knives, a steel wand. Hair the colour of winter sunlight curled over her forehead from under her white cap. She had a tranquil authority that her master lacked as she smiled and nodded briefly to people on the tiers, then bent to her task. As she placed the last knife into a graduated row, Maurits spoke.

'Welcome brothers and sisters in presumption. If you brought a closed mind with you, please leave at once, because today I will prove that a hallowed truth is, in fact, a wilful lie.' With raised brows, he scanned the tiers. 'No stampeding feet? No one afraid of heresy? I applaud you, then, for the only true heresy is ignorance.'

The little pillows of his cheeks gleamed in the light pouring down from the roof windows as the blue eyes assessed his audience.

Ned heard a mutter in the tier just below him, but the man, severely dressed in black, did not leave his place.

'God, the Great Craftsman, created a perfect universe,' said Maurits. 'Of course! "What a dull Dutch chap this van Egmond is after all!" I hear you muttering to each other. "We all know that. No heresy there."'

Maurits swung his gaze from one horn of the horseshoe tiers to the other. 'But let me ask you: why did He do it? Ah, the old unanswerable question! Merely for His own pleasure? Would He be so selfish? It may be an old, familiar question, but has anyone answered it? Not yet.' He held up a modest, disclaiming hand. 'Not until today. Today, I will dare to give His reason.'

Ned had to admit that the man was compelling. But like an actor. All flourish, no floor.

'I say that God created this perfect universe as a challenge to Man's wit.' As Maurits now scanned the upper tiers, his eyes met Ned's. 'As a challenge to become our true selves, truly Man.'

Ned stiffened.

'Many learned men would call us heretics for seeking to understand any part of God's Universe,' continued Maurits, 'whether Henry, executed this morning and lying in that box there, or the generational organs of a frog. "You tamper with Divine Will," they say. "To seek knowledge is heresy."'

207

He made a traverse of the front tier, peering into the eyes of his listeners, gathering them up. 'Those learned men are fools! The Lord intended us to seek. Our so-called heretical prying is part of His perfect design, and I shall tell you why!' He returned to the centre of his stage, beside the coffin. 'For did He not, by creating Man in His image, set alight the fire of what some men call Soul but which I prefer to call Mind — that questing force which distinguishes us from the beasts and sets us as masters over the animal and vegetable estates?'

The words snagged Ned's mind like a half-swallowed hook. He felt a premonition of danger.

'I say that God created us to question and to discover.' Again Maurits's blue eyes searched to see his effect. 'I also say that while the universe may be perfect, man's understanding of it is not. The entire truth has not yet been revealed to us, by the Scriptures or by any other supposed authority!'

Now there was an audible rustle among the spectators.

'What heretical presumption!' Maurits grinned with satisfaction. 'And from a Dutchman at that! My friends, the only true heresy is to be content with our errors and ignorance. To my mind, true heretics say, "Give up the search to enlarge Man's knowledge." True heretics are content just to sit beneath a tree debating the error-ridden teachings of Celsus and Galen, like parrots, squawk, squawk!' In his fervour, he struck the wooden coffin with a clenched fist. The hollow thud was as theatrical as a drum.

'No! *Observo!* I observe, as the Lord created me to do! We must look, each of us, with clear eyes! We must observe and anatomise every living creature on the earth, in the sea, and in the sky: mice, cats, dogs, eagles, weasels, elephants, horses, starfish. Men. Women. Infants, even.' Here, his eyes turned to some intake of breath or murmur that Ned could not hear.

'Long-dead Greeks and Romans do not hand down the truth like Holy Writ. Nor does God keep truth as a closely-guarded secret, knowable only to Himself. All parts of all living creatures are as accessible to our eyes as the workings of a machine – even

208

those of man. All life is as transparent to our understanding as the engines of a watch. As you soon shall see.' He stepped back.

Ned stared down at the stage, unable now to look away.

The two servants opened the coffin lid and heaved Henry up on to the heavy table. Naked except for a small linen clout over his genitals, he flopped and wobbled like a drunk being put to bed.

'You will note that he still remains flaccid.' Maurits straightened Henry's nearest arm. 'He was hanged only two and a half hours ago. He will very soon grow rigid as I work but will have softened again by tomorrow. So.' He contemplated his subject, then gave the arm a reflective pat. He turned to his audience. 'A perfect machine. Made by a Master Craftsman.'

The man in black on the lower tier was now talking angrily into his neighbour's ear.

Maurits glanced in that direction. 'Yes! This man on the table is a machine like all the others: the cat, weasel, starfish, et cetera. No different at all. And as we look at each of them, one by one, with infinite patience, we will come to know them all, as we would learn of watches by taking them apart . . . This poor creature here, as well as any cat or dog.'

He took Henry's wrist in his hand. 'We will understand that his muscles and sinews are merely ropes and levers. Operating thus . . . thus and thus . . .' He bent and straightened Henry's arm three times. 'But . . . !' He glared around the tiers. 'We *must* be permitted to believe the evidence of our eyes . . . even when it contradicts the edicts of the authorities!

'Then, by reason – because the earth and the numbers of creatures on it are finite – we *must* one day arrive at the time when we will have examined every part of every living creature . . . not in my lifetime, I suspect, but one day. And then, *by reason*, we *will* have perfect understanding. *By reason*, Man will know all that God Himself knows of His Creation.' He held out black-clad arms to welcome them into enlightenment.

'No, Master van Egmond, we will never equal God in understanding!' cried the man in black, on the tier below Ned.

209

'You presume too far! Misled by your rumoured reputation, I came here to observe morbid anatomy, not to clap at the antics of a heretical, foreign clown. Pray excuse me.' He clambered over feet and shouldered his way up through the crowd to the exit.

Just what I myself would have said a short time ago, thought Ned.

'The only heresy is ignorance!' Maurits called after him. Some of his audience applauded.

Doors banged in the silence, and footsteps faded down the stairs.

'One less deserter than last time,' whispered Shaw.

Ned stared at Maurits. Could the man truly believe what he said? That there were truths in, and of, this world not yet trapped by the authorities? Truths, as yet uncovered by reason, that might encompass even monsters like the one he had become?

Maurits laid one hand on the corpse's belly. 'With all respect to our friend who just left, I too have studied the authorities as closely as any man, and learned much from them.' The deserter had irritated him, after all.

'But I will not say that they are right when they are not! Galen, the high god of anatomists, made two hundred errors in describing the anatomy of man, which have already been disproved by Vesalius and my own esteemed teacher, Fabricius. I merely follow respectfully in their footsteps.'

Is it possible, thought Ned, that, dislocated as I am, Maurits van Egmond might find my place in a Perfect Universe? And perhaps even know what adjustments to make to the engine to put me right?

Then Maurits recovered his good humour. 'We have one advantage over those sages of Padua, where I live and work in the Low Countries, with our colder weather. Rather like you English over here. When we're fortunate enough to have acquired a subject, we need not, as they must, rush through our exploration in a mere three weeks.'

His audience were still too stunned to titter.

'We are all doubly fortunate today!' Maurits turned away to take up one of the knives. 'Henry was hanged only late this morning and joins us already, so soon after dinner.'

'Maurits is fortunate in his family,' whispered the young man beside Ned. 'Not everyone is the nephew of a prominent Dutch judge with close friends in London.'

Maurits placed his left hand on Henry's belly. 'Now, before your eyes, I will take apart the watch. I mean to show you that, among his other uncorrected errors, the great Galen, echoed by Vesalius, gave man the liver of a dog.'

Ned's heart had begun to beat in his throat again. Which was his own liver, man or dog-like wolf? Did madness alter the body as well as the mind? He imagined that he lay in Henry's place, about to be dismantled like a watch, about to give up all his secrets to analysis by reason. About to be understood.

Maurits continued in Latin. 'First I divide the peritoneum in a straight line from the pectoral bone to the pubic bone. Thus.'

The blade drew a neat red line down Henry's belly. The edges leaped apart. The assistant leaned forward to wipe the ooze with a sponge.

There were exclamations here and there on the tiers.

'Then, transversely from left to right, just above the tips of the hip bones. Now I liberate the umbilicus, to which I shall return later, to demonstrate its extraordinary venous system.'

A shock of yellow and white amongst the red, and lurking blues.

Maurits was transformed. The performing clown had vanished. His face was now intent, his voice filled with a contained excitement. His passion to explore overflowed on to everyone around him.

'This milky membrane beneath the skin is the omentum which covers the eight abdominal muscles.'

The skin was pulled up like a shirt to show the private inner belly.

'. . . the muscles . . . to move thus . . . and thus . . . Now, with semicircular cuts . . . thus . . . I lift up the omentum to show the stomach in the peritoneal cavity.'

A mind willing to risk unknown roads, thought Ned. So confident of throwing light into the shadows. With his shaky Latin, he soon lost his grasp on the thread of the lecture. Maurits, corpse and assistant drifted like boats left far out by the tide, but the eager enthusiasm to enlighten still warmed him.

A woman in the first tier fainted and was carried out. A moment later, a young man also left. Maurits continued as if unaware.

'. . . perfection of these natural positions of the organs, suited to their functions . . . the body's engines . . .'

Blades flashed and floated in Maurits's hands while his assistant held, tugged, balanced, wiped. Henry's ribs were cut with a saw and opened like the double doors of an icon. Maurits lifted the stomach free and set it aside while he turned to the guts. 'Observe how neatly packed! Twenty-eight or thirty feet of gut in so small a space,' he exclaimed. 'I shall measure it later. What greater wonder do you need in this world?'

As firm as a raspberry, knitted together, rounded and defined.

Maurits had torches lit as the light from the roof windows began to dim. Then he pointed out the rich reds, yellows, blues and startling whites with fervour, as if they were a sunset or painting and not the emerging wonders of the viscera.

Ned frowned against a stab of pain in his temple. The torches made his head swim, but he could not look away.

Maurits prodded, probed, snipped. Then, with a final snip, the shift began, like the first stones in an avalanche. The guts tumbled away from each other, fell apart, lifted out like a string of sausages. Henry became meat on a butcher's table.

The perfect machine made by the Master Craftsman was a charnel, a wreckage, a tangle of membranes and tissues, which seemed to jump in the torchlight, animated not by a spark of Divine Light but by whispers and the breathing of dark creatures in the underbrush.

Grandfather, thought Ned suddenly.

A giant fist gripped his chest. Now he could neither swallow nor breathe. He was attacked by something more than qualms at what he saw.

Please God, don't let the beast come now!

He leaned on his hands and breathed deeply. His heart hammered. A tremor spread up from his feet into his legs. Then began to vibrate in his chest. He gripped the rail.

Go away! I won't let you . . . I can't! Not here!

The anatomy theatre had gone. William, Maurits, the crowd were vague and distant. Ned and the beast pressed head to head, will to will, dyke to sea, in a place not quite in the world.

Give way, it wheedled. It would be so easy to give way.

His right temple exploded into a sudden dark pain. Black pain filled his head.

If you give in to me, said the beast, this will pass. The world will be my problem. You can rest.

He stood with his eyes closed, trying to steady his breathing.

By miracle, he felt it draw back, eased his guard. But the beast had prised open his shell.

He was ambushed by a memory that had been hidden for years. His grandfather, before he was tied to the stake, before being dressed in his pitch-covered gown . . . his grandfather's belly flapped open like a parcel. The neat coils of his belly were hooked out like snakes from a burrow. Ned had seen it many, many times in his head, in sleep, but never so clearly as now. Before today the details had slithered, blurred. Today the image arrived at its true and final form, which would never leave him.

He clung to the rail in front of him. Felt the flames, the clinging pitch-covered gown. He was his grandfather, then a wizard at the stake. A shadow dancing in the burning coach, smoke searing his lungs, his hair flaring like dried grass.

He cried out.

Imagination and reality melted together to make one truth.

His grandmother's hot grief filled him. Her passion washed through him again. The weight of coins and children dragged at his strength. Forgive me! His purpose returned with a jolt. He had almost forgotten, distracted by his evil fortune. It was even more urgent now, for he might not have much time. If he were to die for witchcraft, or be imprisoned as a madman, it came to the same thing. Malises, dead-end. Finished. His grandfather's death, his grandmother's self-sacrifice and labour, even Francis's death, for nothing. The Nightingales would have won.

'Ned?' whispered Shaw. 'Are you ill? Do you want to go . . . ?'

Ned shook his head fiercely and held up his hand to ward off his friend. 'Wait . . .' he whispered.

This is merely imagination, he told himself. As you imagined being a dog or the great bronze gong. But the dream held him, insinuated itself into his being, like the beast. He could not entirely return.

I must save myself. I must wrench the corruption from my body and soul, whatever it may be. I am the only reason for the lives of an entire family. I must live to give them a purpose on this earth.

No more despairing thoughts of drowning himself in the fast dark currents of the Thames. His next move, so momentous that his thought and will were paralysed by the prospect. As when he was six, wondering how to assail Jerusalem. Must choose right!

Was Maurits his saviour?

The terror rose into his throat.

'. . . the rope of gut divides into its own separate kingdoms . . . Observe now the venous structure, like internal rivers . . . Here, the bladder and shining claret-hued kidneys.'

Ned opened his eyes. William Shaw's anxious face hovered close to his own.

Colours seemed brighter than before. Ned drowned in those intense reds and blues as Maurits split the kidneys like exotic fruits, then laid them aside with the other cuts of meat. Maurits,

214

his assistant, Henry, remained distant, but the anatomist's voice sounded unnaturally loud, beating like a drum in Ned's head as the lecturer turned to the spleen.

Everything can be explained, if you will embrace this Dutchman's heresy. It might be as simple as that.

Ned felt infinitely fragile, a membrane holding apart two horrors. He gripped the rail in front of him, closed his eyes again and listened to his own being, alert as if lost in a night-time forest, for the smallest sounds and signs that the beast still lurked behind his shoulder here in the tiers of the *theatrum anatomicum*. At the same time, Maurits van Egmond's words sailed up, precise and crystalline, to lodge deep in his being.

Everything can be explained in time.

Fabric rustled around Ned like forest leaves in a high wind. He opened his eyes. The audience was poised, mouths a little open, shining eyes fixed on Maurits.

'And at last, the liver,' Maurits boomed. He freed the wine-coloured organ and held it aloft for them all to see.

'Is this the five-lobed liver of a dog?' he demanded in triumph. 'I can see only two lobes here. Does any man fear to look lest he be forced to change his mind? Heresy or truth? Is this not the triumph of observation over authority? I say again, there is no truth which cannot be proved by direct observation! There is no darkness which the light of observation cannot reach!' Again, he seemed to speak directly to Ned.

The physicians crowded round. People climbed down from the tiers to look more closely in the uncertain light. The liver passed from hand to hand.

'Two. Indeed, only two!'

'I confess that I doubted . . .'

'A triumph . . .'

But Maurits's blue eyes found Ned's eyes among all the others, as if the message were for him alone.

When the last of the spectators had gone, Maurits leaned wearily against the polished rail of the bottom tier and stared absently at

215

the disassembled Henry while his assistant repacked the tools into the chest. The anatomist looked tired at last, his true years now apparent, a man still in his prime, but no youth.

The liver still lay, rosy and glistening, on the table beside Henry's knee, a single step on the way to universal knowledge.

Ned climbed down the stairs to the stage. At close quarters, he stared at the dismantled criminal. 'Can you find madness? What cog or wheel contains the soul?'

The assistant lifted her head from her task at Ned's tone.

Maurits exchanged glances with her, then shoved himself upright with an impulse of the shoulder blades. With absolute confidence, he said, 'Given time, I can find it.' He paused, then added with disarming precision, 'Or at least the organ, or engine, where it resides.'

When Ned hovered uncertainly, Maurits reached out and gripped his elbow. 'Come downstairs to dinner,' said Maurits, 'as I forgot to feed you last time. And I'll show you something to convert you to the New Philosophy.'

Ned was weary, and wanted to hide away to reflect on what had happened that afternoon. It was too soon to begin dealings with Maurits.

'Come on, Malise! Or I'll think that you took offence last time.' Maurits now took a firm grip on Ned's arm. 'Janni, see that our subject is placed in the cellar for the night.'

As they went down the winding stairs much more quickly than Ned had climbed them, he asked Maurits, 'If you don't think me mad, what then?'

'Are you certain you don't anoint yourself with henbane and thorn apple like those poor stupid women who report their dreams and find themselves arraigned as witches? Do you also believe that you fly?'

'No!' said Ned hotly. 'And I don't much prefer that hypothesis!'

'A hit! A hit!' said Maurits good-naturedly. 'But I must at least consider every possible explanation.'

216

'How are "possible explanations" different from hypotheses?'

'Explanations don't need to be proved. On the contrary, taken together, they clear the mind to be open.'

'As I know that I have never used that witch's salve you mentioned, what remains?'

'Possession.' Maurits glanced at him with his pale blue eyes. 'Which I myself have witnessed.' He trotted down two more stairs. 'And my colleague who visited you thought that if you were not mad, you might indeed be a *vir*-wolf.' Maurits tested the word on his tongue and studied Ned keenly now, in spite of his tiredness.

Ned could hardly say the words. 'A shape-shifter? Do you, a man of reason, believe in such things?'

'I neither believe nor disbelieve in such things. Had no chance to observe 'em. I once travelled to Turkey to see a pair of savage children. And I've heard from good witnesses of men who eat those whom they've murdered. But I've never seen man and wolf in one body.'

They arrived at the door of Maurits's chambers.

Maurits stood back to let Ned enter. 'Other men, of unproven reliability, claim to have seen such a one, a *loup-garou*, *vir*-wolf, werewolf, what you will. And many travellers record the existence in the Andaman Islands of the *cynocephali*, men with the heads of dogs, like the dog-headed St Christopher. I must keep an open mind.'

A manservant shucked Maurits from his gown and helped him into a housecoat.

'Let me show you some of my own drawings of the liver,' said Maurits. 'Come sit here at the table.' He began to haul one of the chairs across the wide planks. 'I must wait for daylight to observe you properly, but I can at least begin. Take off your cloak and sit.' He pointed at the chair.

Ned bristled. 'I did not come to be examined!'

Maurits lifted a pile of drawings from a chest on to the table. 'Here, you can see a true image of the two human lobes . . .'

Ned nodded, then nodded again. His clarity of purpose in

217

the anatomy theatre had begun to fade. Having resumed his irritating, self-involved, slightly clown-like qualities, Maurits seemed less and less like a saviour.

A strong kick sent the door flying open. The young woman assistant came in with a tray. 'For shame, Maurits.' She placed the tray on the table. She looked briefly at one of the papers as she set it aside. 'Your guest is waiting for refreshment.'

'Ned Malise is not a guest, Janni. He will become a colleague once he understands what we do here, and believes. We shall collaborate. He may hold the key to my future reputation.' Maurits left the book, dug under a table against the wall and returned with a black Chinese lacquer chest in his arms.

Ned felt a quiver of undefined alarm.

'Poor Ned,' Janni replied tranquilly. 'I hope he understands what he's doing.'

'He wishes merely to obey the classical admonishment . . . so said Solon, Socrates, indeed, the god Apollo himself at Delphi: "Know thyself".'

'Just be careful how well you let him know you,' she said to Ned. She laid a friendly hand in passing on Maurits's shoulder.

'I haven't let him do anything yet,' said Ned hotly. 'And I don't know that I will! I'm not another Henry!'

'Yes!' said Maurits to Janni, ignoring Ned's outburst. 'Do please rub my neck. It set rigid with rage yesterday afternoon during a dispute.' He put the black lacquer chest on the floor and dropped on to the nearest chair after sweeping off its load of recently unpacked books.

She stood behind him and gripped his shoulders with strong fingers. He groaned in pleasure and closed his eyes.

Mistress as well as assistant after all, thought Ned. No mere acolyte would touch so easily. He wondered if she were equally intent in her studies. Nevertheless, her presence comforted him.

'Alchemy,' Maurits said. 'Your thumbs send quicksilver running through my veins.'

218

'A proposition that wouldn't stand investigation.'

Maurits opened his eyes and raised his fine blond eyebrows at Ned. 'Behind me stands the constant test of my philosophical rigour.'

He shook gently under the woman's hands, like the deer-hound when John Nightingale had scratched its chest in the orchard at Tarleton Court.

I don't like this overconfident, uncivil little man! Ned thought suddenly.

'Ned still doubts,' Maurits said, his eyes still closed. 'I shall show him my toys . . . Stay where you are, Malise, the long table's best for this demonstration. Janni, bring the candles closer.'

He moved from under her fingers and opened the black lacquer chest.

A flat, painted-wood clown hung between two sticks, a child's gaudy fairground toy. When Maurits squeezed the bottoms of the sticks together, the clown hanging between them flipped rump over heels as his double strings untwisted. 'D'you see how he works?'

'Without straining myself.' Maurits was either mad or mocking him. Ned recrossed his long legs and glanced at his cloak.

Maurits reached into the chest. 'And this?'

Ned took the enamelled egg and flipped open the lid on its side. 'A watch,' he said, letting his indignation show. Did Maurits imagine that one must attend university to have seen such things?

'Do you understand how it works?'

'In general . . . by springs and levers and other forms of clockwork.'

'And what is it for?'

'To tell us the hour.' Ned blushed with irritation.

'In other words, you couldn't make it nor explain it, but you know what it does and, roughly, how it does it . . . that's good enough. So long as you see that there is no mystery here

– just metal, wrought by the hand of man, into a mechanical form, which so agitates itself that it speaks to us of an idea that is grasped only by the mind of Man – of Time. That last is vital – the watch does not understand what it does and yet it helps to shape an idea that has busied philosophers for centuries.'

Ned nodded shortly. He eyed his cloak again. He could not take much more raising and disappointing of hope. Now he just felt very, very tired.

'Patience,' said Maurits, clearly amused at Ned's suppressed indignation, and pleased at having read it so clearly. 'The New Philosophy will not be rushed.' He reached again into the lacquered chest.

Janni placed a third candlestick in a semicircle with the others, lighting a small arena on the tabletop. Ned looked to her for enlightenment, or at worst, a complicitous glance, but she looked so serious that he concluded she was as deranged as her master and likely lover.

He squinted at the candles, then glanced uneasily at the darkened window. 'The New Philosophy may have infinite time, but I must return to my lodgings.'

'Sleep here.' Maurits glanced up from the chest, where he had plunged both hands. 'If it pleases you, that is.' He looked now at the woman, as if seeking her approval for this remembered civility. 'Why not? We have more than enough room. My host and his family are still at their country estate. We've no one to please but ourselves.'

He turned one hand vigorously within the other, then set on the table a tiny enamelled metal peacock set with jewels. With a faint grinding of miniature gears, the metal plumes of its tail sprang apart into full display. Scratch. Click. Click. Click. Scratch. Scratch. Green, blue and lapis lazuli, the enamelled metal plumes scraped against each other. The minute jewelled eye glittered. The peacock then walked the length of Ned's thumb, stopped and again opened and closed its fan, humming, grinding and quivering all the time with mechanical effort.

'Not as simple as the watch,' said Maurits, his cheeks flushed, his abrupt manner softened by his enthusiasm. 'But nevertheless animated by the same mechanical principles. Now, look at this creature.'

He wound up a bear, of brown rabbit fur, which lumbered awkwardly along the polished wooden tabletop in pursuit of the peacock.

'Help me, Janni!' A painted metal elephant swung its trunk as it walked. Then a rhino bobbed its head and spun its tail.

As it waddled near the table edge, Ned turned the peacock back into the candlelight.

When the peacock began to slow, Janni rewound it.

Maurits rewound the bear. 'Do you see yet where I'm tending?'

Ned shook his head, still irritated, but he also itched to pick up the bear and peer closely.

'And now!' Maurits animated a monkey that banged on a drum, then a hen that hopped, stretched its wings, flapped, and pecked at the floor. A crocodile crawled after a mouse, its jaws flashing in the candlelight. A tiger dipped its head again and again to a bleeding deer, and chewed with squeaking jaws.

Janni corralled the miniature beasts as they threatened to dive from the table, set them upright when they fell over and wound them up again as they slowed. 'We have most of Eden here.'

Whirring, scratching, clicking and rattling, the tiny menagerie danced on the table. Some jewelled, some painted. Metal and wood. Each creature, filled with apparent purpose, headed off to a horizon of its own. Looking as the real world might look if you were an eagle, or a god.

'Do you agree that there is nothing magical here? Nothing mystical or arcane?' asked Maurits. His forehead and cheeks gleamed damply in the warm candlelight. 'All mechanical?'

The scene had a pleasant madness. A miniature Paradise run amok. A renowned and well-connected Dutch anatomist racing back and forth along a table like a four-year-old after clockwork toys. And his assistant just as intent and serious as he.

221

Maurits animated a second bear, more finely wrought than the first, which juggled three minute balls along a curved wire as it danced in a circle. Then a singing bird that flicked its tail, turned its head with a small truthful motion and dripped out a falling string of notes.

'Note that the creatures grow more complex, but are all still animated by clockwork.'

The monkey beat its tiny drum. The bear and elephant marched. The tiger chewed. The juggled balls jerked up and over, up and over, along their wire. The real animals were made more real in Ned's imagination by these simulacra.

'And now . . .' Maurits set down a naked male human infant. It lay on its back, jerked its tiny legs and waved fists the size of peas. Then a quick glittering thread of liquid arched from its male organ and splattered on the tiled floor. 'Man!'

Ned smiled in spite of himself. He almost liked Maurits in this mood of childlike delight. He leaned forward in his chair and picked up the rhinoceros which spun its tail. Its hindquarters vibrated against his fingertips as if it did indeed contain life.

'Do you see yet?' Maurits demanded eagerly. 'That these are not toys but a Philosophy of Nature made concrete . . . epitomes of the larger world in which all living things are a form of mechanism. The larger world is infinitely more complex, of course, but it is merely a question of degree.'

'I still see no space for the soul,' said Ned.

'Aha! But did you not agree that the springs of the watch contained the essence of certain abstract thoughts?'

Ned nodded reluctantly.

Out of the lacquered chest came a miniature monk, sandalled and tonsured, clutching an ale jug in one tiny fist. When set free, the holy brother waved his jug and pinged out the tune of a filthy tavern song.

'So kiss my arse, disdainful sow. Good claret is my mistress now,' sang Ned in harmony.

'You know it?' cried Maurits. 'Do you see? Even immorality can be encompassed with ease, here within universal laws of action. And if immorality, then sin. If sin, then good and evil. If good and evil, why not soul?'

Ned wanted to disagree but could not think how.

Maurits re-wound the monk as the song slowed. 'The babe is like the bear, but more complex. This holy brother is like the babe, but still more complex. Man himself is more complex than any of them, but it is only a matter of degree. Your case is yet still more complex than simple Man, but again by a few degrees.'

'More difficult than that, surely!'

Maurits took an eagle-headed, lion-bodied beast from the chest. 'A griffon – some would say an impossible, unnatural monster. In reality, just like all the others – same springs, same wires, just differently arranged. The New Philosophy leaps over all false distinctions of natural and unnatural. If a thing exists, then it conforms to the universal rules.'

Maurits was too clever. Ned could not debate with him. But there was something, not quite grasped, that he did not like.

Maurits knew it. 'You're not converted yet? You are no more inexplicable than this griffon.'

'Except, as you said, in considerable degree,' his assistant added gently.

'Given time,' said Maurits, 'I will find the cogs and axles that animate your wolf, whatever its cause. Then we can cure it. Cut it out like a boil.' He leaned forward and found Ned's eyes. 'Stay the night.' His will pulled like the current above a waterfall. 'Stay here tomorrow and I can begin to measure you.'

'You must continue with your demonstration tomorrow,' Janni reminded him.

'Ned must stay until breakfast in that case. I can at least begin.' Maurits turned his full fervour on to Ned. 'I shall find the engines that animate the wolf. Cut them out, as easily as an abscess, and free you forever!'

The simplicity of Maurits's philosophy disarmed him. Once you had accepted it, it cut through all dispute.

All Ned's life, his spirit had leaped eagerly and blindly to its

223

destination, then waited for reason to make its orderly way by the longer road. Now, he told himself, he must put himself into the hands of his reason while his spirit lagged behind.

With the side of his eye, he caught the woman's glance, regarding him with total concentration, her hands cupped around the baby. Her large, dark-blue eyes dominated the slightly bony, though attractive, face, which was softened this evening by wisps of angel-blonde hair fallen from under her embroidered cap. He felt himself shrink, drawn into the eyes, falling into a well. He frowned and stiffened.

She smiled and still looked at him.

'What do you see, Mistress?'

'Better than you think.' A simple statement, without coquetry.

It was that as much as Maurits's will and his confidence in his New Philosophy that nearly tempted Ned to stay. But he went back to his lodgings all the same. Perhaps it was as Maurits had said, terror at the prospect of self-knowledge. But he was not yet ready to put himself into the man's hands.

18

By the end of September all the lords and ladies and rich merchants had returned from their summer estates. The streets filled again and grew noisy at night. At Somerset House, rehearsals began again for the Queen's masque.

The royal marriage had unexpectedly taken a turn for the better. Though neither faction could or would say why, the Queen had now fallen in love with the King and he with her. (One obstacle had been removed when, some time previously, Buckingham had been knifed at Portsmouth by an army officer with a grudge.) It was said that she now adored the King passionately and would do anything to keep his favour, even though most of the country accused him of either bloody tyranny or dithering, and the Scots were preparing for war.

Then disaster. The Queen's close friend Lady Carlisle was taken with the small pox.

'The Royal Hen and I have both used your cure!' Lady Ann told Ned. 'She would rather suffer the plague now than lose her looks, just as the King has fallen in love with her at last.'

Lady Ann was doubly grateful to him because she now carried her first child and feared that it might be scarred in the womb.

Soon, thought Ned, when the cure has been seen to work, I can stop fearing for my life . . . can ask for my reward, leave London for the safer obscurity of Tarleton Court. Make myself a workshop in one of the stables . . . Marry . . .

225

For a flash, he was lying again naked, with the young, naked Marika in her enclosed box bed.

Before I think of marrying anyone else, he thought, I shall insist on seeing her, just once. To speak and see the expression in her eyes.

He could not think how light he would feel at last when he let slip the weight of his vow to his grandmother. He sometimes imagined that the beast would leave him then. Then, he would in truth be free to marry. He could never ask any woman, least of all Marika, to wed a man who was part beast.

In the meanwhile, he began another lute, a Christmas gift for Lady Ann's younger brother. While working with his tools, feeling a shaving lift smoothly away from a block under his chisel, laying out the diagrams of perfect harmony on a thin flat board, he recaptured the perfect silence which singing had once made in him. Otherwise, the loss of his voice weighed like grief at a death. As long as the beast threatened to share his soul, he knew that he would never have his singing back. In the evenings, he sometimes held the new lute which he had made for himself that summer, stroked and held it, listening to its hums and vibrations, its tantalising promise of music.

Though he went into society as little as possible, for fear of his beast, he steeled himself to accept when Sir George Tupper of the South Java Company invited him to a party and masque shortly before Christmas. The money which Francis had invested in one of the Company's voyages to the Dutch East Indies was still bobbing back to England on its return voyage. It would be another year before any profits were returned. Sir George, being one of the King's men, was not a close friend, but after the death of Francis he had at least been a cool moderating voice.

Sir George's house looked almost finished now, though here and there squared blocks of rough stone still waited above window arches and in door pediments to be carved into lion masks or vegetable fantasies. A footman in silver and white took Ned straight through the high-ceilinged hall into the garden at the back of the house, overlooking the Thames. Though it was late November, Sir George had had the conceit of a party in the open air, like the old ice fairs.

Ned paused at the top of the steps just outside the garden door to find his bearings. Torches flared and smoked everywhere, while braziers burned to keep the guests warm. The corners of the walks and parterres were marked with starry flags and silver nets filled with glistening wooden snowflakes. Cages of finches and larks hung from poles fashioned in the shape of icicles, the birds' cries inaudible among the hundred raised laughing voices of the costumed guests. The rasp of catgut being tuned came from the string consort on the raised terrace which gave on to the wide empty darkness of night sky above the river. Half-visible behind a fallen canvas wall stood a cart bearing an enormous cage. Waiting behind the bars stood three women, whom Ned had seen passing in their carriages. In spite of the chilly evening, they wore silver and pearl ropes, phoenix feathers, and very little else. To his right was the window of the parlour where Francis had died.

In the gust of warmth that rose up to meet him, the heat of the massed bodies rivalled that of the braziers. The perfume of the guests mingled with that of potted roses, the oily torches, sweet herbs burning on the braziers, rotting vegetation and sewage. For a moment, he wanted to fling himself gratefully down into that collected warmth and bathe in it. But such sociability was no longer safe for him.

Too many torches, thought Ned uneasily. Their unsteady dance made his head swim.

He took in a breath and set off to find his host, Sir George.

'Good evening to you, sir . . . to you, ma'am . . .' He bowed his dark head left and right.

'Master Malise, I trust that you will dance with me!' cried a young woman in blue. One of Francis's heiresses, but low on his brother's list. He bared his white teeth in a forced smile.

'Ned!' cried another voice. 'How good to see you . . . !'

God's Blood! Everyone's here tonight. Once I would have

been overjoyed to be part of such company. As for Francis . . . !

The torchlight juddered. The voices beat at his ears. He felt his beast lurking just outside the dark garden walls.

I should never have risked coming, he thought. I'm not in a humour for merrymaking . . . I'll pay my respects to Sir George and leave. With this press, he'll never notice.

He looked up at a torch, then out across the soothing darkness of the Thames, lit only by the wherry fireflies. He felt a thought drawing near, out of that darkness, a promise of enlightenment. The torch. He poised, waiting for the thought to arrive. But it escaped again. For, as he turned, he saw John Nightingale.

He was certain. Though the man wore a silver half-mask, he knew him. Fully grown and neatly bearded now, with hair the colour of acorns. Almost his own height. But the set of the shoulders, the way of turning his head, were Nightingale's.

I must be imagining! Ned told himself. Up to my old tricks. For how could he dare to be here? Dare to be in England even?

The consort struck up the introduction to a pavane. Ned circled urgently round the outside of the crowd as couples took their places to dance, but he found his way blocked by a splendid fellow in silver-embroidered silk with rolling breakers of lace washing around wrist and knee.

'It makes you want to weep – an upstart, a nobody! Dancing with Lady Holmes . . .'

Ned tried to move past him.

'The woman dressed as Allegory . . .'

Ned already saw. The handsome woman in a vaguely Grecian robe with silver ribbons in her hair was dancing with Nightingale.

Older than when Ned had stared at him across Francis's body. But the same man, for certain.

'You know him?' His companion drank and glared over his glass at Nightingale. 'I'm amazed! I heard that he grew on a cabbage stalk somewhere in Hampshire.'

Yes, I know him, Ned wanted to say. He killed my brother

228

and never stood trial. I believe that he let a beast into my head. 'How does he dare to come here?'

The man gave him an odd glance. 'You hadn't heard? He's the new favourite of our host. Made a fortune abroad for the South Java Company, in some speculation or other. And wouldn't you know, a Dutchman helped him to it.'

'Dutchman?' Had Nightingale been hidden in Holland then, while Ned was looking for him in England?

'Had a marvellous name,' said the man. 'The Dutchman . . . Coymans!' He snorted. 'Coy . . . mans. Hard to forget, isn't it? Well, the man may have been coy, but the woman, his sister, certainly wasn't!' He spoke with bitter satisfaction and glared again at Allegory.

'Coymans's sister?' Ned repeated stupidly. How many could there be? He felt something crack deep inside himself. A splitting. A release. The box opened.

Leave now, he told himself. Don't speak another word! 'What was her name?'

Now the man looked straight at him, with a slight frown. 'Some foreign twisting of the good English name, Mary. Don't tell me you know her too!'

All the time Ned had looked for him, he was in Ned's city. Making love to the only woman Ned loved.

Ned saw Marika naked in bed with Nightingale, those pale breasts with their pink nipples in his hands. His mouth on hers . . .

'Coymans?' Ned repeated, very gently so that the rage boiling up from the tops of his thighs might not escape. He must contain it at any cost, for if it did escape, it would level Sir George's house and all those around it. It would crack the sea walls, and boil the Thames dry. He was a secret lightning bolt. The fuse of a primed cannon which any of the torches could light. 'How did you hear of this?'

'His serving man swaggers as much as his master and babbles more. She weeps for him still. Or so I'm told.' Ned's companion seemed very far away.

229

Just then the dance ended. Beyond a clot of people, the man lifted his silver mask and laughed to his partner. It was Nightingale, beyond doubt. The juddering torchlight winked from the silver mask shoved up on to his forehead and the strands of rumpled hair that fell over it.

Ned thrust his way past his companion, towards Nightingale. He had no reasoned intention, only to unleash his fury. The wolf left the shadows and leaped on to his shoulder.

'Let me through!' Ned trod on a train of cloth of silver and knocked one of the icicle poles askew. The nearness of the wolf gave him strength, propelled his fury.

Sir George himself came from the house, threw an arm across Nightingale's shoulders and led him back inside away from the party.

Ned followed. To Sir George's great parlour, the room where Francis had died. He should have taken that as an ill sign, but surged onward, blind and inexorable in his rage. He pushed aside the footman who tried to block his way, and stood, breathing hard just inside the door with the apologetic footman behind him.

Three faces turned to the invader: Sir George, John Nightingale, and a tall thin man who sat beside the fire while the other two men stood. Ned was too much beside himself to recognise the attenuated grooves and knife-edge nose of Lord Mallender, one of the King's arrangers. He charged at Nightingale. The footman seized him from behind. He shook the man off, but by that time Sir George had shouted for two more men.

Held fast, Ned tried to speak, found that the string between thought and speech had been cut again. 'Justice!' he managed to say. 'This murderer . . . you were witness, Sir George.' He stood panting, with clenched fists.

Nightingale looked quickly at his two companions, neither of whom seemed either impressed or alarmed.

'Yes, I was there, Master Malise. And like many other of the witnesses, believed that your brother's death was an accident.' Sir George turned to Nightingale. 'You too made accusations . . . Sir James Balkwell, among others, more than half believed you.'

'It's old business, Malise,' said the man seated by the fire. He stretched out his long legs. 'In any case, if Nightingale can make as much money for me as he did for the South Java Company, he could earn himself a pardon several times over for any crime he chooses to commit. I have more pressing matters to think of now than stale allegations. Good evening.'

The three footmen forced Ned back through the entrance hall and out into the front courtyard. Left alone on the cobbles, in the light of two fluttering torches, Ned did not know whether he was man or beast. He rode a current, helpless as a twig to swim any other way. He took a position in the street, in the shadows just beyond reach of the torch set into a holder by Sir George's gate. He did not care if Nightingale came out alone or protected by two dozen armed men. He would kill him.

He swam in the darkness, unable to say how time passed. Not himself, but a fierce creature, alert and implacable, intent on its prey.

The distant string consort whipped itself into a frenzy of punished catgut. He did not recognise their tune. A chorus of exalted female voices reached him faintly. He did not know their song. The guests cheered and applauded. He did not know what they did or why.

Then he saw it all: in the torch and candlelight, the naked shoulders of women gleamed with a delicate film of perspiration. With each step, their sandalled feet darted from under their draperies. They laughed into the eyes of their dancing partners. His prey was among them, touching them, flushed with wine and triumph and glinting with malice, drinking deeply, his arm now across one of the naked shoulders, his fingertips carelessly brushing her breast, hardly able to speak for laughing, 'You should have seen the cur kicked away!'

It seemed to him that he truly saw it. His hand clenched on the hilt of the short Flemish dagger which he always

231

carried now, even when courtesy demanded that swords be left behind.

Marika raised her smiling face to Nightingale's . . .

He paced along the wall, shaking his head and growling deep in his throat.

The guests left slowly at first. A carriage. Then another. Voices shouted with laughter inside the walls of the garden.

Ned swung into a prowl, back and forth along the wall, which seemed less solid than his imaginings. He needed to strike the brazen gong, shake thunder from the clouds, cut out Nightingale's heart.

The string consort still played, more softly. He knew the tune but could not remember its name. But it called up Marika. He pushed the picture away. He wanted to kill her too. Better not to think of her at all.

More carriages left the forecourt. Sir George shouted farewells from the steps of his house.

Would the man never leave? Ned needed to confront him while his rage still boiled.

Four guests accompanied by servants left on foot, to walk the short way home to apartments in Whitehall.

Ned prowled to the corner where Sir George's wall met the river. The garden now seemed silent. As he returned to his post, the members of the consort came out of the gate and turned with their instruments in the direction of St Martin's Lane.

He suddenly feared that Nightingale would stay the night as Sir George's guest. He had to kill the man tonight. He would never again be supported by such sure rage. Tonight his sinews would uncoil of themselves, the blade would strike by itself.

But he was already slipping back into himself.

Go back in and find Nightingale. Kill him in front of Sir George if need be.

If he waited another half-hour, it would be too late.

He almost bumped into him in the shadow of the arched gate. There was a beat of silence while they looked at each other in the orange light of the torch.

232

'You again!' said Nightingale. 'Like a fool, I came to the party unarmed. I should have thought to borrow a sword before I left.' He kept walking forward. As he spoke he raised his hands in front of him, palms out to show that they were empty. When they reached chest height, he suddenly lunged forward and shoved Ned violently backwards.

Ned's shoe slipped on the edge of a drain.

Not again! He twisted and hit his left shoulder against the wall instead of his head. He's too close, he thought.

They grappled and then stood locked in an ugly, grunting balance, Ned's dagger-hand pinned to the wall by Nightingale's shoulder. They struggled like sea against dyke. Not moving, just tensed muscles, locked knees and gasps of breath. Neither broke. It seemed that they would stay locked there forever.

'This is not how . . . gentlemen should fight,' said Nightingale in his ear. 'But then neither of us is a true gentleman.'

The white heat of Ned's rage suddenly cooled. He had waited too long after all. Weariness began to suck at him.

Nightingale went limp. Caught off-guard, Ned lost his balance. While he regained it, Nightingale broke free and stepped back. Ned prepared to parry a renewed attack.

'Don't trouble yourself,' said Nightingale. He turned and began to walk away.

'Turn around and fight,' Ned wanted to shout. 'One of us must kill the other! Fight and let fate decide where the right lies! Set us both free!' But he could not speak. He sank down on to his heels against the wall. Even in the dregs of his rage, he could not stab the man in the back.

Nightingale half-turned. 'I won't be arrested for common brawling in the streets. Go away. I must prepare to return to Amsterdam.' He began to walk away again. 'To get my satisfaction, I don't need to kill you!'

'I don't need to kill you.'

What did he mean by those contemptuous words? They feel like

233

part of the thought that still eludes me. The hole in my thoughts where my salvation may lie. I strain to remember.

Or did he mean that he would tup Marika again, for whom he didn't even care?

Ned slept heavily and woke the next morning in his own lodgings, with a faint memory of the night watch helping him home from outside Sir George's house.

Sir George's private parlour! Lord Mallender . . .

He could remember enough of that first part of the evening to be appalled. He rolled over and buried his face in the pillow. He could not believe that he had done such a thing, even in a rage.

Made a dangerous fool of myself. More enemies.

Did the wolf come?

There was a blank in his memory that ended with John Nightingale's voice in his ear. 'But then, neither of us is a true gentleman.' And then, 'I don't need to kill you.'

He turned back over and sat up, chilled. He knew that the wolf had come, whether he remembered it or not.

Any moment, he thought, there will be a knock on the door. A constable. Soldiers.

Later that day, Shaw reassured him a little. The Queen's circle seemed to know nothing, or at least not to care what happened at parties given by a new-made protestant knight and member of the South Java Company. In any case, the Queen's masque was near performance. The intricate dances and the fine points of costumes filled everyone's thoughts day and night.

Four days before the performance, as Ned stood in a parlour in Somerset House, discussing the wings of his demon costume with a court tailor, he felt a shift in the air, one of those small quivers that might have been an earthquake, or the sound of a distant house crumbling. He found the source. The marchioness who directed their actions in the Queen's absence stood bent towards a steward listening to him, one

234

hand clenched before her face, her thumb pressed against her lips. The other hand was half-lifted as if warding off a blow.

Others in the parlour still chattered, holding up billows of lace and whalebone. A gentleman in the mask of Pestilence was trying to frighten Peace and Obedience, while Famine held out his empty claret glass to a manservant's jug. A Roman charioteer stood twisted before a small looking glass, trying to see his own back.

'My friends . . .' said the marchioness.

Her voice lodged a sliver of ice in his gut. He watched a servant enter behind her with a lighted brazier, smelled burning cypress and rosemary, and knew her news before she spoke it.

'. . . oh, my dear friends. I've dismal news. Our Iris, my dear Ann . . .'

It's not possible, Ned thought.

'. . . is taken with the small pox.'

All faces turned grave. Some of the women began to cry.

At least no eyes turned accusingly to him.

'The Queen orders us to abandon the masque. We must all go to our houses and take what precautions we can against the contagion.'

Ned returned to St Martin's Lane, cursing his brother's credulity and his own. What if the cure itself had carried the contagion? As it had been meant for the Queen, the question would surely arise. He did not know what to think or do.

And he had unfinished business. A half-made lute for which Shaw had already paid him. The boy who had not yet smiled.

How long did he have?

The question was answered late that same night while he was packing his tools into their chest.

'Let me in, Malise. I'm alone.'

Ned unbarred his door.

Maurits van Egmond, late and unannounced, no manservant attending him. 'I heard the ill news, my friend. Small pox in the court, very near to the Queen. Some say that the contagion

235

came from a supposed cure, which was to be your gift to the Queen.'

So the word was out.

'Has anyone yet said "treason"?'

'The word lies on the air like foul breath.'

He did not ask about witchcraft. 'Will people believe that I would want to kill the Queen?'

'I sail for Amsterdam early in the morning,' said Maurits. 'I advise you to come with me.'

'So urgent?'

'I fear so.'

He was not truly surprised. Justice wears many cloaks.

Later, he was to ask himself why he did not stop to wonder that Maurits van Egmond counted himself so close a friend.

SEVEN

19

I may live! I have remembered! All those whispers of wizardry and spells have unlocked my thoughts. In a blast of clarity, I caught those elusive words by their tails, now grip them tight, chew, chew, chew! Extract the delicious juice of their meaning.

Legal fact.

Forget madness, melancholy and pressures on the brain!

I must tell the magistrates that I am under a spell. In my head, I'm already free! By law, the wizard who enchanted me is to blame for my crimes and, by law, must hang in my place.

I know whom to blame.

When he stood staring at me after he killed my brother, John Nightingale was casting the spell that changed me to a wolf. That is why he later said that he had no need to kill me! He had taken his revenge already!

Think it through again, Ned. Imagine the magistrates' questions . . .

Nightingale stared overlong into my eyes across my brother's corpse. Shortly after that, my headaches began, which surely were the first signs that his spell had worked! Then he vanished from a locked and guarded prison and no one saw or heard him go. A mere youth! Then evaporated altogether, until he reappeared, mysteriously now in the highest favour. What more proof does anyone need that the man's a wizard?

And he's an Englishman. While I at least am Hollander by nurture. I can defend myself to the magistrates in their own tongue, with a good, nasal Amsterdammer twang.

239

I stretch my limbs among their chains. I flex and straighten my fingers which were restored to feeling by Maurits's ointment. I feel hope.

My lute. I can bear to think of you now.

And Marika! My darling, I may live.

Let's celebrate!

She settled those lovely buttocks, which he had cupped in his hands, on to the chair. She wore only petticoats and was in bare feet, for who could see them? She parted her legs just a little to steady herself before the keyboard. She raised her hands to the left keyboard, not quite touching the keys. Lifted her eyes to his. Straightened her head as she drew in her breath before the first note. The cold air filled with beautiful tears. *Lachrimae Antiquae.*

Why do you play doleful Dowland's seven sad pavanes?

'Flow my tears . . .'

Dowland then, if you will . . . Don't rush at the keys, my darling. I have time . . .

Now after The Old Tears, play the New Old Tears. And now the Sighing Tears . . . Enforced Tears. A Lover's Tears . . .

Will you begin again?

He took up the long-necked, half-pear of his lute, placed it across his body just so, left hand curved tenderly around the fretted neck. His right hand tested the nineteen strings. He lowered his left ear to catch the note as he raised his right arm to the delicately-angled peg box to retune a string. The string tightened across the peg box, the soul of the lute. He smiled at her. Ready.

My tongue sees her. My eyes smell her. My hands taste her. My whole body hears her.

How much did she tell me and how much do I imagine? In this darkness, shadows breathe and swirl like mist into new shapes. I hear the melody of 'True Tears'.

240

20

Mevrouw Cats drew her breath and stretched to get a better view through the uncurtained window of her neighbours' house.

The little slut might as well be standing naked in the street.

In the dining chamber, a public room at the front of the house, into which anyone could see, Marika Coymans stood absolutely still, with hair uncombed and in bare feet on the tiled floor wearing only her bodice and petticoat, naked arms not in the least covered by the fur-lined cloak that she had flung over her undergarments.

(Fur in August! sniffed Mevrouw Cats.)

Shamelessly she had adorned her indecency with gold rings on every finger, two gold filigree bracelets set with rubies, a toothy pink coral necklace and a pearl-edged double portrait of her dead parents hanging between breast and navel on a chain of small gold snakes, until she looked like one of those fashionable, fanciful engravings of savage royalty from the New World. She had also twined around her throat and wrists six ropes of pearls (Mevrouw Cats counted them enviously) and pinned askew on her bodice front a large pearl which hung from a silver bow set with diamonds. Diamond eardrops winked through her curling uncapped blonde hair.

She looked like one of those savage Carib queens screwed up under the bowsprit of an East India merchantman, all

241

curves and bright paint, hair and wooden clothing flying in the sea winds.

Mevrouw Cats glanced up and down the street to see that the early-morning egg-seller, the baker with his handcart and the assorted children were not watching her pry, then rose on to her toes to see better.

The dining table with its mermaid legs, the paintings, the statues, sideboards and chairs had all vanished. The vast black-and-white tiled floor of the Coymans's dining chamber looked as bare and cold as an ice floe.

'The higher the monkey climbs, the better you can see his tail,' her husband had said when she told him what had happened in their own street, four nights before. 'And the farther he falls.'

God does indeed punish the wicked, thought Mevrouw Cats with a thrill of satisfaction. The downfall of another person is exciting enough, but when it is also morally instructive one can feel free to enjoy it.

The young woman suddenly moved.

Mevrouw Cats stepped back.

Marika Coymans paced out the twenty-foot length of the vanished table, counting silently as she went. Right down the centre, between the eight pairs of invisible brocaded chairs, lifting her elegant bare feet through the heavy wooden stretchers that braced the table legs, her hips gliding through ghostly candelabra and invisible bowls of fruit. Twenty feet. Where the far end of the table should have been, she stopped.

Here Justus had sat for the last seventeen years. She rubbed a bare sole across the cold empty tiled floor in disbelief. Then turned her head quickly, as if to catch the Venetian mirror unawares, before it too could vanish.

Gone, glass roses and all.

Still paralysed by astonishment, she wrapped her arms around herself under the cloak and turned slowly on the spot to see once more that all the walls were still as bare as she had thought.

This is how things are now.

And, to my astonishment, I still stand, still breathe.

The house even smells empty, she thought. Without the damp wool of the carpets, the sweetness of beeswax polish, the moist animal smells of the people who had lived in the house until last night. No cooking smells. No fires. No horsey gusts of her brother's groom or salty reek of the maids. No brother Justus and his trail of wine, tobacco and musk.

She bent her head to sniff her cloak. Then lifted her hand to her nose. She, at least, was still enclosed in her own mist of rosemary and rose, like a fragile protecting skin.

She stood, with her hand still under her nose. Naked of their curtains, the windows stared like eyes without brows. The blank, whitewashed plaster walls had been stripped of their pictures and hangings. Chairs, side tables, sideboard, table carpets – all gone. The candlesticks, warming pans, the red and blue Venetian glass. The silver birdcage.

Her brother was gone and had taken their familiar life with him.

Justus, come back for me! Please come back!

She caught herself.

Marika, don't!

She sank down in a delayed collapse of petticoats, closed her eyes and stretched out her hand to touch a mermaid's back. Eight of them had held the dining table on their heads, thrusting forward, at just the height of the diners' hands, a pair of disturbing, globular mahogany breasts, polished by the hands of countless male guests. Panope and her seven Nereid sisters had been Marika's friends and comforters when she was very young.

She imagined that she stroked the walnut curve of the mermaid's comfortable scaly back. With her eyes closed, she could still see the patient ears and friendly smile. She felt a rush of tears boiling up again. Opened her eyes.

Don't lose your grip, she told herself. Or you might never regain it.

She threw her arms wide to the bare walls, defiantly. This is the truth! You do not dream. Get accustomed to it now!

Appalled, Mevrouw Cats inched closer to the window again. Such distracted gestures! Distracted . . . mad . . . I'm certain!

With her arms spread wide, the young woman spoke to the empty room.

Mevrouw Cats felt a fearful thrill beneath her breastbone and crossed the fingers of one hand. Casting a spell now?

Anything was possible. The brother and sister had always been the rotten apples in the street, under all their surface trappings of respectability – the big house, the carriage, the clothes. Wealthier than any other family on the street, but then where did the money come from? Admittedly, they kept up a good front. The windows and all other visible parts of the house had always gleamed brightly. Their servants had always kept the front *stoep* spotless and scrubbed the street in front of the house each day, as was required of every householder. (Mevrouw Cats now glanced sideways at the steps and drew a sharp disapproving breath.)

And where *did* the money come from, eh? Justus Coymans traded in the wind, was what her husband said. With other men's money, but always sure to take his share. 'And often plays outside the rules,' her husband had said. 'But no one complains so long as he makes them richer.'

And then there had been the visitors. Mevrouw Cats couldn't help noticing, the noise some of them made leaving for home after curfew, when all Christian men were safely in bed: the painters, musicians, sea captains, men of no apparent rank or business, the painted women who wore feathered hats and were clearly little better than *bordeel* whores. The Jews, Englishmen and other foreigners. (A friend had whispered that she had once even heard Spanish, the language of Holland's long-time enemy, through an open window.)

It's so true, Mevrouw Cats thought, that a man is known by his friends.

She peered avidly through the uncurtained window into the ruins of a world safely distant from her own, whose dark unseen currents had excited her for years. Ever since the parents died and the brother became head of the household. It was a wonder that the Church Council hadn't summoned the pair of them.

The new truth even sounded different.

Marika listened. The house had always throbbed with a dense music from first light until Justus chose to sleep. Now, just a faint snap from the oak panelling in the entrance hall. A creak from the great dog-legged oak staircase. The sound of her own breathing. No pots clattered in the kitchen, no servants' voices called and whistled, no hounds clicked across the acres of tiles. The dining chamber was as still and empty as the inside of a bubble.

I must think what to do.

But she could not think. She had fallen and was thrashing in terror, trying to stop in midair.

She turned her head, her eyes caught by a movement.

A wide-eyed face stared at her through the window.

Suddenly alight with a white, blinding fury, she scrambled to her feet, stepped on her petticoats, cursed. 'Didn't you see enough the other night?' she shouted, half-choked with everything she hadn't said then, when it might have mattered. 'Shoo!' She ran at the window, waving her arms as if scaring chickens.

Mevrouw Cats jumped back, shopping basket clutched like a shield, wide plump cheeks aflame. She looks like a real savage! she thought. Not just a wooden one. Snarling, half-naked and wearing fur. But what can you expect? That brother of hers has a great deal to answer for.

I've predicted something like this for years, she thought as she rushed on in her black skirts and starched apron towards the vegetable stall at the corner of the next street. She hoped to meet a friend over the heaped peas and pyramid cabbages, so she could make a gift of this latest news.

245

Marika stood glaring at the window, shaking with rage, her arms still half-raised. Then they fell to her sides.

The coral necklace which her brother had given her when she was eight to protect her against evil spirits was of little use against neighbours.

Justus, what did I do to make you leave me behind?

The people you love always leave. Against their will at times, but they go. And, as for the rest, expect nothing at all. At that moment, her rage embraced them all.

Marika had heard the neighbours, when she was a child, murmuring in the street when they didn't see her listening behind the shutters or in the cool stone niche in the side of the *stoep*.

'So sad,' they said. 'Such a pretty little thing. It can't be right for such an innocent lamb to be raised by an older brother like that. He leaves her alone for days with just the servants.'

He's a wonderful brother! she would rage silently in her hiding place. What do you know about it? And I don't mind being left alone!

'He uses that little girl like a wife,' they said, then quickly added, 'no, no, I don't mean that. But like a grown woman, not an innocent child. He lets her consort with all those types, stay awake until all hours. Leaves the shutters and curtains open so that the whole world can see her there at one end of the table, her little head falling into her plate.'

He also failed to make her wash enough and to take her to church on Sundays. But they disapproved most of what gave her the greatest joy – his gift of a monkey for her seventh birthday.

'A vain, restless, lascivious little beast, the symbol of all of Man's worst faults. Why not give her the steady honest affection of a lapdog?' the mevrouws asked. 'A creature that can be taught.'

As for the girl's own education, she might as well have been a man or an English noblewoman, with all the Latin,

246

Greek, Hebrew and heathen books her brother bought for her. He even hired a wickedly expensive Swiss pedagogue to tutor her.

'What use can she possibly have for all that?' they asked each other. 'What husband wants a wife who speaks Greek but can't light a peat stove or scour a floor with sand?' (What do I want with a husband who wants that of me? she would silently retort from her hiding place.)

Nevertheless (Marika noted), the mevrouws and their husbands did not encourage a more wholesome, improving friendship with their own daughters. For children, in their untamed ignorance, were the Devil's natural prey, and he was subtle enough to take advantage of a parent's misguided compassion.

At an early age, hidden beside the *stoep*, Marika began to understand that if Justus had been poor, she would most likely have been taken away, for her own protection and for the good of her soul. She would have been placed in one of Amsterdam's many orphanages to be properly raised by godly women, who could teach her the skills of a good housewife and mother, and how to play her proper part in the ordered wellbeing of her nation.

But her brother's wealth kept them safely united in their shared, disreputable splendour. He armoured her in coloured silks and Brussels lace, French hats and the finest of knitted silk stockings (so she overheard her maid saying to a neighbour's cook). He shielded her with linens as sheer and soft as cobwebs and defied his enemies with a four-horse carriage which had to be lodged (expensively) outside the city walls.

As she grew older, she began to understand her brother's other weapons: favours done, favours owed. He invested his money in other men's ventures and invested their money in his own. He sailed close to the wind so that they could sleep with a clear conscience. He made allies at the Bourse.

He also dispensed patronage – in Amsterdam and Leiden, the wine-sellers, spice merchants, jewellers, bookbinders, weavers,

247

leather dealers and importers of Chinese porcelain, all explained to their wives why any man who spent so much couldn't really be a bad fellow at heart.

He paid generous taxes. And now and again, he put a powerful man into his debt with a stunning speculative return.

His greatest weapon, however, was a surging, self-centred vitality. He believed that he could do anything. (Naturally, Marika believed it too, for many years.) His belief was so great that he swept many others along, even if, now and then, a new-made enemy stepped sourly out of the ranks.

So, in spite of rumours about his sharp-dealing, his scandalous raising of his sister, and the questionable nature of his guests, the pair of them were left alone. At the same time, they gave increasing entertainment to the street and, indeed, to the entire *burt*, as Justus drank more and grew increasingly careless of the general opinion, and Marika grew up.

'Shaped to be a wife and mother.' The mevrouws squinted at her full skirts and tight-laced bodice as she passed in the street with her maid when she was thirteen. 'Even with that height and those wide shoulders.'

When she turned seventeen, they asked, 'What is that brother thinking of, to keep her by him for so long?' They stopped calling her an innocent lamb.

Instead, they began to say how much she resembled him. The same wild gold hair, which he stroked as if she were a pet dog. The same blue eyes with lids as rounded and smooth as cowrie shells.

'Nothing like her poor modest mother,' said the mevrouws, now more loudly, with glances in her direction.

Even more beautiful than her mother, her brother said.

'Young lady, my sister!' Justus would cry down the length of the dinner table as he raised his glass. 'Isn't she lovely!' Then his rabble of guests would smirk and blush and offer more toasts.

He loved to stroll beside the canals with her on his arm, he said. 'Let other men envy me and wonder: sister or mistress?

What a shame that we live in a republic, *onzele schaapje*, or I would make you a princess.'

More than anything, he said, he loved to gaze down the length of the dining table, past the debris of his largesse, the leavings of his cronies, toadies and gulls. Past the curled apple peelings, the crumbs of cheese, the empty sauce boats, the still-overflowing bowls of plums and grapes, the bones, the spilt wine, the greasy mouths smoking clay pipes, and large male hands holding knives or the frail stems of green glass *roemer*s – to see her face.

'Like a light, my lambkins. A beautiful angel.'

At twelve, she had stared into the house's many mirrors to try to detect what he meant. But she didn't see it. Nor why men wrote poems to her forehead, for example ('as open and clear as a sunny sky') and then to her mortification, recited them at Justus's dinner table.

Too wide, was her private verdict.

They wrote poems, too, about her mouth, as sweetly curved as Artemis' bow, and songs about the delicious shadow cast by her lower lip on to her goddess-like chin (too firm, she judged). And odes to limbs like Artemis, (too tall for a woman) and her other Olympian attributes.

She concluded that Justus was blinded by his blood tie and that the others all flattered her to win her brother's favour. The only testimonies that she even half-believed were the drawings of her made by one of Justus's protégés, who was a painter and knew how to look. Along with her good bones and seductive smile, the artist also captured amusement, irritation and uncertainty. From time to time, to her discomfort, he also caught her watching her life take place around her but without her, and recorded her remote, assessing eyes.

She ached for true compliments from Justus, the ones she tried to deserve by doing her best to help him earn the money that kept them safe. If, for example, to further one of his dealings, he needed her to smile, to flirt, to sing, then smile, flirt and sing she would. She told herself that nothing she

249

heard whispered about him was as bad as it seemed. She made excuses for him in her heart and tried to make him happy. She needed him and sometimes he rewarded her by swearing that he needed her.

'My support and solace. What would I do without you? We must stick together, eh?'

When he said such things, she felt her shoulders ease and the permanent knot in her stomach loosen. She had a purpose in their life, after all. He did need her. Until four nights ago, they had been a team.

She had been learning a new English piece on her virginal, in the unlit dusk of their main parlour, across the hall from the dining chamber, when he came home. She waited for him to come in at once, as he always did, to lean on the back of her chair, nuzzle her neck and tell her of his latest triumph over yet another rich fool. Instead, his heavy footsteps passed rapidly through the hall and climbed the large oak staircase to his chamber. She began the piece again. The notes sprang out from the strings and alighted softly like moths on the curtains and hangings of the room.

He would be back down shortly with a gift, a small surprise which he was most likely preparing for her in his chamber.

She sometimes felt that his gifts were given in place of something else, but she did not know what it might be. She didn't mind. He gave what he was able.

The next phrase of the music turned into delicate spring rain, each note as precise and clear as if it dripped from a leaf.

Still he did not come down. After the final cadence, she stopped playing and listened in silence to his purposeful footsteps on the floor above her head.

A tiny quiver of unease pricked at the back of her scalp.

In the hall their maid, Lore, stood on a chair, lighting the candles in the chandelier that hung on a chain from the ceiling. A slow blooming of warm yellow light fell on to their father's portrait on the far wall, rich and stern in the black silk that his colourful son never wore. In the dim light, his eyes seemed to seek hers, but in her present unease Marika would not be tempted to look back.

She had known the truth since she was very small. Her father's portrait was blind. Fish swam through his real eye sockets. And her mother's. Somewhere in the Mare Britannicum off the German coast, sunk by a storm along with her father's ship and its cargo of Baltic oak. She had smiled politely at well-meant stories of angels and Heaven. At six, she refused to believe in a God who let accidents like that happen.

At the top of the doglegged staircase, she listened at the closed door of her brother's chamber. Justus crossed the floor and crossed back. Then made a quick, purposeful zigzag. Then a pause and the rustle of papers.

The panelled wood door was firmly shut. He never shut his door against her unless he had a whore in bed. And she was certain he had been alone when he had come in.

'Justus?' As she waited she stared at Madam, their mother, hung on the wood panel to the right of his door, a small painting for private contemplation, not a pendant to their father for public display in the hall. A pretty, richly-dressed young woman with dark brown hair and familiar, spacious brow met Marika's eyes sideways, her full mouth, which had given such sweet goodnight kisses, clamped into a firm, official line.

Justus claimed to see a disapproving guardian spirit in the cracked blue-grey pigment of the eyes. Try as she could, Marika saw only fish, hermit crabs, and finger bones drifting across salty mud. She looked away.

'Justus?' she said again, more loudly.

'Not now, lambkins.' His voice was harsh even through the thick door.

She was certain he was alone. She opened the door and went in.

Her brother stifled a curse. 'What do you want, sweet?' He laid down on the table at his side the pair of gloves he was holding, as if surprised to find them in his hand.

251

His chamber looked as if she had interrupted a thief ransacking it. Saddlebags stood open on the floor beside his small travelling chest. Shirts and jackets lay thrown higgledy-piggledy on the floor. The door of his cupboard hung ajar. Heaped papers slid askew across the red Turkish table carpet, beside his gloves. His fire was alight, in August.

A frozen hand gripped her throat.

'You're going somewhere?' she asked as casually as she could manage. 'Why didn't you say . . . ?' She looked again at his travelling chest. And both saddlebags. 'Where . . . ?'

'Bruges. A sudden . . .'

Into Flanders, out of the United Provinces altogether. Into the Southern Netherlands, Catholic territory controlled by the Spanish enemy in the war that went on and on.

'Bruges is an enemy city.'

He searched his wall cupboard as if he had not heard. She grew more and more frightened.

He left the cupboard and returned to the papers on the table. His hands were unsteady. His usually ruddy face looked pinched and grey.

'Justus, what's the matter? Are you ill?'

Of course! she thought. He is going to visit a famous physician! But why in Bruges? We have physicians of great reputation in Leiden, or even here in Amsterdam.

'No!' he snapped. 'I'm not ill.'

He glanced distractedly through the papers on the table, put some in his saddlebag, kept others in his hand.

She bent and picked up a shirt. 'Take me with you,' she said with false lightness. 'I would enjoy an adventure.'

'Not this time, lambkins.' He still avoided her eye.

She drew a calming breath. Give him a chance, still, to look at her. To reknit this sudden terrible rent in their collusion against the world. 'Something's amiss, isn't it?'

'It's not like you to pry, lambkins! Studying to be a wife?' He crossed to the fireplace, threw in the papers he held. With one hand, he leaned on the carved overmantel of Neptune

252

with his net; with the poker in his other hand, he stirred the flames, crumbling half-burnt fragments of other papers into ash.

Then abruptly, he seemed to collect himself. He swung back to her, out of rhythm, flashing his teeth under his moustaches as he did across the dinner table when reeling a new gull into one of his financial schemes.

'Don't smile at me like that!' She flung herself across the space between them before he could speak, trapped his neck in her arms. 'Justus! Look at me. Tell me the truth. Where are you going and when are you coming back?'

'I am going to Bruges, you silly goose.' He put a large square hand on each of her wrists and detached her.

'I know when you're lying! I've seen you do it often enough.'

'Don't be a fool! You know how I junket about on my affairs.'

'Justus, this is no junket ... not into Flanders, among enemies. I won't let you pat my cheek and fob me off with a muff or some other trinket this time. What business can you have with the enemies of Holland? What has happened?'

He set aside four papers he pulled from a bundle on the table, glanced through those that remained and then thrust them into the fire.

'Tell me!'

He smashed at the burning papers with the iron poker.

'"Stick together," you said. If you love me, tell me. You know that you must or you'll drive me distracted. You don't love me or you wouldn't terrify me like this!'

He leaned the poker back in its place, ran a hand over Neptune's walnut tail. 'All right, lambkins, since you insist and as I've no time for games: I'm wanted for murder. You asked, so there it is, plain and unvarnished.'

Terror swilled under her ribs. She could not speak.

'I hope I needn't tell you I'm innocent. But my enemies grow ambitious and a warrant for my arrest is being signed at

253

this moment. Or so I've been told by someone whose ear I trust. Thank God for favours owed . . . !'

He's speaking too fast, she thought.

'You're not a murderer.'

'No, lambkins. I just said that I'm innocent.'

'Then stay and defend yourself! If you're innocent, you'll be acquitted.'

His words were right, but his voice and face were not. Think about that later. More urgent matters to settle.

'Oh, my unworldly darling!' He darted a quick look at her, then returned to his study of Neptune's tail. 'Do you truly believe that I can trust in the fair-minded justice of my fellow men, when some of them owe me money and others blame me for losses caused by their own stupidity? There's no such thing as a small enemy. Man's justice is a nonsense. And as I can't test the Lord's justice until I die . . . until then, better a living dog than a dead lion.'

Tremors began, just above her knees. 'Whom are you supposed . . . to have killed?'

'Does it matter? You won't know him,' he said, suddenly ferocious. 'Why do you slow me with this interrogation! It's some tradesman I once had dealings with. And I don't know why I'm supposed to have killed him, because I didn't do it, do you see? The bailiff may be on his way here now. Do you want me to be taken now because of you? Let me get on!'

Her knees dropped her hard on to a joint stool. She watched him.

From cupboard to chest, to saddlebags. He picked up the papers he had set aside on the table and put them into a leather pouch on the bed.

He knelt beside his travelling chest, crammed in a pair of shoes.

Hard as she tried, she still could not craft an acceptable tale in her head to explain it all. She put that problem away as well and addressed the most urgent one. She stood up. 'I must come with you! I can be ready . . .'

He slammed the chest shut and looked directly at her across its arched lid. 'Rika, Rika. You must see that if you flee with me, you'll be held guilty too. Stay here and play the innocent, as you know so well how to do. Put them off my track. Use those smiles of yours. Maybe a few tears . . . why do I instruct a mistress of those skills? You're safer here than in the Spanish Netherlands, don't you see?'

'But why somewhere so dangerous? Why Bruges?' she asked again, numbly.

'Because, war or no, it's the most tedious city in the world, and therefore, no one will think to look for me there. In any case, this affair will die down in time . . . get sorted out. I shall come back, I swear. Meanwhile . . .' He rose and sifted through a heap on his bed. 'This will keep you until I can make arrangements . . . get word to you. Take heart. Be brave. I need you here to protect my back . . . keep our house safe for me while I'm gone. Here.'

He tossed her a leather purse. 'Hide it well.'

The purse fell, heavy, final and terrible into the hammock of her skirts.

'And now, lambkins, you must let me get on!' He began again to sort and pack.

She watched his spiky movements, with more questions trapped behind her pinched lips like nausea. He made a final rummage in his safe cupboard and closed its door. An impossible truth began to shape as she watched him.

'I'd rather risk danger than stay . . .' she began.

'And now . . . *voyons*.' He rushed past her out of the room. His footsteps pounded down the stairs.

She stood up from her stool, crossed to the leather pouch on the bed, slid her hand in amongst the papers inside and pulled a couple out from the rest. She flicked one half-open. It was written in Hebrew. Without the spectacles which Justus had given her, she could not read it easily. She took another folded paper from the pouch. But before she could look at it, she heard him on the stairs again. As she passed the table,

255

she snatched up a few more papers from the sliding piles on the Turkish table carpet, stuffed all the papers up under her stomacher and sat on the stool.

Surely he can hear my heart across the room! she thought. But he did not even look at her as he added a loaf and three flasks of beer to his saddlebags and strapped the bags closed. He buckled the leather pouch from the bed on to his belt, then turned back to the saddlebags.

'Take these down for me to the back gate. I'll leave by the garden, empty now at supper time.'

She stood up, scarlet with guilt, but he was past noticing. He, who had never before allowed her to carry even a shopping basket, now slung the heavy saddlebags over her shoulder.

Once down the stairs, she picked up her spectacles from the virginal lid.

Justus had recently had the centre of the brick-walled garden grubbed up and laid out in the current fad for horticultural mazes. In the centre, small green pegs of young box bushes stood in interlocking rows. Around the perimeter, blush-white roses arched out from girdles of grey sage and iron-green germander and dropped their petals on to the brick-paved walks. The warm evening air was spicy sweet with their exhalations. She was alone. A pair of shears and a pile of wilting weeds lay on the walk near the alley gate, but gardener and gardener's boy had gone.

She skirted the newly-planted centre with its infant maze, to a marble bench hidden from sight of the house in an alcove of dark green yew. There was still just light enough in the garden to read by. She had to smooth each document against her knee to hold it steady.

The first paper she pulled from under her stomacher was an unpaid bill for twelve loaves of West Indian sugar.

No help to me there, she thought, with a sinking disappointment. No cause there to flee the country! She set it aside and took up the second. One she knew that she had taken from his pouch.

256

In Spanish. But she understood the words for 'a licence' and 'silver'. And for 'The Spanish Netherlands'. She frowned at it for a moment, then set it aside. The third paper, heavy with a broken red wax seal, was the one from the pouch in Hebrew, which she, with her inappropriately masculine education, could read after a fashion. 'Pay to the bearer of this instrument . . .' Her eyes leaped to the figures of the sum specified.

Come back to this one later.

She glanced towards the house and snatched up another paper, also from the pouch and also in Hebrew. The next was in Dutch. Quickly read, it commended its bearer to the reader, had been signed by a member of the St George's Militia in Amsterdam, and was addressed to the Governor of a Dutch Caribbean island.

Her hands bucked and shook so that the paper nearly leaped from her lap.

She had known that he was lying. Not Bruges, after all. Silver trading and an introduction to a distant island governor.

The Caribbean.

He was leaving for good. Her brother was going to abandon her.

She lifted her head and stared past the shears and wilting weeds. This time, she could not build a structure of excuses and reasons that would stand.

A stripe of silver darted through an eye socket. A dark sea sucked at the boat.

She heard rapid footsteps. She folded all the papers and shoved them back up under the whalebone and canvas of her stomacher.

He wore his travelling cloak and was burdened like a pack horse.

'So, lambkins,' he said, avoiding her eye again. 'I'll send word as soon as it's safe.'

'You haven't eaten dinner,' she cried, in desperate unreason.

'The least of my concerns. Give me the bags, there's a sweetheart.' He added the saddlebags to his already awkward load.

257

She stood facing him. The moment felt impossible. Could not be taking place.

'So, lambkins,' he said again.

'Please, take me with you, Justus!' she begged. 'I won't mind a ragged life.' She could not imagine the Caribbean, but equally, she could not imagine Amsterdam without him.

'Don't be a goose.' He suddenly looked lost, as he did from time to time, when he didn't know she watched him.

'Please, Justus!' She flung her arms around his neck. 'Dear God! I can't bear it.'

'Let me go, lambkins,' his voice said into her hair. 'I can't bear this either! It's too painful for me. I must go!' Then he kissed her face, her forehead. 'You'd hate to be the cause if I were to hang.'

She released him and stepped back. 'Goodbye, then.' The girl who said it seemed far away.

'That's better. That's my republican princess.' He nodded. 'It will all sort out! I swear I'll come back for you. I'll send for you.' He flashed his teeth. 'If anyone asks after me, I've gone to London. Open the gate for me, there's a helpful little lamb. Keep the house safe for me while I'm gone!'

She watched him dwindle down the walled alley that ran behind the garden. When he turned the corner into the street without looking back, she closed the gate. She leaned her forehead against the heavy wood of the gate as she tried to fumble the bolts home. Her fingers failed. Her muscles lacked strength. She was as insubstantial as a skeleton leaf.

At last, when the gate was secured, she turned back towards the house, and found herself standing in the midst of the green pegs of the new box maze. Her bones were rods of ice, but a boiling of tears pressed against the backs of her eyes. If she let them flow, they would melt her away.

'Madam! Are you feeling ill?'

She hadn't heard Lore approach.

Her maid's face was anxious. 'I'm sent to call you to dinner.'

258

Had the girl seen him go, all burdened, by the back way?

While the maid watched her in silence, Marika turned and twisted, doubled and redoubled, around endless corners to get out of the maze. Numbly, she went into the house, sat at the long table and stared at her brother's pewter plate, his knife box, wine glass and empty chair. She put down her spoon still brimming with an untasted, unrecognised stew.

'You might as well clear his place,' she said to the serving maid.

After supper, she wandered about the house, unable to settle, waiting. She opened the lid of her virginal and fingered the keys. Then closed it again. She went into the garden and stared at the rear gate. She picked up two rose petals and dropped them again.

I'm waiting for men to come to arrest my brother, she thought. The idea seemed an unreal nonsense. But nothing else seemed real either.

He had not escaped them by long. The silver knocker thumped hard on the thick oak front door just as she came in from the garden this second time.

Each thud shook her like a physical blow.

'Lore! The door!'

She chose a seat facing the door, on the marble bench at the far end of the front hall, beside their great oak china cupboard.

The maid opened the door. Five men stood crowded on the *stoep*.

'Mevrouw Coymans? I'm Under-bailiff Rits. May I come in?'

Swimming underwater, she asked him to take one of the chairs beside the marble bench. The other four men followed him into the house. They bulked large, even in the space of the hall.

Keep smiling, keep moving, like seaweed, she told herself. Distract his eye so that he can't see to your heart. Speak so he won't have a chance to say what he has come to say. But her

259

tongue was dry and her mind hollow. She could not remember what Justus had asked her to say.

Rits leaned forward on the front of his chair, elbows on his spread knees, turning and turning a harmless-looking rolled document in his block-like hands.

'When will your brother return?' He nodded encouragingly.

She frowned in thought. 'In three weeks, I believe.'

Don't offer too much. Wait for the questions.

'Where did he go?'

'London.' The watchful, pale blue eyes studied her face. She tried to breathe in against the constricting band around her chest.

'His groom seems to think that he has gone for longer than three weeks.' He gave a terse smile, as if he had won a debating point. 'Does he often travel alone, without his manservant?'

'If you speak to my servants before you speak to me, mynheer, I see little point in this conversation.' The beginning of anger loosened her tongue. Careful, she warned herself. Just in time, she remembered to ask what he wanted with her brother.

Almost apologetically, he said, 'To arrest him for murder.'

She was ready for it. She blinked. Then frowned again. 'Forgive me, but you must be wrong.' She stood up.

Rits did not stand. 'Please sit down, mevrouw. There's no mistake. I have the warrant here, if you care to read it.'

'Give it to me!' She took it with shaking hands. 'Oh! I can't read it in this light. It's absurd. My brother? I don't believe you or your silly paper!' She thrust the paper back at him. 'Please leave his house at once! I won't listen . . .'

'Sit down, mevrouw!' No please this time. 'I must ask you to stay here on this bench while my men search the house.'

She ignored his order to sit. 'If I say he's not here, I expect to be believed! And didn't you just tell me that our servants confirm that he's gone? Here, not here! Which way will you have it?'

260

He too stood up at last, just avoiding real offence. I've done this before, his manner now said. I have the experience to smooth the way for us both, if you will only permit me. 'Oh, I'm quite certain that he's gone,' he said, 'but I must be satisfied absolutely, don't you see? Just think how foolish I'd look if it turned out that you and your servants all conspired to say he'd gone, when he was still hidden right here as we talked! And then escaped after we had left.'

'My brother is all bluster and show,' she said. 'Only a fool would take the show for the action. He wouldn't hurt anyone. Whoever signed that warrant is either simple or mad!'

'He took action enough when he stood to lose five million guilders.'

Silenced by disbelief, she stared back at the satisfaction in his pale blue eyes.

'I would have known . . . !' she began.

'I hope for your sake that you did not.' Rits cleared his throat. 'I'll see that my men disturb nothing.' He nodded past her shoulder. The four men sprang alive, as if he had lifted a spell.

Three pairs of heavy feet mounted the stairs. The fourth man crossed the hall into the parlour.

Rits watched her as they climbed. 'Do you fully understand, mevrouw, that if you lie to protect your brother, you share his guilt? Privately, between us, and I speak now as the father of a girl only a little younger than you, I advise you . . . lighten your soul and the legal penalty by telling me now all that you know.'

'I've already said all I know! But if I did know more, I wouldn't tell you now! I won't be threatened like this, about something so impossible!'

The pale, assessing eyes slid over the great, heavy, carved cupboard with its silver ewers and porcelain plates, the paintings, the banners, the gilded leather cushions on the bench, the striped Spanish matting on the floor.

'Come, come.' His civility slipped at last. 'The whole world knows what kind of house you two keep here. Your brother has

261

always sailed close to the wind but never tipped over before. Don't play innocent, mevrouw. I might believe this display of indignation from my own daughter, but from you . . . no, I think not.'

'Lore!' called Marika.

Wide-eyed and reluctant, the maid appeared from the kitchen.

'Please open the door for Mynheer Rits and his men.'

'Don't try to protect him at your own cost,' said the bailiff. 'I have men at the seafront and all the city gates. He won't escape by boat or by horse. I think he won't get off this time.'

Lore opened the door and fled towards her chamber. Marika stood beside the door. 'Go away, Under-bailiff Rits!'

She heard Lore's footsteps fade up the narrow stairs at the back of the hall.

'He'll pull you down with him.' Rits raised his head to listen to the progress of the search overhead, a dedicated man not unpleased with his work. 'I assure you, the *spinhuis* is not a pleasant place for young women used to a privileged life.'

She glared out of the door through the heavy dusk towards the glinting water of the canal. The shadow of a man leaned against a tree across the street from the house.

The bailiff watched her, turning the warrant in his hands. 'And there's another man at the back,' he said.

They waited.

As his men thudded back down the stairs, Marika saw the frightened faces of the cook and kitchen maid at the kitchen door.

'He's packed and gone all right, sir,' said one of the bailiff's men. 'Means to be gone for good, I'd say. Left his safe cupboard unlocked and nearly empty . . . ashes from papers burnt in the grate.'

'Ah,' said Rits. 'So, that's clear, at least. Well, mevrouw, I'm sorry you weren't more candid. No matter what lies you might claim that he told you . . . living here all the time, you should have been able to guess what my men spotted in a glance.'

His glance assessed the portrait of Coymans *père*. 'I'm afraid you'll see me again long before you see your brother.'

As he left, Marika heard the kitchen door close again.

'Lore!' she called. Her serving woman did not come back down. She went to the foot of the narrow stairs and called again. The girl still did not come. She flew up the stairs in the rage that she had not dared to unleash on the bailiff.

The maid was not in Marika's chamber, nor in the dressing room, nor any other room on the first floor. Marika climbed the dark narrow stairs to the attic rooms where the maid slept. As she reached the top of the stairs, she felt a scurry and sudden silence, as if a cat had scattered mice.

'Lore!'

She pushed open the door into the little room under the roof, next to the cubicle where peat for the fires was stored. In the faint light, she could see that the bed was neatly made. A stool stood on the rag mat. Otherwise, the room was empty. She knelt beside the wooden chest that was the only other furniture, felt inside and dropped the lid again. Empty. She stood very still for a long time, with her hair brushing one of the sloping beams. Then she went back downstairs to her own chamber.

Lore had lit the night candle in the pierced iron morter, and laid out Marika's nightgown before she had gone.

Marika took the candle in the morter and went down into the front parlour, where she sat silently at her virginal. From time to time, careful feet passed the door. In the rest of the house, doors opened and closed quietly. The servants were leaving.

At first, she thought that she should interfere, fill sandbags, try to plug cracks. But she felt the surge of a current too strong for her to fight.

She touched her finger to a single note.

Is my brother a murderer? What do I think? Privately, now that I don't have to defend him to anyone?

She hit the note again, harder.

Justus could be a scoundrel. Selfish, but no more than other

263

men were. And he hungered. She was closer to him than any other creature alive and thought that she understood his hunger.

Nothing was real to him, not even his life, or he could not be so careless of it. He had to be able to lay his eyes and hands on a thing before he could believe that it was real. Therefore, he needed to acquire. Whenever he felt a little lost, as even the worst and most successful scoundrels can do, he would follow his own tracks back through his life along the trail of his purchases.

More than once, she had watched him take a piece from the cupboard – a porcelain bowl, for example, a piece of the blue-and-white Chinese *kraacke-ware* he had bought with his legacy after their parents had died. As he caressed its milky porcelain surface, he seemed to reconfirm the solidity of his own flesh.

Here, he seemed to say, is proof that I existed seventeen years ago, for it was then that I bought this inarguably tangible cup.

He had mapped their lives with paintings, pewter cups, and silver chargers three feet across. A *tableau mort* of a gourd and dead hare marked the spring of the late freeze when they had skated together to Leiden. The Venetian mirror surrounded by glass roses arrived with her first monthly show. A double portrait of brother and sister nailed down in his memory her tenth birthday, when she had officially taken her place at the table and faced him down its length past the faces of his artists, his musicians, his gilder and carver, his investors. (For Justus likewise believed most in the reality of his fellow men when he could buy either them or their work.)

Would that supposed five million guilders have made him hope to buy immortality?

She looked from the window again. The watcher still leaned on the trunk of the canal-side tree. They had not taken him yet.

She would allow that he could be guilty of sharp practice.

264

But sharp practice does not make a murderer, she told herself. However, once you slide across the moral line, are you not like a skater on smooth ice?

She went to the kitchen. To her relief, the cook was still there, shaking out the washing cloths and hanging them to dry over chains and bars in the big fireplace.

'Seven guests invited tomorrow,' the cook said. Her tone made it a question. She did not comment on the bailiff's visit.

'I don't expect them,' said Marika tersely. The kitchen looked as it usually did. A copper pot steamed gently on a hook at the side of the fireplace. The small charcoal-burning stove, banked down for the night, leaked threads of smoke. The crockery and pewter plates reflected the cook's single candle. A brindled cat had tucked itself into a shadowy loaf shape on the window ledge.

The cook nodded. 'And Mynheer Coymans?'

'What do you think?'

The woman wiped her hands on her apron and untied it. They exchanged a steady look.

'Thank you,' said Marika.

The woman shrugged and ducked her head in embarrassment.

Marika said goodnight, and went back up the stairs to undress for the first time in her life without the help of her maid.

As she raised her arm to lift her collar away from her neck, one of her bracelets caught in her hair at the side of her head where she could not see it. She tugged, tried to release herself with her other hand. The knot pulled tighter. Tears started into her eyes. She stood for a moment, her arm welded to her head, fighting an overwhelming panic and the urge to get free by any means. To tear herself free by brute force, yanking the hair out by the roots. She suddenly wanted to sob like a desperate infant. But she forced herself to untangle herself slowly, hair by hair, until her arms and neck ached.

★   ★   ★

It took her most of the next morning to reconstruct herself, in one of her best gowns and her diamond eardrops.

A watcher still stood beneath the tree.

He got away! she thought with exultation. He made it past all the men of Mynheer Under-bailiff Rits! She nursed the exultation to hold other feelings at bay.

By mid-morning, she had received two notes of polite regret for the evening meal.

As the sun reached its midday peak, no guests came, not even the limner Saski, the artist who served Justus as the recorder of his life, dined with them nearly every day and had been in love with her for years.

At noon, she finally sat down alone, defiantly, at her place at the end of the long table, and rang the bell.

After a pause, the cook herself appeared with a tureen. 'I'm sorry, mevrouw, the serving maid had to go visit her mother. I'm all that's here to serve.'

Marika nodded. She picked up her spoon and stared at her plate. She had not yet begun to toy with the vegetable stew when the silver knocker began to thud against the front door again.

They've caught him after all.

She went herself to open it.

266

21

'I have a warrant to enter this house and confiscate the possessions of Justus Coymans, to be held by the City Council of Amsterdam, against fines to be levied against him on his failure to present himself to answer to a charge of murder.'

They hadn't caught Justus after all!

The under-bailiff had brought eight of his men this time, and five horse carts which waited in the street. Four *shutters* with muskets guarded the carts.

Shocked, she tried to close the door. It struck an ox-like shoulder.

'Don't obstruct us, mevrouw. Your own arrest could be quickly arranged.' Rits stepped past her into the hall. 'Greed and vanity. There's a moral here for any who will look.' He signalled his men to begin. Two of them stepped to either side of her father's portrait.

Coymans *père* gave a little start, then toppled forward from the wall. He was carried out of the house which he had built and propped against the side of one of the carts. The other men washed through the hall like a tide.

'Keep the house safe for me,' Justus had said. Did he guess what would happen?

Dazed, Marika watched the tide suck out the walnut pot stand and the rest of the pictures. One man brought a ladder and climbed up to unhook the polished latten chandelier. The dining table and the silk-upholstered chairs floated past her, on to the carts. A rolled-up carpet bobbed past her head. Followed by silver candlesticks, the globe, ebony knife-boxes, the silver birdcage, and Justus's pierced latten footwarmer. Then the plates, painted jars, silver jugs and baptism gifts from the heavy carved oak china cupboard in the hall. Then the cupboard itself.

'Those are my books,' she said to a man bent under an Indian chest covered in copper.

He kept going as if she hadn't spoken.

'Leave them, I said! They belong to me, not to my brother.'

He swung the chest on to a cart.

After a moment of paralysed astonishment, she looked around for the bailiff. He was not in sight. She ran up the stairs.

I should have done this before!

On the landing, she lifted her mother's picture from the wall and took it to her own chamber, where she hid it in the bed, under the coverlet. She grabbed her small Venetian looking glass, her coffer of oils and unguents, all the books she had in her chamber – her mother's velvet-covered Bible, a bestiary, two classical histories, Ovid's *Metamorphoses*, the copy of Aretino which Justus had given her for her eighteenth birthday – and thrust them all likewise under the covers of her bed. Unlike Justus's gilded wood-framed bed, it was a vast cupboard built into the wall and could not be moved.

Then she unlocked her wall cupboard and, trembling as if from cold, put on every piece of jewellery she owned – necklaces, ropes of pearls, two gold rings, bracelets. She hid the papers she had stolen from her brother back under her stomacher. After a moment, she threw open an Indian dressing chest and pulled out her fur-lined cloak and wrapped it around herself. Then she put everything else in her cupboard – an ivory fan, an armful of linens – under the covers of her bed and closed the curtains. As an afterthought, she threw in her pierced latten footwarmer as well.

Two of the bailiff's men came into her chamber and lifted her dressing chest between them.

268

'Those are my clothes!'

The bailiff appeared on the landing. 'Your brother bought them.' He waved for his men to carry on.

She stood in front of her bed, white-faced, while her room was stripped of its furniture. But the men did not try to move her aside.

When they had left her room, she went back out on to the landing. Justus's dressing chest and another rolled carpet were just turning the corner of the stairs. The chair of her virginal was being carried through the hall below her.

'No!' With a shout of fury, she ran down the stairs. 'Justus did not buy that! It's mine, from my mother! You don't have a warrant for my possessions!' She wrested the chair from his hands. Turning back towards the parlour, she met the virginal, already swimming out. 'And leave that! The whole street knows that it was a gift to me from my mother.'

They carried the virginal into the hall. Now beside herself with disbelief and rage, Marika ran out on to the *stoep*. 'Mevrouw van Ryn!' she shouted to a woman passing in the street who stared at the carts. 'Is the virginal mine?'

'Mevrouw, please!' said the bailiff to Marika. 'This is not the . . .' He tried to pull her back into the house, but she clung to the iron railing.

'Don't touch me!' she screamed.

The woman rushed on, head down.

'Please,' said Rits. He looked unhappily at Mevrouw Cats, who leaned on the railing of her own *stoep*, agog at the excitement. He took his hand from Marika's arm.

'Mevrouw Cats!' shouted Marika. 'Tell him. Is the virginal mine?'

Before the startled woman could reply, Rits said to his men, 'Put it down! There, mevrouw, it's done! Calm yourself. I shall ask the magistrates for a decision . . .'

'Put it back where it belongs!' said Marika. She followed them, still breathing hard as they carried it back into the parlour. Then she stood with her clenched fists pressed on to the closed lid of the keyboard while they finished stripping the house.

The bailiff made a final tour to see that nothing of value had been missed. Satisfied, he returned to the parlour, where Marika still stood guard over her instrument. 'That's it. So, goodnight, then, mevrouw. You may stay in the house until the court decides what to do with it.'

'Stay in the house?'

'I believe that the house belongs to your brother.'

'They would take the house and throw me out?'

'If your brother doesn't return to stand trial.'

'What am I to do after that?'

'There are the alms houses, as you've lived here in the city for more than two years. But I'm sure your brother has something better up his sleeve.' He left.

She stood for some time leaning on the closed lid of the virginal. The house darkened as night fell, but no one brought a light from the kitchen. She opened the lid, sat down at the lower half of its double keyboard and began to play. The thin, watery notes rattled off bare walls no longer softened by curtains and hangings.

I didn't do very well at protecting the house for you, Justus.

She went to stand on the staircase and listen. Absolute silence, except for the great staircase itself which still creaked and muttered. No live creature moved in the house, not even the cook. Marika was alone.

She returned to the virginal and felt for the keys in the thickening dark. But then her fingers stiffened. The silence in the house was the held breath between lightning and thunderclap. Suddenly she couldn't breathe, for terror. Like a child, refusing to look into the dark because she knew it held something terrible, she left the chair, stumbled up the dark stairs and felt her way along the landing to her own chamber door.

In her chamber, she moved carefully, wary of furniture that

270

was no longer there. The map in her mind had turned false. She walked through what should have been a table. When her hand passed through what should have been a solid walnut chest, she suddenly questioned even where the walls might be, or whether the floor might not suddenly disappear from beneath her feet.

Keep the lid on. Keep it on tight.

Unspeakable chaos and terror lay in that box.

Head down, fists clenched, she headed for where she prayed for her bed to be.

When she found it, she felt among the soft dark hummocks of mattress, coverlet, blankets and pillows. Her hands touched her mother's picture. With no candle, and no fire in the fireplace, she could not see the rest. She climbed into the bed, dress, cloak and all, pulled the covers over her head and hugged her knees to her chest. Even then, she was still cold.

22

Marika woke from a dream of panic and imprisonment. Her body was stiff, and tangled in muslin, silk and fur. A pearl necklace pulled at her throat. A corner of her mother's portrait had lodged in her ribs. She twisted and tugged, fought clear, sat up in disbelief.

Her brother had fled. Bailiffs had stripped the house. The house itself might be taken away and she would be thrown on to the streets. Justus would come back for her and find everything gone, even her.

The night watch called five o'clock. Then the New Church bells agreed, followed by the Old Church, and then all the others. For a moment, the air was solid with sound. Then there was silence again.

It was growing light, thank the Lord. And was even lighter because she had forgotten to close the shutters. In the pale grey haze, she saw that the bailiff had left behind the pierced iron morter, still holding the candle stub her maid had left. It stood in one corner of the gaping fireplace which was now stripped of the intricate, brass-topped firedogs.

A candle.

I must find light before tonight. She could not face that thick, potent darkness again alone.

She lay down and listened to her heart thudding and to the linen of her bodice rasping faintly against the sheet in time with her pulse. She tried to imagine the coming day, but couldn't. It was too unlike anything in her life before. She closed her eyes.

At least, no one was going to come in and tell her to get up because it was a splendid day and he wanted her company for this or that. And no one would be waiting in the kitchen with her breakfast, impatient to get on with cooking dinner. No one would expect her smiles and flattering attention at supper. And, as her stomach was heavy with a slight, metallic nausea, she need not even go in search of food. She could stay in bed forever, if she chose.

She sat up again, unlaced her stomacher, and crawled out of her gown, which had twisted around her. Then she hid again in sleep.

She slept all that day and all of the next night.

She woke this time to the eight o'clock school bell and a wash of sardonic sunlight in the emptied room. Now she could see the ghostly rectangles of pictures on the panelled walls, and the darker sites of furniture on the wooden floor. Below her windows, day was fully launched. A woman called to a child in the little alley that ran behind their garden, by which Justus had left. Fat, rhythmic thwacks announced the nearby punishment of a pillow or feather bed. Dogs barked. A late cockerel did belated duty. Vendors called in the street at the front of the house, and boatmen shouted warnings on the canal.

She was thirsty and needed to relieve herself. But she lacked the strength or will to get out of bed. And her French porcelain chamber pot was gone.

Someone knocked on the front door.

No maid to answer it now. And I shall never answer the door again.

Go away.

She burrowed deeper.

Again. Not the heavy pounding of the bailiff's fist. Almost timid, like a child. But it was also determined.

Whoever it was knocked yet again.

273

I can't imagine what could happen now.

And again.

And I don't care.

When the knocking was repeated for the fourth time, Marika threw back the covers, shook out her creased petticoat, wrapped herself in the cloak and went down the stairs.

'Mevrouw Cats!' Her prying neighbour, who had watched the loading of the carts.

The woman clutched the sides of her plain white linen apron and ducked her linen-capped head in response to Marika's startled greeting. 'I won't impose . . . won't come in . . .' She glanced in horrified curiosity past Marika's shoulder into the stripped hall. 'Just a quick word . . .' She looked away, into the street, then back with what was almost apology. 'I feel that someone should. For your sake.'

'I applaud your courage in coming at all.' How tongues must have wagged on the street as the carts rolled away!

'Please believe me that I don't hold you responsible for what your brother did . . .'

'. . . what he is *accused* of doing.' And how do you know?

'I only wish to help.' Mevrouw Cats now eyed Marika's cloak, rumpled petticoat and bare feet with an air of confirming something she already knew.

'I'm sure that you do.'

'The steps,' said Mevrouw Cats.

'The steps?' Marika blinked in confusion.

'By good fortune, your maidservant had already scrubbed them, and your share of the street on the morning before . . .'

'The last good fortune of that day.'

'What I am trying to say, is that yesterday and today . . .' The woman gripped more tightly on to the edges of her apron. '. . . no one has washed either the steps or the street in front of your house.'

Marika laughed in disbelief. The shaking of her chest and belly felt too good to stop, so she laughed a little longer.

Mevrouw Cats backed away. 'We all, on the street, understand that you have difficulties – don't think we're unsympathetic. But you are still bound by your responsibilities. Difficulties are never an excuse for not playing your part in the wellbeing of the whole, are they? Imagine what might happen if we all begged off with that excuse!'

'I don't imagine you're ever likely to need to,' said Marika. 'Not in quite the same way.'

Mevrouw Cats ploughed on, eyes down but stubborn. 'I, for one, would never be too proud to get on to my knees and scrub. The posture is dignified by being the same as that for prayer.'

'Which I'm certain that you also do with more grace than I.' With effort, Marika preserved a pleasant tone.

Surprisingly, Mevrouw Cats did not bristle. 'I mean you well, mevrouw. Not everyone does, to be honest, but I blame him.'

Shine! Marika ordered herself. For God's sake, bite your tongue and shine! You need friends, not more enemies. 'It's all a misunderstanding,' she said. 'So please don't talk of blame. But I'm grateful for your good intent.'

The woman nodded, relieved of her burden. 'Good day, then.'

Marika stood for a moment in the entrance hall, flushed out of hiding but unsure where to go now. Sunlight fell in squares on the bare tiled floor and bent against the panelled wall. After a moment, she left the hall and went into the empty dining chamber. She looked up at the smoke-stained beams. Then down again, at the creamy shards of a broken clay pipe which salted one of the black tiles.

Her brother's little province was utterly gone. How confused and lost he would look now that all proofs of his past life had vanished with a mere knock on the door and a bailiff's cart. She began to pace out the length of the vanished table.

275

23

That first look at me on my doorstep wasn't enough! thought Marika when Mevrouw Cats had fled from outside the dining-chamber window. So she came back for a second gander! To see if I were truly gone mad, or distracted or half-dead from shame. And, fool that I am, I gave her more fuel for her gossip.

I should not have shouted at her like that. It will prove a mistake.

She wanted to go back up to her bed and pull the blankets over her head again. But her mouth was now unbearably dry and her bladder ached. She went back into the hall, past the staircase, into the empty kitchen to find water.

Nothing worth either selling or taking had been left. The old iron firedogs still lay in the fireplace, covered in cold ash, but the pot chains in the fireplace dangled slack and empty. All brass and copper pots were gone. Both the peat fire in the fireplace and the small clay charcoal-burning cookstove had gone out. A clay dish for the coals used to light pipes and candles sat in the fireplace, filled with dead charcoal. The cook's rough bed still stood in one corner, but the wool blankets were gone.

On the window ledge, she found two bruised apples. Beside them lay the cook's key to the store cupboard, as clear as a written message. A matching key hung on a chain at her own waist, but only as a formality. The cook had had her money direct from Justus and had controlled supplies without interference from Marika.

276

The copper water cistern was nearly empty. She opened the tap and caught the water in her hand. Then, eating one of the apples, she looked around, dizzied by the vacant spaces she now occupied.

After a moment, she unlocked the treasury cupboard. The silver spoons and pewter plates were gone, as was the Brussels lace tablecloth, but the cook had left a loaf of bread, a knuckle of smoked pork and half a Gouda cheese, as well as the pots and jars of spices and salt. Marika felt unreasonably grateful and cheered.

I won't starve if I don't go out for a day or two.

In the larder, she found an ancient iron pot once used to carry burning charcoal and squatted over it to relieve her aching bladder.

Now as weary as if she had skated from Amsterdam to Leiden, she went back upstairs to her room.

I must light a candle before dark tonight, she thought. But after she had rehung her mother's portrait and laid out her remaining possessions, she had to sleep again. When she woke, the thick, suffocating darkness already filled the house. She could not make herself go out in search of a flint and steel. She lay for a very long time staring at the dark ceiling of her bed. Then she slept again and did not let herself wake until dawn brought renewed safety.

That morning, she suddenly felt brisk. Ready to begin.

She went first to the kitchen for water and to use the iron pot, then walked through the empty rooms taking stock as she had on the first day, but this time she was no longer numb.

I must make a plan, she thought. How to eat. And what to do if the bailiff does come back to take the house. I must find someone to advise me on the law.

Farther than that resolve she could not yet go.

Still taking inventory, she opened the back door from the kitchen into the little red-tiled yard behind the house, tucked into one corner of the irregular rectangle taken up by the formal walled garden. A wooden stool, a fallen broom. A few stacked

277

blocks of peat for the fireplaces. An overturned, woven-willow chicken coop. A pair of her stockings twitching on the drying line. As they were still damp with dew, she left them. She now had one pair, where she had once had forty.

A hen perched out of reach on the roof of the shed.

She eyed it with slight alarm – food when the need arose. If ever she felt hungry again, the hen could become a stew with turnips and dumplings. At the moment, however, the act of achieving this seemed as treacherous and as unlikely as a voyage to the East Indies.

Passing back through the front hall, she heard children's voices in the street outside their door, chanting: 'An ape's an ape and a varlet's a varlet, though he be clad in silk and in scarlet.'

She quickly climbed the stairs to the room she had thus far avoided.

His bed, not fixed in a cupboard like hers, had been dismantled and roped like cords of firewood, the curtains taken down from the tall windows. Even his pewter chamber pot had been taken. A few pieces of discarded clothing lay tossed on the floor. On the way to his cupboard, she picked up a torn shirt and held it to her face. For a moment, he was there again, smelling of tobacco, civet and male sweat.

Holding his shirt to her chest, she crossed to a window. The children below still chanted. When they saw her, they laughed and ran away. She stood for a moment as her brother used to do, looking along the canal that ran to the left of the house, into a wider basin, then on to the sea. From this spy place, Justus would shout out who had just sailed up from St Anthony's Gate and into which side channels they turned.

Must not lose my new brisk sense of purpose, she thought. A far more comfortable state than desolation.

Inside his safe cupboard, which hung open as the bailiff's man had said, she found a half-empty flask of *ginèvre*, an empty jar that smelt of camphor, and two unpaid bills. Under these lay a pair of old gloves stiffened by salt water into the shape of his hands. She pushed the gloves aside hastily and took out what lay under them – his tinderbox. A plain, base metal one, not worth the bailiff's taking.

She sipped the gin. Mistake. She was six years old again and making a face at the spicy heat. Justus laughed as he still held out his glass for her to taste.

She blinked and took a deep steadying breath. Then another defiant sip.

If she were to avoid all the small acts of life that she had ever performed with her brother, she would have to turn statue and freeze into stone.

With the tinderbox and flask of *ginèvre*, she went into her own chamber, took the morter and candlestub from the fireplace and sank to the floor in a puddle of cloak and petticoat to make herself some light.

Suddenly, she rose again and dug among the rumpled mountains of her bed. She had forgotten until now about the stolen papers, and his purse.

First, the purse. She put on her spectacles and counted the contents. One thousand florins.

Enough to live for several months, if she were most frugal. And had a house to live in. But not enough to make a new life from nothing.

She rubbed her nose thoughtfully. Either he did mean to return for her, or this purse was a feeble gesture, a further betrayal.

She sighed and sipped more of the gin. Then she reread the papers she had hastily read in the garden. She had not mistaken them, even in her panic. A letter of introduction to the governor of a Caribbean island. A licence to trade in silver, which one heard that men picked up like casual stones from the open ground in the Americas.

The two letters in Hebrew, which she had taken from his leather pouch, were already shedding dry red crumbs of hardened sealing wax. She spread them on the floor.

279

They were financial instruments of the kind she had seen notaries witness often enough in Justus's private parlour. Addressed to a Jacov Perez in London.

'Dear Jacov Perez . . . Pay to the bearer of this letter . . .' The other was the same.

Now she read and reread the figures in both. Together, they were worth eight thousand English livres. Enough to buy two estates.

And there had been more papers like these in the pouch. Justus might mean to return, but it seemed that he had taken his fortune with him.

So, brother. We must stick together, eh?

With approval, she noted her own chilly self-control.

She crumpled the bill for the twelve sugar loaves and threw it into the empty fireplace. Tinder to start her first fire. Let him come back and ask her for it! Then she crumpled one of the letters to Jacov Perez and threw it after the bill.

Listlessly, she picked up the tinderbox. As she did, her eye fell on the second letter to Jacov Perez, which still lay on the floor.

'Pay to the bearer . . .'

I'm slow, she thought. Unforgivably slow. Why didn't I see it?

She crawled over to the fireplace and retrieved the letter she had crumpled and thrown.

'To the bearer . . .' it said, like the first.

If I have these now, not Justus, then surely *I* am the bearer, not he.

She read both letters again, searching carefully for her brother's name. But again found only 'the bearer'.

Even better, Jacov Perez in London was safely distant from news in Amsterdam. Even the present truce between the two countries did not mean that he would be likely to know about a Dutch bailiff's writs.

Why was I so slow to see it? I believe I can use these as well as Justus! If only I can work out how. Together with Justus's purse . . . And if I sell my jewels . . . I can go to London and find Perez . . .

She could eat. She could clothe herself. Pay for a new roof over her head. Ransom this one. Pay fines. If she decided to do so, she could even go to seek her brother, the Carib silver-trader.

If I can just keep my wits about me.

She smoothed the crumpled letter again, then turned it over to read what she now saw was written on the back.

'Oh,' she moaned. 'Oh, oh, oh!'

Her wits could take no more surprises. She wrapped her arms around her knees and began to rock back and forth, coiled into a tight hard ball, forehead pressed to her knees, jaw clenched, eyes squeezed tightly shut against tears.

On the back of the letter was written: 'To M. John Nightingale.'

24

Justus had called her to his parlour after supper one night to meet a late arrival, and had jovially ordered her to practise her English in charming this new, foreign investor in his schemes. The Englishman had been taller even than she by half a head, handsome enough, with curly acorn-coloured hair and a trim beard.

After Justus had left them alone in the parlour, she had studied his face, its skin darkened by the sun and with a nose once broken but healed straight. No spare flesh on him, that she could judge. Then she saw that his hands were rough, like a peasant's, even though he wore silks and fine linen.

He had looked her in the eye and refused to be charmed.

In vain, she trotted out her repertoire of sallies which usually met with such success among her brother's other marks. Finally, in sudden irritation, she asked, 'Am I tedious?'

'On the contrary,' he replied. 'You fascinate me in the true sense of the word. I fear those charms which your brother so kindly requested for me.'

'It's all in fun!' she protested. 'Don't you English ever permit fun?'

'Only on Saturdays.'

She had stared at him, furious that her civil use of his native tongue gave him the advantage.

★　　★　　★

282

'What did you make of him, lambkins?' Justus asked later as they climbed up to bed.

'His hands,' she said, 'are not those of a gentleman.'

'I agree. But he comes with glowing references from a man I know to be well-placed and well-respected.'

'And conversing with him is like walking with a stone in your shoe.'

'Well, he's no fool. And he carries a heavy purse and speaks for an entire London trading company, wants me to guide his investments. Without risk. I ask you!' He paused on the landing and leaned to kiss her goodnight. 'How could any man resist you if you set your mind on him? Consider him a challenge, as I do. He's far too sharp at dealing. I need him fuddled. Cross-eyed with conflicting desires and distractions. Do your best.'

'When haven't I done my best for you?' she asked, with an edge to her voice.

'Ptsh, settle your fur. I rely on you, completely, as you very well know. I've asked him to dine tomorrow night. Try to swallow your dislike. You'll have your hands full in any case. I've also asked old Captain Pietersen who's begun to beg me again to let him marry you, now that his last wife has died.' He paused in his doorway. 'Sea captains make perfect husbands . . . away for at least two years at a time. Should we consider him?'

'I'm surprised you don't want to marry me to this wretched Englishman with his glowing references and heavy purse.'

'He's a mere agent – the money's not his own. In any case, you'd never stomach London after Amsterdam. Sweet dreams.'

The following evening, John Nightingale smiled at the other company, raised his glass often and amiably enough, exchanged jests. But he avoided Marika's eye.

He dislikes only me, she thought furiously, then looked to see if her brother had noticed her failure.

Justus raised a hand for quiet. 'I've a bone to pick with our foreign visitor.'

283

His guests fell silent in pleased anticipation.

'Well, Nightingale!' Justus glared down the length of the table. 'Not many men have turned one of my own jests against me!'

Marika gazed at the Englishman with arched brows. He tilted his head slightly in question, waiting quietly for Justus to continue.

His neck is far browner than a gentleman's should be, thought Marika crossly. No matter how fine his references may be.

'Yesterday evening, this man arrived here during supper with a letter of introduction,' Justus explained to those guests who had missed the fun. 'Just for devilment, I drew my pistol and held him at gunpoint. "Don't move a muscle!" I cried . . . you all know my little ways . . . how I like my jests. And there Nightingale stood, at bay, in fear for his life, while Saski drew his portrait – wild eyes, slack jaw and all.' He pointed at the young man who now sat sketching with a stylus of twine-bound antimony and paper, midway down the table. 'Then I showed him the drawing, which was the point of the whole matter. He saw that he wasn't going to die, after all, and recovered his composure!'

While his guests laughed appreciatively, Justus waved over his shoulder for the serving maid to pour more wine all round.

'Never mind, Englishman,' shouted one guest. 'We've all been his victim in our turn.'

'But that's not the end . . . do you know what that English bastard did next?' Justus's hair and moustaches flared with delight. 'He snatched my own gun and turned it on me. Demanded my purse! Well! I admit, for a few eye-blinks, at least, I nearly pissed myself! He held me there while Saski drew a most unflattering portrait of my alarm.'

Justus raised his glass to Nightingale. 'Here's to a worthy playmate, my friend! With the balls of a Spanish bull! These other fellows here are grown tame and tedious.'

The tame and tedious fellows laughed, applauded and drank the Englishman's health until he could have lived forever. Saski laid on the table his new drawing of Justus.

'Look how this sly, peeping villain has trapped me now!' Justus held the drawing up. There he was, caught in a few quick lines, the curling, untidy hair and moustaches, hands in the air shaping his tale, the eyes bright with amusement and calculation.

Marika studied the Englishman while he sat calm and still, but smiling, in the midst of the noisy goodwill.

She had to admit that he had a good truthful smile which promised no more than he would give. She watched him watch the other men at the table, her brother most of all. Standing outside, looking in, she thought. Judging us. For a moment, she saw the familiar roistering through his assessing eyes. Saw men at the table as strangers, Justus included.

Her brother was laughing too loudly, his mouth bright with grease, a veiled cruelty in his jesting. She saw how large his bones were, like an ox. And how his hand engulfed the *roemer* of wine, the reddened skin of his knuckles looking even redder against the misty green of the glass.

In comparison, John Nightingale was as fine and neat as a cat.

She felt irritated again, and uncomfortable with a desire to explain and excuse.

He and my brother are shore and sea. Justus is the restless, tumbling force of the waves, the Englishman is the still rock or a dyke wall, against which the waves break and pull back.

But dykes break. Waves find the tiny crack and pound until it becomes a breach. Waves always win.

At that moment, Nightingale turned to look directly at her, with the same assessing curiosity in his grey eyes which he had turned on all the others, without the sardonic challenge of his earlier glances. Gazing back, she mislaid all her easy quips and soothing flatteries. She suddenly realised that she did not hate

285

him at all. She wanted to be safe inside the calm that he kept gathered around him.

I'm about to do something very foolish.

'Be careful,' she said.

He gave her a quick smile of acknowledgement. 'I thought as much.' He continued to study her thoughtfully. 'Thank you.'

Not 'Of what?' or 'Why?'

She did not smile back.

What dangers did I mean? Then she thought, I have just been a traitor to Justus!

She dropped her eyes at last, her pulse loud in her ears. She had stood outside Justus's world before. But she had never been caught at it, except by Saski, who only recorded and never judged. For certain, she had never shared that vantage point with anyone. She could not think what to say next, after such a momentous exchange. She stroked her monkey, curled in her lap, to cover her lack of words.

She tested the exhilaration of treachery. Yes, my brother sometimes sails close to the wind. And I have just made an alliance with a good man who could become his enemy.

What I say actually matters to him, she thought. He heard all of what I meant, not just the words. My usual sallies are too shallow for him – that's why he was so short with me last night and in the parlour before supper.

And now it's too late. His opinion of me is formed. He sees me as my brother's frivolous, shallow, venal sister, and I'm in despair at how to change his view.

The monkey squeaked in protest, twisted from under her tightened hand and leaped down the table in great arcs. Marika eyed Nightingale's head, the line of his throat as he watched the animal's progress, saw the limner Saski sweep the lines of her own head and neck with his detached eye while his hand moved across his paper. She looked away hastily, astonished at her confusion. Her eyes fell to the top curve of Nightingale's left thigh, which lay close to hers at the corner of the table

286

– a long, lean line between the rising curve to his waist and the knee which was invisible beneath the table. She drew in her breath.

Her worldly airs and easy practice, which so outraged the mevrouws, in reality stopped far short of their imaginings. Only Ned had got past her armour of smiles.

Saski passed down the table a picture of Marika watching the Englishman. She looked at it and flushed. Saski had read and exposed her thoughts for all to see. In annoyance, she turned the drawing face-down on the tablecloth beside her plate.

She took a careful sip of wine while she tried to pretend that she had not had these thoughts. Please God, don't let Nightingale look at me now! He will read me just as clearly as Saski did.

The monkey returned down the table in flying leaps between wine glasses, plates, crusts of bread, dirty napkins. It stopped in front of the Englishman and chattered its teeth.

'An animal oracle!' cried Justus. 'Nightingale, you are the fortunate Elect!'

The monkey began to tug at the points that tied Nightingale's sleeves to his doublet. The men around the table laughed and whistled. One murmured to Justus.

'Yes, quite right!' Justus raised his voice to reach the Englishman. 'The little beast is getting you ready for my sister.'

Marika stood up. The silence of her wake was broken as she left the dining chamber, by Justus's voice and a crash of male laughter. When she reached the haven of the parlour, Justus was behind her.

'What's wrong with you? It was all in fun, you know that. Come back, lambkins. The evening's not over yet.'

When she still stood, with her fists clenched on the closed lid of the virginal, he pulled at her arm. 'Don't be a fool. You know how I like a jest. Never worried you before! If you sulk any longer, *I* shall begin to look a fool. Come.'

287

He turned back towards the dining chamber. 'I order you to come back.'

If she had not already betrayed her brother, she might still have resisted him.

She tried to give her attention to the after-supper game of Angel-Beast. She leaned close to Nightingale under Justus's approving gaze. Bent to pick up a card for him. Laughed. Inhaled the warmth that rose from his neck and back. Once, unable to resist, she leaned a little on the headland of his shoulder. She felt his back stiffen and saw his hand falter on its way to a card. He spoke little during the game and, sometimes gaining, sometimes losing, finally lost forty *stuivers*.

He hates this game as much as I do, she thought. Why do I let Justus force either of us into it?

'I shall take Mynheer Nightingale into the parlour and sing him an English song to console him for his losses.'

'A song from you for only forty *stuivers*! What excellent value!' exclaimed a guest.

Justus signalled his approval as they made their escape.

'The rest of us are insanely jealous, mevrouw!' called one of the other guests after them. 'If I lose ten florins, how many Dutch songs will you sing for me?'

What do I think I am doing? she asked herself.

She faced him across three feet of tiled floor. 'Why does it make you so angry when I'm forward?'

'It's your reasons, madam, that make me angry.' He stood tensed, as if ready to flee from the parlour. His grey eyes looked darker here and glinted in the candlelight.

'And what do you imagine these reasons to be?'

His head was only a little higher than her own. 'I feel like a grub thrown on to a pond full of hungry fish.'

'And you think that I'm one of them?'

'Your brother is. And one of the hungriest.'

She looked away. She didn't want to agree. But at least they were speaking real words.

'Isn't the world merely a pond of such fish?' I must move

288

away, she thought. Sit. Go stand by the window. Anything but continue to face him here. She was suddenly hollow with longing.

He took a deep breath. 'I'm very sorry if you imagine that to be true.'

'And I'm sorry if you imagine I'm a fish!'

He gave a quick bark of a laugh. 'Nothing like, I assure you!' They continued to gaze at each other in the dim light.

'There are other seas,' he said. 'Safer ponds. All men are not like your brother.'

How beautiful he is, she thought. How did I not see it last night?

'Forgive my ill manners,' he said after a moment. 'I'm giddy with strange business in a strange land. I don't know your customs . . . A country man turned awkward emissary. If I've offended you . . .'

'No . . .' She shook her head.

The silence was unbearable. He was gathering himself to leave.

'Do you really not feel it?' she asked abruptly, amazed at her daring. Ill-advised, headlong, it was done.

He looked back at her sharply. Then he sighed, like a man who has set down a heavy burden. He raised his hands in submission, giving himself over at last. 'Of course I feel it. What else could have made me into such an awkward, ill-mannered clot?'

'And I thought I knew all those signs . . .'

They stood again without speaking.

I've gone as far as I can alone, she thought.

He reached and took her hand. He pulled her towards him, with a wary question still in his eyes. Then he put his hands on her bare shoulders on either side of her neck. The heat of his palms flowed down into her chest, each finger a separate bar of heat lying across her skin. The sensations set off by his touch distracted her from speech altogether. She sighed. She almost wished that he weren't there, so that she could concentrate on remembering.

289

'So, now what do we do?' he asked her. When she didn't answer, he kissed her lightly. A question.

She took a moment to think about the kiss. Then she said, 'My brother lets me choose my own sweetmeats.' Though she had never tested what he might do if she ate them.

'And if your brother and I fall out?'

'You'll kill me first with too much caution.'

'An English trait,' he said, in a last deflecting levity. 'Learned by necessity in my case . . . but that's another story.'

He kissed her again and pulled back to read whether the messages in her face and her lips agreed.

He's so beautiful, she thought again. And kind. Unlike any creature I've ever known. She leaned into the pull of his arms.

She was all courage now. This was love, at last. She had waited twenty years. She reached for the wonderful firm softness of his mouth. 'Heed the advice of your own English poets and take all that you can get.'

She still flushed with humiliation at the memory.

'Justus, don't fleece the Englishman!'

Tell a fish not to swim.

She waited until Justus went to Leiden for four days to seduce a possible investor in one of his schemes. Then she invited the Englishman to dine, knowing quite well that she intended more. She was certain that none of the servants would report them to the police or the Church Council – good domestic positions in the city were scarce. They soon gave up the pretence of eating, servants notwithstanding. She had led him up the creaking dogleg staircase, amazed at her own ease and daring.

The first sight of his naked body filled her with a pleasure so intense that it made her throat ache. Later, beside him in her cupboard bed, she lay in silent delight, looking at his long arm, bent above his head, the wrist resting on his forehead in sleep.

How that hand touched me.

She leaned forward and sniffed at the rich brew of odours on his fingers.

She lay for a while, his hip against her leg, drowsy, at peace, more warmed than she could remember.

If this makes me a harlot, I don't care. The Church Council can go ahead and summon me. It's not possible that such a feeling is wicked.

She raised herself back up on her elbow, delighted that he was now asleep so she could stare all she liked in wonder and disbelief. In the soft, wavering candlelight, her eyes traced the ridge of his nose and the lines of his mouth. She leaned closer, delighted by the glints of bristle which marched along the soft curve of his upper lip. Then she leaned even closer, to feel his slow, warm breath on her face.

She remembered his hunger and abandon with an intake of breath. Then she sank back again on her own pillow in despair. The curse of clear sight fell on her again. Her real danger was not of summons and fines. She had fallen in love with a stranger who made her see her brother with different, judging eyes, the one sort of man she should have avoided at all costs. A good man, who wouldn't care to swim for long with fish like Justus.

And he had not.

'Take me with you to England,' she had whispered one night.

'You know that I can't share your world either here or there,' he had said. 'I'm a poor man who could never give you the only life you know.' He would not look at her.

'You never meant to love me!' she had cried. 'You came to Amsterdam to taste excitement and now you'll go back to your safe, moral, proper life in England. Where you can be nostalgic and grateful for your escape at the same time!'

Her tears had misled Justus into throwing him out of the house.

'What have you done?' she had cried to Justus afterwards. 'What have you done to make him leave me?'

★　　★　　★

And what had Justus been doing with a paper that belonged to John?

Well! she thought. At least I now know a little better why John left me. And could not look me in the eye. How could he have loved the sister of a murderer and thief?

She looked at the backs of the other letters. The second in Hebrew was also addressed to John Nightingale. She laid those two on the floor and sat back on her heels.

I must wear my stomacher again. I dare not keep these anywhere else.

The bud of an idea began to swell in her mind. Justus's red leather purse surely held more than enough for the passage to London.

Steady, she told herself. She finished the gin.

She put the papers back under the covers of her bed. As she withdrew her hand, it paused on the mattress, where John's hips had once dented it. She snatched her hand away, sipped again at the flask, and picked up the tinderbox.

If the house is taken, where else can I go? Why not to England?

She could not see herself in an alms house lining up humbly for a piece of bread.

If I could go to London to see Perez, I could just as well go to return these to John.

She tried to think no further. But she still saw herself nearing his house. Felt her terror and then the overwhelming relief when he saw her and smiled, even before she returned his letters.

In spite of herself, her imagination leaped far beyond his gratitude, on to babies, herself in the English garden, John's wolfhound at her feet, their infant son on her lap playing with the keys that hung at her waist. Last night, she had thought she would never feel joy again. Now she felt as light as a bubble, filled with sunlit air.

In fact, at that moment, she was startled at how little she was missing her former life. After all, she argued to herself again, if I could go to see Perez, I could go for any other reason I choose.

You are a fool! she chided herself, without paying the least attention to her own warning. And you must wait here for Justus, in case he keeps his promise and comes back.

She went to her bed again and rummaged for the tinderbox. She must stop these galloping thoughts and make herself a fire before the evening grew dark.

She made a little nest of tow, as she had seen the servants do, then struck the steel against the roughened side of the box. A spark jumped and died.

My world is changed, insisted the wayward part of her mind. John might feel that he has more now to offer a fugitive's sister.

She struck with the steel again and watched another spark flare and die in the nest of tow.

A terrible weight of loneliness suddenly pressed down on her. She left her candle and went to the window in her brother's room.

Boats slipped in and out of the basin where the canal widened. Justus might have been on any one of them. She leaned on the sill, breathed in a tarry gust from the port. Then a waft of cinnamon. Then rotting oranges from a spoilt cargo.

Whatever else, I'll manage! she told herself defiantly. Once I get used to the change. People do manage. I'm fortunate. I'm young enough still and good enough looking. If John won't have me and I'm ever desperate enough for company, I could even marry Captain Pietersen.

Except that he'd never have her now. Too old for such an old husband, and spoilt goods.

In the street, a man still leaned on the tree near the canal, watching the house. She nodded pleasantly. You might as well go home, she thought. You'll catch no one by waiting there.

She went downstairs, checked the bar on the front door, went into the kitchen to see that the door to the yard was also locked and barred. Then she went into the parlour, to her

293

virginal with its double keyboard. Her single triumph over the bailiff's men.

She lifted the lid, dusted Artemis and the newly horned Actaeon with her petticoat, then laid her right hand on the keys and played a stretched fourth. Do . . . fa. That odd interval which is not part of the natural progression of harmony. It pulled at the senses. Set the teeth on edge and a quiver down the spine. The devil in music.

Justus was gone, and not just in body. Her brother had disappeared. In his place was a murderer and a thief. And in spite of his protestations, his gifts, his extravagant praise, her brother had not loved her well enough to take her with him. He had not loved her well enough to spare her lover from his rogueries.

She played the odd, unsettling interval again. No wonder troupes of players saved it for the entrance of the Devil or a moment of disaster.

She pulled up the chair.

Back into harmony!

She played a soothing octave. Bottom note, then the top one. Eng . . . land.

Tomorrow, now that I'm rich again, I shall go to the market.

She lifted her head sharply. She imagined that footsteps were crossing the floor upstairs.

Real footsteps. Not just the house talking to itself.

The hairs bristled on her scalp and arms.

She walked silently into the entrance hall and looked up the wooden dogleg staircase. The silence of the landing above felt occupied. She crept half-way up to the landing where the stairs turned back on themselves. The wooden treads creaked under her feet.

She began to believe that she had imagined the steps.

Then she heard them again.

'Who's there?' she called, then cursed her folly. Now the silent listener knew that she was afraid, and alone. She ran back

294

for the enamelled steel Saracen sword which hung on the staircase wall, then cursed again. It had been taken, of course.

'Justus? Is that you?' she whispered. Pursued, wounded, forced back to his burrow.

There was a scuffle and a bang – then the scrape of something large against the side of the house.

Don't be a fool. Run to the front door for help.

She marched fiercely up the stairs to seize the monster by the throat.

A shutter in her room hung open. She looked out into the yard, smelled a strange presence in the air, sweat, panic and dried blood.

With a thump of terror, she whispered, 'Justus? Is it you?'

Nothing moved in the courtyard, or the garden.

Not Justus.

She pulled the shutter tight and dropped the bar. The house seemed made of glass, its walls as fragile as ice.

Then she thought, perhaps it is still in the house and I have just locked it in with me.

EIGHT

25

The Spoon has come with his grey turnip broth. And a white bread roll. And a knuckle of ham.

Another miracle. More of Maurits's prestidigitation. A sign.

Though my unpractised stomach rebels, my soul swallows the ham knuckle, bone and all. It's no more than the twitch of an ear or the relaxing of tail, but that meat and bread, after so much gruel, feed hope even more than they feed the body.

He goes. I now lie on my other side.

I still can't sleep for the excess of hope, triggered by the ability to scratch, and a ham bone.

26

Maurits's carriage took them from the dock straight to the door of his Leiden town house. Four windows wide and five windows tall, twice the width of either neighbour, with high stone steps rising up from the street, and foundations sunk in the mud at least as far as China, the house confirmed the London gossip about Maurits's wealthy and well-placed family. It was an awesome structure, its heavy scrolled pilasters and lintels cross-shadowed by the late morning sun.

'My older brother built himself a new house outside the city wall,' Maurits offered. 'Where there's more room for gardens. I don't like servants moving things about and always prying, so we have the place to ourselves except for old Gerthe. You'll be as safe here as anywhere in the Low Countries.'

Only four boys, two dogs, a water-seller and a *wafflewife* saw Ned climb down from the carriage with his two lutes and box of tools, and mount the steps to the big front door. A very old woman answered Maurits's impatient knock.

Behind the front door, the walls of the entrance hall were covered with painted and gilded leather hangings. The Garden of Eden, somewhat cracked and yellowed, but still full of airy spaces and an infinite manner of creatures, from elephants to caterpillars.

A good omen of safe haven, thought Ned.

'Put down your chest and those lutes and come!' Maurits pulled Ned away from a wistful crocodile. 'Those are the anatomically incorrect fantasies of an Italianate dauber my father took into the house! The true images hang in my study.'

He opened a tall, heavy, panelled door which led into a high-ceilinged room at the back of the house. 'There, on that wall. Now, those hares are well observed!'

At first, Ned did not look where Maurits pointed. Instead, he gawped, dumbstruck, from just inside the door. He had expected a chaste, orderly, secular church for the worship of knowledge.

In Maurits's study, which had once been the chief reception chamber, the vast maze-like pattern of the black-and-white tiled floor had almost vanished beneath furniture, papers, stacked books, rumpled carpets, boxes, candlestands, and dropped clothing. Collapsing piles of papers on the two tables nearly hid the fine but faded Turkey table carpets. A fringed daybed struggled beneath heaped pillows still dented by use, and a tossed blanket. Standing here and there at random, four gold-fringed farthingale chairs covered in blue worsted, each burdened with books, papers or clothes, turned their backs on each other like people not speaking in a huff.

Madmen lived like this.

Ned looked upwards into the dusty haze which hung in the air.

A bulbous chandelier of dulled latten hung from the high, beamed ceiling. Its twelve curling tentacle arms held only one burnt-out candle stub among them. At night all light would have to come from the fire and the four, branched candlesticks, which had dripped wax on to the table carpets.

'There!' Maurits pointed again with suppressed irritation that Ned should be so slow. Then he flung his cloak on to the overburdened daybed and crossed to a large, old-fashioned cupboard with shelves above and closed doors below.

Ned's eyes leaped from clocks to shells to a baby's skull to a stuffed cat eyeing a stuffed mouse. To the skeleton of a cow

301

with horns, a fleshless fox, a sliding heap of drawings on a table. At last he found the hares.

The well-observed hares – a brace slung on a table beside a glowing orange squash – hung above a dentellated wooden frieze at the top of the walnut panelling, canted out from the wall. Ned picked his way closer and looked up. Painted true to life, indeed, hair by hair, even an ooze of blood from the nostril of one.

He turned back to the room, still dumb with amazement and fighting the urge to flee. The huge, carved wooden chimneypiece, painted red and blue and topped by a woollen Turkey-work pelmet, served as a shelf for a family of eggs, ranged in size from that of a man's head down to the diameter of Ned's little finger. On second look, a walking stick in front of them became a stuffed snake. An intricate structure of shelves on the far wall held glass jars which displayed behind their glints a collection of shapes which had once surely been alive or part of something living.

Ned stepped over a live tortoise to take a closer look at the jars, slipped and nearly fell on two books sliding from under one of the chairs. Smells of sulphur, vinegar, and charring mixed with the more domestic smokiness of the fire.

How could orderly observation possibly take place in this chaos?

At Ned's continuing silence, Maurits glanced up. 'The order is in my head,' he said. 'This room is like Life, on which Science strives to impose order.' He dropped a leather-covered folio on to the nearest table. 'On which matter, let me show you some of my own drawings of the liver. Take off your cloak if you mean to stay . . . Come sit here by the fire.' He began to haul one of the chairs across the tile maze. 'I can begin to observe you properly. Take off your cloak and sit.' He swept the chair's burden on to the floor.

Ned bristled. 'I may be a grateful refugee, but I haven't yet agreed to be examined.' Maurits, his benefactor, had

302

changed to Maurits the observer with a speed that made him uneasy.

'Please be good enough to sit. Your irritation with me is understandable. I don't mind in the least. It's merely terror at the prospect of self-knowledge.' Maurits crossed to a far wall and stooped down to riffle among some piled papers. Janni came in with a tray of bread, cheese and a bowl of plums. 'Food before work, Maurits.' She placed the tray on the other table, nearer the fire and a little less encumbered by paper. 'And don't forget that you begin a demonstration this afternoon. Ned will have to wait for your attention.'

Maurits cursed and left his papers to sit heavily at the table with the food. 'Ned and I can't wait! I must find his wolf for him.'

'This demonstration is the reason you came back from London,' said Janni patiently. 'Five physicians and the Praelector himself will be there. You fretted all the way home that the boat wouldn't get you here in time!'

The room made Ned restless. He took a plum and picked his way across the littered floor to look out from the tall, dirty window in the back wall. A garden as chaotic as the study. Maurits did not keep gardeners any more than maids. Unpruned fruit trees and billows of unclipped box sprawled over paths like thick, dark comforters. Here and there in the long grass stood wooden cages, inside which moved the shadows of large birds and other creatures.

Ned looked down at a movement in the grass just outside the window and met a cold yellow eye in a pink naked head with a pendulous sack of skin at the base of the beak. This bizarre head was attached to a black-and-white mottled bird the size of a large gander.

'Not a monster,' said Maurits, without looking up from the book he had taken from a lacquer chest. 'Merely unexamined or unexplained. So far. My Bird of the Indies, bought only last month. Such oddities are commonplace in the Americas, though mine is the first in Leiden.'

303

Is it possible that I am also 'merely unexamined and unexplained'? thought Ned. For that is what Maurits is saying. He raised his eyes. 'What's that roof beyond your walls?'

'The university library. A tomb for books.'

Books. Books had a bad smell in his family. Smelt of brimstone and ashes. Books again.

'What keeps you riveted like that?' asked Maurits. 'I find it a dull prospect. Nothing but green.'

'It's a new city to me,' said Ned evasively.

Books had power. No doubt of that. Enough to get a man burned at the stake, his family exiled, and their fortunes ruined.

'Know thyself,' Maurits had said in London.

A library at a university, an empire of reason. A final chance to act for himself and avoid the pull of Maurits's will. These would be very different books from the ones his grandfather had smuggled into England and died for. Openly displayed on the library shelves, not treasonable. And Holland was not England. Holland had no king or queen to fear books and make them dangerous. He need not be wary of these books.

And I must escape from this room!

'Can a stranger go into the library?' he asked.

'Whatever for?'

Ned shrugged. 'As you are needed elsewhere this afternoon, I could entertain myself there. Make some studies of my own.'

'In the library?' Maurits sounded astonished at such a novel idea.

'My education was flawed, to be sure, but I can at least read! Even a little Latin on a good day!'

'Read here instead. Rest from that appalling journey. Admire my menagerie. I can think of many better ways to entertain yourself.'

'Have some bread and cheese,' prompted Janni.

'You will be seen,' said Maurits.

'But not by anyone who knows me.' Maurits's resistance strengthened Ned's intent. 'I've never seen inside a library.'

'If you insist, I can lend you a scholar's robe. But you'll learn nothing of any use, I promise you!' Maurits sounded inexplicably enraged.

'Still, I would like to try,' said Ned stubbornly. Books had helped to destroy his family. Their power might now help him to put himself right.

27

Wearing one of Maurits's black robes, which was full and pleated like an old man's dressing gown, Ned stopped just inside the library door. So many books could not possibly have been written!

The long side walls were broken by tall, arched, church-like windows. Book presses stood ranked on either side of a central aisle like pews in a cathedral. Each press, higher than a man's head, held at least thirty or forty volumes, every one of them chained to its shelf. Below the books ran reading desks just high enough for leaning an elbow as one stood with a foot propped on the rail provided for this purpose.

Ned breathed in the inspiring exhalations of musty leather and damp paper. He walked quickly down the central aisle, reading the plaques on the presses: History, Mathematics, Theology, Philosophy, Jurisprudence, Medicine. Titles in Latin, Greek, Arabic, Hebrew, French, German, Italian, English and Dutch. On wine-coloured leather, brown leather, black leather. Hand lettered. Printed and tooled in gold. Books without titles. Some were even banded in iron to contain the power of the thoughts inside.

Surely here, in this grand, cathedral-like chamber, among all these volumes, somewhere, in print, in a crabbed hand, in fine engraving or rough sketch, must lurk every truth known to man.

He exhaled. My double nature is in here somewhere. I feel it.

An ecstatic calm filled him. This afternoon, I will find myself. I will not need Maurits van Egmond, nor a physician nor any other man. Not even a man who, like Maurits van Egmond, commands all that lies here and can afford to speak of the place with such disrespect, and must therefore be able to answer any question the Universe might hold.

Then, as he continued down the central aisle, the back of his neck prickled. A cur with a curly tail had followed him, its nails clicking on the wide wooden floorboards behind him.

Can it smell the hidden wolf on me?

It stalked away stiff-legged, towards a spaniel curled at the feet of a scholar who hunched frowning over a volume of Theology. The muscles in Ned's neck and shoulders unclenched. His spirits lifted again.

In Mathematics, two scholars faced each other, braced comfortably on single elbows, talking of the last night's whores.

Such ease in the midst of so much learning! thought Ned with a twinge of envy. He had begun to see just how much he was undertaking in a single afternoon.

So many books! As he walked back towards the entrance door, their combined weight pressed down on him.

On the other hand, no one in the library had given him a second look. No one shouted, 'Imposter! Fugitive! Beast!'

In order even to begin his quest, he decided to ignore Mathematics and Jurisprudence, as unlikely to be relevant to his plight. Which left History, Theology, Philosophy and Medicine.

Where to make a start?

Theology was dangerous. Philosophy, too, threatened ambush. Monsters surely lived in History.

There were four presses of History books.

With a rattling of its chain, Ned lifted down a heavy, brass-studded, leather-bound volume. The text was handwritten in lacy Arabic, its secrets closed to him.

307

The next book he chose was in Hebrew.

The empire of reason was miserly with its secrets. He put the book back. And took another with a title in Greek. Leafed through its orange-tinged pages, spotting words here and there that he remembered from his lessons with Father St Hugh in Amsterdam. He flicked away a dead moth flattened against the word 'ship'.

He turned over more pages, sneezed. He searched for the word, *lycos*, the wolf. No reference anywhere. Nor to enchantment, nor metamorphoses.

Greek was slow going. Not entirely closed, but not wide open, neither.

Then, in Herodotus, he found the word for wolf, but could not make sense of the rest.

As the sun peaked and began to slide down the tall arched windows, he decided that in order to make any headway at all, he would give up on Greek and attempt only books in Latin, English, French and Dutch.

Eagerly, he took down *Polyhistoria* by Solinus. The History of Everything, and in only fifty-seven chapters.

But not everything after all, for it held no wolves. Nor men turned to wolves by Jove, or by any other means. Or if it did, he could not find them.

After dinner, in the mid-afternoon, the library began to fill with still-sleepy students, some barely awake, complaining loudly of headaches from too much ale the night before, bringing with them more dogs and distracting noise.

He leafed through Tacitus, Plutarch, Suetonius, Caesar. The print blurred. Endless battles raged. One dead emperor merged into another. Each general seemed as excellent as the next. The only wolf he found was the kindly creature which nursed the infant Romulus and Remus, later to become the founders of Rome.

He saw how many books remained and noted the lowered angle of the sun. With a silent apology to his grandmother, he gave up on Latin as well as Greek. Shadowy truths might lurk in the black print and sepia script, but they slipped away from him like half-netted fish. What he needed might be there, but he would never see it.

I wish I had paid more attention in my lessons! I saw no need for them then, except grandmother's urging.

Then, with gratitude, he found a book in English – the *Voyages and Travels of Sir John Maundeville*, first written two hundred years earlier, but reprinted many times for the marvels and fabulous tales. On his journey to Africa and Asia, this English explorer had stood at Gaza, he said, at the very spot where Samson brought down the gates, and seen gravel so bright that it could be made into mirrors. Maundeville had visited Prester John on his Indian isle surrounded by flood water from Paradise, and had passed prudently by the entrance to the Perilous Valley – so filled with tempests and thunder and wild cries of devils that it was thought to be one of the gates to Hell.

Among Sir John's cocodrills and long-necked, spotted orafles that could gaze over rooftops, and one-legged men called Sciapodes, Ned found the cynocephali, a race of dog-headed men who lived on an island near India. He read their description three times, then studied the woodcut of a well-shaped manly form with a hound's head, carrying shield and spear. The creature approached an altar on which stood a statue of an ox. Another tiny ox stood on top of the creature's head.

Ned studied the woodcut for a long time. The image was both pleasing and disturbing. It felt significant, but he could not think how. At last, he replaced Sir John on his shelf.

There were far fewer books in English and Dutch than in Latin, Greek, Arabic and Hebrew, but still too many. He found explorations, colonies, ancient voyages, and dead kings. He found the one-legged Sciapodes again, and races of men with no heads, and sheep-plants, and the Antipodes with their feet turned backwards.

Then he found a wolf. In an English translation from the

Greek of a terrible tale of a king Lycaon who ate human flesh and was turned into a wolf as punishment.

He read it twice with a thudding heart, then shoved the book back on to its shelf.

That tale is nothing to do with my case!

Discouraged, irritable and confused, he leaned his head on his hands, elbows on the desk shelf. He had not finished with even one press of History. It would be a labour of years to read all the books that might possibly apply to his case, even leaving out the languages he couldn't understand.

Either I haven't the capacity for this search, or there isn't enough time left in my life, or what I want to know isn't here after all!

But if I walk out of here empty-handed, I have no other reasonable way to turn than to Maurits.

He pulled himself together. Abandoned History and attacked Literature. Discouragement turned to bleak, hollow-bellied despair. A thin sea mist dimmed the windows.

Ned went out into the pale damp evening sunlight to draw breath and try to shake his thoughts loose from the cramping grip of too many words. After a short time, he returned to the library to try again.

Which of you is hiding what I want? he demanded silently of the ranked books. Please! Leap into my hands. Fall open at the healing words! I have so little time!

He attacked wildly this time. Went back for another volume of History, a few more volumes of Literature, tried Philosophy after all. Hauled books down, scrabbled for nuggets, slammed the books back. And he hadn't touched more than a few grains of dust in a desert. He groaned aloud.

'These endless ranks of useless drivel drive me mad too!'

Maurits.

'I warned you not to hope to find Truth in this place!' Maurits shook his head in pity.

'Why are you here?'

'It's too dark to work any longer.'

310

Ned saw that indeed, the presses were now in deep shadow. He hadn't noticed when the candle lanterns had been lit. The library was now nearly empty.

'Go look for truth anywhere but in a library!' said Maurits.

Two students in the aisle leaned their heads together, grinning, and murmured.

'It's my fault that I can't understand,' said Ned, 'with my imperfect Latin, my flawed schooling.'

'Nonsense. Your failure to be satisfied here is a mark of the highest intelligence. I can tell you a few truths! How many presses stand in this library?'

Ned saw the two students exchange glances of knowing anticipation. All other talk in the library had now stopped.

Maurits gave him no chance to reply. 'Twenty-two.' He lifted his voice to be more clearly heard by those who remained. 'But you must entirely discount eight of those twenty-two presses: six in Theology and two in Philosophy. Every book on them is either empty air or superstition.' He waved dismissal. 'No knowledge there.'

He walked back past Ned, a little towards the entrance. 'And over there, in those two . . .' his voice brimmed over with scorn '. . . mere Literature. Of no concern to a man of Science. Fantasies of the imagination – useful when you need fine words to bed a woman, or as meat for daubers who seek an allegory to illustrate. But knowledge? I think not!'

He turned and spread his black-robed arms. 'Ah, but now we have five whole presses groaning under Jurisprudence. I'm afraid that my own father and uncles are responsible for several of those heavy, heavy volumes. Jur-is-prud-ence.' He rolled the syllables with mock pomposity. 'A weighty subject which nevertheless shifts its form with every changing wind of temporal power. Useful beyond doubt – if you must sue your neighbour for the damage done to your cabbages by his pig. But I don't count it as true knowledge.'

He tugged Ned by the sleeve. 'Over here, on the other hand, poor Mathematics earns only a single press – scant lodgings for

311

an impoverished relation! But one of some importance all the same, to our understanding of the Universe . . . in its way.'

He turned and folded his hands in mock reverence. 'And at last I come to Medicine. I swear to you that every book on those two presses will be rewritten in our lifetimes.'

'By you?'

'Yes, by me, and a very few others.' Maurits was unabashed and unapologetic.

There was a smattering of applause and a few jeers. A dogfight broke out in Theology and one of the students left to deal with it.

Maurits seemed not to hear. 'For inarguable fact, I bow only to History, there in those last four presses. The past is eternal and will not change. But it doesn't interest me either. Come out of this place before I burst with fury.'

He gripped Ned's arm firmly to steer him out of the library, nodding left and right, accepting applause, pausing to answer questions. 'Yes, I continue . . . Tomorrow afternoon . . . Yes, at my house . . .'

By the time they reached the door, the cur and the spaniel had been restrained on leads and growled at each other across the central aisle. Ned was so incensed with Maurits that he walked unseeing, straight out between them.

Outside, he yanked his arm free of Maurits's grip. 'That was arrogance, not intellect!' All his awe had gone. He wanted to hit that fair, flat, self-satisfied face and did not care if he lost his safe haven. In his sudden passion, he stumbled over his words. 'You've left me and all other less elevated minds with nothing at all to lighten the darkness of our ignorance.'

'On the contrary.' Maurits shook his head, with an infuriating, confident smile. 'I've cleared the way for that which will answer everything.'

'What's left?' Ned reeled with nothingness.

'For us, for the moment, alas, merely supper.' Maurits looked at his watch, an intricate golden marvel produced from the folds of his black scholar's robe. 'But after we eat, we can make a start with your measurements.'

'I haven't yet decided to submit myself to your observations.'

'But, like me, you can't live without the truth.'

Ned nodded reluctantly.

'Then I'm your best, if not only, guide.'

When they had eaten and old Gerthe, the single, aged servant, had cleared the plates from the table, Maurits unlocked a chest and took out the large book he had been examining that morning. 'Please take off your shirt,' he said. 'Edward Malise,' he wrote at the top of a blank page. 'English gentleman.'

When Ned stood bare-chested in the firelight, Maurits circled him as if judging the merits of a statue or new coach horse.

'*Observo!*' he said. 'First I look. Above all else, I trust my eyes. Even before numbers, I trust my eyes.'

Only Ned's grandmother had ever studied him so fiercely, and that had been to sniff out smaller faults than an invading beast. Again, as with the physician, Ned had the disconcerting experience of gazing back at eyes that saw no further than the surface of his own.

'For example . . .' Maurits tapped Ned's bare breastbone. 'It's clear without any measurement that you have a man's chest or a mastiff's, not a wolf's. A wolf's chest is scarcely a palm's-width across.'

'What else do you see?' After all his resistance, Ned now found that he was intensely curious about what Maurits might discover. He felt giddy with the firelight.

'Your legs are long in proportion to your torso, and your feet are large, both traits shared by the wolf.'

'So what do you conclude?' Ned's voice cracked.

Maurits laughed. 'I'm a long way from any conclusions.'

'How will you arrive at them?'

Janni leaned over and tossed some peat bricks on to the

313

small fire. 'Maurits, it's growing late. We arrived only this morning. You must let Ned go to bed!'

'I observe, I measure and I record,' Maurits said to Ned as if Janni had not spoken. 'Look, here in this book, where I wrote your name.' Maurits's face glowed in the firelight. 'To form true conclusions about the nature of man, for example . . . here in this book I have the particulars of five hundred and two men and twenty women, all of whom either I or Janni examined. Their height, weight, size of bones, length of tongue and penis et cetera. I begin by comparing man with man. I look down these columns for any qualities shared by all these human subjects. If they all have hands, for example, I can then say that the presence of hands *may perhaps* be a defining human trait. D'you see?'

He released a flutter of pages from under his thumb with sensuous delight.

'But then I compare man with the beasts, listed here on these other pages. I have observed and measured as many as I can: apes, salamanders, kites, hens, finches, dogs, pigs, and swans . . . only one wolf, alas, as a student in Padua, but I'll remedy that. And what do I find? That monkeys also have hands! Therefore, hands are not a defining human trait. In this same way, I eliminate all other traits shared by both man and beasts.

'Next, I note the attributes that beasts have but no man does – for example, no man flies. A creature with wings is therefore not a man. And lastly, contrariwise, I can finally deduce those qualities that no animal has but which are common to all men. Man, for example, is the only creature with a naked skin except for small patches of pelt on the genitals, armpits and head.

'When I have recorded every trait of every living creature, which may well take my lifetime, I will be able to conclude, by reason and inescapable logic, that I can then describe the unique and essential nature of man. By this same method, I will uncover where your true nature lies. It may take us time, but we shall arrive, I swear it, and in my lifetime too.'

He set a small clock on the table among the instruments of measure.

'And now, with your permission, I will begin to measure you.'

Ned watched intently as Maurits began to lay out the instruments of order, his scourges of chaos. Measuring string, rules, calipers. With them, Maurits attempted to bite from chaos pieces as small even as his thumbnail, then rebuild them back into an orderly world. Even Ned's own beast might submit to such weapons in the hands of a man who understood their fullest use.

Ned sighed like an initiate at a rite and closed his eyes against the insistent flicker of the fire. He suddenly felt, embedded in his own being, the true power of numbers. He had embarked on a lucid, rational process, an orderly march from darkness into light.

It's unreasonable not to trust myself to him. It's time that I learned to listen to Reason.

Maurits offered a foot-long tube of glass as thick as a carrot. 'Open your mouth. I need your temperature . . . now suck, while I take other measurements.' He picked up a piece of string from the table.

By crossing his eyes, Ned could see a thick central column of mercury, the diameter of a woman's little finger. If the heats of passion as well as the fires of agues could be measured by that objective silver finger, it came very close to measuring the soul.

'Maurits, bed!' Janni said loudly and severely.

'I warn you,' Maurits said to Ned. 'In the name of the New Philosophy I shall take liberties with your person . . .'

Janni crossed to the door. 'Maurits!'

'. . . A few measurements, at least! And Ned must still suck for another half-hour.' He looped the string around Ned's skull, then laid it out along a measure on the table. Then he wrote the figure in the book. He measured Ned's ears and wrote more figures.

315

Ned saw the order of his being begin to take first shape on the clean white page. Hieroglyphs which Maurits would be able to interpret as easily as Ned could read a page of music.

Unable to sleep after Janni had finally prevailed and shown him to his room, he paced the walls, fingered the hangings and eyed cabinets of dusty Chinese porcelain without seeing them, filled with an excitement he could barely admit. He had lived for so long as a blurred shadow of other people's desires. Then he had become a shadow himself, then a thing of indistinct and terrifying outline. A clear, objective light had at last begun to shine on him.

Ned sat up in the friendly cave of his box bed. 'Come in.' Once in bed, with the candle blown out, he had still lain awake in the darkness for a long time. It was late for a visit.

Maurits's assistant opened the door.

Ned straightened in surprise and sudden, startled anticipation. 'Unexpected but welcome. Come in, mevrouw.'

She closed and barred the door. Then brought her candle and hitched a thigh up on to the side of his bed.

Ned swallowed. He did not want to presume what her intent might be, but such ease, at this hour, might be considered strong evidence. The thought caused a lascivious stirring.

'Do I disturb you?'

'No. In truth, I was lying here being tumbled by my thoughts. Hope is a fragile and painful condition.'

She set the candle on the flat at the end of the mattress, so that it lit the box bed like a tiny room. There was a flutter in her manner, as if of indecision, that ran contrary to her usual air of serenity. She had taken off her cap so that her white-blonde hair curled loose around her linen collar.

Perhaps she was not Maurits's mistress, as gossip suggested, but merely his assistant after all. Her long looks in the study may have held more promise than Ned had allowed himself to see. He imagined that Janni might have bitten her narrow

316

lips to redden them for him, and pinched the clean curves of her cheekbones.

'I came to talk of your search for clarity,' she said. 'Perhaps to dissuade you from chasing it.'

'You mean, not to follow through with this investigation?'

She nodded. 'To persuade you that it's not necessary.'

Ned leaned back on his pillows, face hot in the yellowed shadows. He had nearly taken her hand, in an amiable way. Then again, perhaps, she had an odd female idea of persuasion that he would not have expected from her slightly forbidding equanimity.

'Does Maurits know you work against him?'

She smiled broadly. 'Sometimes being the test of his philosophical rigour means keeping him in the dark.'

'Doesn't he smell heresy?'

'Not in me.' She let him stare, unbothered.

'Why warn me off? You're his assistant. Why hinder his work?'

'Maurits is necessary to the world, even more than the world yet knows. That's why I work with him. But I know him well and have seen how fierce his enthusiasms can grow. I see now how interested he has grown in you. You must consider if you truly want to match him question for question.'

'I resisted him for a long time, as you know. Now I feel that I have no other choice.'

'I think that you do.' She looked troubled now. 'What if his interest were dangerous?'

'Mevrouw, what is more dangerous than my corrupt condition? I am a monster. Two creatures take it in turn to occupy my body.'

'Is that so terrible?'

He drew a breath at her ignorance. His thoughts were scrambled by the impossible task of explaining the horror, if she did not see it. 'More terrible than I can say,' he offered at last. 'I'm a treason against nature. *Contra naturam*. You saw how things stood in London! When I could no longer hide it,

317

a doctor would have nearly killed me. My enemies muttered of witchcraft and possession. Even my friends had begun to make secret signs behind their backs. Only influential patrons kept me from being arrested and tried!'

'Live somewhere away from such men.'

'I would rather die than go on living with my beastliness! It will always condemn me no matter where I go!'

'Do you truly know what you're saying?'

'Yes! A dreadful thing has invaded my soul, and I must wrench it out at any cost.'

She stood up. 'Has Maurits taught you yet to be a true empiricist and believe only the evidence of your own eyes?'

'I'm persuaded.'

'Then watch.' She began to undress.

Her instruction was unnecessary. Ned could not have forced himself to look away.

She smiled gently at him as she removed her linen collar, bodice and overskirt. Her shirt. Then she shrugged off the shoulders of her smock and pushed it down to her waist.

His ears glowed hotly as they had not since he was fifteen. He wondered if he still mistook her intent with him and this was some strange, academic seduction.

In the candlelight, he saw two small-nippled breasts, perfectly round, neatly cased in soft skin. Nipples dark pink, set on small saucers of lighter pink and tight with the intensity of her purpose. Fine blue veins showed faintly under the skin like river deltas. The shadow under their fullness was a mere curve, not a fold. She had never nursed a child, for sure.

She put her hands on her hips. 'Am I a monster?' She clearly knew that there could be only one answer. In the candlelight, she was a half-draped goddess, the virginal huntress Artemis, speaking Dutch.

'Hardly,' stammered Ned, now a little giddy with trying to follow this strange event.

'As a convert to the New Philosophy I trust that you are

318

not now offended nor outraged, but merely curious as to what comes next.'

'I admit, I'm curious!' Then he tried to conjure up some gallantry but stopped when he saw that she wanted none.

She untied her petticoats, pushed them over the circular ledge of her farthingale, then undid the wool-stuffed roll and let that fall too. She stepped out of her smock and stood naked in her stockings.

'And now? Do you see a monster?'

Ned gawped for a moment, then looked away. He felt a little angry, as well as shocked, as if he had been exposed in ignorance.

'Am I so monstrous that you must avert your eyes?'

He looked back and still saw what he had seen before. Below the waist, she was a man.

'What do you see?' A severe but concerned tutor putting a question in philosophy.

A youth. Modestly proportioned but undoubtedly male. A nest of fine curling gold hair a little darker than that on her head.

His . . . head.

Ned looked back at the breasts. His thoughts spun as wildly as when the wolf approached.

Two pale eggs of testicles and a pink, hooded penis. The whole machinery looked as soft and unused as a baby's foot.

The creature held its arms away from its sides to invite his scrutiny.

'Monstrous?'

'Strange,' he said. 'Too strange for my brain to . . .'

'All parts work perfectly well.' Janni turned to show Ned wide shoulders, a slim waist and ambiguous hips, from behind not unlike Marika. 'Two creatures in one single body. Like you. But no room for doubt. If detected, I would be dead. *Contra naturam.* A treason against nature, as you said. But I live tranquilly enough, having found a safe haven. Can't you consider doing the same? Accept your beast.'

319

Tears pricked at Ned's eyes, as vague in nature as the nostalgia that he left behind in the realm of the wolf, but more urgent. 'If I were as beautiful as you . . .' He shook his head and scrubbed his face with both hands. 'But we're both still monsters. It can't be denied!'

The creature came back to sit on the bed, skin dyed to a golden peach by the candlelight. 'You won't be shaken in that belief? Aren't you consoled to see that you're not alone, a single horrid blot on the Creation? That there are more of us – in this world, not just in books? We have a fellowship. And we survive.'

'I'm a little consoled,' said Ned after a moment. 'But I still must find and shear away my other beastly half.'

'Then I must tell you what I never speak of to Maurits – whom I once loved, by the way, and who, in his fashion, loved me.' The lower, male half settled itself squarely cross-legged on the striped bedcover. The upper, female part tucked a strand of hair behind its ear and leaned back against the hangings which softened the end wall of the box bed.

Ned stared from one part to the other, still in disbelief. He had heard of such wonders, along with sheep-plants and Caribbean savages who carried their heads beneath their arms. Until his own problem began, he would have dismissed them all as superstition. This creature seemed lodged so securely in the world that he felt, in his disbelief, as if it were he who was not real.

'For the first eleven years of my life,' Janni said, 'I secretly felt that I was a monstrous degradation of male and female, just as you believe yourself to be man and beast. Male and female – sulphur united with mercury in a dangerous, haphazard mingling. I felt both principles intact in me, but blurred, like mud and water trampled together. An affront – a heresy – against God's perfect universe. I was terrified, but kept my secret feelings to myself and was raised as a boy. Then, at twelve, I sprouted these, and was exposed to the world for

320

what I was. I believe I narrowly missed being smothered in my sleep by my father.'

A cramp bit into Ned's gut.

'My mother guessed his intent, gave me what she could – a ring, a silk jacket, a little money and bread – and sent me away in secret, while he milked the cows that evening. I left our village for the crowds of Amsterdam, where I found work as a servant, now disguised as a woman – which indeed, I preferred. But I was discovered each time – the master groped or a fellow maidservant spied. At last, I decided to accept my degradation and flung myself among the lowest, most despairing, most base creatures in Amsterdam to await destruction. But to my surprise, I prospered. I won a small reputation in a *musico* favoured by men with jaded sexual palates. I was still monstrous, but my monstrosity made me a modest fortune (in my eyes). The *musico* owner hired me a room, and my lovers kept me temporarily safe from those who would have the world cleansed of imperfection. I was young enough to think only from time to time of throwing myself into one of the canals. Then tales of my strangeness reached my Master.'

'Maurits?'

'No, he and I are equals. The two pans of a scales. We met later at the university. This man came into the *musico* and hauled me out of bed where I was with an admiral.

'"I have come to be your guide through the flames and back to life," he said. And I dressed and walked away from my livelihood. I remember how the revellers fell silent with jugs at their lips as the two of us passed through them on the way to the door. I was shaking and telling myself to go back to my admiral, but my feet knew better.'

Ned wrapped his arms around himself.

'"You have given yourself to *putrifacio*," said my abductor. "When the blackness appears, you must rejoice."

'I've trusted myself to a madman, I thought. And I hadn't liked the sound of those flames. But I still went with him.

321

'"Did you take me only to be your servant?" I asked, when I saw that he had lodged me in the kitchen of his house.

'"Your long journey begins here," he answered.

'I still thought that he might be mad, but I was impressed by something in his manner, and by the instruments and apparatus in his study. And though he had no wife or mistress, he never touched me except in paternal affection.

'At first, I dusted, then I asked questions. He took me as a student, of both material chemistry and his hermetic philosophy. With the help of his eyes, I learned to see the truth of my own strange being. Not as a degradation of truth but as a metaphor. An earthly image in corporeal form of the unknowable *Anima Mundi*, the soul of the world, the source of life which is neither male nor female but encompasses both. Just as you embody the principle of Mercury, of change and rebirth.'

Ned shook his head violently. 'I've heard these things before, from foolish old women and old men who try to replace their lost potency with imaginary powers.'

'Then you haven't listened widely enough!' said Janni. 'Try the universities and not the fairgrounds! And you haven't listened closely to me.'

For the first time Janni showed impatience. 'I don't offer witchcraft, or the easy alchemical lore of the common *souffleurs* who juggle metals out of greed. And my story's not merely a cheering tale of rising from whorehouse to university, neither. I'm offering you another shape of the truth. You will either fight it with a thousand weapons or know it at once.'

Ned finally let his eyes be captured by the intense blue gaze.

'There is room in Truth for the unknowable and its metaphors as well as for Maurits's mechanical, rational observations.'

'Too many truths!' cried Ned. 'I've only just accepted Maurits's way!'

'At least consider that in your changeability, you share, like me, the unifying radiance of Mercury as *Anima Mundi* . . .'

322

Ned gave a single bark of bitter laughter.

'But like the dead man, you still need the purifying fire,' said Janni severely. 'Your opposites still fight each other, still swill in a muddy brew. You must give yourself to *putrifacio*. "When the blackness appears, you must rejoice."'

'You're more dangerous than the doctors and poisoners!' cried Ned in angry panic. 'Are you telling me to accept the beast?'

'As a beginning.' Janni gave this astonishing instruction matter-of-factly. '*Rotatio*. The turning begins.'

'What do you want me to do? Give myself over to be locked up or hanged? You can do nothing for me, and you know it! Just stone me with more words, more philosophies, more terrors! Unless you're the true voice of the devil offering temptation as I never imagined it – to accept evil as good!'

Janni leaned to pick up the smock and shook it out. 'Hermaphrodites watch over beginnings and ends. Over the decomposition and then the conjunction of the elements. We are the midwives of true births.'

'Like the births of the monsters I fear I might sire if I plant my seed.'

'You know I wasn't speaking of that,' Janni said, composed again beneath the smock. 'We await the true child of your mind.'

'You're tempting me to stay as I am! ". . . swilling in a muddy brew". I would rather die! That's why I don't fear Maurits as you seem to do!' Water pressed on the inside of his eyes until he thought they would burst if he could not weep it out faster. 'Where's your purifying fire now? I'd quench it, for sure!'

Janni offered Ned a linen square from a pocket, then, when refused, retrieved the candle from the bedfoot. 'It will come. You can't stop the journey. You seek self-knowledge and knowledge comes at a cost. The flames will find you in any case, but you've chosen to walk into them blind.' Genitals concealed by the smock, Janni was female again. 'I will stay with you.'

323

'I don't want you! I've finally made a choice!' Ned wiped his face with his hand. What did Janni mean? He still churned with panic. He wanted no more fire of any sort. 'You've unsettled me enough! Go away!'

28

'Wake up, Malise!' Maurits pounded on his door. 'We can't waste time. I must go upstairs and attend to my demonstration in the afternoon!'

By the paleness of the window, it was barely dawn. Ned had not slept since Janni had left him. Now, in spite of the anatomist's urgency, he lay for several minutes with the covers pulled up under his chin, shying away from the memory of Janni's voice, waiting for the moment when his will would allow him to rise. You did not rush at such a day.

'There you are!' Maurits was already at work when Ned went down to the study, inking ruled lines on to a page in a book that was as thick as a Bible. He had not changed clothes nor shaved. His beard stubble glistened red in the light that fell through one of the long windows.

His eager mind never rests, thought Ned. But the room still disturbed him.

Janni was busy with the fire. A graceful female form in skirts again, looking cool and innocent of the night's treachery.

Ned looked away in angry confusion from Janni to the tall unwashed window. Outside, the garden was monochrome in the early light, its precise geometry almost sunk in the dark turbulent sea of overgrown box.

Ned stepped over the tortoise, which had crawled from the wall to the centre of the room during the night.

325

Janni gave him an unashamed complicitous smile over one shoulder, then returned to prodding the fire which took the early morning chill from the room. 'Did you sleep well?'

Ned looked away. 'As well as any voyager on the night before he sails.'

Then he looked back at Janni as she . . . he . . . placed another peat block on the flames, face now intent on the domestic task. Surely, madness must have conjured up the naked creature who had sat on the end of his bed to talk of accepting evil and of purifying fire.

The ancient serving woman followed Ned in with a tray of bread, herring, cheese and ale. Maurits moved his book a few inches for her to insert the tray among the papers.

Janni ate. Ned was not hungry.

Maurits tore a crust from his bread with a vigour that sent crumbs flying across the table carpet, then leaped up from his chair to clear books and papers from the other table. 'We've no time to waste on breakfast.'

'Don't forget that you must continue with your demonstration shortly,' said Janni.

'I said last night in the library that I was busy this morning. I'll demonstrate again this afternoon!'

'So a few students know that you've changed your plans. What of the rest? You must continue this morning.'

'I need a wolf here for comparisons.' Maurits ignored his assistant. 'I must think how to find one. A single example all those years ago in Padua will not do.'

Through the garden window behind Maurits, Ned saw the American bird again. The cold yellow eye in the pink naked head was fixed intently on the uneaten bread in his hand.

'The Praelector is arriving at this moment,' said Janni. 'You must go to greet him. Ned will help me feed the animals, then I shall come up to the theatre.'

Maurits threw down his measuring tools with bad grace. 'When I am Praelector, I shall make such men dance double attendance on me! How can I accomplish any work at all? All

326

right! I go!' He disappeared into the leather-panelled hall in a flurry of frustrated ill temper.

'Does he keep a whole menagerie here then?'

The former dining chamber, large and light, with a fine stone chimneypiece, was now lined with cages and reeked like a dog yard.

'For study, not for amusement.' Janni thrust long fingers through the wires of a cage to scratch behind the ears of a somnolent rabbit lodged on the former dining table. 'We'll merely feed them now. I'll clean the cages later when I've more time.'

Ned accepted a bucket of sunflower seeds and followed Janni's lead, distributing hay, seeds, chopped carrots and cabbage to rabbits, rats, frogs, and birds of different sizes. 'Why didn't you let me be?' he asked. 'I had a firm grip on my truth, however terrible.'

'Words can change the truth.' Janni smiled. 'Does that mean you're reconsidering?'

Ned shook his head violently. 'I'm still fighting you with those thousand weapons.'

Janni lifted one of the rats by the tail and dropped it into the cage of a snake with the girth of Ned's wrist. 'Come outside. I've not much time, but I want to show you something.'

In a small parlour that opened on to the overgrown garden, more books balanced in precarious stacks, more pictures, unhung, leaned on each other like half-made fires. A stuffed lion guarded the door, in possession of all of its teeth but only half its mane.

'Don't touch it,' said Janni, as Ned raised his hand to stroke. 'It's leaping with fleas.'

They stepped out into the intense damp smells of an early morning garden. Birds flicked and flitted among the branches of the fruit trees. A billow of dewy, unclipped box spilled dark wet stains on Ned's breeches. Perfumes lay heavy on the air, as if collected from all the gardens of Leiden. In

327

passing, Janni pinched a protruding sprig from a giant lopsided fist of box.

Ned whistled back at a sparrow, which cocked its head, then replied in turn. Jumping Jack Sprat. Jumping Jack Sprat.

'Can you make it do that again?' asked Janni.

He did.

'A good trick.'

Janni turned through a small iron gate in an overgrown hedge. 'Here we are.'

After the chaos of the house and main walled garden, the order of the hedged physic garden was startling – a stark geometry of plain green marked by occasional muted exclamations of almost accidental colour. In workmanlike rows of small square, weedless beds, outlined by gravel paths, the inmates stood to attention according to their natures, from tiny, clenched thymes to some great lax, cut-leaved giants which Ned could not name. Even in the early morning, a mist of smells had begun to rise, thick, sweet, oily, sharp.

'My kingdom.' Janni bent to whip out an infant dandelion. 'Maurits needs my skills for his studies.'

Ned felt the blue eyes on his face, but stared straight ahead.

'The plants are arranged by purpose or by the condition they treat,' continued Janni. 'There, for example, are remedies for derangements.' Pointing at a confusion of green. 'And there, for hysterias.'

They walked a little along one gravelled path, their feet grating loudly in the still morning air. 'Then, purgatives, like that hedge mustard. And then carminatives to ease wind in the gut. And binders for the bowel. And rue and other herbs of grace for confecting into mithridates, the antidotes for poisons. There, coughs and hiccoughs.' Janni pointed out a woolly plant with felted leaves.

Ned felt the buried message, trying to uncoil like a seed in his mind. He frowned. Did Janni mean to tell him that his wolf might be dosed away with some concoction from this garden? 'Have you wolfsbane then?'

328

Janni pointed to a dark green lacework of finely-cut leaves topped by lax spikes of hooded purple flowers. 'Invented by Hecate from the foam of Cerberus, so they say. So deadly that the Greeks once tipped their arrows with it to kill wolves.'

'Is that what Maurits intends for my wolf?'

'Maurits can't use it on your wolf. In such a dose, it's just as fatal for man.'

Ned crunched along the gravelled walk for a closer look at the wolfsbane. Each purple hood arching over the lower petals ended in what looked like a small sharp tooth. Graceful and sinister at the same time. Its purple spoke of decay.

'It also has kinder uses,' Janni added. 'Some people seek out the hallucinations it brings, and the sleep that follows. It also dries up excess saliva.'

'Janni!' called Maurits, faint and peremptory within the house.

'On the other side of the walk, there, are treatments for fevers and agues, for which I also strip willow bark,' Janni continued tranquilly. 'For swellings . . . painful limbs. And here . . .'

Ned left the wolfsbane, caught up with Janni and dutifully gazed at the crinkled grey-green leaves and thin goose-neck flower stems.

'. . . are the sources of *materia* to calm or to procure sleep, as well as the wolfsbane there, which you have already noted. Henbane, hemp . . . these poppies being chief among them . . . I could grow tedious, but Maurits has saved you with his urgency to begin.'

At the gate, Ned looked back at the physic garden. Why did Janni show me this place? What have I missed? He felt irritated, as if he had been asked to play a game but then was denied the rules. Damn Janni. Every encounter with that creature unsettled him further.

Ned watched the tall figure walking in front of him back to the house. The pale blonde hair had been caught up into a loose knot. The waist was slim, the skirts swayed. Even now, irritated, knowing what he did, he found Janni a serene and

329

lovely creature, an opinion which both confused and frightened him even further.

'Can you amuse yourself here today?' asked Maurits. 'No more wandering about at risk in the world? You'll be safe enough here. The garden has high walls and the gate is locked. No one of any consequence knows that you're here with me.'

'Oh, but they do!' said Ned. 'And will expect to hear from me before long. I escaped with an unfinished lute for which I have already been paid. I could hardly let my friend think I had run away and taken his money for nothing.'

'But it's a friend, you say? Is it a friend whom you trust?'

Ned blinked at the irritation in the man's voice. 'I'm afraid I've compromised you even further than that. For private reasons, I had to tell another man, a patron of sorts.' The boy's father. 'Forgive me if I've put you at risk too.'

'Well, so long as they both wish you well,' said Maurits.

When all human voices had disappeared up the stairs towards the private Theatre of Anatomy which Maurits had built at the top of the house, Ned went back out past the flea-ridden lion into the overgrown garden. The odd American bird had now found a dust puddle under a ragged yew, where it scratched, shuffled its brindled feathers and settled. He sank on to a stone bench. Idly, he watched two robins hop from branch to branch in an apple tree which had once been espaliered tight to the wall, but now fell forward in a deep curtsy toward the ground. He had not slept after Janni had left him. Cushioned by the bushy hedge, he slept now in the morning sun.

Three white wolves sat in the branches of the apple tree and sang, beautifully. Not in howls but madrigals. When he rose from his sleep and went to the window of his room, they looked at him with glowing eyes which invited him to sing the missing fourth part of their harmony. But the window was rusted shut. He stood inside, unable to get to them, and wept in frustration.

★　　★　　★

330

When he woke, he sat looking into the tree trying to think what emotion he had felt in his dream. Then he grew impatient with this waiting. Afraid of growing fearful again. Afraid of Janni.

What if his interest were dangerous? Ned thought that he understood very well what Janni had meant.

But he was not an executed criminal. He was a living English gentleman, a social equal. A colleague, Maurits had said.

Old Gerthe brought him a plate of cold meats and pickles into the garden.

Janni is jealous of Maurits, Ned decided as he ate, still sitting on his bench. An equal in labour but unable to share the public glory, when it comes. Beautiful or no, Janni was a monster. And misery likes company.

Evil should announce itself by ugliness.

After eating, he walked around the overgrown garden, studied Janni's orderly medicinal beds to see whatever it was that he had missed that morning. Then he sat on the bench again and gazed up at the apple tree. Once, the rustle of applause floated down from the top of the house.

You've not much time left to inhabit me, he told his wolf. Maurits is already hunting you down.

He went back into the house and wandered in Maurits's study, looked closely at the ranged jars, eyed the anatomically exact painting of the hares, picked up the rigid, stuffed snake on the mantlepiece. As he turned, he saw the tortoise again, heaving its small world across the tiled floor. The chest in which Maurits kept his books still stood on the table. Ned crossed to it and tested the lid. The chest was unlocked.

He stood for a moment. Maurits had seemed to keep its secrets as fiercely as a dragon. But the lock was clearly open. Then he saw the key lying on the table carpet in the shadow of the box. The ancient authorities would warn him to remember Pandora's box, which held all the evils of the world. But Maurits himself had said that man was made to question and explore.

Observo, thought Ned wryly. He lifted the lid, took out

331

Maurits's book of measurements and drawings. Another book lay under it. Ned lifted it out and opened it.

With a rush of chill, he saw himself.

In the first drawing, done from the front with pen and brown ink, he stood gracefully, one foot a little in front of the other, head lifted and a little turned, one hand raised as if holding an invisible shepherd's crook. Only the face was fully rendered. The rest, though in correct proportion, was in outline only. Numbers written in pencil furred all the margins.

The title of the drawing gave him a second jolt. Where he expected to see 'Edward Malise, English gentleman,' he read, '*Vir-wulf (loup garou)*.' He turned the page.

Two smaller drawings showed the same posture drawn from the side and back. Again, his face and head were fully observed, the rest in ghostly outline, a sketchy map of still unexplored lands.

He hardly knew himself. It was he, but transformed, not into someone else, but into a different thing altogether. His sense of dislocation was greater because some detail was so exact: the tiny bump in the curve of his nose, the direction that his hair curled, even the slightly shorter brow above his left eye. How strange to wait until such circumstances to learn that cold observation had found him so handsome.

The next five pages were still blank.

'*Canis lupus*. Padua, 1628,' Maurits had written at the top of the next page after those, above a drawing of a wolf. Like Ned, the wolf stood upright, on its hind legs, with forelegs spread and turned up from the elbow, in a posture of mock alarm. Again, rendered three times, from front, back and sides.

This time the following page was not blank.

On the next page, the wolf had been flayed. With the fur, skin and all subcutaneous fat removed, its muscles were clearly defined and striped with the lines of the separate muscle fibres. They sat on the bones like a tight, padded suit of underclothes, making the beast look both naked and overdressed at the same time.

332

'*Ecorché*,' said a scribbled note in the upper corner.

The next page showed the exposed lupine viscera, as complex and neatly packed as the executed Henry's had been. All pages had cramped columns of Greek and Latin down the sides, with letters and numbers that corresponded to similar letters and numbers on the body of the wolf.

Ned knew now just what Maurits intended.

He turned back to the flayed wolf. Maurits would not dare! He was surely too ambitious to risk murder.

Then again, ambition was often cause for murder.

'I shall find your beast and cut it out,' Maurits had said in London.

And I did not hear him.

'Ned holds the key to my future reputation . . .'

But William Shaw knows that I left with Maurits. And the baronet, too. Who, as I later learned, had smoothed our way into the South Java Company. And he's a man of some influence who would not let me vanish without question!

And Maurits knows that I would be missed, for I told him so this morning.

The thought was not reasonable. Maurits was a civilised, lettered man.

But also a spoilt and driven brat, obsessed with his pursuit of knowledge, seeming unbound by the usual human concerns. And he was beyond doubt ambitious. What might it do for his reputation to demonstrate the anatomy of a werewolf? Compared with that of a true wolf. He would outshine even the noted Dr Tulp who had examined many lesser monsters to prove or disprove them.

The heavy door into the hall was locked.

He went back to the book. His reason chased itself in circles.

What of Janni?

. . . who tried to warn me, but not clearly enough!

No, I chose not to listen!

333

At a sound from the back of the house Ned dropped the book back into the chest and moved away from the table.

I will escape tonight, through a window if need be, or over the garden wall.

Janni came in. 'I hope your day hasn't been too tedious.'

'Anything but that.' Ned watched Janni lift the dreadful chest from the table and set it aside as matter-of-factly as if it contained nothing but old wool hanks or ancient love letters.

Then Maurits came down for supper from his anatomy theatre at the top of the house, talking of the day's work. His eye was candid, his manner cheerful. Ned examined the anatomist with fierce suspicion. No sign of perversion, of the evil he was imagining. He began to feel guilty for such thoughts.

Was he or was he not a prisoner? He walked to the study door, which Maurits had left open, and gazed into the entrance hall.

'Everyone has left,' said Maurits. 'You're quite safe to go out now.'

Ned ventured into the hall. No one followed. He tried the big front door. It was locked.

'Supper is arrived!' called Maurits. Ned went back into the study.

Are the locks for my protection or my restraint?

Old Gerthe had brought a tray which now stood on the table nearest the fire. Wine, soup, bread, ham.

Ned watched closely, but both Maurits and Janni seemed to eat and drink everything without care. He forced himself to eat and drink a little to avoid comment.

After eating, Janni left to feed the caged animals in the dining chamber. Maurits filled their glasses with a dark purple wine.

'*Oporto*,' he said. 'Don't ask how I came by this unlawful Spanish nectar and I won't be forced to say.' He pressed the glass into Ned's hand. 'A toast, my friend, to the knowledge of tomorrow. I sometimes feel exalted and filled with a rapturous awe, poised always for another step in the direction of total understanding.'

334

'I'm almost beyond feeling,' said Ned. He watched Maurits drink. Saw a tiny dark rivulet run down the pink chin. The Adam's apple heave. Both their glasses had been filled from the same jug. He drank.

Beyond Maurits, he saw the tortoise, not far from the door, heaving the dome of its golden shell on its scaly, claw-tipped sausages of legs towards a dark cleft under a cupboard. A beautiful construction of adjoining plates, domed like the heavens, moving on its own floor, the colour of gold. He thought that he would drown in its heartbreaking beauty.

'Let the machine lift its glass to the enquiring soul. To the New Philosophy!' Maurits leaned across the table and nudged Ned's hand upward to bring his glass to his mouth again.

Even while he tried to protest, he drank again.

The glass fell from Ned's hand. He watched it turn slowly in the air. Tiny candles flashed from its side, the stem, the bell-shaped base. Bright threads of wine trailed like streamers. Then the streamers broke into drops. The glass embraced the floor, flattened itself against the tiles, flung up slow, glittering fragments to meet the last of the falling wine. Then shards and droplets subsided together peacefully on to the meeting of one black and one white tile.

He tried to shout in fury at the trick. His voice sounded very far away and as slow as the blowing of a cloud.

I was a fool not to see it sooner! But if what I suspected is true, why this aid and friendship now that I'm in prison? Maurits has no need to be kind, and nothing to gain from it if he merely wants my executed corpse for his observations.

335

NINE

29

Marika sat bolt upright in her cupboard bed. A suffocating pillow of fear pressed against her face.

It's back!

Waiting in the darkness outside the bed hangings, just beyond the limits of her senses.

30

He lifted his head to listen. He had made some distance, but the baying dogs were closer again.

The wolf leaned briefly against a wall in exhaustion and pain. He needed sweet water to drink, not the salt water of the canals. Needed food. Had snatched a small moon of cheese from an open storeroom but dropped it in his flight when the alarm was raised. He needed somewhere to hide but his enemies had claimed every courtyard, marked every corner with the stench of their urine.

Somewhere to hide. Out of reach of the baying dogs and their sharp hungry teeth. And of the men who carried the torches and guns.

He knew this place, tried to feel its map in his bones. Tried to think where he could safely go to ground.

He knew the smells here, almost drowned in a nostalgic longing he could not explain. Ahead of him, dank salt and sewage. Tar. Wet hemp. Then an exhilarating burst of cinnamon, nutmeg, anise, damp rattan, and delicious fish, spread in wavering layers on the unmistakable, open breadth of the sea air. The harbour, the sea. The smells gave the harbour form in his head. He saw ghostly swaying sails in the darkness behind his eyelids.

But he must not run that way. A dead end.

He had to drink. He dropped on to all fours and licked at the base of a pipe that carried water from the rooftops. Then

340

scrambled to his feet again and veered left into a cupped maze of streets, past the smell of a bakery, which he also remembered. His alley led to an open space made dangerous by light from unshuttered windows. He ducked behind a sleeping cart, slid through a stream of fiddle music leaking from a door. The lantern above the door brushed over his head and naked, blood-striped back. In the shadow of an arched bridge, he paused, reaching for one particular smell, a missing piece of his map.

The dogs were headed towards the harbour now. Would soon find his turning.

He limped on, came to a bulge in the canal where the water had swallowed the earth and swollen like a snake.

Suddenly, out of the night air, he caught a sigh of an odour he wanted. It turned him like a faint, clear, distant trumpet across a field. The dream of another life gripped him with iron talons and yanked at him like a sea eagle with a fish. He knew where he was.

But the dogs were closer. He ran without thinking, away from their voices. Collided with the smell again, in the rope of other smells which tied together the night air. Stronger. He leaped into a run with renewed strength. The baying dogs fell farther behind.

Her room was so still that the concentric rings and purposeful ellipses of the universe seemed to have frozen in their slow swirling dance like water paralysed to ice.

The brick walls seemed as fragile as glass, the wooden shutters as fine as gauze. The tiled roof poised as light as a bubble, ready to float up and expose her to the night sky.

A bird in the eaves, she told herself.

After a few moments of absolute quiet, she climbed down from the bed and crossed to the window to check that the bars were still firmly in place. She held back her thick pale mane and laid her ear to the shutter.

A distant dog-pack bayed. Otherwise, the night seemed still.

★   ★   ★

341

The clamour of his senses swelled. He knew the map well now. Past the resinous tang of gin, past a corner tree marked by every passing dog, and an alley that smelt of goat. Then past a set of steps where a fish-seller's dinghy was always moored.

He climbed the stone steps of a large house, lower and broader than its neighbours. Strange and known at the same time. Panting, he leaned near the heavy wooden front door, careful not to touch it. No thought, just the push of the baying behind him and the soft pull of her smell.

She was one of the many braided currents of air on the other side of the door. He inhaled her warm fierce smell overlaid with something dark blue and sweet. The hair on his neck bristled. His many hungers weakened his knees so that he reached to steady himself against the door. But he pulled back just before he touched it.

Her smell belonged in another place on his map, a place which still escaped him. Another surge of near-memory pressed again at his awareness, as insinuating as a cat. But again it drew back, leaving a sense of loss and the intense desire to snap his teeth. He wanted to howl to loosen the knot in his throat.

But the dogs were coming!

He ran back down to the street and urinated against a tree two houses away. Then climbed the steps of another house, wiped his palms under his bare armpits, and pressed them against the bottom of the door. He listened.

His pursuers were now only a few streets away.

Urgently, he left his scent-mark on two more doors. Then he loped back past two other houses to the corner of the cobbled canal-side street. He turned left and left again into the deep narrow channel of an alley which ran between the backs of two streets of houses and stopped outside a locked iron gate in a high brick wall.

Here.

The dogs behind him had reached the bulge in the canal. A mastiff in the neighbouring courtyard growled.

He ran back to a pile of pungent horse dung in the mouth

of the alley, smeared it on his hands, face, chest and the soles of his bare feet. Ran back to the gate. Climbed it, tearing each stiffened muscle from its anchor as he did. Found himself in a formal garden of paved walks, thorn-spiked bushes, tiny hedges, the smells had changed, no place to hide.

Behind him, the sound of dogs baying had been joined by men's shouts.

He scaled a lower, internal wall, woke a sleeping hen, knocked over a broom and dived into a pool of shadow beside a stack of peat. The mastiff in the next courtyard flung itself, raging, at the intervening wall.

Just a rat in the courtyard, Marika told herself. A cat.

The shadows of the room jumped as the candle flame juddered in the pierced iron morter. She listened to the furious dog in the courtyard next to hers.

You locked it out, she told herself firmly. Whatever it is. On the other side of solid wood doors and shutters.

She climbed back up into her bed. This time, she left the hangings open, to hear better. She closed her eyes.

She opened them again. Unreasoning terror still had her by the throat.

Why deceive herself? That had been no rat. And what were those other dogs tracking? Coming closer.

She opened the shutters and looked down into the kitchen yard and garden. Nothing moved.

She sat on the edge of her cupboard bed, astonished at what she knew she was going to do. She didn't feel brave. If anything, she was angry. Justus's flight had planted a little serpent of anger just under her heart. She had felt it growing, swelling in her chest, brewing venom in clear golden drops.

Now a serpent of terror lay coiled down in the dark courtyard. If ignored, it would grow and grow each night until it overwhelmed her. She must face it now while it was still a relative infant. Her own angry serpent gave her strength.

343

She hauled a petticoat over her shift.

As she stooped next to pick up her bodice, she paused. Why dress unless she expected to meet something? Someone.

She tossed the bodice back on to the heap of skirts on the floor. A shawl and petticoat would do.

I won't find anything at all, she reassured herself.

The dog-pack was now two streets away, a hunting pack in full voice. Its baying echoed off the backs of the houses across the alley.

She took the morter and candle in one hand and the knife from under her pillow in the other. Went down the creaking dogleg staircase on bare feet into the dark sea of the hall. The speckled light of her candle carved out a very small hollow in the darkness.

She reached the door into the courtyard and the garden beyond. Raised the bar. Then terror exploded up from under the dark waters of her mind.

It gripped her in its talons, a great, keen-eyed, hungry shape. Her breathing was paralysed, her limbs lost their strength. Her blood stopped, like frozen canal water. Her heart faltered, her will bled away. She was opened. Unwalled. The hungry shape, if it wished, could reach into her and snatch out her soul.

She stood with her hand on the door latch, trying to breathe again.

If I retreat now, she thought, I will never be able to leave my room again. Just starve there until I die of terror.

She opened the door. Stepped outside into the surprising brightness of the night.

In the courtyard filled with the light of a three-quarter moon, the air was softer, less hard-edged than inside the empty house. The breath of all the men, women, children and animals asleep in the nearby houses and the streets of the *burt*, the breath of all the thousands of sleepers in the entire city, lay like mist. Above the breathing of the city she heard the dogs. Night in the courtyard was inhabited in a way that the dark of the house was not.

344

'Is someone there?' she asked unsteadily. Then she lowered her voice to a sudden eager whisper. 'Justus! Is that you? Have you come back?' She stepped farther into the yard. Oh yes! Please let that be the answer! Justus, returned.

At the far end of the courtyard beyond the low gate into the garden, near the stacked blocks of peat, the shadows reshaped themselves.

Then, stillness again.

'Justus?' she repeated, uncertainly.

The shadows shifted again, grew to human height, moved closer.

She couldn't move at all. This was real fear, not the child's nightmare fear she had felt in the kitchen. Her scalp quivered. All the hairs on her arms and legs stood straight up, pushing at the fabric of her shift. After a moment, she whispered, 'Please, Justus, is that you?'

It moved again. Pale moonlight fell like cobwebs across the large head and bare shoulders of a tall, half-naked man. He raised his head and listened to the dogs.

She held up the candle in the morter with an unsteady hand. The fragmented yellow light showed a mask of filth, matted black hair.

He made a noise deep in his throat.

'Who are you?' she managed to ask. Her voice croaked.

He moved towards her, reached for her.

She stepped back. 'I have a knife! If you don't mean harm, say who you are! Or I'll call for help.'

They poised in moonlit silence.

Dogs bayed at the mouth of the alley.

'You're the one they're hunting, aren't you?'

Without warning, he ran at her, seized her in his arms and forced her back through the door into the dark cavern of the kitchen. The morter clanged against the tiled floor and rolled, spinning the candle flame into nothing. She opened her mouth to scream but could not. He released her so suddenly that she staggered. She heard the door close and the bar drop.

She still held the knife but had forgotten it. The kitchen was black. She heard them both breathing. Found herself sitting on the floor. Her legs had finally buckled. The knife handle slipped in her damp palm.

'Who are you?' she finally asked again.

He did not reply.

'By everything you hold sacred, don't frighten me so! Please speak!'

She still felt the shock of his body against hers. His unnatural heat. He was large, taller than she. Even from several feet away, she could still smell fish on him, smoke, horse dung and a strong feral stink.

Dear God . . . ! she said to herself. I thought things couldn't get worse! Is this how hunted beasts feel? All her senses burned through the darkness trying to find him. Every inch of her skin turned to ears and eyes.

Not Justus. Too tall. Not wide enough in the chest. Or so she thought she remembered. The details of their staggering entrance back into the kitchen were understandably confused in her mind.

How far from me is he now? She scrambled back to her feet. Eased slowly towards the door from the kitchen into the hall.

No bar on that door from the hall side. Must get to my room. Lock and bar, on the inside.

Took another silent step.

His clothing rustled.

She fumbled down the leather strap and found her knife again. Don't speak now. Play his game.

Another slow, careful, quiet step.

He gave a cry that set her hair on end again. Then the weight of his body hit the floor.

The kitchen was absolutely still.

He's dead, she thought in wild disbelief. I'm standing here in the dark with a strange man dead on my kitchen floor!

After a moment, in which she found it difficult to think,

346

she decided. Light. Get another light and look. Can't think about what I don't know!

She turned and felt her way from the kitchen into the hall, where she unshuttered a narrow window on one side of the door. The plaster walls began to jump and sway with the light of torches and lanterns outside in the street. She listened to the shouting and the dogs for a moment, then, with a thought of regret for the missing sword, went up the stairs to her room. She found the tinderbox under her pillow where she had left it, but put it down again and felt her way through the shadowy upper hall towards her brother's room.

As she crossed the landing, fists pounded on the front door. She went into Justus's room, barring the door behind her, and opened a shutter at the front of the house.

The street below was bright with torches, alive with dogs, watchmen, constables and militiamen. A dozen armed *shutters*, and another dozen pikemen. Mynheer Cats stood at the top of his steps in his dressing gown with a sea of dogs swilling around his feet, while his wife, like Marika, looked down from an upstairs window. Her neighbours on the other side also leaned from open windows. Four dogs sniffed at a canal-side tree, then began to zigzag from house to house.

A man wearing the yellow scarf of the militia heard the shutters and looked up.

'Ah! You're there after all, mevrouw!' he shouted. 'As you live alone, we were particularly concerned. Our dogs have tracked an escaped felon to this street!'

She pulled her shawl closer to hide her petticoat bodice. 'Why is he wanted?'

The man hesitated, looked at his eager audience, then said, 'For murder.'

'Murder?' She heard herself falter. It could so easily have been Justus, after all.

'I don't wish to alarm you, but the dogs tell us that he has been in the alley behind your house. They were most interested in your back gate.'

347

But he wasn't Justus. He was another murderer. In her house.

Supposed murderer, she corrected herself. And perhaps dead.

A dog sniffed at the bottom of her door. Three others ran down the street towards the corner. Two others still worried at the tree.

Tell the militia. Turn him over to them and be safe.

She looked down at the churning of dogs and lights. The glints of lantern light on steel. The *shutters*' muskets. Two militiamen thrusting their pikes up into the branches of the tree.

Safe. But, in her present life, what was safety?

Bam! Bam! Bam!

Another militiaman pounded on a door to her right along the street.

Marika quivered. Then she shook her head. An action seemed less like a lie than words. A postponement of decision.

'Well, mevrouw, keep all your shutters and doors well locked and barred till we catch him. Don't open to anyone! We've mounted a watch on the street. If you hear anything, just cry out. And if you need us, give a sign.' He stood looking up for a moment as if to give her the chance for a sign now, a secret motion of hand or face, as if the fugitive might be standing close behind her with a knife or gun.

She thanked him and closed the shutters. Stood for a moment, half-lifted the shutter bar from its slot, then dropped it home again.

Not yet. He has lost his senses. I won't tell them yet.

Back in her room, she opened her shutters to let in the faint light glow of the sky. She made a nest of tow by feel alone, with shaking fingers. Judged the distances in the semi-dark. Struck flint on steel. A spark flared and died. And another. Then the fire caught. With the candle wavering in the morter, she went back downstairs to the kitchen.

Not dead.

He was asleep. On his side with one arm stretched up across

348

the lower part of his face. She dared to squat down and hold the morter close to his face.

Not dead after all. I suppose it's the better way.

He sucked in another ragged breath and exhaled with a faint keening of pain. His head was large and shaggy, the hair black and matted, dusted with what looked by candlelight to be a thick black powder. The visible, upper part of his face was a black, streaked mask. Impossible to read anything about him. His nose, however, had a familiar arch. She was not entirely surprised. A great many men had at some time or other eaten at their table, had imagined a haven, however tenuous and fleeting, in their house.

He stopped breathing.

She prodded him gently. Then a little harder.

'I go!' he shouted suddenly. 'I will leave this body willingly!'

'No!' she cried. 'Stay! Come back!'

His eyes opened. He stiffened and stared straight ahead into the darkness as if he waited for something to happen. After what seemed to her like a very long time, he sighed and fell deeply asleep again.

She fetched her coverlet from her chamber and laid it over him.

What on earth are you doing? she asked herself, as she stood looking down at him. Are you so lonely, or turned so mad that you will shelter murderers just for their company?

She went up to her chamber, barred the door, wrapped herself in her cloak and tried to sleep.

In the heavy, still turn of the night, when the sick most often die and cats go home, she woke again.

Something scraped against her door. She forced herself to go and listen with her ear against the wooden panel.

Again. Near the base of the door. Clothing.

A chilly hand clamped tight on her neck.

He was there. Had woken up and now waited outside her door. Like a cat by a mousehole.

349

You fool! Why didn't you tell the militia? You could pay for that foolish indecision with your life!

She sat on the edge of her bed waiting for dawn, wide awake, watching the door. As she grew colder, she put on her unlaced jacket under her shawl and cloak.

The full measure of my folly, she thought, is almost humiliating – that I was soft enough in the head to give him my coverlet.

Daylight fell through the still unshuttered window. She sat up abruptly. She remembered the whole implausible night except for the one or two hours of resisted sleep.

So, to call the militia, or not?

She tiptoed as quietly as the creaking floor allowed, to listen at her door.

Impossible to know whether he was still there or not.

Hair's-breadth by hair's-breadth, she eased the bar up from its iron cradle. Listened again. Then cracked the door open wide enough to take her little finger.

He was still there. His ragged bulk lay stretched across the doorway, wrapped in her coverlet, still asleep, facing her door.

She eased the door open a little more. His black hair stood up in crusted spikes. She leaned closer to see better in the dim light of the shuttered landing, but the hem of the coverlet shaded his face.

Quietly, she closed the door again.

Before she took matters any farther, in whatever direction, it was clear that she must now dress herself. At last. Even without a maid, reason should tell her how.

First, tie sleeves to bodice.

No, first, stockings. You've no Lore to unroll them up your legs, and you won't be able to bend down once your stomacher and petticoats are on.

But her stockings were still in the courtyard. Hang stockings! Who would see, under all her skirts?

350

In bare feet and smock, she put on her two petticoats, the blue and the red, one on top of the other, tied them in front, then twisted the ties round to the back. Farthingale pulled up next and tied into place.

She paused to listen again at her door. She could smell last night's fear in her armpits and taste the fur that it had left on her teeth.

Then corset, always difficult, even with help. Impossible without.

She tossed it on to the floor.

Now, the bodice, worst of all, but essential. She laced it in front, twisted it, jammed her arms through the armholes, was caught in a corkscrew twist of muslin, buckram and whalebone.

'God's teeth, eyes and toenails!' She flung one of Justus's favourite oaths at the naked walls. But with this man in the house, she could not walk around in her undergarments. She would just have to learn to walk around feeling twisted into a spiral. She leaned on her bed and lifted her feet, one after the other, to try to put on her slippers. She grunted in frustration as the whalebone stays of her bodice cut into her ribs, dropped the slippers on to the floor and shoved her feet into them any old how. She took Justus's red silk purse, then tied the ribbon of her knife back on to her sash.

Armoured at last, she opened her door again. He still seemed to sleep. She lifted her skirts and stepped over him. He stirred but did not wake.

The stairs were kind. She achieved the bottom with only three loud creaks. Listened for the sound of his breathing from above, and escaped through the front door. After a moment, she locked it behind her. If he wanted to flee, he could leave by the back.

The street astonished her. So unchanged, unaware. She blinked in the daylight at the water-seller, the playing children who had taunted her, a man fishing at the canalside. A carriage.

351

She watched it pass, did not know the faces inside. The whole of her familiar world seemed to have fled along with her brother.

Her neighbours had already gone to market, so she had no one to outface as she left the house.

Then she saw what had changed. Two militiamen stood guard at the end of the street.

Go tell them! They could take him before he even woke.

She turned in the opposite direction, towards the New Market. An empty stomach hinders thought.

But in the New Market, eight armed *shutters* walked among the market crowd. And then she saw a tighter crowd massed around a posted bill. She knew at once that it concerned her sleeping murderer.

'. . . but how does one know?' a man said. 'One minute a man, the next, a monster. He might be any of us here.'

She shouldered her way to the front.

'Take your turn, mevrouw!' said an irate woman's voice.

'. . . an ill omen . . . !' the man's voice continued.

It was worse than she had imagined.

'BEWARE,' the bill warned. 'BLOODY AND SAVAGE ACTS. A villain claiming to be an Englishman but who speaks Amsterdammer Dutch. Black hair and of more than usual height . . .'

Her man so far. No question. Except for the English claim, of course. He hadn't spoken a word about anything, except in his nightmare. In Amsterdammer Dutch. Hardly conclusive. But black hair and unusual height . . .

'. . . pale eyes and dark brows . . .'

The brows, yes. Haven't seen his eyes yet, by daylight. What colour were they when he stared so last night?

'. . . without warning, takes on the fiendish temper and bodily shape of a wolf . . .'

Her eyes began to jump and skitter across the black inky words.

352

'. . . this degenerate did kill a flock of nine laying hens and did kill and eat a five-year-old girl . . .'

Marika blinked, swallowed and began to read again from the beginning, scrambling from word to word in haste. But the words remained unchanged.

. . . a five-year-old girl . . .

She read again. This time she noted, '. . . is accused by many God-fearing witnesses, the same men who valiantly, at peril of their souls, did first apprehend . . .'

She shook her head but this time read on to the end, barely hearing that a woman near her screamed and began to cry.

'. . . a reward for his capture or for any intelligence leading to that happy end. May The Lord Protect Us.'

A chill crept under her scalp, down her neck and washed over her shoulders. She read once more, carefully this time, still disbelieving . . . a five-year-old girl! Her stomach clenched with nausea. Her heart began to jolt against her ribs.

She had spent the night alone with him in an empty house.

'I tell you, it's an omen,' said a low voice in the crowd.

A *shutter* stood by a cheese stall, not eight feet away.

I have only to walk eight feet and speak.

. . . a five-year-old girl . . . Such evil does exist, I know.

But the man asleep on her floor?

If I don't hand him over, I'm as much a criminal as he. For so I was told, on the subject of my brother. But as I'm already such a criminal, I am also free to make my choice on other grounds.

She walked to the quayside and stood looking far down into the water of the Damrak. A large sailing ship swayed at anchor to her right, moored outside its owner's warehouse in the heart of the city. She watched the tip of its mast for several minutes.

He could have killed me last night, if that's what he intends.

Unless he was too weak last night. And has now recovered his strength in sleep.

She moved on to a fruit-seller and examined an apple.

Had he truly eaten his victim? A child?

353

Says whom? The authorities, whom I have come to know so well?

But even the possibility of the child!

She turned the apple over and over in her hand under the vendor's watchful eye.

I will say: I know where your murderer is.

But she couldn't imagine choosing of her own will to open her door to the militia and bailiffs. To watch them hustle him out, as they would have hustled her brother. In some odd way, he already felt like her guest.

She still turned the apple in her hand.

'Are you buying, or not?'

She paid. Then saw that she held two apples in her hand.

I shall make up my mind about him for myself.

She had known at the time that she should never have laid her own coverlet over him.

'You came back.'

'You're still here.' She kept her voice level.

He was sitting on the stairs wrapped in her coverlet. 'No place is safer for me than another.' His voice was as hoarse as a man cut down from hanging. 'Don't you know me?'

'We had a rough introduction last night.'

'Desperate creatures forget their breeding. Forgive me. I'll stay over here now. Don't cry out, I beg you!'

'If I were going to betray you, I would have done it by now.' She stared up at him. Beneath the bruises and the black dirt, she began to pick out a familiar terrain. The eyes, the arched nose. And those pale, incriminating eyes. 'You might introduce yourself now, however, as you seem to be sitting on my stairs, wearing one of my blankets.'

'I need you to tell me who I am!' He looked down at her with a fierce, poised urgency.

Then she recognised him. 'Ned!'

Ned Malise. Too much changed. Taller, broader, older, and in some way damaged.

354

If much else happens to me, she thought, I shall contract brain fever. A half-dead former lover, now! Whom I treated very badly. On the run from the law and likely to turn me outlaw too on his behalf!

Seeming eased by her recognition, he sat back again, still watching her.

'Are you their murderer?'

'I'm the one they're hunting. I don't know if I'm a murderer.'

'Why did you come back here?'

'I don't know that either.'

Is that madness speaking in him or not? she asked herself. His former open, searching nature seemed darkened, just as his former beauty was now obscured by filth. She could see, all the same, that his cheekbones stood higher than she remembered, and the blade of his nose was sharper.

'If I'm to shelter you, you can see that I must have answers to these questions.'

He said nothing.

'Your description is posted in the market.'

'Ah.'

After a moment, she went into the kitchen and laid the two apples on the table. Then stood looking at them.

He followed her. 'I swear – as far as I can be certain of anything – that I could never knowingly have done that to the child!'

But only so far as you know, she thought.

He came closer, until he stood behind her. Again, she felt his heat, sensed his height, heard the effort of his breathing, smelled the fish, the smoke and the feral stink. She could not move. This is how hunting beasts eat, she thought. When the time comes, their prey can't move. Why was I fool enough to come back to the house?

He reached past her and picked up one of the apples. 'I need a jacket.'

She turned and looked up into his eyes which were startlingly pale against his filthy skin. Dropped her eyes to his hand, which held the apple. She remembered those long fingers very well.

Then she fled upstairs to her brother's chamber where she snatched up the discarded jacket he had left on the floor and pressed it against her face.

What am I doing? Dear God, whatever do I think I am doing?

'I must go out again,' she said when she had given him the jacket. 'I meant to buy food before, but was distracted.'

'Is there water? I need to drink and clean myself.'

She showed him the cistern in the kitchen and set the tinderbox on the table. 'And if you want it hot, you could try to light the fire.'

The crowd gathered in the New Market was even larger than it had been in the morning, but now grouped, one clump still jostling around the placard, while other gaggles formed around people touting fresher news of the beast.

She paused to listen to a young man of twenty, with blunt features and sharp eyes, who had collected a particularly large audience.

'. . . I spotted the beast itself, just as it crossed a canal bridge, fleeing the dogs,' he cried.

'By what signs did you know it?' shouted a man in the crowd.

'By its eyes like lanterns!' he said. 'Though as a good Christian, I didn't like to look directly for fear of being struck dumb. It was as large as a man, and ran upright, just like a man!'

Marika left him to his awestruck audience and shouldered her way in to read the placard again. The words had lost much of their power since she had talked with Ned.

Ned Malise was gentle to a fault. If she were honest with herself, his gentleness might even have cost him her juvenile love. At fifteen, she had been smitten by the promise of danger in his looks, then been disappointed to find them gracing a

356

youth as young as herself and even more inexperienced. As awkward as a pup though not without charms.

She shouldered her way back out of the crowd.

What would I have chosen to do if Justus had not put such a firm hand on my tiller?

And whatever Ned's obvious misfortune might be, marriage to her might have shoved him quite a different way.

I was not bred to love, she told herself firmly. To shine and beguile, yes. But also to keep a firm grip on my own heart. Apart from Ned, when so very young, she had loosened that grip only once. And regretted the pain ever since.

Another Englishman.

She bought a roasted chicken, cheese, bread, two uncracked cups and a pair of earthenware plates.

As she turned away from the potter's stall, a young woman thrust a pamphlet in her face. Without her glasses, Marika squinted to read.

'*The Prodigious Monster, or the Monstrous Wolf-man, being a true but degenerate Relation of the cynocephali from the islands of Nicobar.*'

Beneath the words, a naked man with a wolf's head gnawed a booted leg.

'It's God's own truth about the Amsterdam Beast,' said the young woman, who wore an amulet against the evil eye around her neck. 'Five *stuivers* only. Its history and appetites. The auguries – what this monstrous appearance means for Holland.' She offered another pamphlet to a passing youth. 'Only five *stuivers*!'

Marika paid.

The pamplet listed precedents for such cases, both ancient and modern: the cannibal king Lycaon and his followers, turned wolf for eating human flesh, who could be redeemed only if they abstained from eating more human flesh for seven years.

She turned the page and found the Cynocephali, a dignified race of dog-headed men who worshipped oxen. St Christopher was said to be one of their number.

She read on, to the final precedent: the three werewolves of Poligny as verified by the notable Henri Boguet in his *Discours des sorciers*.

Of these last three, she read, one had attacked a traveller, in the form of a wolf. The traveller wounded the wolf and tracked it home. But when the traveller arrived at the house, he found the wife bathing a man's wounds.

Without her glasses, Marika squinted at the dense print. A second man was told by the first, now a servant of the Devil, to strip and apply a magic salve. Shortly after, he became a wolf. He had confessed . . .

She began again and forced herself to continue. He confessed to eating a four-year-old girl while in this shape, and to finding her flesh to be delicious.

Her fingers trembled as she turned to the next page. As wolves, both men had mated with real wolves, she read, and claimed to have had as much pleasure in the act 'as if they had copulated with their wives'.

The pamphlet at last turned to the Amsterdam wolf itself.

She did not notice the crowd around her beginning to thin out, headed home for the midday meal.

The pamphlet's author recorded two sworn eyewitness accounts of how this devilish beast had torn apart a flock of hens and devoured them raw. The first witness, who had had the foolish audacity to gaze directly at the beast, had been struck dumb by a single glance from its eyes and could not raise the alarm nor speak at all until the following Sunday.

Marika snorted gently. God save me from such eyewitnesses! Poor Ned! The other witness, who had kept his faculty of speech, she therefore concluded, had not dared to look closely at all.

In the learned opinion of two wise men, Amsterdam's own wolf-man was a sure sign that the Spanish wolf was poised to attack the Netherlands once again. As a coda, the pamphlet gave his name. Edward St Stephen Malise. English gentleman, soi-disant.

Marika tucked the pamphlet under her stomacher. There was matter there that she needed to digest. Among all the rest, the pamphlet said that when the Beast of Amsterdam was captured, he was to be stuffed and put on show at the next *kermis*, or fair.

It's all superstitious nonsense, she decided.

But then, she knew of other cases from her own reading. Such revered authorities as Lycosthenes had described a dog-headed monster presented to the emperor Louis the Pius. And manticores that were lions with human heads. Antipodes with their feet attached backwards. Satyrs and tailed men.

Not only Lycosthenes, but many others, equally trustworthy. The famous Amsterdam physician, Dr Tulp, had himself only recently recorded dissections of diverse monstrosities. Some he had explained away but others he had found to be genuine.

You don't know this new veiled Ned, she warned herself. The youth you once knew could have changed beyond imagination.

Certainly, the apparent circumstances of his life had left her imagination behind.

Ned Malise, perhaps. But not as she knew him. Was he changed enough to be dangerous? And when would he start to remember what he had forgotten?

'Ah!' cried a woman passing by. 'Now I know! My lovely mouser. Disappeared last night. That monster took her!' She began to weep.

'Never mind your cat, mevrouw!' said her male companion. 'The Lord sends such monsters, *contra naturam*, to punish and admonish us. This beast's a portent: Holland will be devoured by the Spanish wolf. You can read it right here! It must be true!'

'Why didn't you say at once who you were?'

'Would I have been any more welcome?' He lifted a hand to cut off her reply. He was wearing Justus's jacket. It was short in the wrist, but wide enough in the shoulder and served at least

359

to half-cover his naked torso. 'I don't know why I came here. I'm sorry. Now that I've recovered myself a little, I shall leave again at once. Now, before my hideous corruption infects you too.' But he no longer had the strength even to stand. He sank back on to the floor.

She had discovered him waiting near the front door, and he had followed her into the kitchen.

'What hideous corruption should I fear?' she asked. If he carried contagion, she had already been too close. 'The plague? The small pox?'

'Nothing like that! But my presence has already infected you, unless you call the militia at once.'

'I've already lied and turned them away last night, while you slept.'

'Fool!' He looked at her with what seemed real despair.

She set out the two plates and pulled the roast chicken into pieces. 'Your reputation swells by the hour. You're credited with two more cockerels and a cat since last night.' She glanced over her shoulder to see if she could detect any signs of wolfishness in him. He was eying the chicken hungrily.

In her absence, he had tried to wash. With cold water only, for the fire was still dead. Though his skin was still streaked with dark smudges, his long, strong nose, dark straight brows, fine cheekbones and full lower lip had been lifted out of the former confusion of filth. He'd had more success with face than hair, however, for his dark curls were still dusty and matted. And she now saw dried blood above his left ear.

'Two cockerels and one cat? That's all?' His voice was edged with irony.

That was new too. I must get him out of the house, she thought. For a great many different reasons. Aloud she said, 'The streets swarm with militia, all watching for you.'

At her invitation, he attacked the chicken. 'Perhaps you could vouch for me on those cockerels and the cat at least.'

He's innocent of the murders. She knew it, quite suddenly.

360

His eyes are the feature that condemned him, she thought. That pale grey, rimmed with black lashes. At fifteen, they had made her feel shivery. And she was not alone, she was certain.

Otherwise, only his long arms and shins suggested the fine-boned strength of a wolf.

It was enough for the ignorant to lump together with coincidence and brew into firm conviction.

'You can't leave just yet,' she said. 'Not with the hunt still in full cry!'

'I'm more grateful than I can say for last night's haven, but I must go. Thank you for not giving me over. I don't know why you took the risk!'

'The law has no friends in this house.' She gestured at the empty shelves, the fireplace stripped of pots and chains.

'Forgive me!' He changed direction at once and seemed truly mortified by his blindness, not to have seen before. 'Sweet Lord! What happened?'

Justus's flight, the bailiff, the stripping of the house, were all related in a few terse words.

Speechless, he paced the bare walls, went into the hall where he slid a hand across the dusty rectangles left by the absent paintings. 'Poor Marika.' He went to the parlour door to look into the hall. 'Even the chandelier.' He moved stiffly and carefully. 'But that's all the more reason for me to go at once. Can't you see? You could hang for sheltering me!'

She did not reply.

He lifted the bar on the kitchen door. 'I ask only the favour of being allowed to keep this jacket for the moment.'

'Stay here, you fool. For another night at least.'

'Not worth the risk to you.'

'You don't know your full danger.'

'Believe me, I think I do.'

He was leaving. Walking out into the arms of the militia.

Reluctantly, she pulled the pamphlet from under her stomacher.

He read it quickly.

'A stuffed exhibit at the fair!' He dropped his forehead on to his knees. 'It's almost comical.' Then he shuddered.

That 'comical' reassured her even further that he was innocent.

'In truth, I don't think I'd get far this evening . . .' He shuddered again. 'I should never have sat down.'

'I'll make a fire,' she said. 'I feel cold all the time now.' She had almost forgotten the forward rush of human discourse, each person pushing the other onwards in slides and jumps.

He said nothing, but watched from the far wall as she built a mound of kindling and peat, as she had watched the servants do, then held the candle underneath in a pocket she had left. She leaned forward and gently blew on the tiny tongues of flame.

The fire grew until its light danced and jigged against the kitchen walls.

'Now,' she said briskly. 'Come sit here by the fire so that I can see how badly your scalp is torn . . .'

He hesitated, then sat beside her, turned his head away and closed his eyes. His hands were clenched on the tops of his thighs. His wrists were brown and scarred where they emerged from the cuffs of Justus's jacket. In spite of the fire, he began to shiver.

'Shall I fetch my coverlet?'

He did not reply, but ignored her, his eyes tightly closed as if groping for an urgent memory.

She had resolved not to be discomfited by his closeness, for any reason. She touched his large head gently with one hand. 'You've a lump on the bone here,' she said. 'You need a surgeon.'

'It's coming!' he said suddenly.

'What is?' She frowned and pulled back. His face looked odd, taut, a little askew.

'Not now!' he said urgently. 'Oh, God! Please, not now!' He covered his eyes with his hands.

'I can . . .' she began.

'NO!' he roared. Without warning he surged to his feet.

362

She scrambled up too but he sent her staggering backwards with a blow of his arm. She fell against the passageway door, hauled the knife up hand-over-hand along its hanging strap, and braced herself for another attack.

He stood with his head lowered, growling deep in his throat.

The flames filled his head with a dark pain that blinded one eye. The shadowed floor stretched and swirled like oil on a puddle. The giant fist closed around his ribs, while the bubble of horror rose up under his heart. He heard a distant scream.

He braced himself and waited, poised against the doorway, neither in nor out. The beast stalked closer.

The bubble of horror shifted from under his heart into his throat. His lungs laboured against the squeezing fist.

A faint voice called, 'Ned!'

Body and the floor melted together. The hall door, a clay cup, a panel of Delftware tiles set into one wall, all began to slide from their former, mappable positions. Sounds beat at his ears. His head reeled under the attack of competing scents that clamoured to be read. Warnings that the beast drew near.

It pressed against his shoulder, leaped up, insinuated itself into his head, then began to reshape him as if he were made of hot sugar.

The muscles between his ears and jawbone shifted on the skull. His scalp contracted. His skull bent into new angles to accommodate his altered muscles and to contain the pain in his temple. His arms and legs stretched and grew thinner.

He fell through the doorway, away from one self, into the other.

I am not myself.

But he had already lost the thought.

The blur of sound and smells began to clear like mist. He could read each separate detail again: peat and sweat, the rancid dust on the floor, mice, mud, apples, roasted chicken, the smell of iron from the dried blood on his head.

363

The woman's foot grated on the tiled floor as loudly as a heavy iron-bound chest. He tilted his head toward her. She backed away a little into a tunnel of blackness. Made a gasping sound. The folds of her skirts scraped against each other as she moved. Her fear nearly drowned all her other smells. He held her steady with his eyes.

He took a careful stalker's step towards her, watching her, holding her always on the point of his gaze. She backed away until stopped by the wall, shouted a warning. Her teeth pulled away from her lips in a snarl.

He didn't want her to bolt. Or to fight.

He unlocked his gaze, retreated a little, yawned elaborately to signal disinterest. Then lay down on the floor. Patience was the key to a successful hunt. He rested his head on his hands and watched to learn what she would do now.

Ned woke in a deserted kitchen. He saw the room clearly by the bright daylight that leaked in around the closed shutters. The fireplace still held a fixed spit and a few pot chains but it had been emptied of pots, pokers, spoons, hooks. The rest of the room had likewise been stripped of plates, bowls, bottles, baskets of vegetables, hanging onions, caged birds, hams, bacon flitches and all other such food and chattels. A single ageing leek had rolled against the tiled base of the wall, where it had begun to sprout a white tentacle from the centre of its tightly-bundled sea-green leaves.

On the floor near him sat a clay cup. He stared at it, then at the remains of a roasted chicken. He picked up the cup and held its thick glazed rim to his mouth.

He knew now where he was. He remembered her hand holding the cup . . .

The hair rose on his arms and neck.

What had he done to her?

He looked down quickly at his hands. There was no blood on them. No blood, no torn flesh, no half-chewed bones on the floor.

How can such questions even be in my mind?

'MARIKA!' he shouted.

He sank back down on to the floor.

What had happened last night? The wolf was a fading dream, impossible to see in its parts.

He closed his eyes, tried to get a grip on the dream.

Then he leaped to his feet and ran into the hall. No blood there neither, nor was there any sign of Marika.

She's gone for the militia! he thought. Then he ran up the stairs.

The door of her chamber was locked. He went slack with relief. She must be inside, had locked it. Safely alive.

'Marika! Don't fear, it's over. I'm myself again!' He was giddy with fever and fear, nothing else. And she must still be alive, uninjured enough to climb the stairs and leave no trace. I did not . . .

But there was only silence beyond the door.

'MARIKA!' He pounded with his fist. 'You must tell me what happened!' When she still did not answer, he thumped the door again in frustration. 'The Devil take you, then! Either speak to me, or call the *shutters*, one or the other!' He sat on the floor beside the door and rested his hot forehead on his knees.

He heard a muffled, angry exclamation from the other side of the door.

The bar scraped, and she jerked the door a small way open. She held her knife. 'Are you trying to call them here yourself?' she demanded with quiet fury. Then she saw that he was sitting on the floor. She opened the door a little farther and let her knife drop to swing on its cord. She stepped past him to open the shutter of a landing window. A patchwork of red and blue fell across her face as she turned back to face him with the width of the landing between them. She crossed her arms over her breasts.

'Tell you what happened?' she repeated as if she had only just heard him, and stared at him with a wry unfriendly smile.

365

She had put on her skirt and overbodice with sleeves again that day. Rumpled and twisted, with dangling points and laces awry, she was fully armoured nevertheless. Though her laces were as approximate as her knots, and her hems rimmed with dirt, her bright hair sprang out around her face with its customary vigour. 'And why should I call the *shutters*? Whatever else happened last night, you did not turn wolf.'

3 1

She still would not turn him over to the hunt. That first night – only the night before last, she thought in amazement – revulsion at the mob in the street had stopped her from turning him over to the militia. But now? How did one know a murderer? She had not thought her brother to be one either. If indeed he was. In any case, she could not let Ned stay here. Not after last night.

Along with all the other reasons . . . she felt hot as she remembered his hand closing around her ankle. He was so weakened that she had easily fought him off. And he had suddenly fallen into that same deep sleep as the night before. But he would heal.

In the daylight falling through the landing window, she saw spangles of light on his wrists and forearms. But no sign of a hideous corruption.

'You don't remember last night?'

He shook his head.

So Ned-the-man had played no part in that humiliating little comedy. She flushed with shame that she had been mad enough from all the strange goings-on that she might have given in to an advance that he did not even remember making. 'And you disown your actions last night as those of the wolf, not yours?' It might seem to some to be a convenient excuse.

'Were they so terrible?' He followed her into her room when she turned to fetch her Venetian looking glass from her bed.

367

She shrugged. 'Look at me.'

He turned to face her assessing stare.

'Your eyes don't shine like lamps, as that young man in the market swore they did. And they clearly haven't struck me dumb . . .'

'Because I'm not a wolf now.'

'Bite me,' she said. She held out her hand.

He glared at her. 'Don't mock what you don't understand. Please don't make light of it.'

'Do it!'

He leaned and took the fleshy side of her hand in his mouth as gently as if it were a dove's egg. She felt his teeth, and the warmth of his lips.

'Go on. You know that you want to!'

He released her and shook his head. 'I still don't remember eating the child, if that's the memory you wanted to awaken. And you're a fool to have taken that chance!'

'I'm a fool, for sure,' she said. 'But not that sort! Ned, please listen to me. Last night, I saw no wolf!'

'Give me your glass . . .'

As she put it into his hands, someone knocked on the door.

'Stay away from the window,' she said urgently.

She locked her chamber behind her, put the key in her bosom, and turned the heavy key in the lock of the front door.

It was an officer of the *burt*.

'I came to see that all's well with you, mevrouw. A neighbour thought she heard a man's voice in your house this morning, shouting.'

Marika managed to look astonished. 'Is my helpful neighbour certain that the voice didn't come from the alley behind the house? I often hear drunks there. I assure you, if a man had been shouting in this house, she would also have heard me screaming as well!'

As the man hesitated, she began to close the door. 'I'm grateful for your concern for my safety.'

368

Don't forget to smile!

She smiled gratefully.

He remained planted on the doorstep.

'Did my neighbour wish you to search my house for her imaginary man?' she asked lightly.

He shifted his weight to the other foot and peered past her shoulder into the hall. Then looked at the closed shutters.

'You're most welcome,' she said. 'But of course, you will need a suitable chaperone. I'm alone here in the house . . . you understand.'

'No, no. Of course.' He touched his hat. 'Well . . . Good morning, mevrouw.'

Half-way down the steps, he looked up again. 'And you won't forget to wash the steps and street, will you?'

'I won't forget.'

Marika glanced at the street as she closed and locked the door. A man still stood under that tree by the canal.

I'm now the accomplice of a supposed murdering monster. Of whose absolute innocence I'm not entirely sure. In law, I am now beyond excusing. I must be mad, with the law already set on my brother, and the house in jeopardy!

Her knees suddenly turned traitor. She went to sit on the bottom step of the staircase.

How have I arrived at this? I could be hanged. I could be burned.

The alternative was to turn Ned over to the police, almost certainly to be killed. Then flayed, stuffed and set up on display.

She bent forward as if in pain and rested her forehead on her knees. She tried to imagine turning him over. Even to save her own skin, she still couldn't do it!

Is it possible, she asked herself, that I enjoy the taste of danger?

She went into the parlour, where she opened all the shutters. Next, she went upstairs and threw wide the shutters over the windows in Justus's room, also at the front of the house.

369

Nothing to hide here in this house! So there!

They would just have to be careful.

Ned tried to hear who was at the door and what Marika was saying. He had begun to feel dizzy, but in the normal way, not with the slithering migrations of floor and wall that preceded the arrival of the wolf.

Marika climbed back up the stairs. 'My neighbours have already been busy, and eager to suspect the worst. I've opened the shutters to deflect suspicion. We must be silent, and take no chance of being spied through a window.'

Instead of answering, he leaned one hand against her chamber wall.

'Are you ill?' she asked in alarm.

'Hot.' His back was a bed of burning coals, and the heat seemed to be spreading to his head.

'Indeed, your forehead sears my palm! Come!' She had to help him walk to her bed. 'How long have you been this way?'

He lay down on the bed with a groan, rolled on to his side to save the broken skin of his back.

'I must get help,' she said. 'Find a physician . . .'

'No!'

She touched his cheek. 'I must! I don't know what to do for you. You're very ill! Your heart is accelerating like a runaway horse. Please, Ned! Let me fetch someone!'

He stared at her in such searching desperation that she feared he was losing his memory again and had forgotten who she was.

'Ned!' Her own heart quickened. What if he died? Then she thought grimly that compared to the task of getting rid of his body, hiding him was child's play.

'Ask for Josie or Catryn.' Suddenly sure, he gave her clear instructions and the name of a Blomsloot *musico*. Then he closed his eyes and seemed to give all his strength to the act of breathing.

32

Marika ran to the Torn Petticoat.

In the shadowed interior of the empty *musico*, an elderly maidservant washed the tabletops with a cloth that smelt of sour beer. A finch hopped from side to side along its perch against the wall. Somewhere in the shadows at the rear of the large room, a man was tuning a fiddle.

'Closed,' said the woman shortly. 'Come back later.'

'I must find an old friend. Josie Jugs.'

'A risky friend. She's dead of the pox, five years ago.'

'The Dainty Dane then.'

'I said we're closed!' Head down, rubbing hard. 'And we've enough whores here already.'

Marika found a coin in her purse. 'Or Catryn the Corset. You must know one of them!'

The woman looked up from her sour rag.

'What do you want with Catryn? She's retired. A great-grandmother twice over.'

'Where can I find her?'

When the woman scowled, Marika offered the coin.

Catryn studied her with suspicion, noting the diamond eardrops and badly laced corset. Even in her disorder, Marika might appear mad, but never poor. The woman in the Torn Petticoat notwithstanding, she could never be taken for a common *musico* whore.

371

They stood in a dirt-floored courtyard, near St Anthony's Gate, which Catryn shared with a tanner. The stench of hides and chemicals made Marika's eyes water, but Catryn seemed not even to notice. She had set a small, rough table on the dirt for dining in the open air where there was light to see.

An interesting place for Ned to have an old friend, thought Marika.

'I have a message from Ned Malise. He sends you his love and respects. He'd come himself, but he's in trouble and needs your help.'

'Neddie?' cried Catryn. 'The poor little lamb! I never thought to hear of him again!' She embraced Marika and held her tight against odorous layers of clothing. Her bulk would have suffocated a shorter woman than Marika. 'A welcome messenger! Sit, and speak! He must be a handsome man . . . Oh, I'd like to see him now! He was a lovely boy. Is he here in the city again? What's his trouble? What can I do?'

Marika took a stool beside the little table. It was ironic, in the circumstances, to hear him described as a 'poor little lamb'.

'Neddie, Neddie!' Catryn wiped her eyes and poured a little ale from an earthenware jug. 'That grandmother and her big ideas! Has life treated him more kindly since she died and that brother took him away to England?'

'Not so well as it might.' Marika could remember that he had had a grandmother, but Catryn's meaning escaped her. Ned's childhood had begun to appear as mysterious as his wolf. 'He needs urgent dosing. Sent me to ask where you and your friends turn when you need a physician's help, but without the physician.'

'Poxed or boxed, do you mean?' Catryn's nostalgia took on a sharper edge. 'Not to the physicians, for sure! Is it for you?'

Marika blushed scarlet. 'Nothing of that sort, I assure you!'

'Well.' Catryn's manner stiffened slightly. 'I thought. From the way you spoke of him.'

372

'I'm an old friend.' There was no time and no need to tell Catryn everything.

'I see.' Catryn eyed her with scepticism. 'Well, as another old friend, I'll give you a name – an apothecary turned cunning man, but he knows everything a physician knows and more.'

Marika hesitated. 'Is he discreet?'

Cathryn snorted. 'He was expelled from the guild, but practises all the same, if it's the law you're worried about.'

It was dusk when she left the shop of the cunning man. She set off for home at a near run. Once it grew dark, the watch stopped anyone caught not carrying a lantern. And she was terrified that she might find him dead. How fast can a heart beat before it whirs into silence?

Also, the cunning man had frightened her.

Standing under the stuffed crocodile which hung from the ceiling, she had asked only for something to bring down Ned's fever.

He gave her a decoction of white willow bark, with instructions. 'And what else?'

'What do you mean?' She had glanced around guiltily, as if expecting *shutter*s to step from the shadows and demand that she lead them to the fugitive beast.

The stuffed crocodile above her head was dusty and missing several teeth. The tiny shop was littered with half-filled jars, dirty spoons, measures of all sorts, in brass and tin, scales, knives, sieves, bottles.

'His cure begins here.' His voice was firm. His eyes were close together but pleasant, his grizzled beard neatly trimmed. He kept his small clean hands folded like a mouse's paws on the curve of his belly.

'His cure for what?' she had asked. How did he know? What signs had he read?

He studied her face. 'That's between him and me.' He rummaged in a chest of sweet-smelling wood. 'Here's a healing ointment of mallow and marigold, too, in case of need.' He

373

gave her a stoneware pot covered with oiled paper. 'And this is for you, an oriental tincture to give you strength.' He pressed a small glass bottle into her hand. 'No fee.'

She managed to thank him before she fled.

More placards had sprouted on trees. The list of the fugitive wolf-man's victims had grown by four missing dogs, six geese and a side of mutton stolen from a butcher's yard. And a man's body had been pulled from a canal with numerous gashes in the chest and arms.

A man still leaned on a tree in their street.

D'you want Justus or Ned?

She glanced up at the house to see that the windows showed nothing. She felt his eyes follow her up on to the *stoep* and through the front door.

Ned lay restless and hot in the dark, curled on to his side. But still alive.

'Where's my lute? I've remembered my lute.'

'In your lodgings perhaps? I'll fetch it for you later.'

'I can't remember where I lodged!' He rocked his head from side to side. 'I can't remember how I came to Amsterdam!'

She made a tisane of the willow bark. Soaked one of her petticoats in cold water and wiped his face with it. Applied the ointment of mallow and marigold to his head.

'Are they still hunting me with dogs?' he asked.

Once he sat up, wide-eyed. 'There's someone on the *stoep*!' And would not lie down again until she went to look.

'No one,' she said. 'A pleasant change.'

He seemed not to hear, but stared at the ceiling.

'Is your wolf coming?'

'No, no!' he said fretfully. 'Don't be a fool. I'm merely feverish . . . Have we ever made love?'

His face was flushed and burned her hand when she touched him. Without answering, she bathed his face and neck again in cool water. Then, in spite of his protests, she tried to tug off her brother's jacket.

'No!'

374

'Hang modesty!' She untied a sleeve and removed it first. He was too weak to resist her.

She pulled off the body of the jacket. He cried out in pain. Then she saw his back. Scored like a ham with crusted crosshatching. In places along the black lines, slits gaped hot and red.

The sight of it set off a faint internal trembling.

She turned him face down and very carefully cleaned away the crusted blood, while he growled and trembled but kept himself still. Then she applied the mallow and marigold salve.

After that, she bathed his head, neck and arms, until suddenly, after the watch had called one in the morning, his fever left him and he slept.

Marika made a tiny fire in her fireplace and went down into the garden for rosemary and lavender branches to burn to purify the air. She swallowed the oriental tincture which the cunning man had said would give her strength, and finished what was left of the roast chicken. Then she took the folded cloak and removed her stiffened bodice. She would sleep here on the floor of her room. In his weakened state, she had nothing to fear from him, and she wanted to hear if he took a turn for the worse in the night. She must wait till he was much stronger before she told him what the cunning man had said.

He slept all that night and most of the next day. In the afternoon, he suddenly sat up and reached out a hand as if he needed help climbing stairs.

'What is it?' She rushed to the bed and took his hand.

'I've remembered . . .'

375

33

Fragments.

His thoughts heaved like kittens drowning in a sack.

He lay on a packed earth floor. His hands and feet were tied. His head ached. A scratchy piece of sacking filled with dust had been tied across his eyes. Through its coarse weave, he saw a small, blurred unsteady orange light. Around the light lay darkness.

Smells of straw, dung and garlic. And stagnant water.

Something breathed near him.

He couldn't see.

Couldn't see.

On the other side of a wooden wall, a horse thumped and stamped.

Still the breathing, there, near him. Intent. Whatever was breathing was watching him.

He was naked. Lying on a floor. Trying to see through the cloth over his eyes. Whatever was watching him would be able to smell his fear.

'There's a wall,' he said to Marika. 'In my mind. Between here and there.'

He lay taut-limbed. Did not want to remember after all. But want it or not, more fragments arrived, began to settle together into moments of greater and greater coherence.

* * *

376

'We didn't kill him after all!'

'More fools we.'

He turned his head, trying to dislodge his blindfold against his shoulder or the floor. Then he curled forward and used his knees. Shifted it enough to see with one eye.

The wide flared eye of the musket stared back at him.

That's enough.

He lay for a long time with his eyes closed, on Marika's bed. But it was too late. He might as well try to hold back the sea.

TEN

34

'Don't look! The blindfold's come loose!' They turned away their faces and made signs against the evil eye.

Two farmers, one holding a torch, the other the musket, both wearing rosemary sprigs on thongs around their necks.

'Go tell the others he's come to his senses at last,' said the farmer with the musket. 'Be quick. Don't leave me alone with him.'

Ned groaned and turned his head on the pillow. Marika touched his forehead to see if the fever was on him again, but his skin was moist and cold.

The other farmer jammed his torch into an iron bracket on a post and left at a run.

In the silence, the torchlight wavered across splintery wooden walls. Above his head, beams, supported on posts. Iron hooks, a vast padded horse collar. A tack room. Part of a barn. His head pounded. His mouth was as dry as an old owl's nest. His feet were tied together with a pair of leather reins.

The torch made his head swim, so he closed his eyes again. Though it was still dark outside, cows lowed nearby in hard-uddered pain. Near dawn, then. Not far from his head, beyond a wooden wall, an unseen horse thumped in its stall. He was in a lean-to that ran along one side of the main barn to house the storage rooms and animal stalls.

Pain drummed in his left temple. The air was cool but not cold, and thick, like the inside of a cupboard. Straw needles dug into the bare skin of his back and neck.

Then he heard voices. Heard heavy boots cross the wooden barn floor.

'I say we should kill him and be done with it,' said a new voice.

'That's murder, Verhagen,' said the man with the musket.

'Not if he'd turned beast at the time.' There was a pause. 'It's no murder if you kill a beast.'

He stared up appalled at the men who had bunched just inside the tack-room door. A cold wave flooded down through his chest and gut into his legs. The hairs on his nape bristled.

'Don't you dare look at me!' The knuckles of the man with the musket whitened.

Two of them spat three times.

'I've five-month lambs to protect,' said Verhagen, the man who wanted to kill him at once. A big man. Rough, cold voice. Glint of light on a bald pate.

The pain in his temple swelled, black and huge as a thundercloud, blotted out his senses. Made his stomach heave. He rolled on to his side and vomited on to the packed dirt floor.

I shouldn't be here, he tried to say. I'm . . .

Part of his mind had been cut away. He could not remember his name.

He breathed in carefully so as not to choke on his own bitter fluids, and ran at the blankness again, as if his mind were a horse that had refused a jump. 'I'm . . .'

'Where's Piet?' demanded Verhagen. 'Why's he taking so long?'

'Waiting for the Reverend Steenwyck to do his buttons up, I expect.' Someone snorted.

What is my name? His thoughts scattered and rolled away like dried peas. He scrabbled after them. *Where am I and why?*

Name first. Take it easy. Deep breath. Try again.

What is my name?

382

He could almost see it now – a shadowy trout in muddy water, just a little too far back under the bank.

'Here comes Reverend Steenwyck!'

Voices in the main barn. Men jostled in the doorway. Two more torches which made his head thump with the black pain. More eyes stared down at him. The stink of their fear pierced even that of cow and horse.

'Steenwyck . . . I can't see him,' Ned said. 'But I can't see him!'

'Hush,' said Marika. She laid her hand on his forehead. 'Wait. He'll come.'

And he did. One minute, a mere presentiment, a blur. Then, all at once, there the Reverend Steenwyck was, as clear and complete in Ned's mind as if he had never been missing.

'How can I deal with him, you fools, if I can't get in?' The small, pink, wiry man shoved through the massed bodies to stand looking down at the man on the floor, leaning on his walking stick, wavering with a palsy and breathing hard. He wore an unbuttoned black coat over an open shirt, no collar, and clogs over his leather slippers. A rim of white hair stood straight out from his head in an angry halo. 'Is this your beast? He looks man enough to me.'

'I would feel even more human,' said Ned, who still did not remember that he was Ned, 'if you untied me and gave me back my clothes. And a drink of water.' The clothes were hazy, but he thought he could remember them. Hat. Boots. Sword. 'A drink of water, for the love of God!'

'Hear how hoarse his voice is!' said someone in the doorway. 'Like a devil.'

'You understand me?' asked the old man, a little too loudly.

The minister's presence made him feel safer. 'The chances are that I understand a language I speak.' He was proud of this self-possession in such circumstances.

383

What is my name?

'A fair point.' The white-haired man studied him. 'I'm the minister of the local church which serves these two villages. Steenwyck. Should be in bed. May I ask for your version of who you are? I've heard theirs!'

It was there, just behind a veil. Pressing its shape into the veil.

'He looks as if he's been hit on the head, among other places,' said Steenwyck to the men behind him. 'That might drive a few things out of any man's memory for a while. Who hit him?'

There was a murmur.

'We all did, one way or another,' said a voice.

'I never touched his head,' said Verhagen.

'And no one hit him that hard, I swear! But, look, there at the mark of my nails where my grip on the beast slipped!' A hitherto silent farmer pointed to parallel scratches on Ned's upper arm.

'Ah,' said Steenwyck. 'Your doubled wound! Can't do without that, can we? Proves the case, doesn't it? Absolutely.' He turned back to the men in the door. 'Someone untie him. And fetch clothes and water instead of gawping at his nakedness! And Paulus Janzsoon, put that gun away!'

'With respect, sir, we'll keep him tied, if you don't mind,' said Verhagen.

'Well, I do mind. As the shepherd of your souls, I order you to set this poor fellow free, unless you can convince me that he did far worse than kill two chickens.'

'Chickens?' asked Ned. He tried to remember chickens.

'He tore them apart alive and ate them raw!' protested Paulus Janzsoon, who in other circumstances might have been a cheerful-looking, ginger-haired man of thirty or so.

Steenwyck ignored him and glared into the crowd at the door. 'I'd untie him myself, but my hands are turned feeble servants. Who else has the courage? No one?' He pulled himself up on his trembling legs and eyed the wedge of

384

bodies in the doorway. 'Thank the Lord, I don't need a cat belled as well!'

One of the newly arrived torches beat directly into Ned's eyes. The men's voices swelled and blended into a blurred roar.

No! Not now, please! He knew that he recognised this sensation and did not want it. With all his will, he fixed his eyes on Steenwyck. Tried to see only him. Reached for the single strand of his voice in the Babel.

'I'll do it.' The man who had brought the minister now pushed through the massed bodies into the shed and knelt cautiously beside Ned. The man with the torch moved aside to let him past.

'Thank you, Piet,' said Steenwyck.

Gratefully, Ned turned his eyes on to this brave soul who had stepped away from the rest.

But as he tugged at the knots, Piet's bright orange-blond hair was back-lit by a torch. The bright globe of his head contracted, then swelled again, then sent out waving tendrils of light. The stinks of fish and seawater on his clothes exploded inside Ned's skull. The men's voices tumbled and boomed again around the walls.

He closed his eyes to steady the world. Keep your grip! Keep your grip!

'Ned!' he said suddenly. Edward. Edward James St Stephen Malise. Along with a wonderful ease of body as the ropes fell away from his arms, his mind also leaped free.

'I'm Edward Malise,' he said. He wanted to weep with relief. The booming sounds and piercing smells eased. 'An English gentleman.'

For a moment, a rush of memory made him forget the talk of beasts and dead chickens, forget even the gun. With the torch no longer shining into his eyes, the world steadied.

EDWARD! (Whose voice was that . . . whose ringing tones?) Ned Malise . . . Englishman. Had a brother named Francis. (It's all coming back to me now . . .) And the last

385

that I knew, (I KNEW! I once *knew*), I was wearing a dark wine-red silk suit, brown leather boots, and carrying my brother's sword ... (How did I come by it?) And I had a hat.

He saw the hat as clearly as if it were in his hand: wide brim, soft, curling feather. Hat, red, feather, blue. Yes!

The blond fisherman now tugged at the knots by his ankles.

With a sense of detached surprise, Ned noted that he had long legs, fine ankles, well-muscled arms and generous genitalia, all of these, except ankles and penis, lightly-furred with fine, dark curling hair.

He looked again at the length of his legs.

I am above the usual height.

He stretched his fingers to restore feeling. Shapely fingers on strong but soft-palmed hands, which were now dirty, scraped raw on the knuckles and with black-rimmed nails.

His fingers pressed down on the strings of an invisible lute. Suddenly, he saw himself complete, upright and no longer naked, reflected in diamond-shaped pieces, faint and watery, in a dark window. With that remembered reflection, his entire physical self arrived at a clap: long face with a strong nose, black curling hair cut to his collar, with a little early grey over his ears. Black lashes and pale grey eyes, which several women had said gave him a fierce look even when he meant to smile. No beard.

He looked down again. A tall, narrow, leggy male body, with good hands and feet. Yes!

'I shouldn't move about as you are doing now,' said Steenwyck. 'My parishioners are jumpy.'

'I won't bite them,' said Ned, careless with relief.

Piet the fisherman gave him a quick look that might have been amused.

'There seems to be some question about that,' said Steenwyck.

Ned hardly heard. He might have captured himself, but the world outside the barn was still absent. There was nothing out there but a void. No house, room, or even patch of street where

386

he might once have stood. His world had gone as absolutely as his name.

He began to whistle softly, to calm himself.

Back off. Sidle up sideways. Corner of the eye. Where was that reflecting window? Who else had been reflected in it?

'Here are your clothes, Mynheer Malise,' said Steenwyck. 'Put them on. No court that I acknowledge would interrogate the accused while he's stark naked. And drink to wet your mouth. Then we'll discuss what you were or were not doing to those chickens.'

He returned abruptly to the only world that existed, here in this farm building, which held mysteriously murdered chickens, endangered lambs, a fight that he could not remember, and a farmer who wanted to kill him at once.

'Herman Verhagen, Paulus Janzsoon . . .' Ned lost track of the long list of names as Steenwyck gave them.

'All honest, hard-working farmers,' said the minister. 'None of them drunk last night, so far as I can tell.' Someone had brought a barrel for Steenwyck to sit on. He gained dignity when he could sit down and the palsy that afflicted him was eased. 'And reluctantly I have to say that a few such cases have been proved in court . . . in France, however. It's a pity you can't remember last night.'

Ned stared at the minister. The return of his suit and shirt, washed and pressed by a farmer's wife, had restored his sense that the world did exist elsewhere. Dressed, he could believe in that world now, in an almost religious act of faith. Had he not bought these clothes there?

He raised his left hand to test the tenderness of his head and through the harsh tang of lye soap, caught a whiff of civet lingering on his lace shirt-cuff. He stared past Steenwyck's shoulder. There was another smell on his skin. In his nostrils. He sniffed his hand again. An unpleasant, sickly smell. And he imagined its putrid taste in his mouth.

'Mynheer Malise?'

387

'Look how he stares! And how pale he is,' said a man's voice. 'I tell you, it's not right!'

'Mynheer Malise?' Steenwyck sounded a little impatient, as if he had repeated himself more than once.

'I'm sorry,' said Ned. He blinked.

'I said, it's a pity that you don't remember more.'

His body was rigid with the effort of recalling how he knew that smell.

'Why does it matter what he remembers?' demanded Paulus Janzsoon, the man with the musket.

No! Wait! he cried in despair as his thoughts scattered. Almost . . . !

'It's enough that we all saw him. And there's the blood under his fingernails.'

'I can't remember how I got here,' Ned said to Steenwyck in despair. 'I still can't remember.' Then he heard himself say, 'I was in Leiden . . .'

Why was I in Leiden?

The world returned to him in a clap, like his name. All there at once. The beast in London. His brother's supposed cure for the small pox. The flight to Leiden with Maurits van Egmond, whom gossip said had no right to the name in spite of his impressive house. But between that falling glass in Maurits's house and here in this farming village there was still a hole in his thoughts.

'Herman . . . Paulus, tell Mynheer Malise what you saw last night.'

'We saw *him*!' Janzsoon averted his eyes from Ned, fearful but stubborn. 'Or whatever he was then. We captured the beast, bound it, and then find *him* here, now. Argue with that, if you can.'

Ned finally began to hear what was being said about him. He blinked.

'Did you see him in the act of killing or eating your chickens?' asked Steenwyck.

'Not in the act, as such, but naked, on all fours, clear

enough, like a wolf. And my best laying hen a little way off on the ground, and the pullet a little beyond. Feathers all round . . .'

His wolf had undone him at last.

'I am not in the habit of going naked on my hands and knees.' Ned glanced at Steenwyck. He chose his words carefully. 'And I doubt very much if I killed your chickens. The very thought makes me ill.'

'Maybe now it does.' The farmer's eyes glinted. 'But we saw you! Before you finished changing your shape back again. And you can still hear the beast in his voice!'

Ned stared back at Janzsoon, who averted his eyes and spat on the ground. The hair suddenly stood up on his neck. He had finally grasped the whole truth: these ignorant farmers believed what had only been whispered in London, that he had turned into a wolf in body as well as spirit. They firmly believed that he was a true shape-changer. A true werewolf. One moment a man, the next a four-legged beast. With a beast's senses and terrible appetites.

The frightening truth was that he could not remember enough of the past night to argue the contrary.

'Why should I kill your chickens? I like my chickens on a dish. With dumplings, by preference. Served up by my man-servant, at a table.' He turned to the minister. 'His accusation is monstrous!'

'So far as you remember,' said Janzsoon stubbornly. 'But it all fits . . . your forgetting. They never remember.'

'A dog or fox killed your fowl,' said Ned desperately.

Of course, that's how it had been! And if Steenwyck could keep these madmen from shooting him or hanging him like vermin, he would in the end remember how he had come to be there.

His beast had never hurt anyone so far. But he also knew that whatever he had become in the past night felt different from his London beast. If its nature had changed, what else might it have done?

389

'Wolf or demon, one or the other,' insisted Verhagen.

'That's enough!' said Steenwyck. 'The Dutch Reformed Church does not admit either werewolves or demons. I refuse to choose between them. I expect to see you all on Sunday morning with your most devout and commonsense faces on . . . and filled with remorse for this foolishness.'

Janzsoon's sunburnt face reddened again to a deep mahogany. 'What about my hens?'

'I'll gladly pay for them if that would help settle the matter,' said Ned. 'As a gesture of goodwill only, to be sure, with no admission of guilt. Then I'll return to . . .' he nearly said Leiden but stopped himself in time '. . . to Amsterdam and we can all get on with our lives as before.'

'If not wolf or a demon, then he was bewitched,' said Verhagen. 'We know what we saw, don't we, Paulus?'

'In the dark?' demanded Ned.

'And we know how he was when we captured him. Roaring and raging, beastly howls and grunts. Not a human word among them. A wolf, I tell you!'

Steenwyck stood up. His hand trembled on his stick, but he roared. 'This man is not bewitched! Nor possessed by a demon, nor a shape-changer nor werewolf, nor *loup-garou* nor *versipillus* or whatever clot-pole nonsense you want to call it! I say that you all have an overworked imagination and that he is a troubled soul in want of the Lord's mercy. My conscience will not let me turn him loose until I have talked and prayed with him. He also needs a surgeon.' He turned to Ned. 'Will you come with me to the church?'

'No, reverend.' The large bulk of Verhagen stepped forward. 'A good many of us agree – we won't free him. We have our families and livestock to protect. The devil is his master, one way or another.'

'Then only God, and not a rabble of farmers, can master the devil in him!' Steenwyck's hair seemed to blaze out like rays from the sun. His wrinkled face turned as red as Paulus Janzsoon's. 'Go out!' he ordered Ned.

Clothing rustled as bodies shifted, half-moved to stop him. He braced his shoulders for the blow of a musket ball.

The farmers' story sucked at him dangerously. Much of it fitted with what he felt.

Steenwyck followed him slowly and painfully out of the barn into the still shadowy flatness of the farmyard.

'He needs a proper priest,' murmured a low voice.

'Priests are what the Spanish have,' retorted Piet, the blond fisherman.

In the farmyard, Steenwyck said, 'Keep walking before me. What fools they are! But that doesn't make them less dangerous.' A few steps later, he added, 'It makes me ask myself what I've achieved in my forty years here.'

They crossed the farmyard and went out through a gate. The men pressed close behind, divided into two opposed and angry groups.

'Farmers against fishermen mostly likely,' muttered Steenwyck. 'Both villages are mine. Farmers down here. Fishermen up there.' He pointed.

On the far side of the nearest field, high above their heads, a row of darkened houses perched on the rim of a dyke. Behind the dyke, the masts of fishing boats swayed against the night sky, the boats anchored higher than any of the houses. The sea lay beyond that dyke, higher than the fields, waiting to reclaim them.

Then Steenwyck guided him into a long narrow lane which ran between two darkly glinting ditches. Ahead, the black bulk of the church floated on a raft of paving in the centre of the vast, flat, damp fields, surrounded by the farmers' houses. Steenwyck followed Ned across the paved terrace into the shadows of the porch. He glanced behind, pushed Ned into the church and barred the door behind them.

In the faint grey light from the high windows of plain glass, the shadowed nave was a shock of ghostly white, pared down to such chalky purity that it hardly felt like a church. No pictures in gilded frames. No painted statues.

391

Ned took off his hat, bent his knee and crossed himself.

His grandmother's knobbed fingers sketched a cross. He saw the silver hair escaping from her cap, her straight back. He was kneeling behind her, watching the fly that crawled along laces of her bodice, and shifting from knee to knee on a cold stone floor, trying to keep his mind on God.

Steenwyck raised his white eyebrows. 'Papist?'

Ned nodded. He had also remembered his oath to her.

I seem to move farther and farther from fulfilling it, he thought with a stab of wry despair.

'I'll trust the Lord to work out the differences between us.' Steenwyck fumbled in a box by the door for a candle and tinderbox.

A fist thudded on the church door. 'Let us in!' Verhagen's voice was faint through the heavy wood. 'We will come in and guard the beast!'

Steenwyck and Ned looked at each other.

'Can you see any signs of . . . what they're so sure they saw?' asked Ned intensely. 'Tell me straight.'

'As well as I can in this light, I see only a man who needs treating for his injuries.' Steenwyck hobbled back to the barred door, placed his face close to the thick timbers and bellowed, 'Leave us in peace!' Turning back to Ned, he said, 'And with a troubled soul.'

'No wolf?'

'More like an uneasy conscience.'

'Always that, in any case.'

The door reverberated again under pounding fists. 'We will come in if we have to break down the door!'

Steenwyck slid back the bar and waited just inside the door.

Paulus Janzsoon and Herman Verhagen charged into the church with other men behind them, but stopped when they found Steenwyck blocking their way down the central aisle of the nave. In their wide, woollen trousers, the farmers formed a solid torchlit mass.

'For shame!' said Steenwyck. 'The Lord will protect me. Or do you offer to do His work for Him?'

'We say that the Lord sometimes needs His soldiers on this earth to help out a little,' said Verhagen. 'Please stand aside, sir, as we all mean to come in, whether you invite us or not.'

Steenwyck stared him up and down, making an oblique chewing motion as if trying to subdue false teeth. 'Come in and witness God's work, then.' He stepped back. 'But don't insult the Lord by bringing your guns. I won't have it!'

They consulted. 'We'll leave all but one,' said Verhagen. 'Paulus, keep yours.'

Steenwyck leaned so close as they walked forward over the black-and-white tiles to the chalky altar that Ned was unsure whether he was supported or supporting. The faint orange light of the torches now laid a delicate orange stain on the pale columns. 'Can you weep?' whispered the old man.

'Weep?' Ned gave him a startled glance.

'I'd like you to leave this village alive, to have a chance to put right whatever has darkened your life. True repentance can encompass a touch of show, if you follow me. I leave it to you.'

They knelt, Steenwyck leaning hard on Ned's shoulder as he lowered himself to the floor. 'We'll pray together,' Steenwyck said. 'Search out the stain. God is merciful.'

'Our Father,' he began more loudly. 'Have mercy on Your child, this poor stranger who has fallen among us. Give him a peaceful home in Your bosom . . .'

Ned found tears starting in his eyes, without his will. He gazed up a pale tree-trunk column to the spreading branches of the chalky arched roof.

'. . . lift the weight that burdens his soul. Return him to his rightful self . . .'

A sense of loss and fear pushed at his throat. He felt all a-jangle, as if his arms or legs might suddenly shoot out into the air by themselves, or he would suddenly sob aloud. He wiped his eyes. The tears were no ruse.

393

'Help him to find peace in this earthly life as he will surely find Eternal Rest in Your bosom. Amen.'

Steenwyck stood, pushing himself up this time. 'Prayers may help, but you must remember that each of us is the guardian of his own soul. Whatever it may be, the beast is yours to quell, your wrestling angel.'

'Make him take Holy Communion!' shouted a voice from the back of the church. 'He can't go free unless he can swallow the Communion wafer!'

Answering shouts drowned him out.

Paulus and his group now stood at the top of the aisle, blocking escape, draped in the black shadows cast by their torches. Behind them, Piet and his crew were wedged into the doorway. Hostility crackled between the two groups like lightning.

'I wager he'll choke on it!' Herman Verhagen thumped his fist against a pew back like a stallion kicking the side of its stall. 'We saw what he was last night and know what he is now, even though he's managed to pull the wool over your eyes! I *know* that devil will choke on the holy bread!'

'Give him the wafer! Give him the wafer!' The chorus grew at the back of the church.

Ned met the minister's eyes. 'The wafer is far less dangerous than your parishioners.'

Steenwyck looked at the faces crowded in the aisle and nodded unhappily. He raised his voice. 'Will you all swear to be satisfied then, and let this man go free?'

'If he can swallow the holy wafer, we will be satisfied.'

'Does Paulus speak for all of you?'

A chorus of assent.

'Kneel again.'

Ned felt the pressure of eyes against his back and blessed the minister for making the men leave their guns outside.

Steenwyck disappeared into the dark vestry and reappeared with his coat buttoned and wearing a white collar that lapped in stiffly starched layers over his chest.

394

Ned watched the tremulous old hands go through a private and domestic little ritual with the wafer. His throat felt thick. He coughed.

Instantly, he heard a murmur behind him. Steenwyck's white eyebrows shot up and his right hand shook more widely than usual, as if he had waved away a hornet.

'He'll never do it!' A low intense voice swilled down the aisle like evil flood water and sent a cold current up Ned's spine.

He swallowed. His mouth had been dry since he first came to his senses in the farm shed. Now it was as dry as chaff on a dusty floor.

Suddenly, he doubted. Unthinkable as it was, ragged shards of his memory — a remembered beast — said that Paulus and Herman might be right.

He tried to swallow again. His tongue had become a lump of unresponsive meat lodged at the back of his mouth.

Steenwyck showed the wafer to the crowd at the back of the church.

'Wait.' Paulus Janzsoon and Herman Verhagen came forward to stand on either side of Ned. Janzsoon carried his musket and Verhagen, a torch.

Ned cracked open his parched mouth. Stuck out his tongue to receive the wafer. Nearly gagged.

Janzsoon inhaled sharply. Verhagen held the torch closer to Ned's face. Ned could smell their heat and anger.

For the first time, Steenwyck looked afraid.

Give me the wafer quickly, Ned willed Steenwyck. Before things go further awry.

Steenwyck murmured. For one miraculous moment, his hand was steady. The wafer alighted on Ned's tongue like a moth.

Ned tried to swallow.

But he had forgotten how. In a nightmare of forgetting, his tongue stuck between his gums like a swollen door. He closed his eyes to Paulus, to the muskets, to Steenwyck's anxious eyes. In terror and desperation, he went somewhere else.

He was seventeen. He caught Marika against a soft box hedge and sank his face into her neck. He breathed in her spicy sweat and rosewater. His throat heaved.

He opened his eyes. And then his mouth. A miracle.

'It's gone,' said Steenwyck.

Paulus caught Ned's head between his hands, pressed open his jaw with a heavy thumb and peered into his mouth, while Verhagen thrust the torch so close that Ned thought his hair would catch fire.

He was too weak with relief to protest. The consecrated host had not rejected him.

'Is it not gone?' asked Steenwyck.

'It's gone.' Paulus turned to the group at the back. 'Who else wants to see?'

Ned's head had begun to spin. He closed his eyes to shut out the juddering light of the torch. 'I must get up!'

'You swore you'd be satisfied!' cried Steenwyck. 'Let him go now.'

Ned cried out and turned his head away.

'Why can't he look at the light?' demanded Verhagen. 'Look! He's turning away from the light!'

'It's over,' said Steenwyck. 'You gave your word. Let him go!'

'But why can't the dog of darkness look at the light?'

There was a dangerous silence.

Ned forced himself to turn and stare into the flames of the torch. The church began to jump and judder like the fire.

A bubble of horror rose up from his stomach and stuck under his breastbone. A giant fist began to tighten around him.

He remembered: this was how it had happened before.

No! Please, not now!

The beast was in the church, close, slipping between bodies. It brushed against him, leaped on to his shoulder. The fist pressed it into his head.

He strained to push it back out. He was going to die.

But his will was not enough. The beast grew like coral

into the spaces in his bones. Its muscles lapped around his own, wormed through his fibres like fungus under tree bark. The fist loosened its grip, to give the beast room. His limbs lengthened. His collar choked him. The torch blinded him. Voices drummed like the sea. He pulled at his collar, unable to breathe. Tore the buttons from his jacket as he hauled it off. A scream pierced his skull like a knife. The leaping flames set other fires alight, so deep in his memory that he could not see what burned.

The muscles of his face tightened. The skin shifted on his bones. His ears pulled towards the back of his skull. His nose pressed forward into a muzzle. The weight of a tail lay heavily along the crack of his buttocks. When he moved, silky fur slid over his muscles under the skin, liquid, soft, easy, invisible to the eyes of others. The last whisper of himself slipped down the throat of the beast like a mouse's tail.

He was the beast.

The stench of fear plugged his nostrils. Blind with terror, he struggled through a thicket of warm bodies, lashed by shouts and screams, jarred by the blast of a musket. Sharp stone fragments rained on to his shoulders. He plunged towards darkness and freedom. Reached the door. Was free.

A second musket ball whined past him. He turned, jumped a water-filled ditch, running too fast for pain to catch up with him. An open field now. The darkness thickened. His muscles coiled and released. He ducked low and ran along the flank of the dyke. Across a drainage channel. Then another. Missed his footing, fell. Dark water swallowed him. He burst up through the surface, knew that he must keep running from the voices behind him, scrambled at the bank, slipped on the wet grass, fell, clambered up again. On the bank behind him, a war of shouting raged.

The net poised like a gull, then covered him.

In his new prison, the wolf smelled human terror on the door handle. A layer of fetid human sweat floated around his head.

397

Fear, dirt, and excitement mixed with the overall scent of a mare. Here, near the door was an effluvium of rage.

The door was solid, with a small barred window. A man waited on the other side, out of sight, breathing quickly. The wolf pressed closer to the door, heard an abrupt rustle of cloth and the gritting of boots. He picked out from the tangled smells a wisp of sulphur from a fired gun.

Limping and careful of his bruises, he tested the bottom of all four walls. Cracks large enough for smells and sounds, but not for escape. In the cracks were traces of mice and stale grain.

Then he heard four voices, low and urgent, returned to the door and pressed his face to the narrow opening between two iron bars. The men, out of sight to his left, reeked of rage and sour panic. He felt himself tossed in the centre of all their tumbling words.

He began to dig the earth floor away from one wall. But the brick foundations had been sunk deep. His nails broke on the hard earth, the skin on his fingers began to bleed. He gave up digging and considered the roof. The underside of tiles laid on a wooden frame. Too high to leap, even without an injured leg. No holds on the walls.

No way out that he could see. He lay down on his stomach, braced on his elbows and faced the door to see what would happen next. He lay so still that, after a while, a mouse came out of the wall to carry on cleaning up the scattered grain.

Ned woke with a flash of wellbeing, as if relieved of a weight. Then he remembered the bubble of terror that had lodged in his throat as he forced himself to look into the torch flame.

He was now penned in a box stall in a barn. Untied, this time, but the opening for the horse's head had been boarded over with stout planks. He raised his hands to his face in the dim light, turned them palm-up and back again. Human hands. He recognised the long fingers that used to dance on lute strings.

He touched his face. He remembered feeling that his ears shifted on his skull, his nose stretched into a muzzle. The

398

tickling beneath his skin could well have been the prick-ing of fur.

'Steenwyck!' he shouted.

The door of the stall was locked from the outside.

'Bring me a looking glass!' he shouted into the hazy dawn light of the barn, through the iron bars set into the door. 'I need a glass!'

Something stirred but no one answered.

He resonated with fear like the bronze gong.

'Open the door! I beg you.'

Again, no reply. He struck the door with his fist in frustration. Wiped both hands over his face again and stared at them as if his features might have printed themselves on his palms. Felt the shape of his head again and again.

His ears sat close to his scalp, in their usual places under the dark curls, although his left temple throbbed and was sticky with blood. He bent to feel his legs. His long narrow feet were where he expected them to be, although one was booted and the other bare. His shirtsleeves ended in lace cuffs that covered the tops of his hands, just as they should do. One sleeve, however, hung like stripped bark from his upper arm. He had lost his collar and jacket in his flight from the church.

Unreason seeped into him like wind-born frost. His mind stiffened with the chill of disbelief, his thoughts set solid and tangled like frozen reeds.

I turned beast. In body as well as spirit.

No, no, no, he chided himself. You merely imagine that you did. You let Paulus and Herman seduce you. Like a child told a fairy tale. Imagined it to be real.

But those other memories nudged at him. And there were more memories layered even deeper – terrifying, half-seen ghosts of his thoughts. His hair stood straight on end with the knowledge, bristling on his arms, legs and scalp.

Last night was not the first time.

He was a current of pain flowing towards the warm smell of horse and cow. Then came the shouts . . .

399

A memory. The beast's memory. When it had arrived in the village.

Renewed terror washed over him. Then passed, without a renewed claim by the beast, without repossession.

Perhaps it had been nothing but terror there in the church.

But he knew the truth: he had been transformed in this new way at least once before the time in the church. He was a shape-shifter.

He pounded on the door. Threw himself at it.

'Send me the minister! I want to talk to Steenwyck!' He gripped the bars. Tried to push off the boards nailed to the opening for the horse's head. More than anything, he needed to converse calmly with another rational soul.

'Come speak to me!'

Come speak in words illuminated by human reason. Knit me back again into human society.

'Just a moment . . . I'm already here. Been here all along.' Slowly, the old man dragged himself into Ned's view through the bars. 'I'm sorry, I slept.' His black coat was covered with straw.

'I need a looking glass,' said Ned, past wondering why the elderly pastor had slept in the barn and not his own feather bed.

'If he tries to break out, we'll fire the barn,' warned Herman Verhagen's disembodied voice close outside the stall door. 'We have armed men posted all around it. We'll shoot at whatever runs out – man or beast.'

'I've sent for the municipal physician,' said Steenwyck through the bars. 'But he can't come until midday. I'll stay with you until then.'

'What do you see here in this stall, now?' demanded Ned.

'Oh, my son!' said Steenwyck. 'Nothing more than the man I prayed with in the middle of the night.'

Ned remembered the lengthening limbs, his muzzle stretching, the bubble of horror under his breastbone. The knowledge of death.

400

'But what did you see after the prayers?'

Steenwyck did not answer.

'For the love of God, tell me what you saw!'

'May I approach closer to the door?' Steenwyck was speaking to someone else. He steadied himself by gripping the bars and looked into Ned's eyes in the dim light. 'I didn't see ears, or tail or teeth, if that's what you mean.'

'Do you swear it?'

'I swear that I did not see any of those things.' He hesitated. 'But my eyes are no longer good . . . untrustworthy as my hands. My word does not convince the villagers. And I'm afraid that some of them swear to fangs as well. I hope that a physician's word will carry more weight than mine. You had received blows, including a blow to the head . . .'

'My case is different,' said Ned. 'Men are diminished by injury, not augmented.'

Steenwyck drew his bristling white eyebrows together. 'What are you trying to say?'

'Father, I felt a thing arrive in me, from somewhere else. It was no internal stain. The beast arrived and entered me!'

'No!' Steenwyck gripped the bars more tightly. 'You describe possession! The Church does not accept that possibility. I cannot accept it!'

'I don't know how else to describe what happened,' said Ned in despair. 'I can only speak the truth as I felt it!'

'Listen to me!' Steenwyck's eyes were fierce. 'What you felt was an illusion. Sooner or later each of us must stare the devil in the eye. What happens after that is how human souls are distinguished one from another. Some choose to fight, others succumb. You may choose to give yourself over to his incitements, but he cannot enter you! Nor send some occupying minion fiend. He cannot possess you! If you wish to imagine that he can, then you are truly in danger.'

'I did not choose!' cried Ned. 'I swear that I did not choose! I was taken.'

'That belief is your choice!' said Steenwyck angrily. 'And if

401

you choose it, then the devil has already seduced you. Believe me, I know that power. The devil is good at taking shapes. The fishermen see him coiled under the sea and the farmers hear him snuffling outside their walls at night. I pray with all my strength that God gives you the might to resist.'

Ned remembered again the sense of lengthening limbs, stretching muzzle, the bubble of horror beneath his breastbone.

'Perhaps I am merely mad.'

'Yes, most likely.'

'How odd that I would be grateful to be mad!' Once he had resisted the thought.

'Not odd at all,' retorted Steenwyck. 'A madman has only to let a physician cure him, or to hide in his madness. A sinner has painful work to do.'

The physician arrived well after the midday meal. A short, fair, stocky man in his forties, in a physician's black coat and white collar, he picked his way through the straw on the barn floor like a cat shaking snow from its paws.

There was a long and fiery debate about the dangers of unbarring the door to the stall. Then it was agreed: the physician must examine Ned by sight alone, through the bars.

'He's back in his human form,' Herman's voice explained. 'But might transform again at any time.'

The physician's round pale face appeared at the bars in the door.

Ned stared back into the light blue eyes under almost-white brows, looking for sympathy or at least recognition of a fellow man.

'That's his human form,' repeated Herman Verhagen.

'How do you feel?' the physician asked. 'Can you understand me?'

'Very well. And I feel both frightened and confused.' He made his tone as civil and reasonable as he could.

'Are you a man or a beast?'

402

'I would hope there's no doubt! I'm a man!' Nevertheless, Ned glanced down at his hands and legs to reassure himself that they were still indeed human parts. 'Is that not clear?'

'Hold out your hands.'

A touch defiantly, Ned did so.

'There's blood under your nails.'

'I'm covered in blood from my own wounds!' Ned turned his head sideways to show a dark clotted wound on his left temple, then showed the scratches on his arms. 'I touched my own blood.'

'Now turn around and lift up your shirt.'

Ned nearly balked, but, to keep the man's goodwill, such as it was, he obeyed.

There was a long silence, while the physician presumably examined his back. He heard feet shuffling outside the stall, and a clinking of metal.

'He has the aphrodisiac tuft,' said the physician at last, to someone outside the stall. 'There, just above the cleft of the buttocks.' He raised his voice. 'Do you remember turning beast?'

'I don't know what I remember.' Ned swallowed. He dropped his shirt and turned back to the door. 'But I swear that I never killed any chickens. The blood under my nails is my own. I am a mild-tempered man. I was never a soldier. I am not even fond of hunting.'

'Are you thirsty?'

'Yes!' That he could answer with full conviction. 'I've had nothing to drink since last night and then not much.'

'His case is quite clear,' said the physician to the men outside the stall. 'Pale complexion and sunken eyes. By his own testimony, his mouth lacks saliva. He has all the signs . . . Please turn around and lift your shirt again . . . That tuft of hair on the base of his spine, the aphrodisiac tuft . . . a predisposition . . .'

'What are you saying?' demanded Ned. He remembered similar words from the Queen's physician.

403

'He suffers from a sootiness in his black bile. An overflowing of melancholy.'

'What kind of melancholy makes a man kill my best laying hen?' asked Paulus Janzsoon with open disbelief.

'One in which he dreams that he is a beast. Such occurrences are common.' The physician spoke with assured authority. 'Men and women in a state of distraction often believe themselves to be dogs, cats, hares or, most commonly, wolves.'

Ned stared at him through the bars. 'Do you mean madness after all?'

'I say that he turned beast,' said the farmer. 'Not just dreamt about it. You didn't explain the mark of my nails on his arm, where I laid hold of the beast when we captured it.'

'If he was dreaming, he must have been asleep, so who killed the hens?' called a voice from the back. The blond fisherman pushed himself forward into Ned's view.

'There are three possible answers to your question,' said the physician. 'He may indeed have carried out the bloody acts himself while in a dream-like state. Or else, the devil may have incited a real beast to do the slaughter while this man slept. Or the devil himself may have killed the hens to make it seem that this man is guilty.'

'*Am . . . I . . . mad . . . or . . . not?*' Ned thrust his face against the bars and shouted. 'For the love of God, answer me. Speak to me . . . to *me*! These are human words, are they not? I spoke to you. Reply to me, not to them!'

The physician looked startled and stepped back from the door. Steenwyck stared at the floor.

'What are we to do with him now?' demanded an unfamiliar voice. 'Will you take him away? Lock him up safe in a madhouse?'

'That's up to you,' said the physician.

'What is the cure?' asked Steenwyck.

'Restraint so he can do no more harm. Or a hole in the head to relieve the pressure of the melancholy.'

'Who pays?' shouted another voice.

404

'Just set me free,' begged Ned, filled with a new terror, of dark cells and holes in his skull. 'I swear that I feel entirely human again. Just set me free. I will pay for the dead hens and put as much distance as you like between this village and myself for no fee at all.'

'He's a demon,' said a voice. 'I say burn him!'

'The villages must meet to decide what to do,' said another voice. 'Both upper and lower together.'

'But what if he shifts again and escapes? Someone's child will be next!'

'Just let me know what you decide,' said the physician. 'If and when you are able to decide.' He left, still stepping cat-like through the rank barnyard puddles outside the barn door.

'Sooty bile!' exclaimed one farmer with contempt.

'I still say we should kill him and be done with it,' said Herman Verhagen. '*We* weren't dreaming, whatever the doctor says!'

Reluctantly, Ned had to agree that whatever had happened had not felt like a dream, any more than it felt like madness. Apart from anything else, as the man said, he did carry the mark of Janzsoon's nails.

'Go have your meeting of the two villages,' Steenwyck said fiercely. 'I shall stay right where I am. And I would be grateful if someone would send for my wife.'

The farmers poised, undecided. Ned watched fists clench and unclench on hay forks and spades.

'You heard what the minister said.' Piet's voice again.

Ned now became aware that a second group had bunched in opposition to Herman Verhagen and his crew. Piet the fisherman stood at their head.

One of the fishermen left. A few minutes later, the church bell began to ring, to call the villages together to decide his fate.

I am Ned Malise, English gentleman.

Limping slightly, he paced the walls of the stall.

405

Two farmers had stayed on guard while the others met in the church. Steenwyck sat on a barrel someone had again set in front of the stall door for him. The top of his scalp glowed as pink as a lamb's ear in the strengthening daylight.

My name is Edward Malise. Of London and Amsterdam. These are human hands. With which I make lutes and play them. I am at this moment thinking a man's thoughts, in a man's words.

'Ned Malise,' he said aloud. A man's tongue had spoken.

'This is absurd.' He shouted at the barn roof. 'These villagers are mad. Put a hole in *their* heads . . . see if that relieves the pressure on their brains!'

He swung round and paced in the opposite direction.

'*Pater Noster qui est in coelo . . .*' He swung over to the door. 'Steenwyck! Did you hear? Tell your flock: my tongue can utter a prayer! What possessed creature or demon can do that?'

Without speaking, the minister squeezed a thick slice of rye bread between two bars, then a wedge of Edam cheese. Ned took the offerings. Mevrouw Steenwyck watched him from a little distance away, holding a basket.

'Thank you, mevrouw. *Merci beaucoup. Multus grati. Charin phero. Gracias. Grazie. Danke.*' He raised his voice a little. 'Doesn't that convince? All human words. Never a howl among 'em!'

He bit into the bread but could not swallow, though he had not eaten since he could remember.

Steenwyck's unsteady hand next held up a flagon of ale. It would not fit through the bars, so Ned put his mouth to the opening and caught as much as he could while the minister poured.

The liquid opened his throat. Suddenly he was ravenous. He began to gulp down the bread and cheese. Then he hesitated and forced himself to take small, decorous bites.

Daylight spread inside the barn, setting alight the motes of dust that floated in the air, and glinting on the broken straw of the floor. The light brought reassurance of reason, of life

406

in proper order. A good many men had stood in that second group, the men of common sense and perhaps even goodwill. He might still escape with his life.

Weariness struck him like a club. He sat on the floor, leaning against one wall, and rested his forehead on his drawn-up knees.

Steenwyck's shout woke him. He sprang to his feet, straight from sleep.

'What's wrong?' cried Ned.

'Anneke's missing! Little Anneke!' bellowed Verhagen into the minister's face. 'Missing since last night. The Devil's Dog must have killed her and eaten her, every last scrap, that's why she can't be found.' Verhagen pushed Steenwyck aside and shoved the wide flat end of his musket against the bars.

Ned flung himself to the floor at the base of the door as the gun was fired. A second musket fired. Splinters shot from the far wall. He was out of the line of fire as long as he stayed below the door.

The men outside soon realised this as well. Ned heard the grating of the key in the lock.

'I want to speak to Herman Verhagen!' he shouted hoarsely above the growling of the crowd. 'Herman Verhagen!'

To his relief, the door opener hesitated.

'What do you want from me, Devil's Dog?' Verhagen's voice.

'Do you believe that I am possessed by the devil?'

'Yes, for certain. I do! Unless you are yourself a devil.'

'For sure, that's the devil's own voice,' said someone in the crowd.

'Then, if you are a good Christian man, get me an exorcist!'

There was a sudden hush on the far side of the door.

'I won't have this!' cried Steenwyck.

'Have my devil cast out,' begged Ned. 'As devils have been cast out since man was created. Only the youngest churches

407

deny it.' He was glad still to be on the floor where he did not have to look at Steenwyck.

Still silence outside the door.

'As a good Christian, do not condemn a fellow soul to hell,' said Ned. 'When there is a way to salvation for him.'

'It's a ruse,' said a voice.

'If he killed Anneke, then he must hang for murder in any case,' said another.

'*If* he killed her, you clot!' Piet's voice again. 'She's probably hiding in a barn somewhere, afraid to go home after some mischief or other. She'll turn up, you'll see.'

Verhagen came to the door.

'Surely,' said Ned, 'if I am possessed by a demon as you say, and against my will, then the demon is guilty and not I!'

Verhagen grunted reluctant assent.

'Then find me an exorcist.'

'You're undoing my life's work,' said Steenwyck. 'I think I know what you're doing. But I regret it, and I'm afraid you may come to regret it too.'

'I'm sorry, minister.' Ned did not want to injure the old man further by pointing out that Steenwyck was no longer able to protect him. He had taken the only way he could see to avoid a musket ball through the head.

'I suppose it's safe to leave now.' The old man hovered outside the barred window. 'Verhagen has made you his creature, for the time being at least. They've sent across the border into the Brabant for a Spanish priest.'

Ned nodded. 'Is that child still missing?'

'Yes, but you've bought time for her to be found. I see that. I don't blame you at all. I shall pray that she's found in time.'

'I thank you with all my heart.'

'Now I must go and devise a convincing excuse for my ignorance of what is going to take place under my nose. Even

408

at my age, I could lose my church for condoning heresy. Better to look a fool.'

'I'm sorry,' Ned said again.

'No. I quite understand. Much as I regret . . .' He fumbled for his walking stick and, painfully, left the barn.

35

Verhagen's creature Ned may have become, but it was Mevrouw Steenwyck who continued to bring him food and drink. She was as small and lean as her husband, but her hands were steady, like her eyes.

'Have they found the child yet?' Ned begged when she brought him his evening meal that next night.

She looked at him with pity. 'Not yet, but, please God, they will soon.' She squeezed rye bread and pickled herring through the bars, then held up the ale jug for Ned to drink. 'And not drowned in a ditch somewhere, though even that might help your cause.'

'Do you believe she might still be found?'

'She's run away once before when she feared punishment for some mischief.'

'How old is she?'

'Five years.'

Ned wanted to ask how soon the priest might arrive . . . whether the villagers were likely to kill him first for murdering the child as well as Janzsoon's hens. But Steenwyck and his wife, the only people in the village who did not fear to speak to him, were the only two he didn't like to ask about the priest.

'Please, may I speak with your husband?' he asked as she turned to leave the barn with her basket on her arm. 'I beg him to forgive me the injury to his theology and to come one more time.'

★ ★ ★

410

Two of the three armed guards stood close behind Steenwyck.

What Ned wished to ask was best said without a witness.

'It seems that I, too, am now an enemy.' Steenwyck glared over his shoulder at his parishioners. 'Jan . . . Henriks, in your place I would be ashamed to suspect my old pastor thus. Do me the courtesy of standing aside a little. Your muskets make me shake even more than I generally do.'

The men shifted and muttered. Then they moved back and sat on the barrels brought to let the guards rest their legs.

'I can't help you any further,' said Steenwyck through the bars. 'Except with prayers.'

'Call in the law,' Ned begged in a low voice. 'Deliver me into the hands of the bailiff or a squad of *shutters*. I'll take my chances with the law. It can't be more dangerous than these madmen. At least I would get a trial, among reasonable men.'

Steenwyck shook his head. 'I seem to be under a form of house arrest. They watch everything I do now, for fear that I will denounce them and this exorcism to the Church Council.'

'But it's your right to send for the police! And mine!'

'I don't think you understand.' Steenwyck bent close to the bars. 'These people believe that you are a beast . . . less than a man . . . a bestial fiend who has murdered a child. No matter what I say, and in spite of your request for an exorcism. Until the supposed devil is driven out, they believe they can pen you and treat you as they like, with God's blessings. If I call in a secular authority, you would quite likely be butchered before the bailiffs got past the church.'

'Then the child must be found!' Ned's voice rose.

'That's your best hope.'

'I know where she can be found,' said one of the guards suddenly. 'Slit him open. You'll find what's left of her in his stomach. But it must be done soon, before his gut is emptied. That's how they caught the Beast of Poligny!'

Ned's sinews turned to stone. His bodily fluids turned to ice.

'He swears that he did not do it,' said Steenwyck.

411

'And how would he know? He doesn't remember the hens either. Shape-changers don't remember, and that's a known fact!'

'It's impossible.' Ned was assuring himself as well as his guards. 'I was already your prisoner when she disappeared.'

'He could easily have escaped in his fiendish shape. Who can bind the devil? I say, slit him open, you'll find her flesh in his stomach.'

'You'll not touch him,' said one of the other guards unexpectedly. 'Now that we've all paid up to send for this papist priest of yours, we'll all wait until he gets here! Let him sort things out.'

Ned dropped into a crouch, overwhelmed again by a sense of disorder and delirium. His jaw began to tremble. He could still it only by holding both hands to his face. A muscle above his right eye began to jump. He hugged his belly and rocked on his heels.

How can I know anything at all when all my senses seem to have turned traitor? I think that I remember a beast. How do I know I haven't done what they say?

Because I feel that it is impossible, he told himself. I could not, ever, *kill* a child.

But he had felt a transformation.

His stomach suddenly heaved, and he retched on to the straw.

Green bile and papped rye bread. No gobbets of flesh.

He wiped his mouth, more in command of himself again.

There, you fool! You grow as credulous as your captors. Of course, you did not turn wolf and eat Anneke!

He looked up at the barred opening, but Steenwyck had left. He then thought of calling the guards to witness that he had not regurgitated Anneke, but speedily reconsidered. They might decide again to look further for themselves.

He had begged for exorcism to ward off imminent slaughter, but he now began to wonder whether the desperate request had not risen, in truth, from a despairing soul.

412

He rocked faster on his heels, willing the priest to arrive. Raised a Catholic, however delinquent in recent years, he had more hope than Steenwyck did for the powers of papist heresy.

36

The priest's dark brown eyes burned into Ned's light grey ones with a hungry interest. The long head was held forward, so that his face, the mirror of his thoughts, advanced before his thin body. He had a grey cast to his skin and lines carved from nostril to each side of his mouth. Ned saw nothing of the judge in him, only curious fervour.

A cold, clean hope filled Ned. Here was a man honed as fine as an old knife-blade by wrestling with the devil.

'I must go into the stall with him,' said the priest. 'There is nothing to fear, at present. Please unlock the door.' He spoke Dutch but with the southern enemy's Brabanter accent, a Fleming not a Spaniard. He turned his head at the murmur of protest. 'If you took the trouble to fetch me here, it seems foolish to hinder my work.'

Ned scrambled to his feet as the priest entered the box stall.

'You are most extremely welcome, Father! And I thank you for the risk you take in coming here.'

The priest put out his hand and clasped Ned's in greeting, his eyes still searching deep. Then he dropped his eyes and, still holding Ned's hand, studied the back of it. After a moment, he released Ned's hand. 'I'm told that you asked for me. Do you undertake to take part willingly in whatever I may do?'

'Most willingly, if you can remove . . . whatever has descended on my life.'

'Man's soul is fragile and its enemies are many. I cannot guarantee to help you. Such an end is in God's hands alone. I am merely his agent. In fact, I must first question you to determine whether or not we proceed at all.'

'I will answer willingly.' His hopes rose even higher. The priest spoke to him as to a fellow man.

'And do you understand that there can be danger in exorcism, should we proceed that far?'

'I submit to that danger.' Exorcism could not be more dangerous than having his belly slit open, or more visits by his beast.

The priest nodded. 'You are accused of transforming from the shape of Man into the bearing and physiognomy of a wolf, of uttering strange and bestial sounds, and while in that condition, to have killed two hens. Further, you are accused of the death of the child, Anneke Schmit.' He waved aside Ned's protest. 'The nature of your crimes is of no concern to me at this moment. My first task is to decide whether you are truly possessed or are merely a wizard.'

'Wizard?' Ned repeated faintly. 'I've not been formally accused of that before, Father.'

'A good thing too,' the priest said with unexpected briskness. 'If you're a wizard, I can't help you. It will be held that you take on the strange and terrible shapes of your own free will, and are therefore responsible for all crimes you may commit while in these shapes. You will stand trial for these crimes, and be punished for them.'

'But if I'm possessed?'

'Then you are yourself as innocent as any man here – the victim of the devil directly, or of a charm or fascination laid on you by one of his agents – a wizard or witch. No trial required. But only in this second case do we proceed to exorcism.'

If he were not in truth possessed, as he half-believed that he was, Ned now vowed to himself to simulate. 'What do you wish me to do, Father?'

415

The priest called the fearful guards, blessed them and told them to stand as witness of whatever followed.

'Have you always had that dark hair on your fingers?'

'Since turning man.'

'Have you been examined for the devil's mark?'

'The physician looked at him only through the bars,' said one of the witnesses. 'No one dared look closer.'

'Please remove your clothes,' the priest instructed Ned.

Ned did so, his mind racing to think of any moles or marks on his body that might condemn him.

Slowly, the priest studied every inch of his skin. Behind his ears, in his armpits, even lifting his penis gently to examine the scrotum. 'You have a good deal of hair' was all that he said at first. Then he stepped back. 'No possible sign but the hair. No conclusive marks. Now dress again and kneel here, in front of me.' He threw back one side of the long cloak that disguised his soutane. 'Fix your eyes on this Holy Crucifix. Can you look at Our Saviour's face? Or do you wish to turn away your eyes?'

Ned braced himself and looked, afraid that his eyes might rebel as his throat had done with Steenwyck's wafer.

The painted wood Christ hanging on the priest's breast wore a distant and wistful expression that reminded Ned of the man on top of the Malise Salt.

'I can look into His face without difficulty.' With wonderful ease, he kept his eyes clamped on to the pink painted face under the crown of painted wooden thorns.

'Will you now testify,' the priest asked the two witnesses, 'that he is not repulsed by this holy sight? He is no wizard, or demon. He will never cast evil spells on your cattle or crops, or bring freezing snow and flooding rain.' He put his hands on Ned's shoulders. 'There is no need for a trial. You are not responsible for your crimes.'

Tears of relief blurred Ned's eyes. 'Then I am possessed after all?' Terrible as this truth might be, it at least offered a cure. This holy man would lead him out of disorder and terror back into the world of reasonable men. He embraced any coming danger with a whole heart.

'I must now pose the questions, before I can say. Answer me now as freely as you can. Do you believe that you are possessed?'

'I believe it possible.'

'Do you know of any possible cause?'

'The physician said that it was a distraction,' broke in one of the witnesses.

Ned stiffened in alarm.

'An overflowing melancholy,' the witness continued. 'A dream. But it was no dream. We saw the beast, didn't we?' He turned to his companion, who nodded. 'Even in the dark, you can tell a man from a wolf.'

The priest nodded with satisfaction. 'Uncertainty in a physician is a strong indication that possession is possible. Melancholy itself is a sure sign.'

Ned sank back on to his heels in relief.

'Have you ever felt constricted or stifled?'

The squeezing fist.

'Oh, yes, Father!'

'Or a heavy weight in your stomach, as if a sort of ball ascended into the gullet?'

Ned raised his face in amazement. He had been prepared to lie, to act, to play the cheat, but there was no need. The priest had just described the bubble of horror. 'Yes,' he said quietly.

'Are you ever seized by fear and terror?'

Each time the beast came, he had felt that he was dying.

He nodded. He did not trust his voice.

The priest made a sign of the cross over him. 'These are all strong signs of possession. Do you also feel a lethargy, as if you did not wish to live?'

Ned nodded. He locked his hands between his knees.

'And when you pass wind from your gut, does it ever smell of sulphur?'

417

He felt as cold as death. He held a demon in him after all. 'Father, help me!'

The priest made another sign of the cross and spread his arms. 'You do not alarm me, demon,' he shouted. 'In man, in lion, in fish, you are just the same!' To Ned, he said, 'I will try, my son, but the devil is strong. Prepare to have your heart wrenched from you.'

'I am prepared, so long as you wrench out the demon too.'

The barn had been emptied of the cows and horses which had trampled its mud floor into miniature storm-tossed waves. With a guard set around the village against visitors, the two witnessing farmers, joined by three others, now cleared all dung and broken straw from the far end of the barn opposite the double cart doors. Then they scattered the floor with clean straw.

The priest then directed them to set up a makeshift altar, a table, with an embroidered cloth which he took from his saddlebag. Next, he set out a gilded and painted wooden crucifix and a pair of silver candlesticks into which he put candles. He had the farmers hang four lanterns from nails in the main posts of the barn. He lit the candles on the altar, which spread a smell of honey. He put on a violet stole from his leather saddlebag. Then he knelt to pray. The farmers waited respectfully until he rose again and turned.

He called the earlier two witnesses to the table altar and blessed them again, then sprinkled them with Holy Water. They stood to one side.

'Bring him out to me.'

The high-vaulted space of the barn felt huge to Ned after the confines of the box stall.

'Come, my son. Kneel here, face to face with our Holy Saviour.'

Crossing towards the priest at the altar, Ned felt his limbs weaken in awe and hope. That face had seen demons nose to nose. If Ned had designed him for an exorcist, he could not have been more apt. For a moment, as the dark eyes probed into his, he turned five years old again, and fearful of damnation, confusing priest with God. Then a clean, cold hope filled him, that the truth did lie here, in what was about to take place in this makeshift church. That a demon did possess him. Would be induced to leave again. He was innocent after all. A passive vessel. Responsible for nothing. The demon did all. When it left, he would be himself again.

First, the priest prayed quietly, as Steenwyck had done, but this time in the familiar Latin of Ned's childhood, imploring God's Grace for the proposed exorcism against the wicked dragon.

Next, he cautioned the possessing spirit to tell by some sign its name, and the day and hour of its going out.

Then he laid one end of his stole across Ned's shoulder as a bridge between their souls, and made the sign of the cross to protect them both.

Ned settled himself squarely on both knees, ready to do what he could.

'I exorcise thee, most vile spirit, the very embodiment of our enemy . . .' The priest's request to the demon was lengthy but polite.

'. . . Go out, thou scoundrel, go out, with all thy deceits, because God has willed that Man be his temple.'

He paused. The witnesses did not breathe.

Ned imagined a sensation of something being hooked out of his gut. But it was imagination only.

'But why dost thou delay longer here?' demanded the priest as if to a recalcitrant guest. 'Tarry not!'

Ne moram facias.

He remembered that phrase. For a flash, Ned was five years old again, reading his Latin book. He had corrupted even that source of improvement with sinful thoughts.

'Give honour to God, the Father almighty to whom every knee is bent. Give place to the Lord Jesus Christ . . .' Again the priest made the sign of the cross.

Again the stillness. Ned fixed his eyes on the Crucifix and the candles. He felt most strange. Uneasy. But nothing that could be construed as a departing demon.

Without warning the priest shouted. 'You lean sow, mangy beast, swollen toad, may God set a nail in your skull as Jael did unto Sisera! Tremble and flee at the name of the Lord!'

Ned flinched and trembled enough for two. Please God, take the wolf from me. He knelt upright with his head a little back, open-throated as if holding the gate wide. His uneasiness had nearly grown painful. He thought that he might topple from giddiness.

'Let the image of God be a terror to thee.' The priest seized one of the candles.

Please go! Ned willed the wolf.

'Tremble at his arm, who led the souls to light after the lamentations of hell had been subdued . . .' The priest held the candle near Ned's face.

One awestruck witness whispered, 'His demon won't answer the priest. Look, how he turns away!'

The juddering flame was again thrust into his face. It swelled horribly and grew as bright as the sun.

He shouted and knocked it away. Then shouts buffeted his head like blows. Every sound pierced his ears like a nail. Horror rose from his belly into his throat. The fist . . . the pressure squeezed him into an alien shape. His nose stretched away from his cheeks. A weight . . . a tail . . . lay heavily along the crack of his buttocks.

He snarled and twisted in the hands that tried to seize him, clawed and bit. Broke free. Had nowhere to run. The cart doors flew open and farmers poured in.

No windows. Up a frail ladder, pursued by the baying pack. A stone struck his hip. Then another glanced off his head. Cornered in the hay loft, forced back on to his haunches by a circle of hayforks with tines like rapiers pressed quivering against the surface of his flesh. The farmers prepared to thrust the hayforks home. The man in black shouted, arms spread like a monstrous bat.

'You are the heretics, not he!' shouted the priest. 'Whilst in full possession of your faculties! Take away those hayforks and scythes! Drop your stones! Trust to the power of God!'

The wolf cowered away from the pandemonium of words, from the poised hayforks. Did the only possible thing. Slowly, slowly, sank to the floor into the posture of subjection and defeat. As he moved, silky fur slipped across his muscles under the skin, liquid, soft, tickling slightly, invisible to the eyes of the others. A thought flickered from some other place: this is not possible. He escaped into a deep, deep sleep.

'Your devil or devils did not yield to Christian prayers.' The priest slapped Ned's cheeks to rouse him. 'Indeed, it became enraged. It is therefore not likely to be the simple form of direct possession. More likely to have been lodged by spell or *maleficia*. It may still be exorcised but will need fiercer persuasion to depart. We must make your body an unwelcoming home from which it will choose to flee. Come. Kneel again.'

A second table now stood in the barn, a little way from the altar. And a brazier of glowing coals. A pail of water. A bundle of green twigs, still with leaves.

Ned's head ached terribly. He felt muzzy, roused too soon from sleep. Suspended still between two worlds. Hands thrust him down before the table altar.

Three farmers remained this time, including Verhagen, all three stripped to the waist. They held cattle whips.

Once again the priest blessed them. Protected himself and Ned with the sign of the cross, placed the end of his violet stole across Ned's shoulder.

'. . . Therefore I do adjure thee, most wicked dragon in the name of the immaculate lamb, who trod upon the asp and basilisk, who trampled the lion and dragon, to depart from this man [a cross on Ned's forehead]. Tremble and flee at the invocation of the name of that Lord at whom hell trembles . . .'

Whatever the demon may choose to do, thought Ned desperately through the fog in his head, I must convince. 'I submit!' he cried. 'I depart!'

The priest stepped back, away from Ned, breaking the violet bridge between them. 'Thou lying toad, thou deceiving dragon! The more slowly thou goest out, the more the punishment against thee increases . . .

A whip stung Ned across the shoulders. Then another whip. He was too shocked by the sudden pain to think any longer how to act. He staggered to his feet, into the hands of the farmers.

They laid him face down on the table and tied him fast. Placed the burning brazier under his head, a few inches below his face. Threw on green branches. Smoke. A cloth over his head to catch the thick damp smoke and direct it into his face. He tried not to breathe. Had to inhale. The smoke burned his lungs. He choked. His eyes wept. The whips burned into his back.

'For thee and thy angels is prepared the unquenchable fire; because thou art the chief of accursed murder . . .'

More green wood. Herbs thickened the smoke. He gagged on it.

'Stand back,' cried the priest. 'Stand back lest the demon shift into you!'

The three half-naked farmers fled to the far end of the barn.

The priest took one of the whips and continued the beating.

Breathe deep and end it! begged his grandmother. Dear God, William, breathe deep of the smoke and end it!

'Yield to God who condemned thee in Judas Iscariot the traitor. For he beats thee with divine scourges . . .'

Ned's lungs were on fire. The inside of his head throbbed red. Couldn't breathe. Air black and solid as hot mud. Dying.

Faintly: 'Even if the demon kills you from spite as it flees, you can rejoice that your soul will live!'

★   ★   ★

422

Smoke filled every crevice of his body and mind, the charred linings of his nostrils, seeped into the shafts of his hair. His eyeballs were smoke-filled globes. His lungs laboured to haul at the clean air. His insides were the charred contents of a burnt-out house, destroyed but still recognisable. Terrifying in their vague familiarity.

Like the shapes in the burning coach.

Smoke filled the clearing and burned in his lungs. A comet carved an arc in the dark air under the canopy of trees. A boy fell like Icarus, his hair on fire.

The man and woman danced in their burning clothes in the hot bright belly of the coach.

'Francis! NO!' He dived. The smoke parted like water and closed over him again.

He was himself again. Half-way to death, where else could he go, but onwards?

Back in the stall. Alive. But tied again. His whole life, tied.

A burnt-out shell. Cough out the pain. Coughing ripped at his bruised muscles.

The door opened, quietly. He couldn't see through his swollen, weeping eyes. A single figure. No light. Come on the sly. Perhaps Anneke's father.

Kill me, he urged. Finish it. And you're welcome.

'Fast as you can, my friend! They found Anneke's blood-stained shoe.' The voice was only a breath.

Ned peered through still-weeping eyes. In the near-darkness, the man's hair glowed a little lighter than the rest of him. The blond fisherman. Hands fumbled at Ned's ankles. Then the fisherman whispered, 'I must use my knife, hold very still.'

Ned exclaimed in pain as Piet helped him to his feet. 'I can't . . . !'

'Walk? But you must. Put these on. No time to find boots, sorry.' He went back to the door.

423

Ned jammed his long legs into a wide pair of breeches. The shadowy jacket reeked of wet wool and herring. 'No!' The rough fabric clawed at his raw, split back.

'You must! Verhagen's on his way here with Schmit and some other mad dogs to slit your throat.'

Ned forced the jacket on.

Piet half-carried Ned across the barn floor and shoved him through the man-flap in the big barn doors out into the night.

'Thanks, my friend,' he said to a shadow on guard in the barnyard.

Ned stumbled. Piet cursed quietly, then flung one of Ned's arms over his own shoulders and began to drag him away from the barn across the endless black open space. Ned gasped at the pain in his back and then again for breath. Tried to think how his legs worked. A dog barked, but not too close. They followed a long dark wall. Behind it, cows complained.

A blurred lantern moved ahead of them. Piet waited at the end of the wall, 'Now,' he whispered. 'Last open yard.' The dog barked again, closer.

Then they entered a narrow fenced lane between two high banks, protected from view but easily trapped from either end.

'God's blood!' said Piet between his teeth. The dog had followed them into the lane. 'Go back, sir! Go back!'

A cold tide washed down Ned's neck.

'Go back!' hissed Piet.

The dog advanced, the shadowy curve of its tail poised like a scimitar.

'It smells the wolf,' said Ned. It had tracked the sulphur, sniffed out his damnation.

'We must get to my boat,' said Piet. 'Just up there.'

Ned peered up into the night through the slits of his eyes. The dark thick line of the dyke lay ahead and above them, fringed by shadowy masts.

They lifted their heads together at the sound of shouts from the barn. Ned found strength to run after all, with the dog barking after them. They emerged from the lane, crossed a plank bridge over a drainage ditch, then climbed the dark flank of the dyke by a flight of wooden steps.

Piet turned and threw a stone at the dog, then hauled Ned up the last of the steps. A line of darkened houses lay strung like beads along the dyke top facing a dark confusion of docks and projecting piers. The fishing boats rocked gently, higher than the farmers' fields.

'Easy now. No running here,' breathed Piet. 'We're just off to work like all the rest.'

Ned limped after him along floating plank bridges that linked the solid dock with moorings farther out from the shore. Several boats carried lanterns where the fishermen were preparing for a night's work. The shouts from the farming village were growing louder.

'Not afraid of wolves either, Piet?' The voice came from four boats away, loud across the water.

Piet jumped down into the rocking shadow of a boat. 'Wolves don't like water,' he called back. 'The devil neither. We're safe as holy wafers out here.'

'You found a mate as brave as you are, I see.'

'Stupid, more like.' He was already untying the boat as Ned clambered on board.

'D'you hear that?' called the other fisherman. 'Sounds like more trouble down there.' He paused to listen to the growing furore in the fields below. 'Sweet Lord, d'you think . . . ?'

'Come on, come on, come on!' Piet urged his sail under his breath. The great shadowy stomach flapped, ballooned, tautened. 'You're the most excitement we've seen here since the Spanish last passed through,' he whispered to Ned.

'The Devil's Dog has escaped!' shouted the other fisherman. 'They want every man to search. Come back in!'

'I'm going fishing,' Piet shouted back. 'I've a living to earn.'

The boat moved sluggishly, through treacle. Then Ned felt

425

a breeze on his cheek and the boat surged forward as if a giant hand had opened and let it go.

'Piet, I order you to return to your mooring!' A new voice called across the water. 'You're not carrying a light. Light your lantern and come about! And bring whoever is with you.'

Lanterns now bobbed along the line of the dock. One pulled slowly away from the others, out into the sea after them. Piet steered toward the dark arm of the sea.

'How dearly will you pay for this?' asked Ned.

'I hear that if you set a charm on me I'm completely innocent.'

'Where are you taking me?'

'Amsterdam. Big place, lots of people. Maybe even a few with their heads screwed on straight.' His face was a dark hole under his gleaming hair until he lifted it to look up at the sail. Then the shifty moonlight caught his nose and brow bones. Ned saw tiny moons of fish scales on the borrowed jacket.

'You can get your head down there, man. Or better, go back to England.'

Ned felt terror at the thought of parting with the owner of that amiable voice. 'Aren't you afraid of me?'

'Well, as I'm doing you a favour, I expect I'm safe until we reach Amsterdam. And from what I've heard, werewolves don't eat fish.'

The fisherman's blond head seemed to float in a world far from the one he occupied. The chopping movement of the boat combined with the swirling in his head into a ghastly unease.

He slept again until Piet set him down just before dawn among the swaying lanterns and sleeping ships of the inner port of Amsterdam and gave him five florins.

'In your place, the first thing I'd do is bathe,' were his final words as he pulled back out into the already-busy, pewter waters of the Amsterdam harbour.

★   ★   ★

426

'And somehow I arrived here,' Ned told Marika. He coughed, then caught his breath in pain.

'Turn over,' she said. 'I'll put more ointment on your poor back.'

'There's still a hole,' said Ned. 'Between the falling of my wine glass in Maurits's house and waking up in that cow shed.'

ELEVEN

37

Marika stood at the window of Justus's room looking down at the dark street while Ned slept. His fever had broken around three o'clock and his terrible coughing had eased. She left him in her bed, covered him, and wrapped herself in her cloak on the floor. After an hour or so, she rose again and went down to the parlour to run her fingers silently over the keys of her virginal. Then she felt a need to check that all the doors and windows were locked. Then she had needed air and opened the shutter in Justus's small parlour again.

I seem to have cast my lot with a monster and child-murderer.

No, she corrected herself. With the man who was my first love. I wonder what might have become of us if Justus had not always taught me that love was a trivial indulgence of the imagination and senses. And if he had not warned Ned off.

You wrote that letter of your own free will! she reminded herself. Persuaded by your brother, but all the same, he did not force you with a rod or gun!

All the same, I'm mad to risk hanging or worse for the sake of sentimental regret!

The night felt very still. Then it seemed that all the birds in the canal-side trees began to sing at once. First a single voice, then a fragile babble. A quick winged shape swooped from the top of one tree into the lower branches of another.

431

A purposeful cur trotted into view. Stopped to lift a leg on the lowest step of her *stoep*. Trotted on out of sight.

For a few seconds the sky suddenly filled with church bells ringing five o'clock. When they stopped, she held her breath so as not to disturb the perfect peace. Then a wood-seller came grunting around the corner, a giant bundle of faggots on two short, stocky legs, and the ordinary morning began.

She watched him pass out of sight, then listened to a water-seller in the next street announcing 'Water! Good water!' as if they weren't all nearly drowned in the stuff.

Why did Ned run here to me? From his strange tale, he had run to this house soon after the fisherman set him down at the port. And while not in his right mind nor in possession of his human senses.

A serving woman peered out of a neighbouring door for the night-soil collector. She saw Marika, stared briefly, then withdrew her head.

Marika stepped back and closed the shutter.

I won't go to the market today. My guilty knowledge will blaze from my face. We have enough bread and candles.

The roast chicken was gone but they had the hen. Its time had come.

In the back courtyard, she lifted the basket coop and tucked the protesting hen under her arm as she had seen the cook do. She cupped her hand around the head. She remembered how to do it: take a firm grip, swing the bird in a quick circle, and its own weight will break its neck. It's as simple as that.

The yellow eye looked up through her fingers.

She shuddered and put the hen back under its basket. Then she gave it a little bread. They would eat the hen another day, when she felt altogether stronger.

Back in the house, she watched the street from the window again, half-hidden by the curtain, as she had done since she was a child. Her neighbours stood talking in the street before the house, on their way to early market. Noses wrinkled, mouths flapped, eyes exchanged volumes. Then they rubbed their shoe

432

soles against the disgraceful dirt on her portion of the street and nodded at her equally disgraceful steps.

She was waiting again, as she had after Justus's flight. But this time she must not wait helplessly or a man would die. And so might she. She had to think what to do, where Ned could more safely go.

She pondered the cunning man.

I should tell Ned about his promise of a cure.

But then she thought, whatever that man may have thought he guessed, he could not have known the truth. Sick people will always believe that yet more ails them. 'What else?' was a safe venture, a rogue's trick to imply more knowledge than he had.

Better not risk trusting him ... perhaps he was even a police trap!

That's how he knew about Ned! she thought. Of course!

But she was still uncertain.

When her neighbours had gone, she slipped out to buy eggs from a passing vendor, and a little fresh water from the water-seller, as the water left in the cistern had begun to smell. As she handed over her *stuivers* for the water, she heard distant off-key music. A band, on the Damrak. It drew closer, then passed the end of her street and crossed the bridge to the far side of the canal, leading a procession with animals and trailed by twenty or thirty children.

When the procession had gone, she went back into the house. Ned was awake and standing in Justus's chamber, where he had opened a crack in the shutters. A thin line of light cut across his face.

'They had an elephant!' he whispered. 'Did you see? And a camel, with a monkey rider on its back. There's to be a fair. I used to go as a boy.'

'How do you feel?' she asked in a low voice.

'I must follow them. Find the fair and join the crowds.'

'I think you're mad with fever again, to talk of going to fairs!'

433

He shook his head impatiently. 'I'll be safe there. The other animals will mask my smell.'

'Wait!' she begged. Then lowered her voice again lest they be overheard by someone in the street. 'You're not thinking straight. The dogs will pick you up the minute you go back into the streets. We'll find a safer way to hide you. The hunt may even die down.'

'Until I next turn wolf and start it off again!' He went out on to the landing and sat down on the stairs, still weak from his wounds and fever. 'It will happen sooner or later. In truth, I might as well give myself up now and save everyone the trouble of catching me.' He looked up at her. 'You must call the militia and hand me over. Say that I forced you . . .'

I will have to tell him that there's another possible way, she decided unhappily.

'The man who gave me the decoction for your fever also told me that he could cure your wolf.'

'And you didn't tell me at once?' He sounded angry.

'I didn't trust him.'

'That's for me to judge! You must have trusted him enough to tell him that I was the Beast of Amsterdam.'

'No. He seemed already to know. "His cure begins here," he said.'

'A cure?' he asked. He tapped the uprights of the staircase as if playing a tune on them. 'Not restraint? Or holes in the head? Are you certain that he said "cure"?'

She nodded.

'Then I must go to see him!'

'And if it's a trap?'

'What will I lose except a few more days or weeks of beastliness?'

'You can't go until we think how you can do it safely, without leaving a trail! Please wait! I shall think of a way,' she said.

They both heard at the same time.

How loudly were we speaking? thought Marika in terror.

434

Not a knocking but a scratching. Not a dog. Too loud for a rat. On the *stoep*, outside the front door. Back and forth. Scratch, scratch. Scratch, scratch. A rich, damp scratching. Scratch, scratch. A pause. Scratch, scratch, scratch. Another pause.

Marika waved him into her chamber out of sight, then went down to open the door.

From behind the door of her chamber, Ned strained to hear.

I should never have waited, should have left at once, as I intended, he told himself furiously. I must not be taken here in Marika's house! And if I am, she must claim that I forced her to shelter me.

He heard her voice, startled but not alarmed. Then another woman's voice.

The door shut. Marika's feet climbed the stairs. When she came into the room, he could not tell whether she was laughing or crying.

'Oh!' she said, covering her face with an open hand. 'Oh. You won't believe . . . !' She shook her head.

'What is it?' he whispered urgently. 'Who was it? What's wrong?'

She grimaced and blew her nose on her handkerchief. 'Mevrouw Cats was scrubbing my steps!'

'She was what?'

'She thought that perhaps, in the circumstances, I might need a little help. ". . . And in Christian charity . . ."' Her voice veered towards a laugh and then away. Then, for the first time that Ned had ever seen, Marika burst into tears.

'But the chief thing is . . .' she said, then paused to catch her breath. '. . . is that she gave me an idea . . . How to get you to your cunning man so that the dogs can't follow you.'

She left at once for the market. Half-walking, half-running to get there before the stalls closed. Bought four brown balls of the locally-made, stinking lye soap, in spite of the stall-holder's

435

determination to sell her some sweetly-scented French soap cakes. She also paid a large sum to a spice dealer for a small paper twist of black peppercorns.

Back at the house, she told a startled Ned, 'On to your knees! But rub them with the soap first. Then soap the soles of your feet.'

With the soap and a basin of water, she began to scrub the floor of the hall. When she had done that, she began on the stairs. Meanwhile, she set Ned to work on the kitchen floor and the wall where he had leaned two nights before. When she had scrubbed every inch of the stairs, she went on to the upper hall and landing, where she paid special attention to the floor in front of her door where he had slept the first night.

Ned scrubbed the floor where he had walked in Justus's chamber. Then anywhere he thought he might have touched. This took them until after dark. Marika opened the back door and, in the faint light of the night sky, scrubbed the threshold and a few feet further out. She stared bleakly at the rest of the shadowed courtyard and garden beyond.

Enough is enough.

At least they had erased his scent from the house. Now for Ned himself.

But he appeared urgently in the dark kitchen behind her. 'I hear dogs again.'

'Are you certain?'

'Not yet in full cry. But it's a hunting pack.'

'Beggar-catchers?' She too could hear them now, coming closer.

Ned started to push past her into the courtyard, but she grabbed the back of her brother's jacket. 'You fool, you've no time to get clear! Wait!' She doused him with the basin of stinking soapy water. 'Now rub the soap again on the soles of your feet!'

She pushed him back into the house, up the stairs and into her bed.

The bed must smell of him and his fever!

436

She threw the coverlet over him and half-closed the bed's curtains. Then poured the last of her orange-oil on the curtains. She emptied most of the paper twist of peppercorns on to the floor beside the bed and ground them under her heels.

'How close now?' asked his muffled voice.

'In our street.'

She tossed her stockings on the floor beside her skirts. Working so fast that she nearly dropped it, she rubbed what was left of one soap ball over the door frame and bottom panel. Then on the floor where he had slept. The soap was worn to nothing. The rest of the peppercorns went on the threshold of her door.

She ran down to the kitchen, found what was left of his ball of soap, scrubbed her hands, then rubbed the tiny soap nugget over any part of her that she thought he might have touched. She wanted to rub the walls, the door posts.

He might have touched here! And here! Suddenly the house seemed to reek of him.

She blew out the candle in her hand just as the search party climbed her steps, and sleepily answered the door.

Not Rits this time. A militiaman, in his yellow scarf.

'Mevrouw, we have intelligence that the fugitive beast may be hiding in your house.' He peered at her in the light of the lantern his lieutenant held. 'I have the authority to enter and search.'

If she threw herself on his mercy now, claimed to be a hostage, wept with relief at the rescue, she might still, just, escape punishment herself.

'You haven't found him yet?' She pulled her shawl tight around her shift. A dog was investigating her hem. She tried to ignore it. Behind the militiaman, in front of two other men, stood a stern woman dressed in simple black, hair hidden by a stiffly starched cap. The chaperone.

He offered her the search warrant to read. Marika waved it away.

'You are quite welcome to come in and search without

437

that,' she said. 'But you must forgive my improper dress.' She yawned, then wished that she hadn't. Her heart tried to leap into her throat. 'I wasn't expecting to receive visitors at this hour. Is mine the only house? Poor you. Imagine having to wake up so many people in the middle of the night!'

'Only your house, mevrouw.'

She shrugged and stepped back, grateful for the darkness of the hall. Her cheeks glowed like hot coals.

Followed by the chaperone, the militiaman and his lantern, she led him through the dark kitchen. The dog followed, nose glued to her hem.

Then it suddenly left her to press its nose to some other exciting news. Then it whined and was distracted by another confusing fragment of scent. The militiaman watched it too, with puzzled interest.

Without comment, he glanced around the empty kitchen, his eyes lingering on the puddle of water where Ned had stood.

Before he could notice the wet tracks leading out into the hall, she went to open the back door. 'Do you want to search the yard?' Then she thought to ask, 'What possible intelligence could you have had? One of my neighbours, by any chance?'

The militiaman watched his dog roam with disinterest back and forth across the kitchen threshold, then trot away. 'I don't consider mere gossip to be intelligence, mevrouw.'

Then, as Marika had hoped, the dog erupted into a frenzy of barking at the bottom of the yard.

The militia called his men, who ran with swords drawn. The chaperone stepped into the yard to see better.

While they dismantled the peat stack, Marika wiped away the trail of Ned's wet footprints with the hem of her shift and her shawl. Then went back to the door. The dog investigated the hen under its basket, then, with a cry of triumph, found a scent proclamation on the back wall.

'Will you open the garden gate, please, mevrouw?' called the officer.

In the alley, the dog put nose to ground, barked and raced off.

'Call it back,' said the militiaman. 'We'll search there after.' He came back to the kitchen door.

The recalled dog now showed no interest in the well-soaped ground outside the kitchen door.

Thank God! Thank God! she thought. I had only meant to deny them the beginning of his trail. If Mevrouw Cats had not been moved by charity until the next day, Ned would have been taken!

Eager now to get back to searching the alley, the militiaman looked quickly into the parlour, the dining chamber. Climbed the stairs. Glanced into Justus's room, the upstairs parlour, her mother's old room, the cupboards.

She gathered her shawl even more tightly around her. 'I don't think it will be necessary to search my bed chamber.'

'Mevrouw . . .'

'Until you knocked, I was sleeping soundly.'

They both watched the dog sniff at the bottom of her door. It shook its head as if a flea had bitten its ear. Examined the door panel.

It's uncertain, she thought with a spasm of terror. Any moment, it will recognise the scent from the peat stack.

'I assure you, I sleep alone.'

Shall I risk the bluff of opening the door?

The dog sneezed, shook its head and turned away.

The officer raised both hands in protest now. 'No, no. I am content. It would seem, mevrouw, that our intelligence was only partly correct. Our quarry hid in your stack of peat, not in your house. Then most likely left again by the alley.'

She managed to nod understanding. She held her shawl twisted so tightly around her hand that its fringes cut into her fingers. Then loosened her grasp when she saw the chaperone's eyes on her hands.

Just as it was leaving, the dog stopped to investigate her hem for a long, long time.

439

She leaned for a moment on the front door after she closed it behind the search party.

He emerged, still wet, from the shadows of the cupboard bed. He wanted to grab her, to kiss her, to whirl her around in his relief. But a sudden fierce stiffness defied him to presume. He forced himself to be satisfied with seizing her hand and repeating his thanks again and again.

'He said that the militia have received intelligence that you're here in this house,' she told him.

'Then I must leave now. On their next visit, I won't escape, nor will you.'

'Let them get well clear,' she begged. 'For a short time at least, this house is now safer than anywhere else. Sleep for an hour or two. Don't risk being arrested by the watch for breaking curfew.'

Ned saw her good sense and also was still feeling weak from the fever. 'When they've gone, nearer dawn, I'll go to the cunning man, then to the fair.'

After they ate, in her room to avoid laying his scent in the hall and kitchen again, he settled to sleep on the floor outside her door. 'I can hear the whole house from here,' he said.

But his back pained him so that he could not lie on it and every move seemed to split open a new seam. Every creak of the house sat him up, alert and listening. Every dog that barked at a passing cat had him at the top of the stairs ready to flee.

He lay awake, thinking of her in the room behind him. He listened at her closed door to her gentle child-like snores, overwhelmed with tenderness and despair.

If I were to breed now, he wondered, would I sire wolf cubs? Or infant monsters? He threw his head back, laid his arm across his eyes and wept. At the first glimmer of dawn, he went to her bed to say that he was leaving.

'Marika!' he whispered.

She was tangled in her coverlet and deeply asleep after the almost sleepless night tending him the night before. He

440

hesitated, then leaned down and kissed the exposed tip of her shoulder. Then he went downstairs and let himself out through the kitchen door.

At dawn, a lantern already burned behind the dirty window. Ned put his nose close to the glass and peered through dust and cobwebs, past a pile of books on the window ledge and the uneven line of a half-drawn curtain. Inside the low-ceilinged room, two men sat in the dim light eating breakfast in a small space cleared among the papers and paraphernalia on a cluttered table. The older, with his back to Ned, wore a full, pleated nightgown. The younger, who had a smooth face and moon-pale hair showing under his soft-brimmed cap, was dressed as if he had just come in from the street.

Ned tapped on the glass.

The older man came to the door, wiping crumbs from his mouth. He could have followed any trade but the most arduous. Eyes close together but pleasant. A grizzled beard, neatly trimmed, and small cleans hands which he kept folded on the curve of his belly like a mouse's paws, just as Marika had said.

'Aha!' he said. 'Come in.'

Inside, Ned stood uneasily, unsettled by the familiarity of the man's greeting, the oppressive shadow of a stuffed crocodile hanging just above his head, the two pairs of eyes which studied him with friendly interest. 'You promised me a cure.'

'I did no such thing!' the older man replied tartly. 'I never promise cures – only the way to begin them.'

'Mynheer, I've no time for riddles. Do you sell cures or not?'

The two men exchanged quick glances.

'You'd best tell me what you want,' said the mouse-man quietly.

Ned looked at the younger man.

'His ears are my ears,' said the older man. 'Are you afraid to speak openly?'

441

After a moment, Ned said, 'With reason.' He glanced at the window through which he had peered. Then at the young man. Ned had seen him before.

Did I see him in a place of danger for me? Or is he a face half-seen on the streets?

'Come, then.'

Ned followed the odd pair into a room hidden behind the first. The single window at the back was still shuttered. The older man closed the connecting door so that they were left in a private darkness lit only by a single lantern. Their faces became patterns of highlights on bone. The glass curves of strange apparatus gleamed faintly in the shadows. In one corner he saw a freestanding conical brick furnace.

With a lump of chalk, the older man drew on the stone floor a large circle about six feet across. In the exact centre he set a three-legged stool.

'Sit there. Your words will be held within the circumference of the circle.' He stepped inside the circle himself. 'They will travel only to my ears.'

Ned looked again at the fair-haired youth, who smiled in a friendly fashion and leaned back deeper into the shadows on a bench set against one wall. 'You will think me mad.'

'Don't tell me what I will think. You can't possibly know. What troubles you?'

Ned looked at the labelled stoneware jars and pots ranged on shelves, the bunches of twigs and dried herbs hanging from the beams. He inhaled the lung-tickling mix of herbal smells: fresh, sharp, sweet, dusty. Words required clear thoughts. His thoughts were tangled. He did not know how to begin, or whether he was even able to. To his surprise, he told the story of the eagle which had dropped him from the sky.

'. . . Forgive me,' he interrupted himself. 'I'm wasting your time with irrelevancies.' He felt an unease in confession that was quite different from the intimations of the approaching wolf.

The older man continued to smile gravely. 'You don't know

what is relevant or irrelevant. Please go on.' His eyes remained fixed on Ned's with intense interest.

So Ned lurched on. His tale skipped like a stone on water: the coach, Francis, the countess with the small pox. The blank hole in his memory. And at last he arrived at what he could no longer avoid: the horror of the wolf. The choice of madness, possession or magic. The demon which had refused to budge.

He stopped, now watching the older man with a pleading face.

'Wait there.' The man went to one of the laden shelves and brought a small stoneware jar. 'Have you ever seen a salve like this before?'

Ned took the offered jar of dark green, greasy unguent. Sniffed. His head jerked back and he nearly dropped the jar. The sick, burnt, slippery smell filled him with a violent, unreasonable horror, as if the jar held a rotting serpent. His hair stood on end.

'Yes,' he whispered. 'What is it?' He began to tremble.

'A compounding of henbane, datura and nightshade. Most often applied to the membranes of the body, as in the private hairy parts. Have you ever used it?'

'No!' He was sure. But he had delivered a jar like this for Francis, many years ago. To the wealthy young woman and the crone. But that still did not explain the horror the smell raised in him. 'What are its effects?' He crossed his arms to pin his hands against his ribs.

'In parts, very like your wolf,' said the cunning man. 'Many foolish people, men and women alike, believe that it will give them unimagined pleasure. Whilst they stagger drunkenly or lie in a stupor, it makes them fly, dance, copulate with dreams and with devils. It makes them believe even that they are transformed into the shape of beasts.'

'What is it?' whispered Ned again.

'The cause of the death by hanging or at the stake for many foolish women and more than a few men. Witches' Salve.'

Ned remembered the young woman sitting on the stool in

443

her petticoats. And the sour-sweet smell in the air, and the fierce smile of the old serving woman. He had handed over Francis's jar and tried not to run as he left them.

'Nothing magical about it, just herbs and the knowledge of how to mix them. You're quite certain that you were never tempted?' the older man pressed him. 'No reckless drunken evening, among importuning friends? I've known it used in the highest circles. The more often when the most protected by social position.'

'Never!'

'And you've never hung over the smoke of their burning leaves?'

'Never!' Ned cried again. 'Believe me, I would never experience voluntarily what you describe!' The smell filled his head. The purple sweetness of its undertone caught at his throat. Until now he had forgotten that one quick sniff at Francis's jar.

'I think that you remember it very well,' said the cunning man.

Ned shook his head. 'No, I swear! I can't think . . . ! In any case, my wolf arrived after a blow on the head.'

'So, then. You are certain that your wolf has a different source.' The man took back the jar and returned it to the shelf.

Like a physician, he then asked Ned to piss into a bottle, which he took into the front room and held up to the growing light of the window. 'Your urine is dark and sad.'

Ned rose and followed him. 'Is there any other possible cause than madness or possession? I swear that I'm not a wizard! Could I have been enchanted?'

'There's also good precedent for compound creatures,' said the older man as he continued to peer at the bottle. Again he exchanged confirming glances with the younger man who had followed them both. 'The Minotaur, half-man, half-bull. Chiron the Archer, with horse's legs and a man's arms and head. Anubis the Egyptian jackal-headed god of death. The universe is full of them . . .'

444

'I don't want to be of their number!' cried Ned. 'I want to tear out the beast and return to the untainted state of Man.'

'Not merely to master it?'

'No! I want it excised! I must be purely man!'

'Hum.' The man placed the bottle of urine on the breakfast table between a shining brass scales and a lump of a strange glowing white stone. 'Hold out your hand.' He tipped into Ned's cupped hand the contents of a small vial.

A heavy round silver moon struck his palm, flattened, stretched into an egg-shape, then shattered into bright muscular drops which jumped apart and ran through the cracks of his fingers, as if each drop were a small creature with intention of its own. Some ran up his arm and disappeared into his sleeve. Others hit the floor, rolled, elongated, contracted, split apart, rejoined each other. They slithered, rolled, stretched like glittering oil slicks on water.

He snatched at some as they fell, caught them, lost them again. He felt a kind of panic, as if something vital escaped him each time another silver drop slipped away between his fingers. A kind of terror each time another globule shattered into a dozen glittering parts and escaped again.

'It can't be done,' said the cunning man. 'Let them go. They will reunite in time.'

'Mercury,' said Ned. 'A cure for the great pox.'

'Quicksilver,' the man corrected him gently. 'The soul.' He bent and trapped three globules, which seemed to snatch at each other, commingle and leap together back into the vial. 'One of the triplicity, with salt and sulphur, that is to say, with body and spirit. Or if you'd rather speak as a musician, the triple affections of our minds: anger, moderation and humility, as expressed in the natural registers of the voice: high, middle and low. Or the three styles of expression, *concitato*, *temperato* and *molle*. It is also a poison.'

'I don't understand,' said Ned. 'Just tell me what I must do to be cured! Am I mad or possessed?'

'You're not possessed. I agree with the minister, Steenwyck.

445

Superstitious nonsense. I have no time for it!' He swept up more of the tiny fugitive silver globes.

'Am I mad then, as two physicians have claimed?'

'Not at all.' Before Ned had time to feel relief, he added, 'You are *versipillus*.'

'*Versipillus*?'

'Turncoat, to be quite literal. Possessing a double nature. You have been bound to the nature of a wolf and carry it with you. Your fur is on the inside, unseen.'

Ned stared down at the floor, chilled. With his foot, he nudged a bright silver drop towards another. They embraced, became one again and rolled away under the table. 'How? And how did I come to be so? And what must I do to make myself single again?'

The man rubbed his forehead with one of his clean little paws. 'Oh dear.'

'Is there no salve that's the reverse of that fiendish witches' grease?' asked Ned. 'One that removes nightmares from the soul?'

'What can we do for poor Ned Malise?' the man asked his younger companion. 'He is restless though his spirits are heavy. He says that his sleep is troubled and his thoughts often rage out of control. He wants to change his present nature, as if he believes himself to be under an evil spell.'

'How could I not want to change!' Ned interjected.

The younger man inclined his fair head and studied him. 'Set him to find when and by whom that spell was cast.'

'Hum,' said the cunning man again. 'Stay here.' He vanished into the back room.

Ned breathed deeply. The white belly of the crocodile seemed to brush the top of his head. He wanted to run out of the low, dark room. Escape.

To what?

He glanced at the calm shadowed face of the younger man, who waited in silent ease, thumbs hooked over his belt. That level, interested gaze agitated him even more. He stooped and

446

tried to pick up a half-inch blob of quicksilver. The silver sprang apart into two mocking halves so that his thumb and finger met on nothing.

When the older man returned, he held seven small metal mirrors. 'You must swear not to say where you were given these. The ancient art of the *specularii* is now forbidden.' He gave Ned a small disk of burnished gold, so highly polished that he could see his face in it, a little veiled but clear enough.

'Every day, look into one of these mirrors. The gold is for the Sun's day, the silver for the moon's day . . .' One by one, he gave Ned the rest of the mirrors. 'Mars rules Tuesday . . . an iron mirror. Silvered with mercury, for that god himself on Wednesday, tin for Jupiter on Thursday, copper for Venus on Friday, and lead for Saturn on Saturday.'

Ned accepted the mirrors with curiosity.

'Look into each of them until a misty curtain seems to hang between you and the reflecting surface. Note what phantasmic shapes you seem to see there. Then put away the mirror at once and sit quietly to reflect on the thing you have seen. That is when the true magic takes place.'

'Will I see the witch who made me *versipillus*?' asked Ned.

'I don't know what you will see,' said the man. 'But you will arrive at the truth about your enchantment.'

Ned found that he believed him. 'And then what should I do?'

The man went to the shelves again and brought back a glass jar cunningly blown in rings of white and yellow stripes. He put this into Ned's hand.

'Is this my cure?' Ned sniffed it. With relief, he inhaled a nose-clearing, resinous, minty gust.

'In a manner of speaking. But a cure in the old style. The contents are to be applied to the wounding weapon, not to the wound.'

'Please speak plainly. In simple terms. Is this how I break the spell?'

'Find who or what ever you believe to have cast the spell.

Stand face to face. Rub this unguent on his or her forehead. And ask to be unbound.'

'That is not simple!' exclaimed Ned.

'Simple to explain, but not to execute. I agree.'

As he was leaving, the man gave him a small stoneware bottle. 'And this is for you. Shake it well and swallow twenty drops each morning.'

Ned found himself back in the street, not only double-natured but wearing an invisible fur coat, carrying seven unlawful mirrors, a bottle of potion, and a jar of ointment that seemed very like something his brother might once have peddled.

The whole visit had been so excessively odd that, perversely, his faith was increased. He wished he could tell Marika that she had been right to tell him, after all, that the little man who looked like a dormouse could not possibly be a police intelligencer. That, in spite of what could only be the purest flim-flam, the cunning man had filled him with a totally unreasonable hope which he could neither understand nor dismiss.

He put the wish out of his head. He had come too close already to bringing her down. He stowed the mirrors, the bottle and jar of ointment carefully into various pockets.

I'll try to get to the fair while the soap's still on my feet.

But at the end of the street, with a jolt of joy and alarm, he saw Marika, leaning on a wall.

She made a small gesture of one hand, both greeting and warning, then turned and vanished into a three-foot-wide passage between two houses.

'What happened?' he asked, when he had caught up with her.

'Did you find your cunning man?' she asked, diverting him before he could speak.

He started to answer but saw that she was hardly listening and broke off. 'Why are you here?'

She strode off so quickly that he had to lengthen his own stride to keep up. Her head was down. 'This morning . . . mid-morning . . . Mynheer Rits came to see me again . . . that

448

man's as bad as an ardent lover.' She gave a bright false smile. 'With two love letters this time. The first took the house. He was so kind . . . granted me until tomorrow night to find other lodgings.' She drew a deep, shaky breath and looked up at the narrow strip of visible sky.

'Because you sheltered me?'

'That's the joke. It's nothing to do with you. Justus has now been officially declared a fugitive from the law. All his property is therefore forfeit, everything they took before, and now the house.' She stopped, wrapped her arms around herself and breathed in. 'The other document summoned me to present myself today before the Church Council.'

'Because of their claimed intelligence that you were sheltering me?'

'Didn't wait to find out.' She achieved a laugh of sorts. 'I've learned in the last few days! Shut the door in his face while he was still speaking, and locked it. Then snatched up my belongings, ready in the kitchen, and slipped away by the back door while he was still hammering at the front. I could hear him still banging and shouting as I reached the street. Everyone was watching him and missed my escape.'

She pulled suddenly on his sleeve to guide him down another alley. 'I took your advice and went back to Catryn.' In the dark narrow passage, she gave him the ghost of her dinner-table smile. 'We're both fugitives now.'

He could not rejoice at her bad fortune, but also could not help thinking, she'll have to come with me now!

Catryn wept as freely over Ned as she had done over Marika, but this time quickly banished sentiment. 'I'd do more, if I could. But two strangers in my small lodgings will attract attention. Of course, you'll sleep here tonight . . . I won't turn my old friend and his lady out.'

'I'll go, if you'll keep Marika . . .' Ned began. Marika had not objected to Catryn's use of 'his lady'!

'Don't waste your breath, Neddie boy,' Catryn said briskly. 'We all have bad times. Stay here tonight, both of you, and

449

we'll think of another, safer refuge in the morning.' She led them into the dark, damp interior that stank of curing hides, a single room where Marika had left one small bundle, the removable half of the virginal's keyboard, and the hen.

Ned woke with a jolt on his sack of damp straw on the floor.

It was the bottom of the night, just before the turn. In her narrow bed, Catryn snored with great jolting, irregular, sucking gasps and flutters.

'What is it?' whispered Marika from her nest in the dark.

'Listen.' He pushed the shutter of Catryn's single room open a short way, to let the sound be heard more clearly. His skin prickled. The base of his throat quivered.

The two voices began low, one leading, the other following. They climbed higher and higher, sliding and twisting around each other, never on the same note, but always in harmony. A third voice joined them, on yet another note. Twined with them up and up into the final, eerie teasing rise.

Her straw rustled as she raised herself on one elbow. He could just make out her shape.

'The fair,' said Ned.

'Dogs?' she whispered.

'Wolves. I'm certain.'

The distant howling came again. The three voices climbed, tone by tone. Then a sliding semitone. Then the final eerie dying rise.

'Do you also hear the same harmonies each time?' asked Ned. 'I'd swear that the beasts are singing together in the Lydian mode.'

'Phh.' She breathed out. 'Beasts don't sing!'

'So I always thought too, till now.'

Catryn's snores stopped. They waited until she began to breathe again.

The wolves howled once more. Their voices slowly climbed, twined, arrived, and died.

450

'Yes,' whispered Marika. 'Now I can hear it too. Very like harmony.'

'I must go there tomorrow.'

'You can't!'

'If my nature is truly double as the cunning man said . . . if there is true kinship, the eyes of those beasts will be my mirror.'

There was a long silence. Then Marika said, 'I will help do whatever will make you believe that you do not turn wolf! We'll talk more in the morning . . . or else we'll wake Catryn!'

The howling stopped abruptly. Ned got up and waited by the window, but it did not start again.

'Whatever else ails you, you don't turn wolf!' she whispered to the dark low ceiling. 'Why won't you believe me?'

'I must go alone. You can't take the risk.'

'Why not?' she demanded. 'There's no longer reason to protect me. I'm a fugitive too.' Then, as if she thought that she might sound self-pitying, she added, 'No one will expect the Beast of Amsterdam to have a woman on his arm. And, if you should happen to change shape under the influence of your relatives, I can always say that you're my pet.'

'What is the day?' asked Ned.

'Wednesday.' Marika lifted her head in curiosity. In the feeble daylight that now prodded the shadows of Catryn's hovel, Ned was staring down at a silvered glass mirror he had set on the floor between his knees, dressed only in his trousers and shirt. 'What are you doing?'

'Scrying.'

How fierce he looks when he frowns like that, she thought. And Catryn's low-ceilinged room seemed too small to contain him. She studied the long nose and dark brows. The long slim legs. The dark hair on his wrists.

Is it possible that he has something of the wolf in him after all? That such things can happen?

Justus was not infallible, no matter what she had believed as

451

a child. In fact, knowing what she knew of her brother now, why did she cling to the cynicism he had taught her? Why cling to anything he had taught her?

Because I know nothing else, she thought. Except that little glimpse of another world shown to me by John Nightingale before he snatched it away again.

Her hand went to her stomacher where she had hidden his two letters.

'What are you trying to see?' she asked Ned.

'The truth about my enchantment.'

She almost laughed but stopped herself in time. 'Is this something else that your cunning man said?'

He continued to gaze down as if he had not heard her.

'What do you see?'

'Only myself,' he said in frustration.

She settled back on one elbow. It was probably as well that he did not look at her just now. In the corner of one eye, she could see a piece of straw stuck in her hair. She could imagine how she must look after such a night.

Why do I care?

She got up, picked off straw, and arranged her clothing as well as she could. There was no water in which to wash.

But no mirror, neither, to see the need, she thought. She glanced again at Ned, who still seemed entranced by his scrying mirror. She crossed to stand behind him and look down, to see whatever it was that held him so.

Their eyes met in the mirror. She put her hand on the tip of his shoulder to steady herself, caught by a sense of impossibility. How could their glances meet? She stood behind him. Their two faces looked in the same direction, as did the two wavering faces in the mirror, yet the beams of their eyes did not travel parallel, but each pierced the other's eyes with startled surmise.

'Do you search for a wolf?' she asked roughly.

His hand pinned hers to his shoulder. 'For the future.'

She pulled her hand free. Could not think what might be safe to say.

452

How I've changed, she thought. A mere month ago, I would have smiled and invited an empty compliment. Misfortune is eating my easy wit.

Catryn woke and gave them bread and ale. When Ned told her that they were going to the fair, she found them some old clothes, including a man's hat for Ned which he pulled down to hide his dark brows and pale eyes. They left Marika's belongings with her, and Ned's bottle of potion and ointment jar.

'Come back tonight.' Catryn tucked apples into their pockets. 'I must go sit with a sick friend for a day or two in any case, over on the New Side.' She began to pack a bag for herself. 'Don't break up all the furniture for firewood.' She hugged them as they left.

In the street Marika picked up a pigeon's feather and stuck it into the band of Ned's hat. 'That's better! It makes you look a little foolish and nothing at all like a werewolf.'

She felt foolish herself. Worse than foolish. The day after losing her home and being summoned by the Church Council, she was going to a fair with a fugitive werewolf who had been accused of killing and eating a child.

But what better? Go on! Think of something!

In truth, she was anxious about Ned. His eyes looked inwards and he moved with a tightly-wound force, in strides that even her long legs could not match. When she had stuck the pigeon feather in his hat, he had smiled absently and withdrawn inside again.

They joined a growing crowd that picked its way across the workings of the new canal. After a short hesitation, she took his arm, to make them look a little more like the other early merrymakers who flooded out of the city gate, following the sound of the discordant band towards the fair.

Outside the city walls, Holland stretched away to the horizon, flat, damp, creased by drainage ditches, a flatness interrupted only by clumps of trees, the insect-like machinery of bridges, and a few large country houses inside walled estates.

'Your scent will surely be lost among so many others,' she

453

said lightly. His arm was firm and warm. And though he seemed hardly to notice her at his side, his elbow pressed her hand firmly against his ribs.

'Is your back less painful now?' she asked.

He nodded. 'I'd like you always for my nurse.'

She would have pulled her hand free, but they arrived at the edge of the fair.

In front of the wall of a large country estate, a temporary village had sprouted. Tents, painted canvas booths, market stalls, and cages. Large cages on wheeled carts, smaller ones stacked one on top of another. Inside them, all manner of creatures squawked, squalled, twittered, hooted and yapped. Above this cacophony, a hurdy-gurdy contested hotly with the band.

Marika paid a few *stuivers* to get them across a bridge over one of the small canals. Then bought two crullers from a stand, hot from the fat, and gave one to Ned. But he was too distracted to eat.

Though it was still only early morning, there was already a crowd. Marika glanced at Ned's face and took his hand. His grip in return was so hard that it hurt.

There was a feral reek in the air. A brew of fear and rage spilled from the cages.

'No dog could find you here!' whispered Marika in his ear. 'Not with that stink!'

'Buy your seats now for the next parade of beasts!' shouted a dark-haired man with a piratical plait. 'Marvel at strange creatures from the Indies! Wonder at the unsuspected riches of man's domain! Learn the truth about the beasts!'

'He's a rash man to promise the truth about anything,' said Ned. 'We must sample it before we go . . . Where are the wolves?'

They edged behind the back of a bagpipe player and dodged a rolling hoop. Then passed a bored lion, flattened against the floor of one of the large, wheeled cages.

'The poor thing's dying of tedium,' murmured Marika intensely. 'I'd rather be on the run.'

454

A large group of both sexes and all ages surrounded a tethered elephant. At the urging of a tiny, blue-eyed mahout, a man from the crowd paid for a mug of ale and offered it to the elephant. The great beast gripped the handle with the delicate, probing finger at the end of its trunk and drank, to cheers from the crowd.

Beyond the elephant, a rhinoceros stood tethered by the leg, with an ill-tempered glint in its small squinty eye. 'Ride the rhinoceros! Win a prize.' The crowd here was smaller, and hung well back.

'I think that we may have been followed,' said Ned suddenly.

'Where?' Marika glanced around as if gazing in wonder.

'THE SPOILS OF EXPLORATION!' said an overhead banner strung between two poles. 'MONKEYS! MACAWS! BUFFALO! TURTLES!'

Here and there the local bailiff's men stood keeping an eye on the crowd, looking out for drunken disorder, public lechery and wantonness.

'I don't see him,' she said after a moment. 'Or do you mean one of the bailiff's men?'

'No, there, behind that cage.'

A large smooth cat, sleeker than the lion, with a stonemason's shoulders, flung itself from one end of the wheeled cage to the other. As they pretended to gaze, before moving casually on, it ate their hearts out with its eyes. A ginger-haired youth stood looking at the cat on the other side of the cage.

Their way was blocked by a pyramid of dogs balanced, dancing with jigging feet on each other's backs, while the hurdy-gurdy churned to the end of the tune. On the final note, the pyramid dissolved. Its different springy parts ran off and disappeared behind one of the painted canvas walls. For a moment Ned was reminded of the quicksilver running from his hand.

'There!' Ned gripped Marika's hand even more tightly and pulled her after him towards a banner: 'THE DEVIL'S DOGS!'

His face held the terrified anticipation of a seeker at an oracle.

Marika looked back at the bailiff's man who now stood at the edge of the elephant's crowd. Then spotted the ginger-haired youth again. This time at a sweetmeat stall.

Where else would a young man go, who's hardly more than a boy?

She looked away as he turned in their direction.

The reek was even stronger here. Two of the three wolves had withdrawn as far as they could, to the rear of their cage, and sat with their backs to the gaggle of children who pushed past Ned for a closer look. The third wolf, a large male, lay stretched out in the centre of the cage. As Ned gazed, it yawned, exposing a red cavern fenced with sharp white teeth as long as Ned's thumb. Marika watched, appalled, as it rested its muzzle on its forepaws and gazed up under its brows, straight into Ned's eyes. Then, with a look that she could describe only as despair, the wolf closed its eyes and went somewhere else.

Ned closed his own eyes.

He was the wolf. A current of fast-flowing grey water. His world was wherever he set his foot, new again with every step. He travelled without stopping, pulled by ropes of smells: the faint waft of a female from beyond the hill, pines, cattle, the afterbirth of a tender new fawn. Pulled onwards by the clap of a wood pigeon's wing, the rasping bite of a snail. By the squeak of a mouse – a casual mouthful. He flowed onwards, with his mate, pulled by the exhilarating size of the world, until it stopped short in the pupil of a man's eye and shrank to the size of a cage.

He opened his eyes again.

Where was the devil in these dogs?

He saw nothing so terrible. These creatures had nothing to do either with the beast in his head or with the farmers' wolf.

'Come away,' murmured Marika. 'You draw attention.'

He felt the beginning of an outrage that he could not express,

456

let alone explain. 'I must hear what supposed truth is said about them!' Ned plunged back into the crowd past a monkey which rocked back and forth on its perch, looking into the distance above the heads of the crowd, towards the largest tent where the parade of beasts would be held.

'You don't expect to learn truth in a fairground . . . Ned!'

When Marika caught up, he said, 'If I am to be part animal, I must know the supposed truth about that part of myself!' He plunged forward again into the tent. Though she was cut off by a large farmer, his wife and four blond children, Ned's height, Catryn's old hat and the pigeon feather made him easy to see in the crowd.

Marika saw the ginger-haired youth push into the tent not far behind Ned.

I'll watch from here, she thought. Perhaps he'll show whether he's following Ned or not.

She bought herself a twist of fried potatoes as an excuse to stand, then hovered just outside the tent, on the edge of the milling crowd, where she could look through the lifted flaps and see both Ned and the youth. She wiped her palm across her mouth and glanced around the fairground again. One of the bailiff's men was watching the drunken elephant. The other was not in sight. She looked for a moment at a beggar who stood a few feet away.

She was certain that she had not seen him earlier, when she first looked for their possible follower. One wouldn't forget those once brightly-coloured rags layered so thickly that the man looked like a haystack on legs. She turned to look into the tent again. Ned's hat was just where it had been before. There was applause from the crowd in the tent.

The beggar laid his hand on her arm and whispered, 'Lambkins.'

Her fried potatoes scattered on the muddy ground. Her throat closed up.

He smiled. Under the brim of his filthy hat, blue eyes

457

gleamed at her. His teeth were a shock of white in the filthy tangle of his beard.

Under his cloak of layered rags he wore a soldier's leather jacket but no shirt.

She pulled her arm from his grasp. Held her hands up between them, like a shield.

'Lambkins,' he said reproachfully. 'Surely you know me, though I hope no one else will.'

'It is you!' she whispered at last.

'Didn't I say I'd come back?'

Not like this.

She raised her head and scanned the crowds. A squad of *shutters* strolled along the canal edge.

'Come away from the general view,' she said. He followed her into a beer tent.

I should be happy! she thought. Filled with joy.

She turned to face him. 'Dear God, Justus . . .' She was jostled by two large men with tankards.

'Stop eying me like a shying mare and give your prodigal brother a kiss!' he said when the two men had moved on. 'There's no *shutter* in here to see you now.'

'I despaired,' she said, still with her hands raised between them.

'Foolish lambkins, not to trust her brother. I told you I'd return.'

'Why didn't you take me? Do you know what you left me to?'

He smiled and reached out to pinch her cheek gently with a large dirty hand. 'Aha! That's what all this reticence is about. You're angry with me. My sweet, you'll forgive me when you hear . . . I saw that the house is sealed. Where are you living now?'

'You can't come there!' she said with a stab of panic.

'You haven't by chance married Pietersen?' he cried with forced delight. 'Or some other hapless, helpless quarry?'

'Pietersen was never *my* quarry,' she said tightly.

458

He drew her through the crowd towards one side of the tent. 'Let's find a bench . . . Do you have enough money to buy us ale? We'll hide in the shadows and trade our excellent adventures since we parted.'

'I need to stay here . . .' Then she thought that she would be able to hear from the applause when the show was finished.

'I've thought of little else but coming back to see you,' Justus said once they had settled on a corner bench.

'Justus, did you do it?' She kept her voice very low and looked around the dimness of the tent. A small forest of pipe-smoke columns grew up from the table just beyond their bench.

'Oh, that's all past now,' he said airily. 'I have other problems to interest me now.'

'The problem still interests me.'

'Oh, lambkins!' He leaned close and peered into her eyes. 'You don't truly believe that I killed the cursed man, do you?'

She smelled him, acrid and strong as a dog or sweating horse. When she didn't answer, he took her hand and pressed it to the bare flesh of his chest beneath his jacket.

'Can you feel my heart breaking?' he asked. 'At the very idea that you might have been tormented by such doubts.'

She jerked her hand, trying to pull it free. He held it captive over his breastbone.

The crowd in the show tent applauded again. But not with finality.

'I will confess then.' With his other hand Justus captured her face. 'Look at me, and absolve me if you can.'

'What did you do?' She could barely whisper the words. She felt that she already knew.

'I confess that I have killed a man . . .'

She let out her breath. Her eyes slid away from his.

'But only since I left you. I knew what life might bring – that's why I insisted that you wait for me, safe at home.' His eyes held hers. Then he released her face and stroked her cheek

459

softly. 'I almost regret having raised you so gently, if it means that you won't understand now about the kind of life I had to lead abroad.'

'Life wasn't so gentle here after you left.'

'Then you'll understand all the better that, after all my money was stolen, I had to shift to keep from starving. Not always in the most delicate ways, alas.'

She leaned back against the canvas wall and braced her arms to keep her upright against a sudden giddiness. 'All your money was stolen?' But she had been certain that he had many other bonds safe in his saddlebags. Guilt and compassion swilled beneath her heart. 'Oh, Justus . . . !' I'm sorry! she was about to cry. I'm so sorry. I didn't mean to leave you with nothing. I thought you had so much and were leaving me so little.

'I was careless,' he said. 'I forgot what villains this world holds.'

And she had been so sure that he was one of them. Instead, she was the villain!

'A gang of footpads set on me on the road just over the Flemish border, and took my horse and saddlebags. I killed one of them.'

She burst into tears of relief that it had not been she who had beggared him and forced him into Lord knew what new villainies.

'My poor sweet.' He stroked her hair. 'Don't weep for your big brother. They beat me only lightly, and I've always bounced back. You know me. And, indeed, here I am, just as I promised. At no small risk, I may add. But I would take any risk to find you. I have such plans. I had hoped you might have managed to lay your hands on a little cash.'

Inside the tent the crowd stood facing a painted Garden of Eden where three Dutch merchantmen sailed up over the horizon in splendid disregard of chronology. Just as Ned found a place near the front, the band marched in and took its place just to the left of the painted Serpent twined round the Tree of Knowledge of Good and Evil.

'Welcome, Sons of Adam and Daughters of Eve, to the earthly Paradise!'

The dark-plaited pirate who had touted the show stepped from behind the Serpent's tree. His wide-brimmed hat had now been pinned up flat against the crown above his face. Long ragged green sleeves, like those of an old-fashioned minstrel, flowed from his arms like moss from the branches of a tree. Below the waist, however, he wore rough wool breeches and solid farmer's boots.

'Welcome to the new Eden, right here in Holland, where the lion lies down with the lamb . . .' He sized up his audience. 'And the Spaniard just lies!'

There were shouts of edgy laughter.

'But to be serious – for Paradise is a serious matter – I know that you are, of course, not here just to scratch the itch of idle curiosity. Like all good Dutch citizens, you work at all times to improve your souls. Confess – you're here only because the church is closed!'

More laughter, but a little less than before.

He fixed his dark eyes on a youth, then on a young woman. 'Why do you laugh? Don't you think that I, the Animal Master and Adam's heir, can teach you true morality as well as any minister?'

Dead silence. Some heads turned to look at the bailiff's man, who stood at the back of the tent.

'You! Mynheer and mevrouw Mankind, sitting there, gawping . . .' He smiled again. (Don't take my bullying seriously, said his smile.) '. . . in spite of yourselves, you will leave here wiser than you came.' He paced the front of the crowd, gathering up their eyes with his own.

'We know that God has assigned each beast in His Creation its own duty towards Man. The ox with meat, milk, and the labour of its muscles. The humble bee extracts sweetness from the air for us to eat, and teaches us, by its perfect example, of

461

a perfect civil order – each citizen subjecting himself to the greater good . . . But what of the rest? The *ferrae naturae*, the wild beasts which admit no master?' He paced, hands spread ready to catch any answer. 'What good are they? Do they too serve man, or are they the Devil's creatures, doomed to dwell in darkness?' He drummed out the alliteration with relish.

Ned leaned forward, his knuckles white.

The Animal Master held up his arms. A monkey dropped from a pole into his arms, climbed him like a tree, and balanced on the top of his head.

The crowd laughed.

'Yes!' the Animal Master cried. 'Laughter. The first, and best service paid to Man. Giving cause to laugh in these warlike times is a service beyond price!'

Wearing the monkey like a wobbly hat, he threw out his right hand. Serpent and tree were rolled up smartly by a pair of ropes to show the lion, out of its cage, staring blearily at the ground, attached by rope and collar to a stout post.

'Ahhhhh,' the crowd quavered with one breath.

'Now, here is a service even better for our souls than laughter: a chance to reflect on evil and to ponder the cost of bloodshed and violence.' The Animal Master walked up to a man in the front row and dropped his voice conspiratorially. 'The lion is also a beast in which the physical passions run high. Would you like to touch it in hope of catching some of its virility? No? Wise man! For you might also catch its putrid smell and bad breath that are the cost of sexual excess and too much meat. And what would your wife say to that?'

The crowd laughed. His victim blushed. The painted cloth Serpent dropped back into place.

Where is the wolf? Ned wondered. Surely, he will expound on the wolf!

'Next, the elephant . . .'

Surely, the Animal Master would display the wolf!

'. . . The elephant, closest to man in intelligence . . . and

462

vices. The largest animal found on land, from Ethiopia, beyond the deserts of Sidra. It teaches us true courage . . . and by its bad example to avoid the vice of drunkenness.'

The Animal Master gave the fluid-kneed elephant another mug of ale, which it drank to the applause of the crowd.

The band played a sombre flourish. The Animal Master dropped his voice theatrically. 'Now, a beast of the wilderness, of a place without God. A fierce, blood-sucking persecutor of man, the ravager of his flocks! The Devil's own Dog. What possible service can the wolf perform for Man?'

'My other half,' whispered Ned. 'My half-brother.'

A weary, loose-shouldered wolf trotted in, head and tail down, held between two taut ropes, pulled to the left and right by two muscular youths. It was the large male, which had yawned, then looked into his eyes.

The spectators inhaled sharply. A woman in the crowd screamed. There were furtive rustlings of signs being made against the evil eye.

'This slavering beast,' cried the Animal Master '. . . this Hound of Hell, this Dog of the Devil, is as hungry for blood as its master is for souls.'

Another intake of breath from the crowd, and more rustlings.

'What can it possibly give us except its pelt?'

The wolf lay down and went somewhere else.

'Firstly, this wily and ravenous hunter teaches us cunning and the skills of the hunt.' The Animal Master regarded the supine wolf with a flicker of doubt, but resumed with all his original fervour. 'But greatest good grows out of greatest evil – just as a light shows brightest in the darkest pit. From the worst creatures, we can learn to the greatest advantage of our souls.'

He had them now, the entire crowd, including the bailiff's man, standing silent with held breath, fixed by the burning points of his dark eyes. 'The wolf was created by God to

463

remind us to be always on guard against the forces of chaos and evil. To stand as an example of bestiality, which we must wipe from our souls!'

One of the youths holding the ropes leaped forward, kicked the wolf in the side, leaped back again. The animal sprang to its feet, bristling, fangs bared, as huge as a staghound. Suddenly alive and as terrifying as its reputation, it bucked and twisted. It slashed at the ropes with its teeth.

'Ahhhhh!' quavered the crowd. There was an uneasy stirring and several more screams.

'Don't look into its eyes!' cried a voice. 'Don't look! Or it will take your soul for its master! It will strike you dumb!'

'No!' Ned turned and forced his way through the packed bodies to reach open air. Screams from the audience drowned his cry.

Marika seized his arm as he fought clear of the canvas tent flap.

'Are you turning wolf?' whispered Marika urgently, following close behind.

He shook his head blindly. 'Did you hear him? "We must wipe bestiality from our souls!" But the beast meant no harm. Not till they kicked it!'

'We must go! At once!'

'Lies!' he said. 'Not the truth at all, but lies! *Homo lupus homini*. Man is the true beast!'

'Ned, come away now! We must go back to Catryn's.' She led him away by the arm. 'Help me to detect whether we are followed by either that ginger-haired lout or a beggar in coloured rags.'

They got back to Catryn's hovel without seeing a follower. Catryn had left them ale and bread. Ned watched Marika as they ate in the last of the evening light. Something had happened to her at the fair. She did not even attempt her false brightness but stared silently at her hands and plucked crumbs from her bread with restless fingers.

464

We must leave Amsterdam tomorrow, thought Ned. We've overstretched our luck here as it is.

'I'm tired,' she announced suddenly, and lay down on her straw mattress.

At first when he heard her, he thought that she was praying. Then he heard the intensity and rage in her muffled voice.

Very cautiously, with a desperate tenderness, he eased himself on to her straw mattress and curled himself around her. Amazingly, she did not object. He closed a feather-light arm around her and felt her flesh under the light fabric of her shift. Then he heard what she was saying between clenched teeth – a torrent of oaths and curses that would have made her brother proud. His own name figured, along with Justus, John Nightingale and her neighbours.

At last, she exhausted herself and lay very still. Then she began to shiver. Harder and harder until she might have been a cart over cobbles. He heard her teeth begin to rattle.

'I'll stir up the fire,' he whispered. 'It's all right. Wait. I'll wake the fire!'

He crouched and prodded at the feeble overnight embers in the little fireplace that heated Catryn's hovel. He blew, fed, coaxed. Grew dizzy with blowing, squinted his eyes against the swirling ash and jumping flames. At last he nursed up a quivering bush of heat and light to try to warm her.

He pulled a square of plaited rush matting across the dirt floor for them to sit on, and persuaded her from her sack of straw to the hearth. He sat, hardly breathing, staring through the fine gold wires of her hair into the flames, her weight against his chest, the back of her head against his mouth and the smell of rosemary water in his nose, while she remained elsewhere. He turned his head away from the dancing fire to steady himself with shadows. But the shadows writhed and jumped.

The world shifted.

The wolf breathed in his ear. The pressure began. Let me in.

Dear God, not now! He had never changed with her since

465

that first time. He had thought that she was safe. In her present state, she might not survive another shock. She might not survive what he would do to her.

He fought it, as he had before. But he was too tired now, too distracted by the warmth of Marika in his arms. He braced himself. Tried to force the beast back. Locked. Broke.

He tumbled, drowning, in the familiar terror. The beast grew like coral into his bones. Looked out through his eyes. Began to listen through the trumpets of his reshaped ears to the scraping of her petticoat as she breathed.

No!

But the beast took him. He felt a hideous, ecstatic ease. The secret, silky fur slipped across his muscles and veins, liquid, soft and easy, invisible to the eye. The weight of a tail dragged at his spine. Still holding her with one arm, he began to shrug off his jacket. When she tried to turn, he buried his keen snout in the fragrant warmth beneath her ear.

She had the maybe smell.

Marika had let herself lean back against Ned's large, comforting warmth. She had achieved hollowness, a peaceful absence of any feeling at all. Only her eyes still felt as if they were trying to push themselves out of their sockets. She recognised bottom, where the speed of the dive slows and you don't yet know whether or how fast you will rise again. She had been close before, knew that you don't spurn any handholds to help turn yourself upwards. When she felt stronger, she would make certain that he did not misunderstand her present need.

She kept her eyes closed and let the firelight flicker on her lids. Drifted, pushing away images of Justus dangling like an old sack on the gibbet island outside the Amsterdam harbour. Or Ned.

She saw Justus in the tent, daring her to disbelieve him. Then triumphant at her tears. Then Justus, running away earlier, avoiding her eyes and lying. Forgetting to say goodbye.

466

The face of the *burt* officer at her door. Heard the voices on the *stoeps*.

But he was her brother. The only family she had.

She imagined Justus holding her in his arms at night after their parents were drowned. Saw herself, old and pinched, still sitting at the end of his table, still smiling false smiles with toothless gums.

Cash. He hadn't come back for her at all, but for cash. When she said no, he had left again.

Ned's arms tightened suddenly. He made a small, odd sound, part grunt and part exclamation. His body stiffened. She was startled back into the room and present moment.

'Ned?' she whispered. She turned her head.

His eyes looked into hers without seeming to see her. His expression was so strange that she felt a shock of fear. It had finally happened again.

Without warning, Ned was no longer there. She was in the arms of the beast that looked like him.

She had planned to be coolly observant. To fetch a mirror and show him that he had only a human face – a little altered to be sure, but not a wolf's muzzle. But fear has a way of grabbing the nearest set of empty clothes. All her fears now dressed themselves in the fear of this unfamiliar Ned, with intent eyes, the muscles of his face somehow rearranged on the bone.

She repeated his name, as if it were a charm to bring him back. His face had not turned to a wolf's muzzle, but it was transformed all the same.

A shadow of horror passed over his face. Then his expression brightened. He seemed to see her now, but not to know her. His arms tightened.

'Ned!' She called as if he had gone very far away. 'Come back, please!' She struggled against the fierce grip of his arms.

He buried his face deep in the curve of her neck.

'Don't be a fool!' She pulled at one of his forearms to loosen it.

467

He made a soothing noise and opened his arms a little. He stroked her arms, breathed in the odour of her hair, rubbed his face with apparent delight in the bright tangle at the back of her neck. His hot breath through her hair turned to cold trickles that ran down her neck and over the skin of her chest. She broke free and turned on her knees to face him.

Not a wolf. Not his face. She had been right about that. But he now took off his boots, stockings and jacket, which Ned would never have done.

'What are you doing?'

The muscles of his face pulled oddly at the bones beneath. His eyes looked deep into a private intent.

Perhaps his face did not change to a wolf, but his spirit did!

As he stretched to pull off the shirt that Catryn had given him, the firelight scooped out a wide flat bowl under his ribs and showed a broader chest than she remembered on the youth of fifteen. The scars on his back were healing.

He took off his breeches.

'Stop at once!' Her voice tightened and her face grew hot. She scrambled to her feet.

His hand closed on her ankle. She tried to shake it off.

'Ned, you're beginning to frighten me.'

Still holding her ankle, he lay down on his side with his head propped on one hand, and stared up at her. He seemed totally content.

She tried not to look at the long-limbed, naked body, kept her eyes on his face. 'Please, Ned, speak to me. Don't jest. You make me afraid of you.'

His pale, dark-lashed eyes still regarded her steadily, with intense interest, as if he had settled in to read her for at least an hour. His hand was firm on her ankle and seemed unlikely to let go.

'All right, I'll stay. But you must let go of my ankle so I can sit again.'

When he did so, she was pleased with the success of her small

468

stratagem. She was free. She had also ascertained that he could hear and respond. Something of Ned still remained. And, on balance, it seemed to wish her well, not ill.

She settled cross-legged on the woven mat and gathered up the coverlet in her arms like a shield. She looked away. If she continued to meet his eyes, she would say something with her own, whether she willed it or not.

'Do you mean to make me so uneasy?'

She clutched the coverlet as he rolled over towards her, ending on his back, his ribs against her stockinged soles, still looking up into her face.

'You look a fool gawping at me like that.'

Don't prattle from fear, she told herself.

He plucked her right hand from the quilt and laid her palm on his face. His breath was warm against her skin. When she tried to pull her hand away, her fingertips bumped the fragile half-globes of his eyelids. She left her hand where it was, for fear of hurting him.

With his eyes closed, she could look at his long naked frame spread out before her, recognisably Ned, not that much changed since fifteen. A little more flesh, but the same lean, purposeful musician's hands. The same stretched elegance of calf and thigh. And long slim feet that seemed made for the dancing he swore he could not master. To tell the truth, however, she remembered his face best, dark brows clenched as if in agony, his long thick hair falling into her mouth when he had collapsed on her breast. She had looked at him then, at fifteen, with the same distance she now felt.

He felt even more distant now. While the body was more-or-less the same – broader in the chest and perhaps less racked by awkwardness and self-loathing – her Ned had gone somewhere else and allowed another creature to move in.

He held her wrist lightly, to keep her hand against his face. She found that she didn't mind. Though no longer Ned, he still kept her company. She felt comforted by the press of his ribs against her feet, as if he were a friendly dog. Perhaps he

469

truly was a wolf in body as well as spirit, and she was charmed so that she didn't see it.

'The world is mad, or else I am. Or else I am dead and heaven is nothing like they say, or hell is much cooler . . .'

He kissed her palm, then tasted it. Licked the tips of her fingers. Bit gently at the pad of her thumb.

She stiffened, braced for him to bite with full strength.

His teeth tested the pad of her first finger. She relaxed again.

'And by the way, my friend, once again, you are not turned wolf in any visible way . . .'

Her eyes slid to the dark nest of his groin and his half-swollen penis. An arrowhead of orderly black hair pointed up his belly at his navel, which she saw for the first time to be a perfect oval dish of fold, like a tiny ear. She was a fool if she pretended any longer not to know where they were headed, whether he was man or wolf. She did not love him now, she told herself, any more than at fifteen, but she lacked the strength to change their direction.

Where else and what else would be any better? And what difference did it make?

She didn't know what she felt.

Her hand was a safe place in which to hide all of herself. The adventures of her hand – gentle teeth and a warm tongue voyaged across her palm and around her wrist. She closed her eyes and became only her hand. The cool rivers still trickled behind her ears, down her neck, through her chest and belly.

The tip of his tongue on the small webs of skin between her fingers erased warrants, closing doors, brothers who left forever with averted eyes and then returned in need of cash. In her relief at forgetting all those things, she also forgot to think that the teeth might still close through her flesh.

He lifted himself up and leaned close to her face. She heard him inhale. He licked her mouth delicately, then the sides of her nose. Then her lips again, then he kissed her.

470

She permitted him. Noted the warm, determined question of his mouth, declined to answer. Then kissed him back.

Why not? She had kissed other men for worse reasons, because it would help Justus or placate another admirer. And at least her hand and mouth were awake now.

On hands and knees, he kissed her again, harder. Then he sank back on his heels and buried his face in her petticoat, between her legs.

'You're turned part beast, for sure,' she said weakly. The youth she had known had blushed at a nipple. Now his breath was hot through the thin linen of her petticoat. She placed a protesting hand on his head, but did not push.

To hell with all of it! She let herself be pressed down on to the matting with the coverlet beneath her head. She turned her cheek into the worn wool as he pushed her petticoat up to her waist. He buried his muzzle in the warm musky flower between her legs.

She was not anxious, as she had been with John Nightingale, not distracted by a desperate need to please or fear of a wrong move. Instead of the keen, urgent nugget of hunger that she remembered, she felt a shimmering, a dissolving of her physical envelope, as if she met him somewhere outside of her contained and limited self. When he had collapsed against her breast, she wrapped her arms tight around his neck, her mind clamped hard against a threatening uprush of tears.

Then she opened her eyes and saw the tenderness in his.

Direct, searing sensation rushed into the hollow in her chest. The tears welled dangerously. She sat up in alarm. He reached for her.

'No. Please. Leave me alone.'

She lay down again, willingly, but tried to think of gibbets and hangings, of knocks on her door, black-dressed women narrowing their eyes and whispering on *stóeps*. She dived for the cool, dark, placid waters of indifference, but he hauled her back, from cold safety into hot danger.

She pushed him away, then pulled him back in panic. Cried

471

out in alarm and still offered up the sides of her neck, nipples, insides of her elbows, the small of her back. Bit by bit, she resumed residence in every scrap of her flesh. He entered her again. She clung to him this time with her arms and legs. This time when they finally lay panting, cheek to cheek, the tears came.

'I'm sorry . . . I'm so sorry!' She couldn't stop. The dyke had cracked and let through a hot, undignified, terrifying flood. She cried noisily, in gasps hauled up from the bottom of her lungs, with a force that fitted the scale of all her disasters. He held on to her and rocked her on the mat in front of the fire.

'What is it?' she begged. 'What is wrong with me?'

He breathed into the damp hair of her temples, on to the lids of her closed wet eyes. With one hand, he pulled at the coverlet. With her own arms clamped tight around his ribs, she slid slowly deeper and deeper into a soft sleep.

When she woke some time later, she found two survivors of a shipwreck, clinging to imagined safety even in their sleep. She pulled away.

The crack under the shutters of the unglazed window had just begun to lighten.

'What's wrong, my love?' She saw him wake fully and feel where they were.

She sat up and pulled her feet under her to make distance between them. She turned her head to the grey embers in the fireplace.

'You needn't fear the beast. I'm Ned again.'

'I know. I can see it.' She dropped her wide brow on to her kneecaps.

He watched her for a long time in silence. 'Come with me. I know that's a vile invitation. But please come!'

'Why?'

'Don't you want to come? I can't leave you behind now.'

'Because we made love?' She lifted her head from her knees. 'Do you remember that we made love?'

He frowned, troubled, then nodded. 'Yes. Or rather, I feel

472

that we did.' He looked down at his own naked body. 'It seems likely.'

'And what besides lovemaking do you propose to do with me? Ned, I mean, not the wolf.'

He sat up and leaned over to coax the fire awake again. She watched him think as he worked. The scarred muscles of his bare back bunched and flattened when he prodded the embers. 'We'll make a new life together, away from Amsterdam. Somewhere. England, away from London. Scotland . . . they still have wolves there.' He half-smiled.

The fire twitched. He looked at the tiny tongue of flame thoughtfully, then set down the poker. On hands and knees, with his genitals swinging at the base of his belly, he reminded her of the wolf of the night before.

'I don't need saving.'

He turned to her, kneeling on his heels. 'I'm asking you to be my wife.'

'Oh!' she cried. 'Oh, hellfire and damnation! Don't do that! I beg you!'

'Not to save you. To save myself.'

'Ned, I'm not for you or anyone. I can't love you. Thought I loved a brother once. Now I don't know. And I imagined that I was infatuated with an Englishman – who then spurned me and is your enemy. I couldn't become a wife. I haven't the knack!'

'I'll settle for what we already have.'

'What I have isn't with you. It's with the wolf that you and your doctor want to destroy.'

My member refuses to rise, even in imagination. I begin to believe that the touch of her hand burns my legs. I try to drift off to sleep beside her and wake half-strangled by my chains.

473

TWELVE

38

Still naked on his knees, Ned turned his head to listen. Far away in the early morning city, he heard dogs. A baying pack.

'It's not possible!' Marika said in despair. She scrambled to her feet and ran to the shutters to listen.

His clothes were scattered around the hovel. She snatched up his shirt and turned a sleeve right-side out. Ned hauled on his trousers, found only one sock. Hauled on his boots. His shirt. Justus's jacket.

Marika rummaged in her belongings, then brought him a ball of soap. 'We don't know for certain that they want you. Could they be after someone else?' She lifted her head and listened again. The baying was closer.

He took the soap.

'On your soles! And don't forget your hands! What a joke if it were me they wanted this time.'

Ned scrubbed his boot soles with the soap, then his hands and neck until he stank of lye. 'Where will I be able to find you?'

'I don't know . . . Try here . . . send a message to Catryn. I'll tell her where I've gone.'

'I'll come back for you when I can!' he said.

'Don't say that!'

He heard bitterness as well as fear in her voice.

'Don't be a fool and try to come back! You'll hang. I'll survive. All I must do is repent and grovel. And learn to spin with the other whores.'

477

She looked out into the alley where the hovel stood. A three-quarter moon glowed a cheesy yellow in the brightening sky. 'Go now!'

He grabbed her in his arms.

'Don't get caught!' she said. 'Take to the water if you can. Try to get to the fair. Stay with the animals until you can think what else to do!'

The maenad hair brushed his face. He tried to memorise her. She smelt only of herself now and of lovemaking, without the rosemary and rose oil. His fingers made a desperate inventory through her shift: her ribs, her waist, her hips. He kissed her to memorise her lips. She kissed him back hard, then broke free.

'Go now!' she said. She opened the door. 'Wait!' She ran back to her things and brought him some coins which she stuffed into his pocket.

He leaned to kiss her a last time as he went out.

The narrow alley was a shadow-filled ditch. He turned his head a little to study the complex darkness with the side of his eye. Nothing moved. Nothing out of place. Or too opaque. Or too still.

Left or right?

A watchman in the street to his left called five o'clock. The bells began. Old Church, New Church. St Anthony's Church. The air grew thick and metallic with the sound of bells. Then, abruptly, the night silence returned.

The dogs were closer, but with his scent covered by the soap he might just get clear.

He turned right along the alley, towards the new canal. He would lose his trail in the mud, grab a bucket like an early workman, follow the canal round to the port. Slip out of the city through the early morning traffic, then follow the outside of the city walls till he met the crowds bound for the fair. Then he saw the lantern at the end of the alley.

'What is it?' whispered Marika as he doubled back past her, headed towards the other end of the alley.

478

'Someone's there.' He touched her extended hand briefly. Then kissed her again. But she pushed him away urgently.

'Ned, *run!*'

He ran to the end of the alley. Froze. Waited, unsurprised, angry at himself for having hoped. The light of a window beyond the end of the alley flickered again as something moved across it.

'. . . so eager?' asked a man's quiet voice. 'You must have a pocket full of charms.'

'Just my musket,' said a second low voice. 'Who needs better magic than that?'

Ned pressed himself back against a gate, into an overhanging vine.

He was trapped in the ditch of the alley between the man with the lantern whom he was supposed to see and these others who waited for him to run into their arms. It made no difference that his smell was disguised. They had known where he was and were waiting for him. They had had intelligence. Someone had betrayed him.

He eased out of the arch of the gate and slowly doubled back a second time towards Catryn's hovel, past the backs of two other hovels. Then past two walled yards, perhaps with sleeping dogs. A longer wall along a small orchard. Stable walls. A barred half-moon drain.

He grabbed the iron bars over the drain and heaved. But they sat too firmly in their mortar.

He had only one thought. If he were to be caught, it must be away from here. Marika must not be found.

He jumped at the orchard wall, swung up and topped it, landed badly, stumbled. The hand he put out to save himself sank into something warm and soft. Before his heart could beat again, a demonic screech ripped the early-morning air. He scrambled to his feet, pushed past heavy feathery bodies and ran through short ranks of trees, followed by the cries of the outraged geese.

He climbed a low internal gate into a small formal garden.

479

There were lights and shouts now in the alley behind him. And now a dog in the neighbouring yard barked and marked his location. A shutter opened above his head. A man's voice shouted. On the far side of the yard, he unbarred a wooden door in a high outer wall. Found himself in a narrow channel between cliffs of house walls. He darted left, ran, turned again. Then again. Stopped to gasp for breath and was shaken by a fit of coughing. He saw light reflecting from water.

Now, while he had eluded them, he should take a boat. They would see a moving boat on the water, but if he could be gone before they picked up his trail, he could lose them. Bent low, he crossed the street, towards the reflected light.

One of the large canals, too confused to know which. Went to the edge, peered down for a skiff or wherry. Then he heard the dogs, gaining ground. Cursed the growing daylight.

For one moment, he was tempted to sit down on the cobbles and wait.

This can't go on forever.

Then he began to run, to get out of the street before the hunters turned the corner and saw him. Turned into a shadowed cleft.

The alley led directly into a yard. No cross alley. No back gate. A sheer wall rose three floors. Warehouse or workshop. Tiny windows high out of his reach even if he climbed on to the lumber stacked against the wall. A sawing horse, too low to help. Shavings. Chips. Windows shuttered anyway. He was in the bottom of a brick well.

He searched the roofline for a gap, a low shed. His breath tore at his lungs. How puny man's strength was when put to the test!

Fool! Fool! To run in where he could not see the way out! But he was only a man now. The wolf would have known better!

He flung himself at the back door of the house. Locked.

480

He banged. He heard movement behind the door but it stayed closed.

'In the name of God's mercy, please let me in!'

More movement inside. But the door didn't budge. Word had spread.

He clambered back up on to the stacked wood, as if the wall might miraculously dissolve, or an unnoticed window would let him pass through. He leaned on the wall and searched the yard. No tools left to use as weapons. Nothing but a closed door and the opening of the alley where the dogs now bayed. They had him.

The walls of the tiny yard magnified their ecstatic whoops. The furore shook his bones, rattled his skull so that he could not think what to do next. Their nails clattered on the bricks. The reek of their triumph lifted the hairs on his neck.

The chase was over.

He braced himself for their rush. Already felt the burning agony as yellow teeth stripped muscle from the bone. He saw dark shining spots hit the walls as the dogs yanked and flung their heads, and white bones already being worried in the darkness of the yard.

But the pack did not rush at him. They held him at bay and waited. A huge dog with the lion face of an English mastiff or bandog stepped forward from the pack. It was master until the real masters arrived.

Ned panted and stared into the large dog's eyes, trying to hear through the baying how close behind the men were. The bandog had a mastiff's blocky jaw that would lock on a bull's flank and hang on until either dog or bull was dead. Its bloodshot yellow eyes, netted in sagging flesh, held a suppressed rage that it could never bite hard enough to relieve.

The woodpile shifted under his feet. He scrambled and regained his balance.

Don't fall! he ordered himself. Dear God, don't fall!

He eased himself to the ground with infinite care, still holding the bandog's eyes. Felt behind him with his right

481

hand for a block of wood. Closed his hand on a nothing, a straw, a twig. Useless, but it made him feel better to be armed, if only with a chair-leg-to-be.

Get past if you can.

No use now to turn aside in placation, to lay his head playfully on the ground, or to wag a non-existent tail. He had become prey, and prey did not negotiate. It either fought back or waited for the end. He took a small testing step forward.

A quiver of expectation shook the pack. The dogs realigned, grew less ecstatic, more intent. The leader rumbled in its throat. The hairs at the base of its tail bristled.

Ned risked another step forward toward the mouth of the alley, staring back. 'Down, sir!' he bellowed with all the human authority he could raise.

The bandog lifted its lips from its gums and showed incisors as large as a boar's tusks.

Ned stepped back and looked away. He glanced quickly back. The boar tusks were covered. The tail relaxed slightly.

Ned stepped forward again. 'Down, I say!'

Instantly, the incisors gleamed, the growl rumbled as deep and loud as cartwheels.

Man's authority and wit had failed him. The dogs would hold him here until the men arrived. And the men would chain him, beat him, burn him, lock him away forever in a cell underground. Or hang or burn him.

God help me, please! Holy Mother, send help. Send a miracle.

In the whole accursed yard, there was no flail, no hammer, no saw, nothing! The Dutch passion for order had doomed him.

He would rather be torn apart than lie choking slowly to death over a smoking brazier or choke more slowly in a noose. Even a chair-leg would take the force of the dog's teeth better than one of his bones. For a few seconds, at least. He listened for the men's shouts above the riot of the dogs.

Not yet.

He met the bandog's eyes again. Took another step forward.

Dark spots had begun to blur his vision, made it hard to hold the pack leader's eyes.

The bandog stepped toward him into the lists, backed by two self-appointed lieutenants. The rest of the army bellowed encouragement. Whoop. Whoop. The prey has refused to stand at bay and wait for its fate.

The bandog advanced with a swagger of shoulder, happy to forget its fragile pact of obedience to man.

Ned gauged the power of the shoulders, the thick neck, the block-like jaw. Its weight nearly matched his. How absurd for man to think that such a creature was subject to his will. By what divine fiat? A fraud, exposed here in this yard.

He hefted the wood. Might just be heavy enough, swung with enough force. If he had the chance to swing. Got behind that monster. Maybe. Break its neck. Its skull. Stun it. Slow it, at least. Maybe. And maybe lose a hand or knee. Maybe find himself lying on the bricks trying to breathe through a torn throat.

Whoop. Whoop. Their ravenous glee made it hard to think.

He eased sideways, to circle. The bandog read his intent. Then Ned heard shouts and saw the orange flicker of torches at the far end of the alley.

In that second of inattention, he was hit by an avalanche of rusty fur and snapping teeth. No pain, but the sound of tearing. He saw his sleeve flapping in streamers. Drops glistened, suspended in the air. Then he felt a distant pain in his arm, heard the clatter of his piece of wood as it struck first the wall and then the brick of the yard floor. But he was still free.

Deceived in its first grip, the bandog fell, coiled to its feet and sprang back. Ned tried to spin away from the jaws but felt pain again, high on his leg this time. He lost his footing. Fell.

His face struck the beast's shoulder.

He clawed it into an embrace, his arms around its neck. Squeezed. Like trying to choke a horse.

A blur of torches arrived in the yard. Dimly, he heard the men's shouts above the raging of the dog.

483

The bandog swung its head, its thick neck and heavy shoulders designed to break an enemy's neck or to strip the muscle from a bull's flank. Ned's feet scrabbled on the brick paving. He tried to kick its belly with his other leg, but could not find it. His hands slid on the short coarse fur.

The pain was a blinding white.

The dog swung him out, then slammed him back again against its shoulder, locked on to as much breech as flesh. Then he felt the skin of his leg tear. The bond between them loosened. The teeth unlocked to find better purchase. Once they had lodged again, he was dead, one way or another. There was nothing he could do.

I need the wolf's teeth and ferocity. God in Heaven . . . Lucifer . . . whoever decides these things, send me the wolf! Transform me now when I need it! The beast has ruined me. Send it now to save me!

The bandog leaped. Before its jaws could close, Ned flung himself on to its back and again embraced its thick neck with both arms, his face thrust against the bristling fur. His nostrils choked with dust, loose hairs and the blaring smell of its rage.

Where is the beast? I beg you, come find me now, or I will die!

The dog shook and writhed to throw him off. His torn arm could not choke it. He began to slide, off its shoulders, around its tree-trunk neck into range of the teeth. Pressed against the side of his eye, he saw foothills of black lip and gum and pink razor peaks of teeth. Bristles stabbed his lips and nostrils. He couldn't breathe. Dust and hair blocked his nose, the thick neck pressed it flat. He opened his mouth to gasp for air. His strength was going.

The bandog's raging roared in his ears.

He had to breathe. Opened his mouth again, gasped. His injured arm loosened. It was giving way. He clamped his teeth on to the dog's neck. His only hold. All that kept his own throat from the dog's teeth. His teeth slipped on

484

the smooth hard muscle. The dog bit into his calf, through his boot.

The side of his boot tore away. His arm slipped a little more.

He shifted his teeth a fraction of an inch toward the jaw, searching for purchase on looser skin. Any moment he would gag, sneeze, cough, and then die with his throat torn open. He was a rat now, being tossed from side to side by the powerful neck. He found slack skin on the dog's throat with his teeth and held fast. It shook him from side to side in fury. His single good arm failed, his body came unmoored. As he was flung to the ground, the dog's skin tore under his weight. Its hot blood burned his mouth and chin.

'Don't shoot!' shouted the officer. 'Keep him alive for questioning!'

Ned didn't see the gun. He and the mastiff collapsed side by side on to the brick paving. The mastiff quivered and pawed. Ned's lungs turned themselves inside out sucking at the air. The mastiff's hindquarters twitched and jumped while its life flooded out over the brick.

Ned stared at the dying dog. Most unbelievable in this monstrous, unthinkable turn of affairs was that he was still completely himself. He wiped his chin and looked at his hands. He noticed only dimly the closing circle of pikes and pointed muskets. When the men laid fearful hands on him, he had begun to weep and retch and scrub at his face with the sleeve of his good arm.

So here I am.

THIRTEEN

39

Two unfamiliar, armed men come with the Spoon. They watch him feed me bread, cheese and cold meat, washed down by beer. Then one of them orders him to unlock my web of chains from the staple in the floor.

'Stand up,' one of them tells me.

I laugh. So they lift me between them. Once up, I find that my legs hold me. The torn one is stiff but my stretching and flexing have kept the muscles alive. The bites in my arm and leg are hot, but Janni's ointments have fought off putrefaction. And Maurits's food has given back strength. I take a step.

The dangling chains swing against my shins. I clank and rattle like one of Maurits's automata grown to monstrous size. I can still walk. Unsteadily, but I progress. With a sword tip between my shoulder blades, I clank towards the door.

Today. Something happens . . .

Today, I speak.

I stop walking.

The sword tip presses me onwards.

I no longer feel even fear. I am empty of everything but the need to find words to save my life. I have no thoughts left. I don't know what I will say. I once knew but, just now, it's lost in the thundering in my head.

Upwards. Out of the cellars of the Town Hall. I realise that I will see daylight again. As I make my slow, painful, metallic way up the stairs, I feel the air grow lighter. An inappropriate elation grows in me *like one of Marika's bubbles. When I step up into a shaft of sunlight from a high window, I feel that I will burst. I am both fragile and intoxicated. The light burns my eyes. The air is richly wonderful. Even the stink of the canals is welcome after the unchanging weight of dank mould in my nostrils.*

I am postponing thought.

I am a character in a story and watch myself with great interest: a tall man grown too thin, ludicrously garlanded with chains that get in the way of his feet and bruise his ankles as he tries to walk. Or waddle, I should say, with feet apart like a child with a soiled clout, arms held a little forward and to the side. Dirty and lousy. His chin bristles with dark beard stubble. His mouth feels like an owl's nest. He does not look either reasonable or like a gentleman. An animal, from a fair. A dancing bear, corrupted from true bearness but not anything else either. A creature suspended between two natures, lodged in neither. If I were a magistrate, what would I make of him?

I try to straighten my shoulders and walk rather than shuffle. I gather up the chains at my wrists as if they were the sides of a skirt.

He was witnessing the likely ending of his life. Wanted to be there, but could not collect his scattered thoughts. He tried to pull himself back from his distance, to rejoin the story.

The guards pushed him into a cage with sides of flat iron strips woven into a lattice. It stood opposite a long table at which five chairs were set. They locked his chains to the sides of the cage, then positioned themselves beside it. He hardly noticed them. His attention was on the five chairs for the five men who would decide his fate: the five magistrates.

To avoid causing unnecessary horror to the citizens of Amsterdam, his case was being tried in camera, before a special tribunal made up of representatives of both the Dutch Reformed Church and the municipal governors.

He looked around him, still blinking in the light. The same chamber where he had been arraigned. Modest, panelled in pinkish oak. Two high windows. The Amsterdam flag. A

490

trumpeter lounged against a doorpost, peering down into the flared mouth of his *clarino*.

Painfully, Ned turned to look over his right shoulder. No benches for the vulgarly curious. Twelve spectators sat on chairs behind the cage. Most had been staring at him, but averted their eyes when he turned. Maurits, however, nodded at him gravely. No Janni.

A man who might be one of the farmers. Behind him, a pair of well-dressed merchants. Behind Ned's other shoulder sat two clergymen. And at a small table set to one side, a clerk sharpened his quill pen with a small knife.

He began to wake. The numbness rolled back and with ice-needle clarity he saw where he was. His knees weakened. He gripped two slats in the woven iron cage and felt a burning pain in his left palm. Saw a smear of blood from a sharp burr of bright metal on the newly made cage.

What was he to say? Nothing was left of the man he used to be, or wished to be. What acceptable self should he construct from nothing, to offer the court? A man bewitched by an evil glamour? He could offer them a possible wizard to blame but could not also give them the moment when the spell had been cast. And his own thoughts on that subject had changed in any case. What self could he even imagine? None, for certain, that would arouse mercy in the occupants of those empty chairs.

He heard an odd angry vibrating sound outside the room, like bees about to swarm. A short trumpet blast announced the magistrates. The people on the chairs stood up. Ned turned back to face the front, his head swimming.

First in, wearing a long black pleated gown, was a cool self-regarding man, brown-haired, round-headed, with wide-set eyes, long nose and small mouth tucked up under an upswept moustache.

Ned liked the second magistrate better: altogether softer outlines, wispy hair that touched his shoulders, fleshy, shovel-like chin and questioning eyes. The third was the tallest and oldest, clean-shaven, balding. His face was a confusion of planes and creases, a labourer's face, with a blob of a nose and eyes as steely as a sword blade.

The chief voice, thought Ned. And, sure enough, he took the centre chair behind the table.

After him came a pale-haired nobleman, moving with the steady force of an East India merchantman under sail, who nodded to one of the spectators and sat beside the leader.

Last came a crinkled elder, a churchman, snap-eyed, quick on his feet, who took a chair at one end of the table. He had been the second visitor to Ned's cell.

The chief magistrate spoke at once. 'This case is unique in my memory, and we can find no exact precedent in any legal records in the state of Holland. The known facts have stirred such horror in the hearts of Amsterdam citizens that it would be almost impossible to find a man willing to swear himself unmoved by them. Therefore, and also to protect the people of the city from unforeseen evils, there will be no jury. The magistrates shall rule jointly . . .' He bowed slightly to his left and to his right. 'But they must rule unanimously. In such a case, with such serious consequences, any doubt must be an abomination.'

The bees still buzzed at the edge of Ned's hearing. Then he realised that they were the sound of a crowd outside the Town Hall.

'I need not say that all of you here will observe total discretion about whatever takes place.' The magistrate searched the group on the chairs for nods of agreement.

Ned swore an oath to tell the truth.

Then the clerk read out the charges: killing the dog, Paulus Janzsoon's chickens, a sheep, and Anneke Schmit.

'Mynheer Steen. Speak for the prosecution.'

The first magistrate rose. The brown-haired one with the large, cool eyes. 'My task is simple,' he said. 'As you will hear, the accused is beyond doubt guilty of one of the monstrous charges. Therefore, I will first address that undisputed crime,

492

together with his second, similar, and equally monstrous crime. Show the depraved beast his first victim!'

A canvas-wrapped bundle was carried in, placed on the floor in front of the cage and unwrapped. The dead dog. It now stank.

Ned's temples pounded. He could not breathe.

It's dead! he told himself. But he heard its roar in his ear and felt the power of the thick neck beginning to shake him loose. He sat down on the floor of the cage.

'Do you recognise this animal?' asked Steen. He and all the other magistrates watched Ned closely.

Ned nodded. How could he not recognise it?

He forced himself to look again. The dog lay crook-legged, in the shape its wrappings had imposed. The wound in its neck appeared very small. Its flesh, past the bloated stage, had begun to shrink back on to its bones.

'Is it the same dog that attacked you and which you then killed?'

Ned nodded again.

The magistrates wrote.

'The accused is admirably honest,' said the fifth magistrate, the churchman.

Men-at-arms carried in a second putrid bundle. Ned closed his eyes.

But it could not be Anneke Schmit. They would never have brought a child wrapped like an animal!

It was a dead sheep that he could not remember having seen, let alone killed.

'And do you recognise this animal?' asked Steen.

Ned shook his head. The two dead animals rippled and swam on the unsteady wooden floor: the bandog and the sheep with limp matted wool clotted dark at its throat, already attracting flies. Like them, the magistrates ebbed and flowed, like scraps of seaweed carried in and out by breaking waves. 'No! I have never seen it before.'

If I were guilty, he thought, surely I would remember!

493

He looked at the creature's dull, stupid eyes. But if the man could kill a dog, what might the wolf have done without his knowledge?

But thank God! It was not the child!

The second magistrate rose and looked closely at the two wounds. 'The wound on the sheep's throat is much larger than that on the dog.'

The other four consulted papers, nodded, wrote.

'But similar,' said the nobleman.

'As if made by the same teeth,' said Steen. 'It's as well the militia arrived when it did, or several more valuable hounds might have been lost.' He called to the court officer. 'Bring in the first witness, Willem Schults.'

Schults, solemn, slicked smooth and polished, with a Bible clutched to his breast. The man Ned had taken for a farmer. As he took his place before the magistrates, he looked back over his shoulder at someone among the spectators, as if for support. Ned turned too late to see Schults's ally.

Not from the village. He had never seen Schults before. To his knowledge.

Yes, a farmer, said Schults, after swearing his oath. He kept his eyes turned away from Ned.

Yes, owner of the dead sheep. Yes, he knew it for one of his own by the mark on the ear. Yes, he knew the man in the cage. Had seen him well on the night in question, though he could scarce bring himself to gaze at the monster again.

'Will you please look at him now and confirm that it is the same man.'

Schults held the Bible in both hands, a shield between them. His eyes darted to Ned, then away again. Yes, yes. No doubt about it. He glanced again at someone among the spectators.

Ned listened intently. He was certain he had never seen either sheep or Schults. This certainty would have eased his mind if, in the farmer's stolid conviction and the scratching of pens, he had not heard the beginning of his doom. He swayed under the unbearable weight of his head.

494

Schults had been checking his sheep before bed, saw a man in his field, which lay just outside the city walls. Was about to challenge him when the man stripped stark naked and put his clothes on the ground.

'I've never been to any such field!' shouted Ned.

'The prisoner will not speak until he is questioned.'

'I thought then that perhaps he had a woman there in the shadows,' continued Schults. 'Though I don't suppose it's usual to lie down in fields bare as Adam, however urgent your lust. Thistles and all.'

Mixed frowns and amusement among four of the magistrates. The churchman, seated at the far end, still watched Ned.

'What persuaded you otherwise?'

Schults hesitated. 'Well, he . . .' he indicated Ned with the Bible '. . . made devilish grunts and groans, then pissed in a circle around his clothes. I knew what this meant and felt my hair stand up straight as a brush. He looked straight at me with eyes like yellow lights . . . froze my tongue in my mouth.' Perversely, Schults was slowly gaining confidence and fluency. 'Then he dropped on to all fours and slipped off into the darkness. Only it wasn't a man who disappeared into the shadows, but a beast – something like a man, but covered in grey hair, with a long snout and bushy tail sprouted above his buttocks.'

'Did you make to capture him?'

'I gave chase at first, thinking to give him a wound that would identify him when he changed back into a man, but he was too swift. Then I found the sheep with its throat torn out. And I knew what had done it!'

'No!' cried Ned. Something was very wrong, but he did not know how to fight it. Schults ebbed and flowed in his awareness. Solemn face, incredible story. He could not distinguish the madness of these proceedings from real delirium. How could it help to say 'I am certain that I didn't do it . . . as far as I know'?

'Why didn't you take his clothes so he could not change back?'

495

'To be honest, I was too frightened at first, once I had run a little way after him. Then I did go back, but all I could find was a pile of stones.'

At that, the magistrate with the shovel chin, who had questioned the strength of proof in the two wounds, raised his eyebrows. The older one, at the end, still watched Ned, not Schults. But the others leaned and murmured to each other, and scratched notes.

All five questioned Schults but he did not waver from his story. Nor did he ever look again at Ned.

'Now,' said Steen, 'back to the crime that needs no proof.'

Two members of the militia took it in turns to tell of the chase and how Ned had been taken, and of his supernatural strength and pleasure in the carnage of the fight.

'Strength of a demon. Eyes like lanterns.'

'Did you not say that he was weeping at the moment you arrested him?'

'Yes, for sure. How could he not? He had turned man again and knew what he had done.'

Ned fainted.

When they had revived him with vinegar, the magistrates were examining Verhagen. The farmer was also shackled.

'. . . only through the power of God,' he repeated. 'I swear that the priest never called on dark forces or carried out any superstitious rites! He did nothing but pray over him. The only crime was to fail to ease the soul of the accused. Afterwards, he still fled the light and sought out the comfort of darkness. Yes, we concluded that there was no demon and repented of our superstitious ignorance in thinking that possession was possible. We see now that the evil is part of his essential nature and can't be removed. He was not possessed.'

The chief magistrate said, 'That's just as well, as it's not a circumstance on which we would feel happy to comment.' He lifted his top papers and read one near the bottom of his pile. 'And when we later consider the charge against you and

496

your fellow villagers of practising illegal rites, your help here will be taken into account.'

The grateful Verhagen was dismissed.

The physician who had visited the grain shed was called next, and questioned closely about his diagnosis of madness and the forms of animal delusion. 'The accused is merely mad,' he repeated firmly.

When he had been dismissed, a second physician was called. He was of a different mind.

'The prisoner seemed lucid under questioning,' he said. Nothing like a lunatic in his opinion, beyond the disturbance of mind natural to his present situation in gaol. Whatever the explanation for the beast might be, he was forced to declare the man, at least, to be in possession of all his wits and senses.

'May it please your Honours . . .' Maurits stood up. 'May I speak?'

'Permission granted.'

'I have been treating the prisoner in gaol and argue that he is, indeed, no more than mad.'

Lycanthropia, he said, could cause delusions of being many other animals besides a wolf. He had heard of cases where men and women thought themselves to be dogs, cats, and even chickens. Such madmen might seem lucid in the time between their intervals of delusion but they were nevertheless ill, as much as if they had a wasting sickness or ague. Therefore, he challenged the testimony of the second esteemed doctor.

'If it's mere madness, how would you explain the testimony of Willem Schults? And of the militiamen who arrested the accused?'

'A group delusion while in a highly excited state.'

The militia witnesses bristled. They were good Dutch citizens, not used to being told they suffered delusions.

Ned saw that the magistrates too had been offended by Maurits's brutal enthusiasm for the rational truth. Such clumsiness in a man of his intelligence might almost have been deliberate.

497

'May I have leave to examine the accused?' asked Maurits, unabashed. 'If he is indeed part wolf, in any manner, then he is not an object of dread and opprobrium, but of rational scientific interest. I would determine where he belongs within the natural order.'

'Natural order? Are you saying that such a creature was present in the Garden of Eden?' asked Steen, outraged. 'In the perfect Universe? Show us the text to support that! You're dangerously close to heresy, Mynheer van Egmond. Such evil surely arose after the Fall. This corruption is a mark of the evil Man embraced with the bite of the Apple.'

'Ignorance is the only heresy.' Maurits grew flushed. 'I spend my life fighting exactly such deliberate self-blinding!'

'Sit down, Mynheer van Egmond!'

'May I examine the prisoner?'

The magistrates conferred.

'Two doctors have already done so,' said the chief magistrate. 'We see no need for another diagnosis. Will you sit down!'

What does Maurits think he is doing? Ned wondered. His plan to get me out – if that's what that was – is already foundered! Never trusted him!

Then the clerk read a deposition from the villagers on the disappearance of Anneke Schmit.

'Now, Mynheer Malise,' said the churchman at the end of the row. He stood. 'You have a chance to defend yourself . . .'

It's now! thought Ned wildly. Now I must think what to say! I'm still not ready.

'You were born a Catholic. The court will make allowance for any differences in belief. In the terms of your own religion, and in spite of the denial by Herman Verhagen, could you say that you are possessed by a demonic spirit in the form of a wolf?'

Point the finger, Ned! his body cried. I don't want to choke to death! Cry out about charms! Blame Nightingale! Blame the wizard. Try to offer them a self that will induce mercy!

'Your honours, not a demon . . .'

498

His fists clenched. He held a shining moon of quicksilver in his hand. It shattered, sprang from his hand in a galaxy of gleaming, glinting parts. They stretched, broke, scattered, ran away into the cracks of the floor, the folds of his clothes.

'Your honours . . .' He shut his eyes. Lie, Ned. Say the words that might save you! Grasp on to the only hope you have of mercy. Connive, falsify, hope to please.

He remembered the parallel dreams. The eyes of the menagerie wolf meeting his own.

This may be my last chance in this life to speak exactly as I feel.

The silver fragments reunited into globules, then re-embraced into shining flattened globes, turned into a muscular metallic river.

Deny the wolf!

'Though I once believed otherwise, I am not possessed.'

The silver river flowed back into his palm until he again held the heavy silver egg. He could still feel its weight in his hand.

A rush of relief filled him. The scrabbling panic in his mind settled. He had only to tell the truth. Whatever that might be. And whatever might happen next.

'Do you express remorse for your crimes?'

The words rose by themselves. 'I killed the dog to keep it from killing me. The sheep I deny altogether. And I swear by anything holy that you might ask that I could never kill a child!'

The magistrates shifted in their chairs, looked at each other.

'Come, Mynheer Malise,' said the oldest one, his unspoken champion. 'A witness swears under oath that in the shape of a wolf you killed the sheep. Better to give us some reason for mitigation. Were you perhaps charmed into falsely believing yourself a wolf?'

I searched the cunning man's mirrors and saw only myself. I'm not a gentleman. Hardly English. Certainly not Dutch. No longer a musician. Rejected lover. The only undeniable part of me at present is the beast.

499

He stood poised on a high icy pinnacle from which he could only fall. But he controlled the direction of the fall.

He hardly chose, just spoke.

'The wolf is a part of myself.' He heard the intake of breaths and the ragged canon of sighs. 'Part of my double nature.'

The magistrate was aghast. 'Do you mean to say that you willingly embrace your beastliness?'

'Never willingly!' he cried. 'Don't think that! I loathe and fear that part of myself. I fought it. Tried every means I could think of to excise it. You have heard even from my enemies that I tried. But I have failed to wrench it from my being.'

'Do I understand? You claim that this beast is a part of your true self?'

I believe that it is! he thought with astonishment.

'I can't deny it, or I deny myself.'

Back in the cage, I needed to lie down. Curled against the wall. I had just condemned myself to death, yet felt an astonishing lightness.

Maurits leaped to his feet. 'Surely his words prove madness!'

'We shall say what they do or do not prove,' said the magistrate. 'Sit down, Mynheer van Egmond, or I shall make a formal complaint to your uncle.'

The five magistrates withdrew to consider the evidence.

They returned almost at once. The chief magistrate looked at me.

'We had no difficulty in reaching a verdict,' he said. 'A single witness of unblemished reputation said under oath that he saw the accused transform into a wolf before killing the witness's sheep.' He glanced at his fellow magistrates. 'A natural scepticism might force us to question this testimony if nine other witnesses – all respectable members of the Amsterdam militia – had not seen the accused kill a bandog with his teeth in a similar beastly fashion. A further five similar witnesses saw the accused still wiping the hot blood from his face. These unarguable facts force us to give a greater weight to the earlier testimony about the sheep and to the possibility of his guilt in the death of Anneke Schmit. Furthermore, the accused believes and accepts that he is by nature part wolf.

'We therefore find him guilty of killing both the sheep and the dog. The death of Anneke Schmit remains unproved.'

There was a sound of protest from behind me.

The magistrate frowned, then glanced again at his colleagues on either side. 'Passing sentence, however, is more difficult. First, we must consider very carefully the true nature of the accused, which in turn defines the nature of his crime and will, therefore, dictate the appropriate penalties.'

He adjourned the tribunal for two days.

In my cell — a tall sandglass standing on the stone-flagged floor, with twelve divisions, large enough to measure a day. Another gift from Maurits, no doubt. I could not decide whether it was meant as a promise of quick deliverance, or an ironic taunt.

What have I done?

In chains, I could not pace the walls of my cell.

I knew that I must be mad to have spoken as I did. But I could not think what else I could have said. I was dead anyway. And if I had killed the child, I would die with pleasure.

I saw the bandog's bloodshot amber eye against my own, felt the dry pins of bristle on my tongue. Felt the slimy brick paving under my scrabbling feet. Smelled its rage. Began to slip.

Shook the images from my mind. At once felt its stinking hot breath on my face again. Saw the great bloodshot eye . . .

Marika! Help me!

I lay down behind her, curved against her back and hips. She sighed and eased herself closer in her sleep. I curved my arm around her and cupped her warm soft breast. Heard the baying of dogs . . .

You would be satisfied now, I told her. My wolf is as safe as I am.

★　　★　　★

501

When I at last fell asleep, I dreamed that I ate a small, delicious but unfamiliar roasted bird. When I had finished, I turned to the serving man who waited with water and a napkin for me to clean my fingers. He gave me a child's apron instead of a napkin. I woke myself with my scream of horror and lay on the cold stone floor trying not to retch.

I tried to sing, to turn my mind elsewhere.

'*Agnus Dei, qui tollis peccata mundi, miserere me . . .*' I sang. Could a wolf appeal to a lamb? From all the music in the world, why had I chosen that prayer?

In the courtroom, I felt that I had no choice but to speak as I did. I now thought of Janni's promise of the purifying fire. It had sounded so clean and absolute. I had now entered Janni's fellowship, accepted my fate as a metaphor for change and rebirth, but still swilled in blackness. Self-knowledge must surely bring peace.

And yet. And yet. A knot somewhere deep in my being had loosened.

The story's not finished yet.

When recalled for sentencing two days later, I could just walk unaided and was clear-headed enough to feel terror.

What have I done? I asked myself again.

No cage. Good or bad sign? Again, Maurits was there.

I will not flinch.

'This case has led us to an unprecedented degree of debate and prayer,' said the chief magistrate. 'We were forced to be guided, not so much by what is the truth, as by what it is not. Master Malise, please step forward.'

I looked straight into his eyes so that the man wouldn't think that my weakened legs gave way from fear.

'After long and careful deliberation, this court judges unanimously that you have not lost your wits, for which we would have sentenced you to incarceration for life in a hospital for lunatics. We judge you to be sane and culpable.

'We could not agree unanimously whether or not you

502

change your human shape and lineaments for those of a wolf, although the testimony of the witnesses does point that way.' He glanced to his left in suppressed irritation, at the magistrate seated at the end of the table.

'And there is no question of our considering the abhorrent Roman belief that you might be possessed by a lupine demon.

'However, we do find, with one accord, from the evidence, supported by your own admission, that you do at times assume the character of a wolf. In that state, of your own choice and free will, you commit bloody acts of beastliness.'

I heard rustling among the spectators.

'In adopting the nature of a beast,' continued the magistrate, 'you are guilty of treason against the Divine Order, guilty of treason of the senses. To turn beast, even in part, even in spirit alone, is heresy against the noble nature of Man, giving Evil a free passage through the gates of the human soul. You introduce unreason into the realm of reason, and stand as much a threat to order, in both its religious and civic meanings, as any Anabaptist or other dangerous heretic. Such a thing is intolerable in a civilised state. For all these crimes against both God and State, the court sentences you to death by hanging.'

I look straight into the eyes of the man who tells me that I am to die. Death should cause no more fear than birth. The door in and the door out. I myself invited it.

Yet I imagine that I can will the words back into his throat. That, if I wish it devoutly enough, I can go back a little and step now into a different place.

In six days, I am to hang.

What is hanging to what I have already suffered? Shorter. With a sure end.

I cannot endure it. A reckless rage swells up into my throat. Then his words freeze me.

I believe that he is saying that voices had been raised in favour of hooking out my gut before my eyes. I'm not certain. My

503

ears feel as if they have been stuffed with cloth. I'm seized by a tremor that rattles the chains on my legs.

A man's voice shouts from behind me. He steps forward as I fall.

Maurits leaps to his feet. There is confusion while the witnessing physician stoops to revive me. As I am led away, Maurits talks earnestly and persuasively to the five magistrates. I hear only the treacherous accepting words '. . . before he is hanged'.

So much for my magician.

40

We were alone together in the dark underground cell, my wolf and I. Considering the price I paid for claiming it, I wished that it would keep me merrier company.

We'll ripen for a few days on gibbet island, I kept thinking. My wolf and I. Then they will weight us and sink us. I can't think about what will be done to us first.

I dreamed of flames again that night, and waking brought no relief.

The sound of the key in the lock shook me into icy clarity.

Not the Spoon. The two men-at-arms who had escorted me to trial. They unlocked my chains from the staple in the floor and tried to set me on my feet. My legs buckled from lack of use.

'Where am I going?' I demanded. I had thought I had no capacity for terror left, but now a swilling of ice and flame crumbled my bones and dissolved my sinews. 'It's too soon! I don't hang for four more days!'

For answer, they shoved me up the stairs. At ground level we twisted and turned through corridors I had never seen before.

There must be a secret room for executions!

Then I knew that they were taking me through a minor door to the gibbet island that lay just off the coast . . . or to a place of public execution . . . or that they had changed the sentence and that my wolf and I were to be burned.

In the court room, I had imagined that I could face death

505

with equanimity. But being cheated like this of my last four days set me bumping and yawing like a broken wheel.

We turned a corner into a small back hall, hardly more than a vestibule, and found Maurits. His face was as sober as his clothes: heavy, worthy black cloak, the tall flat-topped hat.

The magistrate Steen and a city official stood with him, passing papers from hand to hand, signing names.

'Your bond,' said Steen.

Maurits leaned over a table and signed again.

'Forfeit after seven days,' said Steen with a hint of anticipation.

The city official witnessed Maurits's signature.

I was hoisted forward numbly, squinting against the slanting afternoon light.

Maurits did not greet me, nor even acknowledge my presence, except as a delivered parcel. 'I'll return him safe enough,' he said. 'And there will be your man Bakker to make certain of it.' He turned to my two escorts. 'It's just outside.'

They took me out through the door and, to my astonishment, hoicked me chains and all up into Maurits's carriage. A man in a leather jerkin and the yellow scarf of a militiaman took the seat across from me, laid his pistol in his lap and stared at a point beside my nose. A few moments later, Maurits climbed into the carriage. He still did not speak to me. Like the militiaman, he settled silently into his seat. After watching the streets pass for a moment, he took a small book from his bag, looked at me as if I were merely an interesting piece of freight, and began to write notes in a tiny hand.

'Maurits . . .'

'Keep him quiet,' he said to the guard. 'Until I can bind his evil so that he can do us no harm.'

I clamped my mouth shut before the guard could think how to shut it for me. He contented himself with pushing his pistol into my ribs.

My head reeled. The daylight, the air, the sight of trees, people going about their business. The smells and sounds. All new, bright and overwhelming after my time underground. Even the court chamber had not prepared me for the intense cacophony of the surface world. The flapping snorts of our horses, the creaking of the carriage wood and the screech of the wheels against the sides of stones, hectoring dogs, cries of a water-seller, the scents of horse, of waxed leather, of damp starch, of the guard's sweat and Maurits's oil of orange, all battered my hungry, fragile senses.

At the same time, I glared, bewildered, at the man who had whispered 'trust me' as I lay on the stone floor of my cell. And arranged food and medicines which had saved my hands if not my life. If he were playing a game now, I felt it would be kind to signal to me. I could not forget the drawings of the dissected wolf, but Maurits had sworn in writing to keep me for only seven days and to return me safely. Whatever his game, it was something else.

As soon as we arrived at Maurits's house, he and Bakker locked me into another cage, high enough to sit up in, or to crouch, but not to stand.

'Sweet God in Heaven!' I shouted, trying to get to my feet, bent double like Atlas trying to carry the world. 'Isn't it enough to have me in chains? Do you have to cage me like one of your rats or rabbits?'

'Go find your supper now in the kitchen,' Maurits told the guard.

He listened while the man's footsteps faded.

'Now tell me that I'm a genius!' he cried. 'My dear Ned! I beg you to congratulate me!'

I glared through the iron lattice.

'Forgive me! I won't leave you in there a moment longer.' He stepped over a pile of encyclopaedias and unlocked the padlock.

I stared at the open cage door, half-expecting it to swing shut again in my face, then I crawled out on to the tiled floor. How could he think that it was safe to set me free?

He took a set of keys from his purse and began to unlock my

507

web of chains. My right wrist, then my left. The chains clanked on to the floor. I moved my arms. Without chains. Silently. So silently that I could hear the scrape of the tortoise's claws on the tiles nearby.

The air burned the raw skin of my wrists like bracelets of fire.

Maurits stooped, grunted and unlocked my ankles.

I was free. When I tried to stand, I saw why he did not fear me.

For the next half hour, I set myself the problem of standing like a man again. I stretched my legs and pulled myself upright by holding on to the outside of the cage. I reached high above my head. I drew circles with my arms. Painfully, I began to walk, from one side of the study to the other, wall to wall. I felt myself turn, felt each muscle slide over the next. In pain but alive.

Remember this feeling, I told myself. You have only six and a half more days to enjoy it.

Maurits watched me. He found a wine jug lurking among the glass jars of preserved fragments, between something rope-like and a fish's head. 'A toast.'

'Another?' Did he think that prison had made me forget? 'Why? In six and a half days I still hang.'

'You won't hang.' Maurits poured two glasses of claret.

'Your bond is forfeit if you don't return me for execution.' I looked in passing at the heavy, panelled door of the study, and the brass lock. 'And Bakker out there in the kitchen will see that you obey.'

'I don't obey the Bakkers of this world.' Maurits beamed at me. 'Tonight, Janni will dose him so that he sleeps.'

I hobbled to the day bed and pushed off Maurits's cloak to make room to sit down. The upholstery was unbelievably soft.

When I refused the glass he offered me, he asked, 'Why do you fear me? Or is it mere petulance?' He drank his own wine with satisfaction. 'Can't you see yet how I've made you a free man?'

508

'The Amsterdam magistrates are crafty fellows,' I said. 'Even Janni can't dose them all into oblivion.'

He sighed in mock impatience. 'Come into the dining chamber and see my device for setting you free.'

The dining chamber was still filled with cages and the feral stink. In the far corner, in a large cage of interwoven iron slats, was a wolf. A huge male with long limbs and feet the size of my hands.

I peered at the markings of its muzzle, the rim of black fur above its eyes. The white around its mouth, the rusty shading on the sides of its muzzle, the caramel-coloured blaze above its right eyebrow.

My wolf. The huge male which had looked into my eyes with despair, then closed its eyes and gone somewhere else. The same wolf that had later blazed with rage, seemed to grow to the size of a small horse, able to devour with its thumb-sized fangs every man, woman and child in the fairground tent.

I remembered the eyes, not yellow, but a dark hazel, flecked with lighter spots, with black lines drawn around them, and black brows above, very like my own.

Maurits leaned close to the grid and peered in. '*Canis lupus*. Dog in its wolfish form.'

The wolf flattened its ears and wrinkled back the skin of its nose, showing the front incisors. It backed away, flattened itself against the far wall of the pen and snarled again.

'By good fortune,' said Maurits, 'the menagerie owner fell foul of local law and had to leave the district abruptly. Was happy to shed some of his baggage.'

It wore a collar attached by a chain to the grid of the cage.

'Unlike you, this creature is as ordinary as the fleas on its neck. A machine of sinew, muscle and bone. Still common in Germany, France and Sweden. Driven out of the virtuous Netherlands along with the devil, or so we're told.'

I leaned forward and stared through the iron grid. The wolf growled again.

'Try to think, man! Don't you see my device yet?' demanded

509

Maurits like an impatient tutor. 'It's a miracle of logic, employing only sleight-of-hand, simple, like all best conceits and devices. Even magistrates can be gulled. Can't you see it?'

He looked enormously pleased with himself.

I shook my head.

'Firstly, no one knows that it's here but Janni and me. Bought it under a false name, brought it here drugged in a roll of carpet. Old Gerthe's afraid even of snakes and rats, so she never comes into this room.'

A wave of giddiness dropped me on to a stool near the cage. A piece of the floor seemed to move. Then I saw that it was a mouse, eating grain fallen from the rat and rabbit cages.

'Think!' urged Maurits. 'Witnesses have sworn under oath that you changed shape. True or false, I shall use that testimony.' He gave up hope of my understanding, and explained as if to a small child. 'The court gave me permission to examine you before you are hanged. I begin my examination, but as I do so . . . oh horror! . . . you transform again into a wolf. And then . . . alas . . . I am forced to kill you in self-defence. You, the wolf, not you, the man. The dead wolf then goes back to Amsterdam as Ned Malise, transformed.'

I gaped at him.

'Mynheer Bakker might have given trouble, but he'll not be eager to contradict any story I tell. Not only did he desert his post, but after his dosing he will have had wicked dreams which he'll believe to have been reality. I shall then apologise and offer to pay whatever fine the magistrates might see fit in such extraordinary circumstances but I can't be accused of anything worse than carelessness . . . foolhardiness, perhaps. And you, Ned Malise, will have disappeared. Died with the wolf! You will no longer exist! And then you and I, my friend, will have all the time in the world for our quest.' He was cock-a-hoop.

I stared unseeing at my still-filled glass. Did he think I was a fool and could not see another way to judge his device?

'There were sceptics among the magistrates,' I said. 'Who

510

didn't believe in the wolf, and didn't need to. They set the question aside and found me guilty of treason to the Natural Order.'

Maurits nodded. 'But enough of them were not sceptics. And I have a reputation as a sceptic myself.'

I remembered his performance in the university library.

'If I profess that, to my astonishment, I was forced to accept the evidence of my own eyes . . . In any case, I shall move you somewhere safer, in case this house is searched.'

'Bakker is asleep.' Janni came looking for us with the wine in one hand and a basin filled with rags, bottles and jars under the other arm.

'Poor Ned needs one of your elixirs,' said Maurits. 'I think his wits are dazed with too many changes of circumstance.' He took my glass and drank it himself. 'Poor frazzle-witted Ned!'

'Wrists and ankles first,' said Janni. 'Then we'll see what else he needs.'

We went back into the study where Janni knelt by my chair and lifted one of my feet.

'Maurits is right,' I said. 'My wits hardly know where I am, let alone who I might be. Gaol has reshaped both body and mind as much as any transformation.' Wincing, I watched Janni's skilful hands bathe my ankle. 'Don't fear to hurt me now. Pain reassures me that my limbs are still attached to me. I haven't thanked you yet, Janni, for sending the ointment that saved my hands.'

Gazing down, I could see the fuzz on Janni's sweetly-curved upper lip above the smile.

'This will hurt still more.' A green poultice, slapped on to the raw flesh, bound in place with strips of linen.

If Maurits believed that I had forgotten what had happened before the prison, that I had forgotten the dosed wine, and had accepted his device at face value, he might give me more freedom . . .

'You're a genius Janni,' I said. 'And I begin to grant Maurits his claim to be a genius as well. I examine his device every

511

way in my mind, and I still can't see a fault.' I saw Maurits's gratified smirk, which he did not even try to hide.

Janni took my right hand and began to rub it with an embrocation which smelled of mint.

'I'm forced to conclude,' I said, 'that Maurits *is* a genius, nearly as great as he himself believes . . . No, even greater!' I watched him swell and blush with pleasure.

He filled his glass again, and one for Janni. 'Ned sees truth at last!' he cried in mock triumph. 'A toast! To our partnership in the pursuit of knowledge!'

'And the cure which knowledge will bring.' I stood, unsteadily. 'To the man who has just saved my life and would also like to save my soul!'

'Modesty should forbid me to drink,' said Maurits. 'But it won't!' He tilted his head back so far that claret trickled down the round, flushed pillow of his child-like cheek.

I took my glass. I also let the wine trickle down my chin, but did not swallow. A former street rat doesn't fall for the same trick twice.

Gerthe brought a tray of supper into the study. We leaned our elbows on the table and scooped up ham and pea soup.

I forced myself to eat, for strength, and only from the common serving bowl. 'What have you given Bakker?' I asked.

'Opium in his wine,' said Janni. 'Gerthe thinks he can't hold his liquor. Then I put him to bed and rubbed witches' salve into his skin.'

'Witches' salve?' My spoon paused.

'I ordered it,' said Maurits, still pleased with himself. 'He'll dream that he flies through the air, mates with demons, suckles at witches' dugs.'

But Janni had read my tone. 'A good use of an evil substance.'

'Tut, Janni. The salve has no morality, good or evil.'

'Good use in place of evil use, then.' Janni glanced at Maurits with suppressed feeling.

'Where do you find your witches' salve?' I asked.

512

'I made it.' Janni looked at me levelly. 'From wolfsbane, henbane and aconite . . . plain, soulless herbs. Maurits is right. The substance itself has no innate virtue or vileness. Those depend on how we use it. Most witches are more fools than sinners.'

I raised my eyebrows.

Maurits did not care for my hint of censure. 'Bakker might dare to confess sleeping on duty,' he said. 'But not the dreams that he's been given. If he does, he's a fool, like all the other poor fools who have confessed and been hanged or burned. The salve is your guarantee of his silence, Ned.'

'Is his life at risk because of me?' I asked.

'Less than yours would have been.' Maurits scribbled as he spoke.

'The truth is, yes, it is at risk,' said Janni, contradicting him. 'We work with dangerous *materia* and must always approximate. One root of aconite might contain ten times the active principle of another.' The blue eyes searched mine for understanding. 'The antidote for opium is foxglove, but that too brings its own dangers. One time I might restore his heartbeat and the next time, kill him. Avoiding murder is the art. But if it helps you rest easier, I swear that I'm tending him as if he were a baby born three months before its time. You remember that I once told you that knowledge comes at a cost . . . ?'

I nodded. I felt that I had begun to nod a great deal. Weary beyond thought. That morning I had believed I was about to hang.

Maurits wiped a piece of bread across the bottom of his bowl, then lifted his head.

All my senses were jolted awake again. A desperate, keening, skin-tingling wail came from the dining chamber.

The wolf had begun to howl.

We froze amidst the debris of the meal as if the unearthly sound had cast a spell over us.

Its voice climbed step-by-step. Still, to my ears, in the sequence of musical intervals that made up the Lydian mode.

513

Maurits shook himself. 'You must silence it, Janni! Urgently!'

'Animals don't react like men . . .' Janni protested.

'Silence it!'

Janni rose and left the study.

'It's calling to its pack mates,' I said. The howl made me want to weep. I also felt very drunk though I had had nothing to drink. Too much happening. Too tired. I fought it. Needed a clear head.

'How do you know?'

'I just know.'

'Come outside,' said Maurits. 'We shall listen for the others and try to judge if you are right.'

I followed obediently. We made our way from the study along the dark, unlit passage, past the racket of the dining-chamber menagerie, where Janni's candle now flickered, and past the flea-ridden lion, into the dark garden. Something rushed away from our feet in the long grass. The yellow-eyed bird muttered in its dust bowl near the house wall.

I considered running. But my legs were barely steady under me. I wouldn't get far. Even unpursued. Tomorrow, I thought. After sleep. And more food. Now, my head was spinning.

'No moon.' Maurits nodded to himself. 'Therefore: it is not howling at the moon. Contrary to accepted "truth". I may have to write yet another treatise. Do you want to howl, Ned?'

I shook my head in the dark. Then said, 'No, it makes me want to cry.' It would die soon, for my sake. I did not want it to die.

'Tender fool.' Maurits's face leaned closer. 'Won't help the wolf. If the creature has no emotions, why waste your own to no purpose?'

'Listen,' I said.

The wolf in the house howled once more. The stretched, eerie notes bored into my marrow. The howl pierced the roof and the sky, crying to whatever lay beyond the dark roof of the world. It pinned me through the heart.

514

'I'm cold,' said Maurits. 'Let's go back into the house.'

'I feel as drunk as a dog,' I enunciated with care. 'Why "dog", Maurits?' I asked. 'Have you ever observed a drunk dog?'

'Only an elephant. And in his circumstances, I'd have got drunk as well.' Maurits headed back into the house. He raised his voice and shouted, 'Janni, I need another jug of wine!'

Janni came out of the dining chamber. 'It doesn't respond. And I won't risk a still greater dose. But if its presence here is known, your device turns transparent, and Ned will no longer be safe.'

'Leave the beast!' said Maurits through the darkness of the little back hallway. 'I've just thought of the answer: there's no wolf! It was Ned who howled.' He laughed. Then laughed more loudly as if, on reflection, his jest was even better than he had thought. 'Oh, no, there's no wolf here, mynheer bailiff. No, no, no! The prisoner tried to sing after supper and howled instead.'

I looked back out into the garden. In the dark, it extended forever. Even with a spinning head and fluid knees, I could try to run now.

I became aware of Janni at my shoulder, reading my thoughts. Waiting. A question floated in the air. I turned to the dim, luminous oval of face. 'The unavoidable journey,' I heard myself say, more or less coherently. 'Began in a place I still can't remember. Continues here.'

'What's that?' demanded Maurits's voice.

Ahead, in the house, the wolf howled again.

Maurits returned to grip me by the elbow as if to guide a blind man. 'Dearest Janni, don't you have to see to friend Bakker again?'

After his assistant had disappeared, Maurits dragged me back to the study, set me on the day bed and covered me with a rug. I needed no dosing that night to fall helplessly into sleep.

515

41

I woke with a child's terror of strange beds and strange rooms. I lay rigid for a moment, falling and falling into nothingness. Then the world steadied. The sun was high.

My mouth was upholstered with feathers. I lay on a low cot, like one a serving man might place for himself beside his master's bed or in an antechamber. Against one wall of a large, lofty octagonal room filled with rainbow light from the eight tall windows of brightly-coloured glass. Above my head, the goddess Flora let crimson catch-fly and blue harebells fall from pink glass fingers. She glowed from behind a grille of iron bars that covered the entire window.

I moved my arms. They were free. My wrists were bandaged where the prison shackles had rubbed away the skin. I remembered: Janni had bandaged them, before supper the night before. My pulse began to slow a little. I sat up.

Janni had also bandaged my raw ankles. Curious, I lifted an edge of the linen wrapping around one ankle. The oozing, weeping ring of flayed flesh had been smeared with a sticky brown unguent. Miraculously, the pain had gone from both ankles and wrists. I touched the unguent, then sniffed it. It smelt familiar, like damp books and burning leather. Like the salve Marika had applied to my back.

I swallowed and tried to swallow feathers. I would die if I did not drink.

I looked at a jug of water set beside my cot. Lifted it, set it

516

down again. Imagined the water on my tongue.

As far as I could tell, I owed my deep sleep to nothing more sinister than exhaustion, disbelief and my first comfortable bed for days.

Just rinse your mouth. Don't swallow.

I took some water in my mouth, swilled it round deliciously. I meant to spit it out but suddenly my throat rebelled. I swallowed.

I waited, but all seemed well.

I waited a little longer. Then greedily drained the jug.

I closed my eyes for a moment against a wave of giddiness, but it passed. I waited. Still no slowing of time, no fading of the world.

Nothing in the water after all.

I was unbound, I had been covered. I fingered the fine wool of my blanket, noticing as I did that the finger with which I had touched the unguent had gone numb. Beneath me was a feather mattress.

I tried to tell myself that these were good signs.

I lay back down to consider the wonderful comfort of being able to lie down, on a bed, with a feather mattress. The sensation was so unexpected and so wonderful that I also began to believe I might survive after all.

As I was drifting back towards sleep, I heard a slow heavy breathing behind me.

I sat up fast, then had to wait for some time for the earth to stop spinning around me. Then I cautiously opened my eyes and looked to my right.

The wolf lay stretched out on its side in a cage set against another of the eight walls, eyes closed, the skin of its belly slung like a hammock below its heaving ribs. It did not respond to my approach.

I supported myself on the cage and looked down at the beast for a long time, holding out thoughts that hammered to be let in.

Then I roused myself to see more clearly where we were and what this building was.

517

The doorway had an iron grille on the inner side, like the windows, made of decorative spirals welded to solid iron vertical bars. Outside that was a massive oak-panelled door. I tried the handle of the grille, then squeezed my hand through to try the oak door. Both were locked, and neither lock held a key.

I crossed to one of the windows. We sat high on a mound, most likely artificial, above an overgrown canal whose banks were swollen with rushes and leaning grass. The thin ribbon of open water wore a coat of fluffy green scum punctured by the rotting bow of a sunken skiff.

Beyond the canal stretched a wet, flat landscape, striped with glinting irrigation ditches, on and on until it folded down over the far line of the horizon like a cloth over the edge of a table. In the far distance, grazed flea-sized sheep. Closer, I saw fields studded like an embroidery with the tiny French knots of cabbages. But not another human soul.

From the opposite window, where Daphne flung glowing, green leafy arms to the transparent sky and laughed back over her shoulder at an off-stage god, I looked down on long grass and weeds where a garden had once been. A weathered stone arm waved from under a nearby hummock of tangled bindweed and ivy. I saw no house to go with the garden.

I pushed. Behind its bars, the iron window frame had rusted shut. The iron grille on the door, however, was new.

I needed to sit again and returned to the cot.

I looked again at the high ceiling, the bright glass windows. A pavilion – a folly – used for banqueting, perhaps, or sitting after supper to drink wine and eat candied fruits while the sun set across the watery fields. Now, besides my cot and the wolf's cage, it held only an iron-bound wooden chest large enough to hide a man, a smaller plain wooden box, a couple of stools, and a pair of tables stacked one upside-down on the other.

I stood up again, this time with less difficulty. My prison stiffness was slowly leaving me.

The large iron-bound chest was empty. The plain wooden box held sawdust, so fresh that it still smelt of pine resin.

I stared at the box. The feathers were back in my mouth.

The box in Maurits's Theatre of Anatomy had remained tucked away under the dissecting table because his subject was dead and did not bleed.

Then I heard men's voices and ran to a window.

Maurits waded through the long grass with a leather pouch slung over his shoulder. Behind him, a young man carried the chest of instruments.

As they reached the bottom of the steps that led up to the door, I looked again at the young man, at the grave oval face under the soft, squashy cap and the strand of fair hair that fell over his forehead.

It was the young man whom I had seen at the shop of the cunning man. And liked, and almost trusted. The layers of deceit and possibility jammed my thoughts solid.

I had known that such a transformation was possible, even likely, but it set off a trembling above my knees and a bee hum of unease at the base of my throat.

Was he the source of the militia's intelligence?

Janni was as handsome in male guise as in female, but how a change of pelt alters a creature!

Still with me, as you promised, I thought grimly. But not quite as I expected.

I listened to keys grind in the locks.

Maurits entered jovially. 'I apologise . . . the day's half gone. Janni kicked me awake, saying that Bakker wasn't to be kept dreaming just so I could sleep off a booze.' He dropped his pouch on the floor, flung his cloak into another heap, thrumming with fervour and impatience.

Maurits cannot know that I saw the book! I decided. No man is such an actor as that.

Janni moved faster than I remembered, less tranquilly. He made himself busy by the wolf's cage. With his back turned, he had denied me his face. I looked at the broad shoulders

519

under the male jacket and at the long legs, trying to see the woman whom I had trusted.

I could not think how to behave. 'Where are we?' I hoped that it sounded like a plausible question.

'An hour and a half by boat from Leiden, by wind alone, without a tow.' As he spoke, Maurits crossed to stand by Janni and look down at the sleeping wolf, the fingers of one hand tapping rapidly on his thigh. 'A pavilion on a family estate – not our chief one, I hasten to say – rented, ever since my parents died, to a farmer who shelters his sheep in the great chamber of the house and his second horse in the hall.'

He laughed over his shoulder at my expression. 'No, not another madman who keeps a menagerie in his dining chamber. My father tore down much of the main house for stone to build the one in Leiden where I now live . . . he would have none of your common brick! It's a ruin now, the sheep are welcome to it . . . Janni, where's Ned's dinner?'

Janni opened a pouch and handed me a parcel of bread and a cold lamb cutlet.

'Eat while I explain,' Maurits ordered me. In mid-flight, he veered to the cage. 'Its breathing is very shallow, Janni. Are you sure you didn't give too much?'

'I have the antidote here if need be,' said Janni patiently, but without the old, grave tranquillity. I imagined that I felt a new tension between them.

I tried not to stare suspiciously at the food. To eat it or not – which was the greater risk?

I was taller than Maurits, but he had weight in his favour. Facing each other, fairly and equally armed, I would have won, hands down. But Maurits had Janni, whose position was unclear. And Maurits was on guard, no doubt about it, even through the smiles and earnest lecturing. Above all, I must not let myself be drugged again.

Had they locked the grille again? The key was not in the lock.

'Will you help take measurements while the beast still sleeps?' Maurits asked me. 'It will save time.'

Was it possible he believed that I had not yet understood that I was to be flayed and anatomised like the wolf in his engravings? Most likely whilst still alive, or else why the box of sawdust? Alive to keep me fresh for as long as possible. And the wolf as well.

I did not see yet how to save either myself or the wolf. But, at all costs, Maurits must continue to think me a witless fool, so numbed by prison that I did not yet see the drift. I must stay free, unbound, and undosed with any more of Janni's devilish potions. I must pray that my own wolf did not choose this time to visit. I must not look at the box of sawdust, for if I did, knowledge would be naked in my eyes.

'Of course,' I said. And made a show of swallowing a yawn.

Maurits studied me for a moment too long, suspicion in his pale blue eyes.

Then Janni and I measured the wolf. Janni called out the numbers and Maurits wrote them into a book: width of chest, length of leg, diameter of ankles, waist and knees, length of tail. I made exhaustion the excuse for slow deliberation in all my movements.

The wolf had light bones for its size, and foot pads larger than my outspread hand. Standing on its long slim hind legs, it would be as tall as I, while its tracks would suggest an even larger beast.

With Maurits impatiently urging us on, we mapped the wolf's ears, paws, structure of withers and hip. Then I helped to turn the great beast over and pulled back the black gums so that Janni could count and Maurits record the number and shape of teeth which could have cracked off both our wrists.

Janni's face was closed as we worked. My sweet ally had vanished and left a changeling in the form of this deft, withdrawn young man.

The wolf snored through all these manipulations. When it sneezed, Maurits asked me to hold open the jaws while Janni poured in more of the tranquillising brew.

521

'Opium?' I asked, with what I hoped sounded like innocent curiosity. I stroked the wolf's coat, which was rough and patchy from captivity. But its muscles were still powerful, the teeth fearsome. I felt odd handling it with such impudent familiarity.

'Opium doesn't calm beasts as it does man.' Janni gazed anxiously at the snoring wolf and placed a hand against its heart. 'It works on them only as an ointment to dull local pain, but not for sleep.'

Nausea began to tickle my stomach.

We rolled it on to its belly again, so that the long blunt muzzle, ridged with rust-coloured fur, rested on its huge white forepaws.

Maurits seated himself by the head and began to sketch the exact colour markings of the head, slowly and with great concentration.

In the fading afternoon light, I watched him work his way down the wolf's body, noting the markings of its pelt. He reached the tail.

'Finished.' Maurits tapped together his drawings to square them. 'That brings us to your pelt.'

Hot bile burned in the back of my throat. Now I would be flayed.

Still feigning ignorance, I held out my hands palm down, to show the dark, incriminating fuzz on the backs of the first knuckles.

'I meant your inner pelt. If you are *versipillus* and indeed have fur inside your skin.'

Janni was locking the wolf back into the cage, face out of sight again.

Maurits took my hands and turned them over to peer closely at the insides of my wrists. 'Until we look, we must resort to hypotheses. First, that you are not *versipillus*. In which case, we won't find fur on the inside of your skin and never will. Because, in that case, you are merely mad or possessed. Not in any way a true wolf.'

522

In spite of me, my hands jumped in his grasp. His touch made me ill.

'Come to the window where the light is better.' Below Narcissus, he peered at my inner wrists again.

'The second hypothesis is that you and the wolf are two separate creatures fighting to occupy a single house. You are *versipillus* only when you have transformed to your wolfish state. In that case, we won't find fur under your skin if we were to look now when you are in your human form.'

He pressed down on my inner arm with his thumb, and studied the veins beneath the skin. 'Thirdly: we find fur, even now, while you believe that you are entirely man. In that case, you are a true werewolf, a creature compounded of two commingled parts, both man and wolf. As in the Minotaur or Chimera and other such compound creatures, these warring parts coexist at all times, but dominate each other in turn, just as good spirits and ill temper can take it in turn to rule a single man or woman.'

I knew what he would find, but had no intention of saying. Above all, I had to stay free and in possession of my wits.

'The question,' said Maurits thoughtfully, 'is how best to determine which is the truth.'

'I'm quite sure that you intend to look,' I said.

Maurits let out a little breath. 'With your permission?' He held my wrists, looking into my eyes.

'I have said that I must learn the truth about my nature, at any cost.' Although that had been some time ago. I knew more than enough now. 'If I understand you correctly, by looking, we can prove or eliminate at least one of your three hypotheses,' I added earnestly. Could Maurits truly believe that I would willingly invite him to begin his voyage of exploration into my body?

'I do believe that you mean what you say! You surpass my expectations,' said Maurits without even a whiff of irony. 'You choose as I would choose in your place. Not many would.' He meant it as a true compliment.

We now openly entered into a new time. I looked at

523

Janni again, trying to gauge how he would jump if I jumped Maurits.

He dropped my hands and clapped me on the shoulder. 'I said that Ned would be a worthy colleague, didn't I, Janni? Equal in fervour if not in education!'

I listened hard to his tone. It was just possible that I had cozened him.

Maurits told me to rub a dark brown sticky ointment on the skin of my arm. It stank of damp books and burning leather. The numbing salve again.

'Apply a little more,' said Janni, who now stood behind Maurits watching us.

Janni, the academic colleague, I thought bitterly. The likely one-time lover and now colleague in Maurits's obsessive criminal search for the minutiae of Truth.

As I rubbed more ointment into my skin, I caught Janni's eyes, hoping for a flicker, a wink, or any other sign that I might safely make my move.

Janni took the stoneware pot from Maurits, replaced the lid and turned away. This desertion nearly tilted me into panic. In spite of all the good reasons not to, I had been certain that Janni was benign. I knew that my reason was often faulty. Now I could no longer trust my unreason neither.

Maurits lifted a small steel blade from his wooden chest.

'Can you feel this?' He pricked my arm lightly with the knife tip. The skin was numb.

I shook my head.

'Will you watch or avert your eyes?' He pinched the skin, feeling for slack. 'How great is your hunger for knowledge?'

I swallowed. 'My curiosity is even stronger than my stomach.' As indeed it was. If he found fur, I must attack without caring about the odds.

I felt pressure and a faint sting. His first opening of my flesh. A red line welled up on my skin. Then I felt tickling warmth as a trickle of blood ran around my wrist.

Maurits made a second cut at right angles to the first, as

if beginning to draw a square. Then he gently prised up the small flap of skin.

I saw only white-spotted, red flesh before the blood welled up and drowned it. No fur.

Maurits wiped my arm with a piece of linen and took a lens from his instrument chest. He wiped and peered again through his lens. Then he shook his head.

There was no pelt. The cunning man had been wrong. In spite of his assurance which I had believed.

'A creature with a double nature,' the cunning man had said. Then I saw suddenly the meaning of his words, of his magic mirrors, and what the magic of his salve might be. If I lived, I had a mission to England beyond the setting of the Malise Salt on the table at Tarleton Court.

I stood numbly. 'It's proved then,' I said, feeling a rush of ill-timed joy. 'I'm not a constant compounding of man and wolf!'

Not a werewolf! Not a *loup garou*!

Yet what I had claimed in court had also been true. Fur or no fur, my wolf and I were on intimate terms, like it or not. We fought for tenancy of my body. I envied its strengths and ruthlessness. It left me snatches of its dreams and had made love to my woman.

Maurits took fresh lint from his pouch. 'I have seen pictures supposedly drawn by eyewitnesses which show werewolves with the heads and bodies of wolves, but with human limbs. Therefore, the skin of the arm is not conclusive. We must also examine that of your back.'

I fumbled with the shirt buttons, for all the fingers on my right hand were now numbed by the ointment.

Janni had disappeared.

'Would you be good enough?' Maurits offered the ointment pot again. 'Or else I won't be able to handle the knife. High on your right shoulder . . .'

With effort, I made myself turn my back on Maurits.

Again the pressure and trickling heat.

'No fur.' Maurits sounded disappointed.

'So, I am not a *vir*-wolf after all.'

'Only a positive makes a proof,' said Maurits. 'The absence of fur merely suggests the possibility that you are not.'

I did not press him to say what else he needed for positive proof, for I was certain he would want to find it.

'I must look under my own skin now,' he said. 'To compare.' He opened the salve again and had me apply it to his left forearm. Then made the same cuts in his own skin.

'The same as yours.' He looked both thoughtful and disappointed.

By the time Maurits had dressed both our wounds, less expertly than Janni, but workmanlike, the light had gone.

Janni returned with food and a candle lantern.

Maurits replaced the knife in his chest of instruments and uncorked a wine jug. 'A good day, if not long enough for greedy curiosity.'

Sailing close to the wind. Testing me. 'A good day,' I agreed. I watched Maurits drink. Detected no trick.

Janni lit the candle in the lantern, then set out a raised meat pie, dried dates, bread and a Gouda cheese.

'Not too much to drink for either of us tonight! Not like last night,' said Maurits.

I watched them both as they began to eat. Janni ate very little, but Maurits seemed careless of what he picked and chose. My stomach screamed for food and drink, even though my wary gullet had clamped shut against it.

'Not hungry?' Maurits gave me an amused, knowing look and helped himself to another slice of the pie. I nearly fell into the trap of acknowledging his amusement.

My throat closed in remembered warning, but my stomach insisted. At last, I ate.

'Where will you sleep?' I asked, trying not to wolf down the much-needed food.

'On my boat,' said Maurits.

When Janni had cleared away our supper, we all three went

outside to relieve ourselves over the side of the steps. Maurits and Janni both stood below me on the staircase.

I looked into the dark, overgrown garden.

Knock Maurits down and run! Take your chance with Janni.

As I had the thought, Maurits looked up, smiled, and put his hand under my elbow to turn me back through the door.

Behind him stood Janni, who had not met my eye, waiting in the darkness. The new, male Janni, in the freedom of a man's clothes. The better to match me in a fight. While I hesitated, gripped by an unnatural slowness, Maurits locked the iron grille between us.

'Sleep well,' he said cheerfully as he closed the outer door. 'Tomorrow we will begin to get to the heart of the question.'

I listened to the sound of the second key and collapsed on to the cot.

'To the heart of the question.'

My ribcage swung open like a pair of church doors. My exposed heart, naked and indecent, tried to tear itself free and escape, but it was tied in place by slimy white-and-blue strings.

Over and over, I rehearsed the moment on the steps – perhaps my only chance to escape. I remembered the unnatural ease with which Maurits had turned and guided me.

I yawned. A sweet silky sleep reached for me. The wolf already snored.

I sank back, slow and heavy.

Slow, drifting into sleep like a cloud.

No!

I struggled to sit up and fell back again on to the feather bed.

But Maurits and Janni had both shared the wine jug. And the bread and meat pie. I made certain before I touched any of it.

The dates. Dark as half-burnt wood, and sticky. In a racketing of thought, I tried to see our dinner again in every detail. I could not remember with certainty that I saw either Maurits or Janni eat one.

Janni, Maurits's accomplice, had prepared last night's wine and the ointment. And the dates. Janni, as double in heart as in body, had betrayed our supposed bond in monstrosity. I had been wrong to trust. 'I will be with you,' indeed! Still not wanting to believe it, I felt the pain of amputation.

With my teeth clenched, braced upright against the wall, I fought the soporific drug.

You gullible fool!

My life is short and another minute of it is now passing, I thought. And now another. And another. I'm counting my life down to nothing. Won't waste even a second in sleep, which is death's shadow.

But whatever was in the dates was stronger than my will.

Cold early-morning light shone weakly through Flora's catch-fly and harebells. I recognised the dryness in my mouth. But this time I could not drink, even if there had been a jug at my side, for I lay spreadeagled on one of the previously stacked tables, arms and legs stretched tight, wrists and ankles tied, stripped naked and covered with the wool blanket.

Last night on the steps had been my last chance to escape.

Fool, fool, fool! A slim chance is better than none!

I turned my head, already knowing what I would find.

The wolf lay on the other table. On its back it was longer than I. Janni's calming draught had worn off. The eye that I could see was wild with terror, the eyebrow arched in a very human expression of fear.

'I'm so terribly sorry! If it weren't for me, you wouldn't be here.'

The pale wild eye swivelled to fix on me.

'At least, I understand why I'm here.'

The beast whined. Its long body convulsed as it struggled again to break free.

528

'Steady, boy. Steady.' I had to look away from that eye. If I added the animal's terror to my own, I would flood away what was left of my reason.

The wolf heaved and twisted against its bonds. Its panting rasped at the air.

'Poor, poor Hound of Hell. Steady, or you'll kill yourself on your ropes.'

On reflection, that might be a better choice than waiting for Maurits.

I tried to raise my head. The box of sawdust now stood beside the wolf's table.

The wolf gave another keening exhalation.

'Easy. Easy.' I began to croon, to try to soothe that desperate struggle on the other table. The wolf's panic had begun to infect me even through the last false ease of the opium.

Terror began to thud in my temples, wipe out my thoughts.

'Steady,' I crooned. 'Steady, brother.'

I must not lose the character of man. That was my part. I must think for us both!

'An ape, a lion, an ox and an ass, do show forth man's life as it were in a glass . . .' My cracked lips moved, my dry throat forced out a creaking imitation of song. '. . . the hawk will kiss the azure sky . . .' I imagined that the animal was a little calmed by my attempt at music, though it was barely better than a beastly grunting. When I next listened, all I heard was its panting. I turned my head.

The eye had closed, though the narrow ribcage heaved. At my silence, the eye opened again.

'. . . and the owl cries, To-whit-to-woo . . .' I resumed.

'I'm pleased to find you in good spirits,' said Maurits.

The wolf whined and convulsed again at the sound of his voice.

'Please don't misunderstand your ropes.' Maurits locked the iron grille door behind himself and Janni, cutting off a brief waft of green grass and canal water. 'They're not from any ill will, I assure you.'

'Thank the Lord for that mercy!' It might be my part as Man to think clearly but, in truth, I doubted whether thinking was of any use now.

Maurits set his chest of instruments beside the wolf's table. 'I admire you, Malise.' He opened the chest and began to lay out his knives. 'I admit that, until yesterday, I doubted your determination to pursue truth to the end. But when you allowed me to look under your skin, I saw that at last I've met a kindred spirit as keen in the hunt as I am. One who understands the need to sacrifice the concerns of his own trivial life, just as I understand the need to set aside my own natural repugnance . . .' His voice rose to the excited, elevated tone that I had heard in the library when he was destroying all human knowledge. 'You, like me, see that a single life is nothing compared to the universal understanding towards which we are working. Even Janni wavers at times.' He shot his assistant an accusing glance.

'Then why am I tied like this?'

I heard the tiny metallic voices of the knives and blades. Then the heavier clunk of the mallet, the scrape of the saw.

I heard the first hint of apology in his voice. 'Today we set off on our final voyage of discovery – to compare your anatomy directly with that of the wolf, part by part, until we discover exactly how you, a *vir*-wolf, differ from a true wolf, and how you are the same.'

He crossed to stand beside me. 'Whether your condition arises from madness or from a true double nature, it will leave its signature on your anatomy. And I shall be the first anatomist ever to embark on the voyage to find that signature. I won't have you changing our plans.'

His voice now had an edge of defiance. He was still sane enough to understand, at least in part, what he was about to do. 'In your place, I myself might hesitate to set off. So I've tied you like Ulysses to the mast, to help you resist your own weakness. I like to think that, like Ulysses, you might even have asked me to do it.'

'I would not!' I said between clenched teeth.

He patted my shoulder comfortingly. 'I've brought the tincture of opium to kill the pain. Don't feel shamed to ask for more.'

He leaned his face over mine. 'And don't fear – I shall still give it to you, even when you're no longer able to ask. You will feel very little except a deepening drowsiness.'

He pulled back the blanket covering my nakedness, measured a line on my belly, then crossed to the wolf, to compare. 'I never entirely trusted you not to change your purpose. It was only reasonable for me to make some plans of my own.'

I suddenly saw answers to last questions that I had not yet had time to ask myself. 'How did I get to the village?'

Maurits nodded in cheerful acknowledgement. 'I thought that an excellent device, the sleight-of-hand. If your London friends followed your trail they would find only your arrest, a trial and then the terrible final transformation.'

'You gave me to the villagers!'

'An anonymous gift.'

'I didn't kill the chickens?'

'Of course not.'

Hot relief flooded me, even there on the table. 'And I did not kill the child!'

Maurits shook his head. 'Against reason, too many of the villagers were at first inclined to let you go. Something more than chickens was needed. Even so, against all reason, the fools still refused to call in the law. First you begged for exorcism and then you escaped. It cost me a lot of time and money to pick up your scent again.'

The ginger-haired youth had followed us at the fair, and then back to Catryn's hovel.

'And then you set the dogs on me in Amsterdam!' He had planned this perhaps as long ago as in London. No. The exploration perhaps, but surely not the rest. Not before I told him that I had friends who might miss me if I disappeared.

'Did you murder the child? As you mean to murder me?'

'To add to Man's knowledge,' Maurits corrected me. 'To learn, as you yourself once wanted to do more than you wanted to live. Don't disappoint me. Your death will be nothing like the undignified, scrambling resistance of murder, or the slow suffocation of the gallows. Your life will creep away slowly, without pain. And before it does, you will come to know yourself. The death all men pray for.' He turned his eyes from me to the wolf and back again.

'Your device will fail. You'll be discovered.'

We turned enemies in an instant. I saw him understand that I was a fraud after all, and a liar. Worse, that I could embrace ignorance when knowledge was possible. And worse yet, that I had fooled him.

'Why? Nothing has changed,' he said fiercely. 'I will still perform my sleight-of-hand. The dead wolf will still go back in your place, as Ned Malise transformed. No one will look for you, Ned Malise the man, because you won't exist any longer.'

'Marika . . .' I stopped myself with a curse.

'Don't fear, I have her safely out of harm's way. With the law as lenient as it is towards the gentler sex, one doesn't get many chances to examine a woman.'

I heaved against my bindings and howled.

How could Janni permit this? Unless there was a deeper, more evil passion between the two of them than I had ever imagined. I turned my head. 'Janni! Help me!' I bellowed, knowing that it was no use.

There was to be no help from anywhere. My beast and I would have to sort ourselves out alone. And that poor wolf on the next table depended on us to save it, or it was certainly dead.

I felt myself begin to struggle wildly, like the wolf. Our grunts of effort mingled.

Steady, Ned. What are your weapons? Have you any now?

'. . . An ape, a lion, a fox . . .' I sang in my head. Steady, boy! Don't frighten human reason clean away!

Where was Maurits vulnerable? Only weaknesses, vanity and arrogance. How could I attack those?

'. . . he will only care how well or ill you argue your case,' Janni had said of him.

A faint whine. And still the panting. The wolf's, and my own.

Think for the two of us! The part of me that is man must reason all these poor animals out of this dreadful discord, this shouting of demons and clanging of brazen hell-gates!

'When the cock begins to crow . . .' Once, when I sang, I had known where I was.

Maurits looked startled. The wolf whined again.

My thoughts would not settle. I swung, I groped. Perhaps the reasoning man alone could not get us out of this, after all. I turned my head to look at the wolf.

Maurits measured down from its breastbone, then went back to his chest to pick up a small knife.

The wolf whined again. To my ears, a terrified question, not the grating of a badly-oiled machine.

My own wolf and I would die together, in a horror partly of my own making. The beast on the other table was innocent of any crime other than being itself. It would die for my sake. I could try to save it, even if I could not save myself.

I would try, even though I now felt Janni returned and standing guard close above my head.

'He will only care how well or ill you argue your case,' I heard Janni's words again.

'I've reached a startling but unarguable conclusion,' I said to Maurits. 'That you are a fool!'

I was rewarded by seeing him fumble his blade. He recovered from his surprise, snorted and replaced the knife with another.

'As wilfully blind as any scholar whom you attack.'

'It won't work,' he said. He studied the wolf again.

I had to break his rhythm. He must not make the first cut, or he would have begun, irrevocably.

533

The wolf whined. What was left of a rational man heard it and knew what to do.

'I can refute your mechanical philosophy.' Janni's clothing rustled near my head. No doubt ready with some fresh subduing brew, waiting for the master's signal.

This time Maurits half-turned and smiled at me. 'You can't make me stop. I don't care if you've lost your nerve.'

Just engage him in debate. Break his rhythm.

I persevered. 'You are wrong in one of your fundamental assumptions.'

'Am I? Praise the Lord that I've been warned!'

'Beasts are not mere simple machines, larger versions of your clockwork toys. They have souls, like men.'

'Have you notified M. Descartes of his error? Or the faculty at Leiden? At Padua? Or Paris? Or the Church Synod, for that matter?'

But at last he turned to me, away from the wolf, his interest engaged. 'Debate won't save you, Malise. I'm sorry if you feel sudden regret, but you first chose this road of your own free will, as Janni will be witness.'

Sadly, that was correct. Janni had tried to dissuade me and I had impatiently dismissed the warning.

'Your earlier resolve was nobler than these feeble taunts,' said Maurits. 'With the help of your case – the first anatomical examination of a *vir*-wolf compared with that of a true wolf – I mean to be Praelector of Anatomy without the long, dull apprenticeship . . . within five years. You can't begin to understand the difficulties that the Church, the law, the superstitious rabble, throw in the path of Reason. Fabricius was exiled for presuming to examine God's perfect handiwork. I've known men fined into ruin, even hanged! Every faint glimmer of enlightenment is hard-won . . . even the true number of lobes in Man's liver. I am a crusader in the cause of Reason. Do you think I'll change my opinion on anything because an ignorant English musician tells me that I'm wrong?'

534

'Never,' I said. 'I would not presume.'

'What do you intend then?'

'To make you change it yourself.'

Maurits snorted through his small nose like a pony. 'Irresistible! Do I detect the threat of a budding hypothesis?' He folded his arms and waited expectantly, but with the blade still in his right hand.

I shut my eyes.

Hole in my thoughts. Breathe. Wisps . . . Grab them!

'The gift of Art is a manifestation of man's soul,' I said.

'That's an assertion, not even hypothesis. And a commonly known truth at that.'

Think, Ned!

'I say that the wolf has Art. Therefore the wolf has a soul and is not a mere machine.'

Maurits laughed aloud. 'If I had you in class in the Academy, I'd scourge you from the gathering. What do you make of that, Janni? "The wolf has Art!" A beast has Art! Another assertion! This time, unsupported.' But he had now joined the debate with as much relish as irritation.

'I will demonstrate that my assertion's true.' I wished that I had Janni in my sight.

'By its nature, the soul can't be demonstrated. That's why I don't waste my time on it. Leave it to the theologians.' Maurits began to lose interest again.

'Can Art be demonstrated?'

'Of course! By its actions and artifacts . . . none of which the wolf has.'

'And is music an Art?' I was gaining confidence in my direction.

'Of course!' He turned back to me, impatience mixed with relish.

I could have sworn that he had begun to enjoy himself.

'Set me free,' I said. 'Give me the remaining days of my release by the court. And some other things that I will tell you. I swear that I will demonstrate that the wolf has music

535

and therefore, Art. And, therefore, by reason, that it, like Man, has a soul!'

'The physicians were right after all. You are mad.'

I took a breath. 'Because I dare to question what you think you know? Oh, Maurits, I think you're afraid to look clearly because it might force you to change your opinions!'

'You begin to irritate me.' He studied me thoughtfully now. 'And are heretic to almost every philosophy, old and new! There may have been one or two authors in the past who would have agreed with your extraordinary assertion. But it's against the thrust of present knowledge.'

'*Observo*, Maurits. You of all men, closing your eyes and refusing to look!' Even the anger in his eyes was better than the earlier, over-confident fervour. 'Or do you fear to tackle a greater question than the number of lobes in a man's liver?'

Maurits's wide pink cheeks flushed dark red. He breathed more heavily.

'If you close your eyes now, a small part of the universe may remain in darkness forever. "The only heresy is ignorance." Now, Maurits, where did I last hear that?'

For a moment, I thought that he might simply cut my throat in rage.

'I know when I'm being baited,' he said, after a few moments. He drew a deep breath and exhaled so fiercely that his halo of wiry, sandy hair quivered. 'Still, as a man of reason, I must concede that you've quite correctly reminded me to be true to my own principles. I must let you make a fool of yourself trying to demonstrate the undemonstrable. Until then, I can't be absolutely certain that I'm right.'

He was silent for several moments, eyes on me, but unseeing. Then he nodded to himself. 'You're right, I have nothing to lose. *Concedo*. I will watch your demonstration. But you won't have saved yourself – after that, we continue.' He looked at Janni, who gave the slightest of nods.

'You can have only three of the remaining days.' He began to put away his knives.

536

'I must have all five!' I knew the direction of my road now, but not what lay at its end. I would have to travel and trust.

'But I must have at least two to examine the wolf, even if I save you entirely for after I send it back. Three days, no more! What else do you need? You must work inside this room and not for any reason, nor on any pretence, ask to go out.'

I nodded agreement. 'But you must set the wolf free in this room. Undrugged and out of the cage.'

'Undrugged and free?' he asked in disbelief. 'And just where do you plan to be? I said that you must stay locked in this room.'

'I shall be here with the wolf.'

For the first time I felt that I had gained a slight advantage. Maurits was genuinely alarmed.

'I can't let you do it! I won't have you damaged.'

'I won't be,' I said with false confidence. Though I would rather have the wolf tear me apart than be gradually sliced into a display of butcher's wares as Henry had been. Even if it were entirely painless.

The key turned in the lock of the iron grille. Maurits and Janni were on the outside, the wolf and I inside, both unbound and at liberty, with a pan of water, and a dead hen. The wolf still lay in its cage, but the cage was unlocked.

Maurits, now armed with a pistol he had brought that morning in his bag, had kept outside with him two cow shins, with hoofs still attached, which I had ordered along with the hen.

In the morning, after Maurits had untied me, Janni and I had restacked the two tables and pushed the box of sawdust back against the wall by the iron-bound chest. Maurits supervised with the pistol in his hand. Janni kept a safe distance between us at all times but, just once, I managed to catch his eyes with my own.

I could have sworn that he gave a minute nod of encouragement before looking away. A moment later, after Janni had left in search of the cow shins, hen and other supplies,

537

I decided that I had created this reassurance out of my own desperate need.

Now, in the early evening, the wolf began to shake itself out of its torpor. When it lay dizzily with its head at last lifted above its forepaws, I opened the cage door far enough for it to escape into the room. 'Hello, brother.' I set the pan of water just inside the cage, then sat myself down against the wall, close by, with the dead chicken at my feet. I whistled softly to myself. My thoughts were clearer today. Tentatively, I tried a few vocal exercises. The fist did not grip my throat and close off my voice. I crossed back and drank a little of the water Maurits had brought for the wolf, to relieve my dry mouth. Thinking was still like climbing a steep hill, but getting easier. I whistled again.

'Did you give it opium as you did me?' I asked Maurits, whose watchful face hung close to the grille. I wanted the wolf to grow used to my voice.

'No, Janni told you – it doesn't procure sleep in beasts.'

I began to whistle again and watch the wolf. No doubt, it could hear my heart beating from where it lay. It had heard the whistling and watched me with bleary eyes. I began to sing, very quietly. Very carefully. Songs I had learned in the Blomsloot. Dry and rough as it was, my voice still flowed unimpeded from my throat.

A little later the wolf sat up on its haunches. Some time after that, it clambered to its feet, and stood swaying gently like a man decanted from a tavern, drunk and unsure which way was home.

Four songs later, it staggered to the pan of water and drank most of it. It lay down again, still inside the cage, near the door.

'This could grow tedious,' said Maurits. 'How long will your demonstration take?'

'I have three days.'

'No more than that,' he said testily and unnecessarily. 'I won't lose a rare chance to examine a mature wolf.'

538

The more unsettled he was, the better.

Suddenly, the wolf was out of the cage. On its feet, it was monstrously large. It advanced three feet towards me, peeled back its lips in a snarl, then fled to the far side of the room.

I faltered for a beat, but kept singing quietly, one of the songs I had sung to Marika on the day we first met. I stared at my hands, dangling from my bent knees, and eyed the wolf sideways.

I had assured Maurits that I wouldn't be damaged. Now that the wolf was free, I wondered if I had promised wrong. I knew the wolf's ferocious reputation better than anyone.

The wolf advanced again. Stopped half-way across the room. Growled without peeling back its lips to show the gums. Advanced, then fled again.

'An amazing coward for so fierce a reputation,' observed Maurits.

I offered the chicken with my foot. Stretched my leg and pushed it a little farther towards the wolf.

'Come eat then,' I said as steadily as I could. 'If your belly is ready.' I pulled my foot back. My outstretched leg seemed a more tempting meal than the damp, limp-necked hen.

The wolf streaked across the floor, snatched the chicken, retreated to the far wall and turned its back to eat. It looked over its shoulder at me, then buried its muzzle in the feathers again. Checked once more that I still had not moved, ate again.

I unclenched a little. In comparison with the bandog, the wolf so far seemed astonishingly mild. I half-closed my eyes and hummed. A song in the Phrygian mode. Then the Ionian. My voice slowly loosened. Cracked less. I felt a pleasant buzzing in the bones of my face. Apart from my purpose, singing had begun to feel good again.

How ironic, I thought, that music may begin to return to me just as life seems set to go.

The wolf finished the chicken and curled up on the floor, as far from me as it could get in the room. It seemed to sleep

539

but, every so often, the eyes opened under the black brows, then shut again.

Tedium began to drain my fear. I closed my own eyes. How slowly the poppy retreated! But the wolf and I had little time. I changed to the Lydian mode, which Marika and I had imagined we heard in the howling, the night before the fair. I hummed, sliding up to that unsettling, stretched fourth note that belonged nowhere in the harmony of the universe. The Devil's Note. *Diabolo in musica*. Each time I climbed towards the Devil's Note, I felt an uneasy shifting under my heart, a faint memory of the approach of my own wolf.

I wanted to sing in a different, more comfortable mode, but this was the wolf's music. I hummed. Again and again, climbed through my discomfort back to safety. I hummed. Then I dozed. Hummed again. Woke with a start, heart drumming, senses alert.

Across the room, in the dim evening light, the wolf sat upright, staring at me. Straight into my eyes. Its gaze felt like the pressure of a hand.

I stared back, heart suddenly racing. Then I began to hum again in the Lydian mode, and turned my back on the wolf. I heard it walking across the floor.

It's no more than one of my old canal-side friends. It's no more than a dog. I mouthed the silent words like a charm. No more than a large dog. A large dog. A large dog.

I felt it sniff me from behind. A nose touched my ear. Slowly, I raised a hand and offered it for examination. The great russet-streaked head moved into the side of my vision. I saw it peel back its lips and nip my shirtsleeve.

'No!' I exclaimed before I could stop myself. The wolf fled again to the far wall.

That was where we still found ourselves when it grew dark.

Maurits poked water, bread and cheese through the iron grille. 'You seem still a long way from proof of lupine Art.'

'How long does a single demonstration of anatomy take

540

you?' I retorted. I decided that this meal, if no other, was likely to be safe to eat. I ate and drank with pleasure and the appetite of renewed, but undefined, hope.

Maurits wrapped himself in a quilt and slept on the steps outside the door. I could not see where Janni slept. The wolf and I slept curled against opposite walls.

I woke in the grey before dawn with the wolf looking straight down at me. Its muzzle was five inches from my nose.

'Good morning,' I murmured with stiffened lips. 'You look better than yesterday.'

Ears pricked forward and tail held high above its back, the wolf put its nose to my mouth, then moved back to my nose.

I made myself breathe gently. In and out. In and out. As if my blood hadn't frozen solid. The wolf sniffed my mouth again. Then sat down on its haunches.

I imagined an assessing look in its eyes. Was I edible or not?

Moving very slowly, I offered the rind of last night's cheese.

The wolf half-snarled and backed a little away when I moved. But it came close enough again to snatch the cheese rind from the floor, its ears rolled flat back against its skull. It retreated only a few yards.

I looked at the size of its teeth as it dispatched the cheese rind. 'Maurits!' I called quietly. 'Wake up!

The wolf pricked its ears but did not move farther away.

'Steady, old boy. I'm going to get you some real breakfast . . . Maurits!'

When he stirred in his blanket, I slid carefully along the floor to the grille. He unlocked the grille and opened it cautiously, just enough to pass through a cow's shin bone. He relocked the grille, but I had now induced him to unlock it at least once at my command.

I held the shin out to the wolf. The force of its strike on the bone nearly dislocated my shoulder. The wolf loped away again, and again sat with its back turned. I heard the cow bone crack between its teeth.

541

This time, after it had eaten and slept, the wolf returned to where I sat to examine me with open curiosity. At first from behind as before, but then it moved around to the front to test my face, both hands, my ankles. I leaned forward and sniffed back, offering my face as I had learned to do on the canal side with my curly-tailed friend.

Nose-to-nose, it met my gaze again. I imagined an intelligence in the yellow-flecked eyes and felt an absurd desire to explain to the beast what I had to do. I wanted to beg its help.

'This animal mastery that I'm witnessing now is enough in itself to hang you for wizardry,' said Maurits. He aimed for scorn but missed. In spite of himself, his voice was hushed.

Janni woke and came to stand looking over his shoulder.

'I didn't know you had the knack of mastering animals,' said Maurits. 'Or is it only wolves?'

I didn't answer. The wolf was too close. Without breathing, I reached up and laid my hand on its withers. Still as rough as when I had stroked its sleeping body. I scratched. Moved my hand a little. Scratched again. The tail swung. The ears flattened slightly. The wolf lay down like a dog at his master's side. I moved my hand to the thick ruff on the scruff of its neck.

I breathed out. I felt wary and respectful, but not afraid now. Under my hand, the huge animal also felt wary, but calm.

'This is all most astonishing,' said Maurits, still hushed, but with rising impatience. 'But it's only a fairground trick of animal mastering so far, nowhere near the human Art you promised me.'

At the sound of his voice, the wolf had turned its attention to Maurits.

'Wait. And be still!' I ordered under my breath. I had to accustom Maurits to obeying me.

The wolf growled, rose and trotted to the grille. It bared its fangs. Maurits backed hastily away, though he was safe enough on the other side. Then the wolf stiffened. It seemed to see the freedom beyond the grille. Ran at the grille, crashed into it. Leaped at it and fell heavily back again. Then it began to run in frantic circles around the room. It flung itself again and again at the walls and grille.

'Damn you, Maurits! You've just cost us all that I've gained so far ... Steady,' I said to the wolf. 'Steady! Don't hurt yourself. Those walls are too strong even for you.' I talked and sang. Soothed. Sang. Loudly now, willing my music to calm the frightened, frustrated beast. My throat slowly opened in remembered freedom. Though some notes still cracked, they belonged to me again. Born from my true thoughts and will.

The wolf slowed, stopped leaping at the walls and grille. At last it stopped running and sat again, facing me but at a greater distance than before.

I talked and sang like a mad fool.

It lowered its muzzle to its paws and, as it had in the menagerie, went somewhere else.

I watched it. When it woke again, calmed by sleep, I patted the floor, as if inviting a dog to play. The wolf looked astonished. It did not respond, but stared at me with even greater interest.

'Why not play with me? We're in this together.'

'I don't understand what you're doing,' said Maurits. 'Don't think that you can somehow trick me into letting you go ...'

'Quiet! Each time you speak, you alarm the beast again and lose us time.'

To my gratification, Maurits obeyed my order and shut his mouth.

Janni had disappeared.

By the end of that second day, the wolf came to lie quite naturally beside me for several moments at a time. I shared my cheese with it again, then again laid my hand lightly on its ruff. When it curled up to sleep, only a few feet away, I edged closer to the vast grey flank. Very slowly, I curled up against the wolf as I had curled up when a small boy. The wolf sighed. Its fur was very warm against my skin. In spite of the circumstances, I was filled with a

543

deep calm. I was six years old, and a wolf. Unbelievably, I slept well.

'Our last day,' I whispered the next morning as we breathed into each other's nostrils. My sense of peace had fled as soon as I woke. 'I need your help. This wonderful companionship is not enough. We have a hypothesis to prove.'

And a half-formed plan to carry out. Whatever else he did, Maurits must not kill this wolf.

'Your last day . . .' said Maurits through the grille.

'Quiet!'

'I shouldn't . . .'

The wolf veered away and began to circle the room, close against the walls.

'Maurits, do as I say, damn you!' I breathed urgently. 'Or you'll undo yesterday's work. We're very close now. Have your book ready to note whatever you see and hear.' I had no idea whether or not I lied.

I heard the rustle as Maurits again obeyed me. When I looked, he sat pressed against the grille, watching intently, book and pen in hand, a man always eager to learn.

The wolf continued to run circles around the walls. Whenever it paused, we sat companionably shoulder-to-shoulder, my hand resting lightly on the scruff of its neck.

'Help me repay your gift of last night,' I begged softly.

I began to sing. Dowland, this time. My voice was not yet itself but it would have to do.

A pale eye turned my way. The wolf cocked its ears. Looked away. Then straight back at me. The muscles of its throat quivered.

Suddenly, I knew that I was not merely buying time with false hope.

Please! I begged the wolf, without speaking. It's daylight, and there's no moon, but please.

I began to sing a Lydian scale. Climbed step-by-step . . . *do re mi* . . . Again, as I approached that unsettling, off-centre note of 'fa', anxiety tightened my body. I felt a pressure in my head. Then I passed on and climbed back to *do* again, and the sense of home. The pressure eased. I did it again, but sliding this time, my voice modulated into the ghost of a howl.

The wolf stood up and stared intently into my eyes. Its throat quivered again. I heard a faint, hollow whine.

Please, I begged it.

It stretched its head forward and up. Made a hollow trumpet tube of its muzzle. Its jaw quivered. It howled. It raised its head higher and higher as the notes of the howl climbed. The fur of its ruff trembled.

'Maurits, listen!' I whispered, and joined it again. Miraculously, in full daylight, the wolf and I howled together. And again. It threw its head back farther and farther until the hollowed muzzle pointed at the sky. I heard that it was leaving space into which I could weave my own notes. I adjusted my tune to the wolf's. In the Lydian mode, our voices climbed, entwined in harmony, but always on different notes. The wolf's voice seemed to resonate in my body. My own howl vibrated in my chest and throat, scoured deep into my belly. It was a direct wound, an opening into my most profound being. I was a pipe. A conduit.

'Listen, Maurits!' I whispered.

Our voices crisscrossed, approached danger, became lost, then found order again. As we arrived home at the top of our climb, our voices came together in a moment of perfection. Then came a moment of perfect stillness.

I had hoped, but never expected this wonder. Our music ran round the inside of my skull, polishing it smooth and clean.

For a time, as I looked into the animal's eyes and felt my way upwards through our music, fearing the Devil's Note less each time I approached it, I forgot Maurits altogether, lost in the wonder of this unbelievable, unimaginable song. If this was my double nature, I gloried in it.

Then I recalled myself, and why I had wanted this music so badly.

'Can you hear it?' I whispered urgently, as I drew breath to howl again.

Maurits stood at the grille, open-mouthed, too astonished to speak.

It did not matter whether he had heard the music or not. But he was entranced. That was all we needed.

'The other bone, Maurits!' I whispered urgently in the next pause to draw breath. I could feel the wolf begin to draw back from the howling. Its eyes slid away from mine. It would stop soon. I needed to act now.

'I'm nearly there. Bring me the other bone! I'll hold the wolf fast. Bring the bone!'

I had no trick to fight him with after all, just the force of my will.

We howled one last time. I laid my hand on the wolf's neck and prayed that Maurits could not hear that there was nothing more to prove. That was the music, the Art, the soul. More than enough for me, but perhaps not for Maurits.

The grille door opened. Maurits edged cautiously a foot into the room. I gripped the wolf by its scruff with all my force.

'Now!' I told it quietly. I felt it gather its strength.

'GO!' I said. And released it with a push towards the freedom beyond the half-open grille.

My other self. Live! And I will take whatever comes next.

Maurits screamed as the huge beast, leaping past him, knocked him to the ground.

'Janni! Stop it!' shrieked Maurits.

Beyond Maurits as he scrambled white-faced to his feet, I saw the wolf jump the overgrown canal, land awkwardly and streak away, bumping a little in its gait, but not slowed. Janni stood on a lower step and watched it go.

'Janni, you fool . . . !'

Too late, Maurits fumbled in his bedding outside the door, found his pistol, raised, then lowered it again as the wolf dwindled and disappeared. His child's face was a mottled greenish white from fury. He turned the pistol on me.

546

'You pig's arse! You've achieved nothing! The beast will either be shot by a farmer or run back into captivity with its pack mates.' He was close to tears. 'A senseless waste of an opportunity I'll most likely never have again!'

'If ever you wanted affirmation of a soul, there it was! Hypothesis proved!' My whole body still resonated. I cared nothing for Maurits now. Music had returned to me in a way I could never possibly have imagined.

'You didn't help yourself, believe me! You're still a monster. Your double nature will still bring you down, wherever you run! You could have died nobly, a sacrifice to man's knowledge, instead of in a trap or noose. To think that I gave you credit for man's wit and sensibilities!' He came into the room and slammed the grille behind him.

'You gave me credit for being more like you than I am.'

'I never gave you that much! You were a fool if you believed me. You're half-beast for certain! Get into the cage while I think what to do with you.'

I watched the muzzle of the pistol find the line to my heart. 'No.'

'Surely you can see that with this gun I must ultimately win any argument.'

'I have enough reason to see that you won't shoot me unless you must. A bullet would most likely kill me and, dead, I will decompose. You want me fresh, for as long as possible.'

'I may change my mind on that.'

'The bullet will also destroy what you want to examine. I don't think you'll shoot, unless from wounded vanity. And you're far too reasonable for that.'

We stood looking at each other.

'A dilemma,' I said.

'Sit down where you are then,' said Maurits after a moment of thought. 'Try to wait me out if you like. But I'm well-fed and don't have traces of opium still in my body. I also have Janni. You will have to sleep before I do.'

I ignored the order to sit. Instead, I circled the walls as the

547

wolf had done. I was unbound, undrugged, whole in body. I had gained ground. But to exploit it further – how, I did not yet know – I had to stay awake.

Janni brought food and water from the barge.

Maurits backed out of the door and pissed over the side of the pavilion steps. Then he drank from the water jug Janni had brought. He offered me the jug.

I laughed.

'Please do drink,' said Maurits. 'I would rather that your veins didn't collapse. You might as well.'

The air grew hotter as the sun rose. Maurits watched me from the door as I continued to pace around the walls.

Finally he grew irritated. 'Look!' He drank from his jug with one hand, his pistol still in the other.

I looked at the water drops still running down the pink round cheeks. Another trick, I thought.

'Janni!'

Janni's head rose obediently up the steps. He stood close behind Maurits, not beside him. 'Maurits wants you to drink, Ned,' Janni said sternly and shook his head.

I stared for a second. Could no longer make sense of anything. It was all over. I was outnumbered two to one by madmen. Maurits had a gun. I couldn't outwait, outwit or outfight them both. But I flung myself at Maurits all the same. While I was alive, I would not be bound again. And the wolf was free.

'Wait, Ned!'

It happened too fast to see clearly. The blast of the pistol trimmed the hair above my left ear and punched a bright hole where Flora's pink glass hand and arm had been. With hardly more fuss than a raven shaking out its feathers, Maurits lay senseless on the floor.

I recognised the method from my brother Francis and the Blomsloot streets. Except that Janni did not now go through Maurits's clothes to find his purse.

I shook my head. My left ear felt plugged with a thick cloth.

548

'You fool!' said Janni. 'Why didn't you wait another two seconds? Pretend to drink? Help me, for God's sake! We must work fast!'

I helped to heave Maurits up on to my table, where Janni strapped him down with expert hands. As Maurits began to mumble and protest, Janni pulled down his lower lip and rubbed a green, greasy ointment on the inside of his lip and around his gums.

'What are you doing, you abomination?' demanded Maurits foggily. He tried to turn his head away.

Janni held the small stoneware jar under Maurits's nose. 'I had some left after dosing Bakker.'

The smell uncoiled towards me. A green slithery smell with undertones of sickly purple. The rotting serpent. Francis's Egyptian Salve. The witches' salve. 'No!' I shouted with a horror I could not explain. 'You must not!' I felt the trembling begin again.

'Did the wolf that visited you in the village feel like all the others?' asked Janni.

I had wondered, but had never been able to think clearly about my own questions.

'He used it on me?' I whispered.

'Your own wolf doesn't arrive and depart on order. And he needed you to be wolf-like when he left you at the village. With the slaughtered chickens and a rumour, that should have been enough to see you arrested.'

Maurits convulsed and began frantically to try to hawk and spit.

'That is more than mere observing, Maurits!' I said.

Maurits had wound me up and pointed my life towards the killing of the dog, the transformation of my body to stone in prison. Towards a false living of my last day of life.

'And without the salve, your transformations don't last long enough,' said Janni. 'The villagers didn't see your wolf, but his!'

The dry mouth, I thought. The sickness! And I had not felt

549

that sense of fragile refreshment that usually follows the sleep that follows the wolf. I began to feel a tentative rising of joy. The wolf of the village was not my wolf! I understood now. Did not have to try to make room for it in myself with all the rest, which was more than enough.

'I agreed to Bakker because I wanted to believe in your rescue by sleight-of-hand. Gave you the chance to disprove my suspicions,' said Janni to Maurits. 'Until you forced belief.'

While Maurits, now wild-eyed and straining, clamped his teeth tight together, Janni pulled out each of his cheeks in turn and rubbed more salve into the hollows at the back of his teeth, as one doses a reluctant dog.

Janni stepped back and looked at him with a pinched face while he washed his hands carefully with water from the jug.

'And how soon would my turn have come? A *vir*-wolf and a hermaphrodite, Maurits, two monsters one after the other! What a temptation for a man of your dedication and fervour!'

I thought again with astonishment of the little flurry that had put Maurits on the ground, then remembered Janni's days in the brothel. I sat down on the floor. A man's wits can take only so much.

'Come!' Janni hauled me back to my feet, fiercer than I had ever seen or imagined. 'Move your rig! Help me with this chest.'

'Oh, *sheisse*! Oh, God's tears . . . !' Maurits gurgled and hawked, trying not to swallow. He tried to spit sideways on to the floor. 'I'll see you displayed, Janni! Before you hang.' His shouts already sounded a little furred. 'I'll cut down your corpse and pickle the pieces in a jar! After I've diced you into atomies!'

We lugged the iron-bound chest out of the pavilion. Janni turned back and locked both doors. Then threw the two keys, one after another, in high powerful curves into the canal.

'Monstrous guttersnipe!' Maurits shrieked faintly through the thick oak door. 'Traitor cockatrice! You obscenity, *contra*

550

naturam! You're dead without my protection! You should have killed me! You're both dead!'

We staggered sideways down the steps with the chest between us, then loped and stumbled, with the long damp grass grabbing our ankles.

I felt drunk with relief. A little out of control.

A disembodied stone arm waved from a pillar of bindweed and ivy.

Janni was not a traitor after all. Janni was still a friend. Janni was benign. My judgement had been sound. I could trust my senses in that at least. And against all odds, I seemed to be free. Then I stopped so suddenly that Janni nearly fell over the chest. 'Marika!' I said.

'Safe.'

'And is the child still alive?'

'We go to them next. I thought it best if Marika looked after Anneke while I could not. Now, please move again. We must all be well away from Leiden before Maurits is found.'

'We? You're leaving Leiden?'

'Your wits are still fuddled. Of course, I must leave after what I just did in there. What do you think he'll do once he's freed? And apart from anything else, you're not fit to move more than twenty yards alone.'

Captivity and dosing had taken their toll on my muscles. I stopped and sat down on the chest. 'Why didn't you kill him? He's right, that was the reasonable thing to do.'

Janni looked away from me, out over the canal. 'Judgement is not my part in life. I did worse than kill him. My old master would grieve and I'm already ashamed.'

My scalp prickled. It frightened me to see Janni looking uncertain. My just-recovered, benign Janni.

'We can't turn witness to the law, any of us,' said Janni. 'But he couldn't go free! There is also the matter of the child. Taking her served him two ways – it inflamed the villagers against you further, and gave him a rare subject to examine at his leisure, a young female child. The parents of any who die generally don't

551

like to give up the bodies for examination, even to physicians.' Janni almost seemed to be apologising.

'And Marika?'

Janni nodded. 'You heard him say his intent towards her. I swear that he has never gone so far as murder before! I would know, I'm certain! But then he has never before faced such temptation.'

'He surely would not have anatomised even you!'

'Oh indeed he would,' Janni said bleakly. 'I know now. He must at least have thought it, from the beginning . . . how could he not? It would be unreasonable to deny the arrival of the thought . . . but to act on it . . . ! And he would have expected me to offer myself freely. To question even as I died, a willing sacrifice to that god-like understanding. Sometimes he half made me feel that he was right and I was wrong. If he were me, I swear that he would have anatomised himself!'

I remembered how Maurits had looked under his own skin.

'He is mad but not a hypocrite.' For a moment, still staring out over the canal, Janni seemed like any other mortal testing the metallic taste of betrayal. Then he hoicked at the handle of the chest. 'Keep moving. Rest on the boat.'

'If I'd had the strength, I think I would have killed him,' I said. 'Or let my wolf kill him. Why is turning him beast worse than killing him?'

'He built a fortress of reason around his madness, impregnable to any truth that couldn't be measured. I've forced unreason into him like corn into a Strasbourg goose. Addled his crystalline thoughts, propelled him into a maze out of which he may or may not find his way. He'll rut with demons, visit places in himself that he won't ever be able to measure and record in his book. He won't even be able to publish his observations for fear of arrest! I tell myself that the experience may break him, but it might also lift him into a richer, more balanced state of reason. Far beyond the number of lobes in a man's liver.'

'He seems to me to have got off lightly,' I muttered as I staggered on towards the canal and the waiting barge.

'But judgement is not my part in life.' Abruptly, Janni stopped talking.

'When we return the child, we must alert the law,' I said. 'And as none of us can do it safely, Piet will have to do it for us.'

We set down the chest on the canal-side beside the barge, under an unpruned, lichen-covered apple tree. I lifted my foot to step across the gap of green water into the next part of my life, then paused, breathing hard. 'The other salve your master gave me, Janni . . . The cunning man was your master, was he not?'

Janni nodded.

'Is it truly an antidote for spells?'

'It depends on how it's used. At the very least, it heals putrefying wounds and whitlows.'

I looked down at the barge waiting to take me to Marika. And to whatever would come after that. Too much had happened too fast.

I must not just stumble forward numbly. I must . . .

I did not know what.

I was spinning. Dizzied by flashing fragments of possibility, of self, of other selves. By being still alive.

'Into the boat!' said Janni.

'Wait . . . !'

I must choose how to use the salve. I understood that much. Not so simple as it might first appear.

'We've no time . . .' said Janni. Then stopped.

'I need a moment to collect myself,' I said, more coherent than I felt. 'Before I see Marika.' A part of the truth. I reached out to steady myself on the tree trunk.

Fires burned in my mind. A lean shadow flickered between trees. Knives and cold stone.

My lungs ached as I still struggled to catch my breath. I thought I caught a glimpse of white bone. 'Boo!' said Death. 'Nearly got you! Twice!'

'Is your beast coming?' asked Janni urgently.

'No . . . I don't know.' I found myself sitting on the ground under the apple tree. Then I flung myself back, arms akimbo, into the grass. My fingers clutched the rough stems as if I might otherwise fall off the world.

I must finish whatever it was that I began back there with the wolf. Must know what I am offering Marika. Have too much at risk. Must not leave this place till I know.

Looking up through the leaves at the sky, I thought I remembered my first sight of it, in my grandmother's arms.

As I gazed up into that clean, empty space, I began to catch my breath at last. The spinning slowed.

'I think I'm almost back,' I said to the sky. 'But not quite as I was, like it or not. *Tant pis!* Too bad. But that's the way it is.'

A single black cross hovered, high and tiny against the brightness.

I was the eagle.

The spinning stopped.

I lay on the wind and looked down at the little four-limbed creature spread out akimbo in the grass under the tree. Nothing but space around me. Under me. The salty wind smoothed the feathers of my breast as it glided over them. The top of the tree shivered below me like water in the sunlight.

I lay, breathing slowly. 'Go away! I'm thinking. Must do without help.'

'Do I leave you after we've come this far together?' Janni's voice sounded far away.

Tarleton Court. Marika. John Nightingale. Francis. Grandmother. My wolf. My chest of tools. All were still there, all waiting for me to decide what to do next. Not for anyone else.

My wolf, most urgent. Embraced perhaps, but it could still hang me, no matter where I fled. Can't ask Marika to . . .

Janni gave a strangled noise of impatience. 'Surely I left you alone for long enough! Perhaps even for too long. You saved

554

your own life today, one way or another. Learn to accept help when you need it! There's no shame in that!'

'Wait!' I said desperately. 'Please!'

I squeezed my eyes shut, to hold my thoughts in place and not let them escape up into the quivering, sunlit leaves of the apple tree. One of them had whispered that I might yet master my wolf . . . as much as Man can truly master a beast.

I opened my eyes and stared up again through the flickering leaves.

The wolf stirred. Though I had invited it, a sudden fear chilled me nevertheless.

I closed my eyes, then laid my arm across them.

When the shivering light was hidden by my arm, the wolf pulled back.

The same whispering thought had tried to reach me across the dark Thames on the night of Sir George's party. But this time I caught it. On the night of the party I was still heeding the authorities, who said that I was mad, or possessed, or a shape-shifter. I had listened when told that I feared the light because the Devil, who was in me, loved only darkness.

'I think I know what summons my wolf!' I said aloud in astonishment.

Light.

I thought again about the circumstances of each of my wolf's visits: the flickering sun, the torches, the firelight when Marika dressed my wounds. The unsteady firmament of the Queen's Chapel.

Light, but only shifting light. It drew me into its coming and going. When it changed, I followed. Dark and light. Dark and light.

'First I'm one, then I'm two, then I'm one again,' I said.

Like the silver globules which the cunning man made leap apart and then together again. It was a mystery, painful and dangerous like most mysteries, but a bearable one. And one in which I was no longer a completely helpless victim.

Just as some dreams, instead of fading when you wake,

555

remain in your mind, as solid and real as written messages, so some moments take on a pivotal density, as if the fluid running away of time is slowed a little. The senses clear. The mind soars. Your thoughts ring like music. You know that you must pay attention.

In such a mood, I accepted this mysterious truth as mine.

I also saw now how the old ecstatic sense of a shift in my being – in music, in joy – was the brighter cousin of the darker wolf.

I had told the truth to the sky. Against all reason, I was back in the Universe, though I could not yet see clearly how I had arrived there. Surely, after all that had happened, I must have been touched by a special grace to find myself here, alive, about to see the woman I loved, and filled with the conviction that all would be well if I would make it so.

I sat up, then stood, a little unsteadily. 'Since the trial, was it all a test?' I asked. 'Is this still a test?'

'Oh, no. You chose, every step of the way.' Janni reached out, grabbed a wrist, pulled me towards the barge. 'But I'm saving your life now whether you like it or not.'

I resisted. 'Only if I like. That's how it must be from now on.'

We balanced, eye to eye. If we were to fight, I had the advantage of height and reach, but our strengths were evenly matched.

'What *is* your part in life then, Janni?'

'Being a metaphor.'

I was looking into the golden eyes of a lion.

'Not even you,' I whispered. 'Let me go.'

Janni released me, cocked his fair head and raised a cheerful eyebrow. 'Well then, command me!'

556

FOURTEEN

42

Marika heard a man's voice call her name above the nearby, wavering cries of the sheep. 'Stay here!' she whispered to the little girl. Nothing and no one in the world could be trusted any longer.

But the child whimpered in her half-sleep and clung to Marika's neck with arms like iron bands.

'Please! I don't know who it might be!' Then she gave up and carried Anneke with her to the door. If there was danger, she doubted in any case that she could escape with the still-drugged child. She opened the door which protected their chamber and stepped out into the roofless great hall, dishevelled, damp, with straw in her hair and filled with the fury of a woman who has been pushed beyond reason.

The former great hall was open to the sky and seething with sheep. In the ivy-hung gap, where the heavy main door had once been, stood Ned. He had leaned one hand against the stone door post as if to steady himself.

Marika stepped forward, scattering sheep.

'You're alive!' she and Ned cried at the same time. Then Marika stopped, reining in her indecent joy. Behind Ned was that strange creature who, wearing skirts, had shaken her awake and then, wearing breeches, had hustled her from supposed safe haven in Leiden to this country ruin, only to abandon her with a half-dead child. With hardly an explanation and only terse instructions to keep the little girl warm and to

559

feed her a few drops at a time from a stoneware bottle of vile-smelling liquid.

'What do you want?' she asked with as much self-control as she could muster. 'Either of you?' Want nothing, risk nothing. Risk nothing, fear nothing.

Shock replaced the joy in Ned's eyes. 'I've come back for you.'

'Why?' Justus had come back too, in hopes of a little cash. And left her again. 'And as for you!' She turned on Janni. 'What the devil is your game? Are there only madmen left alive in the world?'

'Is that Anneke Schmit?' Ned's voice was so roughened that she saw now why she had not recognised it when he called her name.

'Yes,' said Janni. 'I had to leave her before I had time to rouse her fully from Maurits's dosings. He never understood the fine degrees of danger . . .' Janni pushed through the sheep and unclamped the child from Marika's neck. 'Let me take her now . . . her colour's better than when I saw her last. You've done well.'

'The poor little girl!' said Marika. She felt light-headed and slightly detached from the world. 'According to that thing in there . . .' She nodded at the room where Janni had disappeared with Anneke '. . . Maurits van Egmond nearly killed the child in order to keep her *fresh*!' She glared at Ned as if she hated him. 'Have you and Maurits managed yet to excise your wolf?'

He crossed to her and put his hands on her shoulders. 'Didn't Maurits tell you what happened in court?'

'I didn't believe him.' She tried to ignore the heat of his palms and the images it raised in her head. 'I know that your whole life was bent on removing that curse. It wasn't reasonable, what he claimed you had said.' She looked at his odd expression. 'You did refuse to renounce your wolf?' The light-headedness grew worse. 'Oh, you are a fool! What possessed you to say such a thing in court? You threw your life away!' Even light-headed, she noticed that he did not flinch at the word 'possessed'.

560

'Because it's true. And because you wished it.'

'*I* wished it?'

'"What I have is with your wolf," you said, "which you and your doctor want to destroy."'

'You said it for me?'

'How else can a man on his way to the gallows declare his love?'

'Oh, *merde!*' She burst into tears. 'Oh, oh, oh!' She wiped her nose with her sleeve. Be careful, she warned herself. His life is fragile. This moment is rare and will pass. 'What kind of love is that, to declare itself when it is about to vanish?'

'I have much more to say to you, but, for your sake, not yet,' he said. 'I must go to England.'

She heard the hesitation.

'I have business with John Nightingale.'

She had been right not to trust the permanence of his return into her life.

He looked away from her. 'I have an unbinding to do and a vow still to fulfil.'

'As it happens,' she said, 'I have business with him too.'

43

The next day, we took the child back to her village. All of us, for Marika came too, with her single bag, keyboard and hen, having no other way to turn. I was sorry to have her company under such duress. But I did not know whether I would still be alive in a month, or where I would go, or what I would now make of my life. Like a man underground, I was feeling my way towards my destination, intent on getting there, filled with hope, but without light or other sign to say that I went the right way. I did not let myself think about her business with John Nightingale.

We moored a little way along the coast and Janni set off along the dyke tops with Anneke on his back.

He had brought my belongings in the boat from Maurits's house, where they had stayed since I first arrived from London. As I searched among them to be sure that my lutes were there and unbroken, I felt the heavy metallic shape of unfinished business and knew that I was right not to press Marika now into making a bargain that could never be in her best interest.

Instead, while we waited for Janni's return, I took my ashwood lute out of its wrappings for a short time and caressed it with joy at our reunion. I did not play or sing, for fear of attracting attention to us, and wrapped the lute again quite soon, so that the glue and strings would not soften in the damp sea air.

To fill the time, we talked a little of what had happened to each of us since she had touched my fingers in farewell outside Catryn's hovel in Amsterdam, each very careful of the other and thinking more than was said. I didn't think that she realised what Maurits had intended for her and will never tell her. 'What is the day?' I then asked.

'Wednesday.'

Wednesday. *Mercredi*, Mercury's day.

While she watched me, I took out the mirror of the quick-silver god. I stared into the gleaming surface for a very long time, trying to scry the future, but still saw only my own face.

In the afternoon, she curled her long limbs into a nest of cloaks in the bottom of the boat and slept as if she had not slept for several nights. I kept watch and took shameless advantage of my freedom to study her.

That evening, she and I watched a tiny light grow slowly larger across the water. When it pulled alongside us, I recognised the boat. It had carried me out of danger once before.

'Anneke is with her parents again,' said Janni. 'Piet here told them the name of Maurits and where to find him, and enough else to be sure that the child's story is believed.' He looked at me. 'Not so lightly, after all.'

44

One customs boat challenged us in the lower reaches of the river, just past Greenwich, but finding no cargo of value, let us pass without further question. Piet sailed us up the Thames past the docks, under London Bridge, past St Mary Overie and the stews of Bankside at Southwark on our left, the city on the right. We moored for the night at some steps in Southwark opposite three big new houses along the Thames. Then, while the others rested in an inn, I went in search of Sukie at the Bear and for news of Will Shaw. Late that night Will and I toasted each other fervently with ale and exchanged news. I gave him a fairly accurate version of what had happened to me. I also gave him his almost-finished lute, told him who might varnish it for him, then string and tune it, and tried to return his money, but he would not have it back. As an even greater gift, he told me that the baronet had been asking after me to give me a piece of good news.

Shaw raised an eyebrow, but I could not, from discretion, satisfy his curiosity.

The next morning we sailed on upriver, past the Battersea Marshes, the mouths of the Fleet, the Wandle, the Tyburn, the Effra, Falcon Brook and the Brent. We sailed on past King James's New Park on the flat land by the Thames, across from Syon. Then past the crowded, domed towers of the Richmond Palace on the river's edge, a little upstream from the New Park.

Piet landed us in the afternoon at the edge of some flat water meadows by a great sweeping curve of the Thames at Petersham, a half-mile above the palace. Beyond the water meadows, which were dotted with grazing cattle, Richmond Hill rose towards the high wooded plateau of Richmond Forest, on the edge of which Will Shaw had told me we would find John Nightingale. When he also told me of the man's recent misfortunes, to my surprise, I had felt no joy.

Janni and I shook Piet's hand as if wringing off his arm. We clapped each other on the shoulder, exchanged good wishes and blessings. Then we all waved goodbye as he sailed away back downstream. He had told me that the return of Anneke had more than earned him forgiveness for the suspicion of having helped me to escape.

I paid a small boy who was watching the cattle to look after our tiny heap of bags and boxes. Then I stopped a man walking along the riverbank and asked him where in Richmond Forest I might find the new house-to-be of John Nightingale.

Curiously, he studied our party of three, me in my ragged finery, Marika equally bedraggled, but wearing diamonds in her ears, and Janni, miraculously clean and serene as a nun, who was dressed and travelling as a woman, partly to keep Marika proper company and partly from preference. He looked at the heap of our belongings.

'You have strange friends,' the man said. 'I wouldn't be seen to hang on him myself!' But he pointed upwards towards the plateau and a little farther upriver. 'Go find him while you still can!'

I watched him pass on, back towards Richmond, then glanced at Marika. When I had told her that morning of the turn in Nightingale's fortunes, she showed no more than a friend's concern. But I felt her reluctance to meet her old lover again and suspected a lingering fondness.

We walked upstream along the muddy riverside path, through nettles and elderflower. A flotilla of wild ducks landed on the river, their feet running on the surface, wings beating backwards as they settled. They swam in parallel with us for a few yards, then suddenly clapped up into the air again. On our left, in the water meadows, the cattle had begun to question, with the occasional querulous moo, whether it was not yet milking time.

My eyes followed the line of the ridge high above us to our left, right on the lip of the escarpment, where the man on the towpath had pointed. Even at that distance, I knew him. The seed of my grandfather's murderer and usurper of my birthright. The boy who had wept in the orchard. The fiery Icarus. My brother's killer. My nemesis. I frowned to see more clearly across the distance. A man only a little shorter than I, with acorn-coloured hair and a short neat beard.

He was striding away from us along the very edge where the forest plateau fell steeply down to the water meadows. Beside him, head down and tail up, trotted a deerhound whose withers reached almost to his hip – not the same one which he had stroked in the orchard, I told myself. Envy, and other emotions too complex to describe, blurred my thoughts. I tried to shake them off. Whatever it proved to be, I must see the moment of our meeting clearly and cleanly. This was my last chance to unbind myself, no matter what form the release might take.

Reason and magic churned together in my mind. Nightingale had struck the blow that had invited in my wolf. But I no longer believed that I could shed that disturbing, dangerous soul mate of mine. For better or worse, I had acknowledged that thing of darkness as my own.

So what must I ask of Nightingale?

I felt in my pocket for the pot of ointment given to me by the cunning man, the antidote to enchantment, which I was to rub on my enchanter's forehead while I looked into his eyes and charged him to release me from the spell.

'John!' shouted Marika, as he was about to vanish into a stand of trees. She knew that I turned to watch her. 'John!'

The distant figure stopped, listened, then located us as we

566

climbed up away from the river. He did not come down to meet us, but waited, it seemed to me, warily. As we neared the top of our climb, the deerhound trotted down to sniff at our legs and feet.

'Marika!' Nightingale called uncertainly and began to slide and scramble down the slope.

Then he recognised me. 'You! I thought you'd slunk back to the Low Countries after trying to poison the Queen!'

Janni, he hardly noticed.

I climbed the last few yards. We stood face to face.

'Have you come to gloat?' He felt for his sword, did not find it, put his hand on his dagger instead. 'I could change my mind about the need to kill you.'

Panting from the climb, Marika caught up with me. 'Just let him speak.'

'I'm not in a listening humour.' He turned and climbed back up the hill away from us. We followed. The dog bent her nose to my right knee.

Behind Nightingale, set back from the lip of the escarpment in a grove of oaks, I saw the first workings of the house Shaw had told me of. Raw ditches, planks, piled bricks, shovels, picks, buckets and sacks.

'You catch me at a bad time,' he said bitterly. 'It seems that His Majesty gives gifts and takes them back in the next breath. First gives me this land to build an estate. Then just a few weeks later I learn that he means to make a closed hunting park, surrounded by a high wall . . . which will run just there, between you and me.' He pointed with angry jabbing gestures. 'My new barn, already rising there, will lie inside the wall. My fields there, outside the wall. As for my house, the cursed wall will run right between the dining chamber and the jakes!' He glared at me. 'So, Malise, you see that I'm not in a humour to discuss our *vendetta*.'

'I want . . .'

'Can't you see when a man's at the end of his wits?' He moved closer, as if he meant to throw me back down the hill.

'If I weren't in such bad odour with the law myself, I'd turn you in for the reward!'

'John . . . !' Marika begged.

'Who told you where to come to gloat?' he demanded.

Janni broke in mildly. 'We had to leave Holland in haste, and have just now climbed down from our boat here in England. Ned always meant to find you, good fortune or bad. He has an embassy to you.'

'I've never yet liked his embassies!'

'I want to end the discord of our war,' I said to him. I closed my hand around the yellow-and-white striped glass jar.

Nightingale looked at me curiously. 'Reckoning blow for blow, surely the amnesty is for me to declare!' His eyes were hot coals veiled with ash.

'Do you prefer war?' I asked. 'Do you need to kill me now? Or can old enmity and new amity live together as conflicting but reconcilable truths?'

The only sound in the clearing now was his angry breathing. In the forest, beyond the clearing, a fox barked. Then the rustling of leaves filled my ears, a soft rubbing together of dry-skinned hands. I smelled leaf mould, a sharper green smell from the bracken above his building site, the intense sharp animal odour which had sprung out from him when he had seen who I was.

I heard my own blood and felt the warm slanting rays of the setting sun as it dropped beyond the open space of the valley. In the corner of my right eye, I saw the river glint in the bend far below us. My back felt the presence of Marika, close behind me, and I could smell her rosemary and rose perfume through the tang of salt water and stink of travel that marked all three of us – Marika, Janni and me. I could hear her soft, careful breathing.

'Once I risked nothing of any value when I risked my life.' I looked over my shoulder at Marika. 'Now my life is more precious to me than I can say. And very new in its present

568

form. Untarnished yet except perhaps by my wolf – which itself may have played a part in returning my true life to me. I have everything to live and hope for, and will try to live with the fears.

'But our battle belongs in the old life which I must shed altogether, one way or the other. If you want to kill me, here I am.'

I held my arms away from my side, open to his attack. 'I will not fight back.'

Now I could not hear Marika breathe.

He walked away and stood staring out over the edge of the escarpment into the hazy distances of the Thames valley. The dog began to follow him, then stopped midway.

'I don't believe that you would stand and let me kill you,' he said at last.

'I would try. For I will not fight you again!'

'It's not reasonable for the battle to go on, I agree,' he said after another silence. 'Life is so generous with other enemies. But the lives of two parents . . . the wreckage of my own life . . . I was punished for your brother's death.' He raised a hand to hold us where we were and walked away into the grove of small oaks. The dog gave me a searching look, then followed her master.

We waited.

I suddenly saw us. Floating. Poised above a valley, on a ridge in a forest in England, among the raw ditches and piled bricks and lolling, muddy buckets of a never-to-be-built house. With no moment certain after this single present one. Our futures lay as open as the vast space of the valley below us, and as hidden in mists. Exiled from all our homes, all our possessions in one poor heap among the wave-like roots of a tall beech tree. My tools, patterns and precious pieces of wood, Janni's chest of bottles, Marika's keyboard. We could hover, fold our wings and dive, or fly, as we chose.

I turned around, astonished by where I found myself and why and with whom.

Marika's brightness was not dimmed by her damp, dirty clothes, but her face was tight.

'Tell me truthfully, did you come here for him?' If she said, yes, I would welcome Nightingale's sword.

She frowned in protest. 'I came with you.'

'You had little other choice. And you loved him once.'

'*Merde!*' She glared at me again. 'Your wolf would not have said that. Are you trying to say that you didn't want me to come with you except from pity?'

I stared at her in disbelief. 'Marika, I don't know where I shall go or what I will do. I have no property, no money. I share my body with an invading beast which puts my life in constant danger if it is detected. Of course I want you, but how can you want *me*?'

'It's beyond reason,' she said unsteadily. 'I agree.'

Janni stood staring out into the hugeness of the Thames valley, hands clasped against her skirts behind her back in a distinctly masculine fashion.

Finally I took courage and asked, 'What is your business with him?'

'Only some lost property to return.'

I remembered my resolve on the canal bank to act always by my own choice. Took Marika in my arms. She leaned back away from me, trying to see my face.

'I'm entirely myself,' I said. 'Plain Ned, no wolf. And if Nightingale decides to let me live, I want you to marry me. Wolf and all.'

'I'm not cut out to be a wife.'

'Don't think that I offer a bargain. How many wives would have a wolf for a husband?'

I caught movement in the side of my eye. Nightingale, with his dog standing at his hip.

Marika and I moved apart.

Nightingale avoided my eyes and stood looking out over the river valley. 'There are great wrongs on both sides, many before either of us were born. And logic says that I must also

570

weigh two parents against a single brother.'

The dog looked up at him, then stepped forward a little into the space between us. I dropped down on to my haunches.

'I'm still too inflamed by my present loss to think straight,' he said. 'There's more to my story: I must leave England. Refused to make way for His Majesty's precious wall . . . incited other landowners in the forest to resist. If it weren't for the private amusement that I suspect I gave Lord Mallender, I would most likely have been arrested for treason.' He waved his hand angrily. 'Suddenly, there's no ground under my feet. I'm uncertain of my own nature. I seem to have mislaid my best self, from fear, or ambition, or rancour. This is no small choice you've offered me. And at a time that is all choices . . . when it seems that every choice I make will set the course of the rest of my life.'

Though Nightingale spoke, Marika watched me. I held out my hand to the dog.

On her great long legs, the deerhound crossed to me. She sniffed at the offered hand, then looked into my eyes with a knowing tranquillity, as if she waited for my understanding to catch up with hers. The scimitar of her tail swept sideways and back. Then she folded herself to the ground and graciously allowed me to scratch behind her ears.

Nightingale sighed.

With Marika still watching me, I ran my hand over the short rough coat, along a continent of delicate bone and tough sinew.

The oak leaves scraped against each other above our heads. Below us, a lark stitched the open hillside to the evening sky in long zigzags of rising and falling flight. The hound thumped her tail on the ground.

Nightingale gave a small laugh and shook his head in mocking disbelief. 'Here I stand, Man the Master, heir to Adam's rule over the beasts. And yet, so perplexed and in a churn, that I can think of no better choice of how to act than to be guided by my dog. I know her gifts for smelling out character. If

571

Aphrodite there, in her infinite wisdom, can show you such favour, I can at least forgive. I pledge an end. That does not mean, however, that I can like you.'

The dog looked from him to me and back again.

'I didn't ask that.'

Rather awkwardly, we clasped hands on it. There are many ways of unbinding.

Marika stepped back beside me again. 'I never doubted your choice,' she said to John Nightingale.

'Then you know me better than I do myself.'

'I would not choose to repeat anything that has happened,' I heard myself saying. 'But, now that it's behind me, I think that I'm grateful.' I shook my head in disbelief. 'Yes. I believe that I am.' I looked at Janni over Marika's shoulder. 'However painful the reshaping, I would not again be the man I was before.' I looked back at Marika. 'Nor wish to be anywhere else but here.'

She gave me a smile I had never seen her give before. Open, glowing and without a taint of flirtation.

Our supper that evening, as Nightingale's guests, outside his half-built barn in the last of the setting sun, with two bottles of good claret, was merrier than any of us would have believed that morning. We laughed immoderately, perhaps excessively, in our relief, as we exchanged mounting tales of woe. When the sun sank, we continued by lantern light inside the walls of the barn. To my relief, Nightingale did not make a fire.

'. . . my best laying hen! And feathers all around!' I declaimed in the thick outrage of Paulus Janzsoon, astonished that I could already relate the tale with such gusto. And my audience whooped with appreciative glee.

'. . . and I asked Lord Mallender, can the King always do just as he likes?' John poured more wine. 'Tax as he likes? Unmake parliaments as he likes? Are you telling me that with an army deserting for lack of wages, His Majesty now would like to pay for a seven-mile brick wall around some of the best farming and grazing land within a day's ride of London!'

We clicked our tongues in sympathy, and Aphrodite thumped her tail.

'And why does he need another park? I asked Mallender.' Nightingale leaned over to scratch her head. 'He has a perfectly fine one made by his father at Kew. And the King's man said to me, "Nightingale, the wall will be built whether you oppose it or not, and it will be as thick and solid as your skull. Don't you see? In offering to buy back your land – at a reduced price, to be sure – the King is doing you a favour!"'

It was more tragical than comic, but we wept with laughter. Sometimes, the laughter tilted almost too far in our relief at laughing at all, but we always caught ourselves and steadied.

Nightingale and I were guarded with each other, and from time to time exchanged startled looks. I had no doubt that we would stumble here and there on the road back from enmity, but we were already bound by being fellow travellers on it.

When we had worn ourselves out with laughing, we persuaded Marika to bring out her keyboard and play for us. She set it up on a block of wood. As the bright notes flew up from the attack of her strong fingers, I imagined the creatures of Richmond Forest creeping closer to listen, as if she were a female Orpheus. I thought I saw them in the gathering darkness: deer, badgers, foxes, squirrels, rabbits, owls. I thought I could hear the rustle of leaves and the scrape of twigs as they crept closer and closer around us.

Then she begged me to sing, and as I could refuse her nothing, I did. I was all music already, from hair to toenail – bones, blood and every fibre of my sinews. I unwrapped my ashwood lute. They all waited patiently while I tuned the strings, which were not damp at all.

I settled its curved, shining body against mine, then hesitated. Here, in the lantern light, after her music, I could not sing fashionable phrases of praise to beauty or the transports of love. Nor could I sing a bawdy whorehouse song. I did not

573

know what to sing. I closed my eyes and entered the still place, feeling for the music in my bones and blood. I remembered a dream which had come to me while I lay on the cold stone prison floor.

'A fairy tale,' I said and began a slow, chilling, mournful melody. A tune for a pipe, played in a cold, high, mountain meadow. A tune for the wind blowing over rocks.

Marika looked startled and a little frightened. The others also looked surprised at this change of mood.

The music unfolded as if by its own will. I sang of solitary maiden and a huge and fearsome wolf made of stone.

The music lightened, grew warmer.

One day the maiden took courage and laid her hand on the great stone head. The stone cracked, grew crazed like an ancient jar. And out of the crumbling dust flew a singing bird.

I lifted them up with me on my voice, into the soul's place of perfect stillness. Marika sat with her head down and her hand over her eyes.

'In fairy tales,' said Marika, breaking the silence at last, 'everything happens three times. You have come back to me only twice.' She wiped her damp cheeks defiantly.

'I'll come back to you again and again and again,' I said. 'Each time I turn wolf, for a start. I'm damned to live in spinning circles of change and rebirth. Ask Janni!'

'I will always lay my hand on the wolf's head,' said Marika.

Then she and I sang together. And then Nightingale proposed a sailors' song, to which he joined in with an uncertain but pleasing bass. Unfortunately for the musical balance of our consort, Janni, like Marika, had, not an alto, but a second high soprano voice. From time to time Aphrodite raised her head and politely stifled a howl in her throat. In spite of the almost accidental chinking notes of a night bird in the bracken, I missed the voice of the wolf.

Before we made our beds, I gave Nightingale the salve. 'For whitlows,' I said.

574

Janni lifted her head from arranging a sleeping nest. 'Don't forget the other.'

After a moment spent considering the stoneware bottle which the cunning man had given me, I tilted my head and swallowed a mouthful of the bitter yeasty liquid.

Accept help when you need it. And who knows what truth might ease my wolf? I might be reconciled to my beast, but I would not deceive myself that as long as it was with me I could live as before.

Then we slept well, if not grandly, under our cloaks, on the heaped canvases which Nightingale had arranged on the barn floor. I slept as if on a feather bed in Paradise, with Marika warmly lodged against my flank.

Breakfast the next morning was a much more sober affair, with cold daylight and the need to plan pressing on us. By midday we had concluded and shaken hands on it, all in a circle, John Nightingale, Janni, Marika and I. There seemed no other way for these fugitives from justice than to launch a second ark. I would at last ask a favour of the baronet, whose ships sailed the Atlantic as well as to the Indies.

But before I braved London, I had a private journey to make first.

The green tunnel was unchanged, except that the bluebells had handed over to red and white ragged robin, purple glazed foxgloves, and lurid pink catchfly. Tarleton Court showed only one sign of change – a formal Dutch-style parterre, still skimpy and immature, laid out in front of the house, the young box bushes like rows of small green pegs.

The shock of recognition took my breath away.

The mud track punched with deep holes by the hoofs of the dairy herd still led back towards the orchard. The chapel still stood among the tipsy gravestones of my ancestors. The outbuildings still leaned casually, though on closer look both the pig house and grain store needed repairs. And a raven's nest now bristled between two crenellations of grandmother's

575

tower. I stopped on the road a little way off to compose myself. My mission was more painful than I had expected.

This time a mastiff came to the gate. Close behind it came a man in his late twenties in rough woollen trousers, who rested the sharp curved sweep of his scythe on the ground and asked how he could help me.

When I asked to speak to the master of the estate, he said, 'I am the master.'

This time, in spite of my worn and soiled clothing, I was invited to take refreshment in the main parlour, which the family also used for dining, just as my family had done. At first, as I stood in the oak-lined doorway, I saw only two things: a long polished wooden table pushed back against a wall, and a carved stone cartouche above the fireplace bearing an ornate letter 'M'. As I walked a little farther into the room, I saw that the lead fireback carried the Malise eagle and two keys. I raised my hand to touch the stone 'M' on the cartouche.

'. . . two generations ago,' I explained to my host and his even younger wife as we ate, in the company of their four children and a small house family of five. I ran my hand across the surface of the table, which smelled of beeswax and honey. 'I never lived here, but my grandmother often spoke longingly of the place.'

William Hutton nodded and smiled.

'How she must have missed it!' his wife said. 'I know that I would.'

'Though I can't keep it as I would like,' her husband added. 'Taxes grow heavier every few months. And drought has cut our harvests for the last two years.'

I nodded and offered my hand to the mastiff who had followed us into the house and lodged under the table.

'After we eat, shall I show you?' asked Mistress Hutton eagerly. 'You must see my favourite room, in the tower. I always sit there to do my sewing and spinning. And the children also prefer it.'

Grandmother's painted flowers had faded. I peered up at

576

ghostly cream-coloured tendrils, the faintest memory of pink flowers and green leaves. By the time my children might have played there, had I had any, the flowers would have gone.

Back in the main chamber, after seeing the other public rooms of the house and revisiting the dog yard, which was just as full as it had been with unfinished tasks, and after standing in the chapel before the tomb of my great-grandfather – also Edward – I sent their young groom to bring one of my saddlebags. I set the bag on the floor beside the polished table.

'I haven't been entirely candid with you,' I said. 'In truth, I want to beg a favour.'

'It does no harm to ask,' said Hutton, still cordial, but a little wary now. As if he thought I might have rested content with dinner.

But Mistress Hutton beamed at me. In my enthusiasm for her house, I had become as good as family.

'With your permission, I would like to leave this here.' I took a large, heavy, cloth-wrapped bundle out of my saddlebag and set it on the table. I unwrapped it.

The Malise Salt had darkened a little with tarnish but was still magnificent. The silver lions' feet, the silver pillow, the saints on the sides of the tower, the dome, all glowed in the early afternoon sunlight falling through the window.

'For how long?' asked Hutton. 'A thing so valuable is a heavy responsibility.'

His wife frowned charmingly in bewilderment.

I touched St Mark's lion, then the stylite on the tip of the tower spire. I lifted the silver dome and imagined that the blue glass bowl was full of sparkling, greyish crystals of salt. I remembered eating a turnip as a quail. I replaced the dome, on which the Spanish demons still warred with the angels. 'It's a gift for you,' I said to Mistress Hutton.

Both Huttons stared at it, speechless.

'It belongs with this house. And I won't need it where I'm going. Keep it or sell it as you please.'

One of their sons, of about six years, put his face close to

577

the man perched on top of the silver spire and frowned into the tiny silver face. Then he stroked the lion.

'You can't . . .' Hutton protested.

'It seems that I just have.' I picked up the empty saddlebag. Its lightness alarmed me in a way I could not explain, but excited me as well.

The mastiff escorted me as far as the gate. I scratched its head in farewell. A short way along the road, I stopped again and looked back.

Tarleton Court had been in my flesh and bone after all. But there was still room in my anatomy for other places too. *Rotatio*.

The cycle shifted a notch.

Now for London.

45

'Thank you for seeing me.' I could not believe my own presumption, nor what I was going to ask.

The baronet shrugged. 'I've invited you often enough.' His smile took any edge off his words.

We stood in the small parlour where he and his steward clearly dealt with daily affairs. When I was shown in, he had risen to greet me from behind a large table heavy with papers and account books. In its centre stood a wooden model of one of his ships, the *Sea Dragon*, a three-masted galleon, complete in every detail, from the tiny stitching on her sails, to miniature cannons on the deck and an English flag at the top of her two-foot mainmast. She had a full rounded bulge to her belly, rather like a lute. Smaller models of two similar ships were displayed on a cupboard against one wall.

He waved me to a chair and sat again himself. 'Well?' He cut me off with a gesture when I began the usual courtesies.

I took a breath and, without ceremony, told him that I needed passage to the Americas.

'Urgently?'

I nodded.

'I've heard the gossip,' he said. 'You took a risk coming back to London.'

'A gamble on your good will.'

'You know you have that.'

'Perhaps not, sir, when I tell you that we are four.'

579

'Four passages?' He thrust out his lower lip and considered. 'Not much more difficult than one, if you don't ask for luxury.'

'Do you know of a voyage that might take us?'

'If you're not particular as to destination, one of my own ships . . .' He turned to point at one of the models on the cupboard behind him. 'The *Sea Horse* . . . sails soon for Chesapeake Bay and Jamestown. Has room for four, as long as none of you is a grand lady.'

I looked past him, trying to imagine crossing a vast sea in such a fragile cup of wood and cloth. And thinking how to describe Janni.

'Two ladies, sir, but neither grand.'

Now came the most difficult question. Together with the uncomfortable thought, which I had fought all the way back to London, that I should have kept the Malise Salt to sell after all.

'As for the cost of passage . . .' I began.

The baronet frowned. 'There's no need for you to ask that.'

I looked at him, not trusting what I thought he meant.

'It will cost you nothing.'

Of course, secretly, I had hoped, in that deep ignoble part of the self that imagines and prays that life might be different from its reality. But I had expected to offer to work for passage, to be allowed time in which to pay, to make lutes for twenty years, if need be, to earn what it might cost. The man owed me nothing. He had already more than repaid any imagined debt for the little I had done, by introducing Francis and me to the South Java Company – for I had grown certain that this had been the case.

I could only blush and stammer in response to his generosity. 'Sir, I'm overwhelmed . . . I can't . . .'

'It's done,' he said, cutting me short again. 'Come upstairs with me now. I'm sure my wife would like to see you once more before you vanish to the New World.'

580

She was seated by the fire in their small private parlour in one corner of the upper floor. The boy stood by her side. An inch taller and freed from his harness, with his hair neatly cut and a recorder tucked into his belt, he was watching his mother's hands as she embroidered a chair-seat cover.

I glanced at the baronet, but his eyes were on his son. My heart began to thud.

The boy turned and saw us. For a long moment he stood absolutely still, staring at me. Then he screwed up his face while, with visible effort, he searched inside his head for who I was. Then his face smoothed out again. He looked straight into my eyes, opened his mouth, and screamed.

A scream of joy, not anger.

He took a step towards me. Still looking at me, he groped at the air with his hands as if searching there for the words and music, and began to sing.

'We be soldiers three . . .'

For a count of four, I could not breathe, then I joined his song. '. . . lately come home from the old country . . .' We finished rousingly, together, 'with never a penny of money!'

'Penny!' cried the boy. 'Penny!' He laughed and clapped his hands in glee. Then he stepped back to his mother's side. She smiled at me and laid her hands lightly on his shoulders, both claiming and caressing, while the boy fixed me with a stare as intense but delicate as that I had exchanged with my singing wolf. His mother stroked his head and back, then rested her hand on the nape of his neck.

The boy gave me a sudden, devastating smile. 'We be,' he sang. 'We be.'

Rotatio.

CODA

Five Weeks Later

How can I possibly be so happy?

I must live the rest of my life with a beast in occasional residence. I stare out at a rough, metallic, endless sea, a spectacle of awesome bleakness that would wither the stoutest soul. Though it's still late summer the sea spray clamps around the *Sea Horse*'s rigging in icy tubes and sparkles crystalline on my beard.

The worth of my entire life can be measured in three small chests two decks down below my feet. I picked weevils from my morning biscuit.

And yet.

Also beneath my feet, Marika is retching into a bowl, only in part because of the *Sea Horse*'s staggering gait. We believe that she carries our cub. She shouted at me to leave her in Janni's care and go on deck. At my elbow leans my other companion – a man who once tried to kill me. And I returned the compliment.

We exchange glances. At the age when men begin to take younger mistresses and think of having their portraits painted, we're headed for an unmapped land of savages, wild beasts, hard labour and possible starvation. He raises his brows in wry dismay. We smile, then look back out to sea. Aphrodite wedges herself more tightly between us for warmth and safety in this strange, unsteady new world.

The *Sea Horse* plunges, shakes like a dog, and rises with water pouring from her flanks. Aphrodite whimpers.

Foolishly, I am light with joy.

Afterword

Modern Neurology and Recreational Drugs

Like the author, as many as one in two hundred readers of *Quicksilver* may recognise some of Ned's symptoms from their own experience, even if they don't share his sense of full animal transformation. In *The Man Who Mistook His Wife For A Hat**, in a chapter called 'The Dog Beneath the Skin', Oliver Sacks describes a young man whose senses seem to become those of a dog. *The American Journal of Psychiatry*, among other serious publications, has described patients who imagine that they are wolves, dogs, rabbits and other animals. The medical perspective on these people in the twentieth century is very different from that in the seventeenth, but the modern parallel with lycanthropy is unmistakeable. A possible diagnosis which Sacks suggests in a footnote to his dog-man, is a form of Temporal-Lobe Epilepsy.

From her own experience with TLE, which is a partial epilepsy producing disorientation, sensory heightening, hallucination, and perceptible behavioural changes, the author had already concocted a possible explanation for the reality of werewolves, even before she found the Sacks footnote, which gave final confirmation to her theory.

---

* Oliver Sacks, *The Man Who Mistook His Wife For A Hat*, Pan Books, London, 1986.

There are, of course, many other phenomena collected under the umbrella myth of the werewolf, including 'wild children', forms of hysteria, and other medical and psychological conditions. (See the following bibliography for some excellent treatments of these.) Most intriguing of all is the possibility, suggested to the writer by glimpses snatched in her research, that some werewolves were voluntary, that the infamous 'Witches' Salve' (which did exist and act as described in *Quicksilver*) was used as an hallucinatory recreational drug, particularly among the wealthy idle classes who in mid-seventeenth-century England had few outlets for their money, and did not fear prosecution in the same way as the more marginal social figures who were most often convicted as witches.

Though Ned is never 'cured' in *Quicksilver*, and leaves England for the dangers (to him and to his wolf) of seventeenth-century New England, he is well on the way to learning to manage his condition. He has recognised what would now be known as 'triggers' for his seizures, and is learning to avoid them. It interested the author to learn that many 'folk' remedies for the falling sickness and other conditions which could well have been forms of epilepsy did in fact contain high levels of vitamin B^6, which is a modern prescribed supplement to other anti-epileptic medications, and which helped bring about the complete control of her own condition. There is a good chance, therefore, that Janni's 'dosings', like the dietary approaches of many modern sufferers, will further help Ned. There is also the chance, though not a large one, of spontaneous recovery.

This final lack of a cure in *Quicksilver*, which might seem to be an unhappy ending, reflects some of the writer's most passionate feelings, and spurred the need to write *Quicksilver*. For her, as for Ned, the sudden arrival of her beast unravelled her life and made many things impossible, including her then career. It was, however, in intensive care, while hooked up to tubes and eyeing the emergency kit on her bedside table, that she began to write again after nearly twenty years. What she then interpreted as a near-death experience, and her later experiences of altered sensory and emotional states, seem not only to have introduced (what was then) a frightening element of irrationality into her life, but also to have released a new creativity.

Though she would never volunteer to go again through the first few years of her illness, she is now deeply grateful for the shaking-up, the re-evaluations, and fresh starts she was forced to make. She acknowledges the 'wellness in the illness' and offers the need to seek out this wellness as a counter to the often bleak and unhelpfully negative advice offered to epilepsy sufferers.

Though medicine has made great advances in controlling the symptoms of all the epilepsies, we have never quite lost our folk terror of the falling sickness, nor as a society worked out just how the epilepsies fit into our social and economic fabric. Writing *Quicksilver*, the author experienced a sense of continuity, of reaching back through history and touching human experiences which today might seem implausible or freakish and meaningless. She hopes to extend to others that sense of belonging to a community (though one less extreme in nature than Janni's community of monsters), and also to help explain a condition which is still, by many people, badly understood. Epilepsy is episodic. The seizures are interludes, not a chronic condition. As in Ned's case, when not possessed by your beast, you are entirely yourself. So far as you are allowed by everyone else.

It is important to understand that TLE is not a single condition, but a collection of symptoms which can have many different underlying causes. Each case must therefore be considered in its own terms.

Also, symptoms like Ned's are not in themselves proof of epilepsy and may often, and more commonly, be found with other conditions. For example, Ned's sharp head-pain and disturbances of vision may also accompany migraine.

Select Bibliography

Wolf and Man

Aristotle, *Historia Animalium* (Loeb editions).

Bomford, Liz, *The Complete Wolf* (New York, St Martin's Press, 1993).

Borges, Jorge Luis, *The Book of Imaginary Beings* (Penguin, 1987).

Cooper, J.C., *Symbolic and Mythological Animals* (Aquarian/Thorsons, 1992).

Douglas, Adam, *The Beast Within* (London, Chapmans, 1992).

Franz, Marie-Louise von, *Redemption Motifs in Fairytales* (Toronto, Inner City Books, 1980).

George, Wilma, & Yapp, Brundson, *The Naming of the Beasts* (Duckworth, 1991).

Jung, Carl, *Man and His Symbols* (London, Aldus Books, 1964) and *Psychology and the Occult* (London, Ark, 1987).

London, Jack, *The Call of the Wild* (Beaver Books, 1986).

Lopez, Barry, *Man and Wolf* (1978).

Ovid, *Metamorphoses*, transl. F.J. Miller (London, William Heinemann, 1925).

Petronius, *The Satyricon* (Penguin, 1977).

Pliny, *Naturalis Historia*, Bks VII–XI (Harvard University Press, 1983).

Thomas, Keith, *Man and the Natural World: Changing Attitudes in England 1500–1800* (London, Allen Lane, 1983).

Magic and Medicine

Balch, J.F, & Balch, P.A. *Nutritional Healing* (New York, Avery Publishing Group, 1990).

Gerard's *Herbal*. From 1636 edition (London, Studio Editions).

Grieve, Mrs M., (ed. Leyel), *A Modern Herbal* (Jonathan Cape, 1931).

Helman, Cecil, *The Body of Frankenstein's Monster, Essays in Myth & Medicine* (New York, W.W. Norton Company, 1991).

Hill, *A Gardener's Labyrinth* (facsimile edition).

Magner, Lois N., *A History of the Life Sciences* (New York, Marcel Dekker, Inc., 1979).

Mann, John, *Murder, Magic and Medicine* (Oxford, OUP, 1992).

Poluin, Miriam, & Robbins, Christopher, *The Natural Pharmacy* (London, Dorling Kindersley, 1992).

Singer, Charles, *The Evolution of Anatomy* (London, Kegan Paul, Trench, Trubner & Co, 1925).

Stockwell, Christine, *Nature's Pharmacy* (London, Century, 1988).

Sutherland, J.M., Tait, H., & Eadie, M.J., *The Epilepsies, Modern Diagnosis and Treatment* (Edinburgh, Churchill Livingstone, 1974).

Thomas, Keith, *Religion and the Decline of Magic* (London, Penguin, 1973).